PRAISE FOR MICHELLE SHOCKLEE

In her trademark style, Shocklee examines the ramifications of long-held secrets while also exposing some of history's own, exploring the often-overlooked sacrifices of the people of Oak Ridge, Tennessee, during World War II. Equal parts heartbreaking and gripping, *The Women of Oak Ridge* is Michelle Shocklee at her very best. A thought-provoking, beautiful, meticulously researched novel not to be missed.

    JENNIFER L. WRIGHT, award-winning author of *Last Light over Galveston*

Gripping from the first to the last page, *The Women of Oak Ridge* is a fascinating exploration of a secret city, its effects on the entire world, and the people who guarded its mysteries. Michelle Shocklee deftly weaves a tale of intrigue with poignant insight into the ways the human soul grapples with the complexities of the past . . . and how past and present can be a gift to one another. Brilliant!

    AMANDA DYKES, bestselling, Christy Award–winning author of *Born of Gilded Mountains*

Compelling and deeply emotional, *The Women of Oak Ridge* explores a shadowed history of our WWII home front. . . . Michelle Shocklee masterfully weaves the stories of two women—one looking forward in hope, the other burdened by the past—into a tender exploration of human frailty, the power of truth, and the freedom that comes only with forgiveness. Readers won't want to miss Michelle Shocklee at her very best.

    STEPHANIE LANDSEM, Carol Award–winning author of *The Fault Between Us*

Told through the points of view of two women from two generations in the same family, the story . . . takes the reader on a rollercoaster ride. I was fascinated by the historical aspects and drawn into the characters' worlds as if I lived it with them. Michelle is a masterful storyteller, and she's outdone herself in this novel. I give *The Women of Oak Ridge* my highest recommendation.

    KIM VOGEL SAWYER, bestselling author of *Hope's Enduring Echo*

Intrigue, danger, and secrets fill *The Women of Oak Ridge* and kept me turning the pages well into the night. . . . If you love historical fiction, you don't want to miss this one.

    ROBIN LEE HATCHER, Christy Award–winning author of *To Capture a Mountain Man*

Michelle Shocklee has once again written a beautiful story. . . . I couldn't put it down until I got to the very satisfying ending. Another great read to add to your bookshelf.

    LIZ TOLSMA, award-winning author of *When the Sky Burned,* on *The Women of Oak Ridge*

The stories of Laurel Willett and Mae Willett are so intriguing as to make one not want to stop reading. I was grateful to be able to answer historical questions for Michelle regarding what really happened in Oak Ridge during the Manhattan Project, and she has captured the atmosphere well and stayed true to the historical elements.

    RAY SMITH, Oak Ridge City Historian and Tennessee Historical Commission Commissioner, on *The Women of Oak Ridge*

Michelle Shocklee is a master at capturing the heart of her characters and inviting readers right into their journey. *All We Thought We Knew* is a poignant story about prejudice, family secrets, and both the sorrow and resilience of lives forever altered by war. A powerful time-slip novel.

> **MELANIE DOBSON**, award-winning author of *The Wings of Poppy Pendleton*

Memorable and moving, *All We Thought We Knew* is a novel of ordinary people who are tested by two wars that altered America. . . . Michelle Shocklee has woven a poignant tapestry of revelations and restoration, heartbreak and hope.

> **AMANDA BARRATT**, Christy Award–winning author of *The Warsaw Sisters*

Rich in description and atmosphere. . . . Through beautifully rendered characters in heart-wrenching dilemmas, Michelle Shocklee asks profound questions about life and family and belonging. An evocative read you are sure to savor!

> **SARAH SUNDIN**, bestselling, award-winning author of *Midnight on Scottish Shores*, on *Appalachian Song*

Captivating. . . . Rich in history and mystery, *Count the Nights by Stars* is a novel that will teach and inspire.

> **HISTORICAL NOVEL SOCIETY**

Shocklee elevates the redemptive power of remorse and the grace of forgiveness in this moving saga.

> **PUBLISHERS WEEKLY** on *Under the Tulip Tree*

THE WOMEN OF OAK RIDGE

THE WOMEN OF OAK RIDGE

MICHELLE SHOCKLEE

Tyndale House Publishers
Carol Stream, Illinois

Visit Tyndale online at tyndale.com.

Visit Michelle Shocklee's website at michelleshocklee.com.

Tyndale and Tyndale's quill logo are registered trademarks of Tyndale House Ministries.

The Women of Oak Ridge

Copyright © 2025 by Michelle Shocklee. All rights reserved.

Cover photograph of woman with bicycle copyright © Magdalena Russocka/Trevillion Images. All rights reserved.

Cover background photograph of plant by Ed Westcott, 1946, US Government Work, public domain.

Author photo taken by Jodie Westfall, copyright © 2012. All rights reserved.

Cover design by Sarah Susan Richardson

Interior design by Cathy Miller

Edited by Kathryn S. Olson

Published in association with the literary agency of The Steve Laube Agency.

Scripture quotations are taken from the *Holy Bible*, King James Version.

The URLs in this book were verified prior to publication. The publisher is not responsible for content in the links, links that have expired, or websites that have changed ownership after that time.

The Women of Oak Ridge is a work of fiction. Where real people, events, establishments, organizations, or locales appear, they are used fictitiously. All other elements of the novel are drawn from the author's imagination.

For information about special discounts for bulk purchases, please contact Tyndale House Publishers at csresponse@tyndale.com, or call 1-855-277-9400.

Library of Congress Cataloging-in-Publication Data

A catalog record for this book is available from the Library of Congress.

ISBN 978-1-4964-8421-5 (HC)
ISBN 978-1-4964-8422-2 (SC)

Printed in the United States of America

31	30	29	28	27	26	25
7	6	5	4	3	2	1

For my girls,
Erica and Kaley
You are beautiful women, inside and out, and you
are each an answer to this mama's prayers!
Genesis 2:22

If the Son therefore shall make you free,
ye shall be free indeed.

JOHN 8:36

PROLOGUE

THE WHITE HOUSE
WASHINGTON, DC

DECEMBER 9, 1941

President Franklin D. Roosevelt sat behind his desk next to a fireplace in the White House, with the United States flag behind him, spectacles perched on his nose, and paper in hand—a calm presence in a room swarming with aides and people rushing around. A half dozen microphones faced him, and a photographic camera stood ready to make record of this, his first fireside chat since the attack on Pearl Harbor.

Someone signaled for silence.

A hush fell over the room.

"Ladies and gentlemen," the announcer said, "the President of the United States."

President Roosevelt's face took on a serious expression as he addressed the nation.

"My fellow Americans," he began, his measured voice familiar to the millions listening. "The sudden criminal attacks perpetrated by the Japanese in the Pacific provide the climax of a decade of international immorality.

"Powerful and resourceful gangsters have banded together to make war upon the whole human race. Their challenge has now been flung at the United States of America. The Japanese have treacherously violated the long-standing peace between us. Many American soldiers and sailors have been killed by enemy action. American ships have been sunk; American airplanes have been destroyed.

"The Congress and the people of the United States have accepted that challenge. Together with other free peoples, we are now fighting to maintain our right to live among our world neighbors in freedom and in common decency, without fear of assault."

He spoke about past relations between the United States and Japan, including meetings that took place mere days before the attack. He reminded listeners that the US had done everything possible to maintain peace. Now, we found ourselves at war. Every man, woman, and child, he said, was a partner in the most tremendous undertaking of our American history.

"I am sure that the people in every part of the Nation are prepared in their individual living to win this war. I am sure that they will cheerfully help to pay a large part of its financial cost while it goes on. I am sure they will cheerfully give up those material things that they are asked to give up.

"And I am sure that they will retain all those great spiritual things without which we cannot win through."

His final words were firm and indisputable.

"We are now in the midst of a war, not for conquest, not for vengeance, but for a world in which this Nation, and all that this Nation represents, will be safe for our children. We expect to eliminate the danger from Japan, but it would serve us ill if we accomplished that and found that the rest of the world was dominated by Hitler and Mussolini.

"So we are going to win the war and we are going to win the peace that follows.

"And in the difficult hours of this day—through dark days that may be yet to come—we will know that the vast majority of the members of the human race are on our side. Many of them are fighting with us. All of them are praying for us. For in representing our cause, we represent theirs as well. Our hope and their hope for liberty under God."

The president fell silent, yet his inspiring words would resonate with Americans in every corner of the country. In big cities and small farming communities. With families gathered around the radio in their living rooms, and soldiers huddled in barracks on military bases, preparing for war.

Deep in the mountains of eastern Kentucky, shivering in the chill of the two-room, coal-company-owned shanty she shared with her parents and younger brother, eighteen-year-old Maebelle Willett heard President Roosevelt's rallying call. To sacrifice and do her part to help win the war. To fulfill her duty as an American citizen. To play a role, no matter how small and insignificant, in defeating our enemies.

After the national anthem ended, she clicked off the radio and stared out the window. Cold rain drenched the earth, making life more miserable than usual. Pa, weakened from black lung, coughed from the next room. Her mother's treasured clock chimed from the shelf above the stove, a reminder she needed to get supper started. Mama would be tired after a long day of scrubbing laundry for other folks, and Harris was always half starved, as were most eight-year-old boys.

Yet Maebelle didn't move.

In that quiet moment, envisioning the world far beyond their secluded holler in the highlands of Appalachia, she came to a decision.

She would answer the president's call. She didn't know what she could do or how she would do it, but somehow, someway, she *would* make a difference in the outcome of the war.

The president and the country needed her.

CHAPTER ONE

LAUREL

OAK RIDGE, TENNESSEE

JUNE 1979

The secret changes everything.

Those four simple words echoed through my mind as I drove down the streets of Oak Ridge, a place I hadn't seen in ten or more years. Although the small town tucked in the hills of East Tennessee looked like any you might find along the back roads of America, this particular community was anything but typical.

The secret made it so.

I glanced at the directions Dad had given me to Aunt Mae's house, but either he'd forgotten how to get there or I couldn't read a map. Being that I'd found my way from Massachusetts to Tennessee without issue, I didn't think it was the latter.

"Come on, Dad," I muttered, steering my Camaro Z28 down yet another dead-end road. The cobalt blue car had been a surprise gift from Dad and Mom when I graduated from Boston University with a master's degree in psychology, making my younger sisters envious. I'd reminded them I had to drive our old station wagon all through college. After the ribbing I'd had to endure from friends about the tanklike vehicle, I deserved a cool car.

The new hit "Reunited" by Peaches & Herb played on the radio.

"I wish I was reunited with Aunt Mae right about now. Why can't I find her house?"

It had been years since our family traveled from Boston to visit Dad's older sister. His job as a vice president of a national insurance company took him all over the country, and he'd stop in to see Aunt Mae when he was in Tennessee. Every few years she took the train to visit us, but the last time she came—wasn't it for the big bicentennial celebration in 1976?—I'd taken a summer job in New York City and missed seeing her.

I pulled up to a four-way stop and tapped the steering wheel. Which way should I go?

I vaguely recalled spending Thanksgiving in Oak Ridge when I was fourteen or fifteen years old, but like most teenagers, I hadn't paid attention to directions and landmarks as we made our way through town. Aunt Mae's house was tiny, that I did remember. I'd slept on the pullout sofa in the cramped living room with both of my sisters, which was not ideal for a girl who preferred to sleep late during her school holiday.

Yet not once during the handful of visits my family made to Aunt Mae's over the years did anyone mention *the secret*. The fact is, I wouldn't know about the secret even now if I hadn't walked into the faculty lounge at the community college last month. My first year teaching freshmen psychology was nearing an end, and like most of the staff, I was ready for a break. I had plans to spend the summer with friends in Maine, eating lobster and enjoying the gorgeous scenery. I'd also hoped to use the time away from the city to finalize the topic of my dissertation. For some reason, I couldn't land on a subject that ignited a fire in me.

That changed the day I learned about the secret.

The recent memory sped across my mind.

The small television in the corner of the faculty lounge had been tuned to the early news that afternoon. Dr. Baca, the school's history professor, sat on the worn sofa in front of it, eyes glued to the set.

"A London grandmother was taken into custody yesterday," the TV announcer had said, his voice and face projecting seriousness while film of an older woman being led away by police rolled behind him. "Letty Gladding is an alleged spy for the Soviet Union, having worked undercover and undetected in British government offices as a secretary for decades. It is believed Mrs. Gladding passed classified information to the Soviets, including materials regarding Tube Alloys, the British atomic weapons program during the 1940s."

"Wow," I'd said, gaining Dr. Baca's attention. "She looks so normal. Who would've ever suspected she was a Soviet spy?"

"Spies come in all shapes and sizes," he'd said. "There were plenty of them in the US during the war. Most were communists." He'd launched into a tale about Julius and Ethel Rosenberg, a husband and wife with two young kids. They'd been arrested, tried, and executed in the 1950s for espionage during the Manhattan Project. Ethel's brother, David Greenglass, who was also arrested for spying, spent time in Oak Ridge in 1944 before being transferred to New Mexico. "Didn't you say you have an aunt who lives in Oak Ridge? Was she there during the war?"

I'd nodded. "She worked at a manufacturing plant, but I'm sure nothing that happened in Podunk Oak Ridge was of interest to the Russians."

I distinctly remember chuckling at my little joke.

Dr. Baca had stared at me. "Laurel, Oak Ridge was a secret city during the war, like Los Alamos. My guess is the plant your aunt worked at helped provide highly enriched uranium for the bomb that was dropped on Hiroshima."

I'd stood in dumbfounded silence.

Tiny, obscure Oak Ridge had a role in producing the atomic bomb? And Aunt Mae was involved? How had I not known this?

After my conversation with Dr. Baca, I'd driven to my parents' house and quizzed Dad about Aunt Mae and Oak Ridge. The next day I'd gone to the university library and read everything I could get my hands on about the Manhattan Project. What I learned convinced me of two things: I'd found the topic for my dissertation, and Aunt Mae's life was a total mystery to me.

Both observations were the reason I now found myself in Tennessee instead of Maine.

I made another half dozen turns, passed a school and a church with a tall steeple, before I finally located the correct street. The homes in this part of town were modest, with postage-stamp-sized yards. I saw the familiar beige residence, set just off the road, and confirmed it was hers by the street number painted on the mailbox. With a sigh of relief, I turned into the driveway and cut the engine. It had been a long trip, and I was ready to be someplace other than my car.

I groaned and stretched as I exited the vehicle.

Mom had worried about me making the trip by myself, declaring all manner of terrible things could happen to a twenty-five-year-old woman alone on the highway. She'd bought me a can of mace, a whistle, and given me five rolls of quarters, making me promise to call her from a pay phone every so often until I reached Oak Ridge in one piece. I spent last night in Durham, North Carolina, with Hannah, a friend from our days at Boston University. When I'd called Mom, she tried to talk Hannah into joining me for the remainder of my journey.

"Mom," I'd said into the telephone receiver, rolling my eyes while Hannah giggled behind her hand, "I don't know how long I'll stay in Oak Ridge. Classes at the community college don't start again until September, so I have the entire summer off from teaching. The research for my dissertation could take a while, depending on how much Aunt Mae remembers about her work during the war and who else I can find to talk with me about those days."

As I headed for the steps to my aunt's narrow front porch, I made a mental note to call Mom as soon as I got settled.

The house looked just as it did years ago. Maybe a little more weatherworn, but still as neat and tidy as I remembered. The lawn had recently been cut, and a window box full of various flowers made a colorful splash on the otherwise plain exterior. An overgrown patch in the back corner of the yard reminded me Aunt Mae enjoyed gardening, yet despite warm weather, it didn't appear as though she intended to grow anything this year.

I knocked on the front door. A dog barked from inside.

A moment later, an older, slightly pudgier version of the woman of my memories appeared. Her chestnut brown hair had gone prematurely gray, so she'd always seemed ancient to my sisters and me. According to Dad, I looked like my aunt when she was younger.

Green eyes squinted behind thick glasses. "Laurel? Is that you?"

The question was unexpected. "Yes, Aunt Mae. It's me."

She pulled the door wider. "My eyesight isn't too good these days. The doctor calls it some kind of degenerative disease with a fancy name. Come in, dear."

I hadn't heard this news. *Does Dad know?* I wondered.

We hugged, then I stepped inside and was immediately transported back in time. Old-fashioned furnishings. Black-and-white framed photographs of family members long gone, along with more recent color photos of my family. The faint odor of mothballs permeated the air, and a plethora of potted houseplants occupied what little space remained.

Peggy—Aunt Mae's terribly spoiled Pomeranian, according to Dad—waddled up, a great puff of light brown fur. The dog sniffed my shoes, peered up at me for a long moment, then padded off in the direction she'd come from, apparently declaring me harmless. I was more of a cat person myself, but the fluffy critter was kind of cute.

"I admit I was surprised when your dad said you were coming down for a visit. I can't recall the last time you were in Tennessee." She closed the door behind me and squinted. "My, you've certainly grown up."

Guilt swept over me.

I'd never made much of an attempt to have a relationship with my aunt. She was an odd bird, ten years older than Dad. When she visited us in Boston, she never seemed to know what to do with my chatty sisters and me. She wasn't up on the latest music or movies or anything else that might interest us. We'd greet her with a perfunctory kiss on the cheek when she arrived and again when she left, with little interaction in between.

"School has kept me busy." Even though it was true, I knew I was making excuses. Earning a master's degree in psychology was no easy task, but a phone call to my aging aunt would only have taken a few minutes here and there.

She gave me a long study. "Harris said you're working on your dissertation. I had no idea you wanted to get your doctorate. That's quite ambitious."

Her tone hinted at possible failure. "It's definitely a lot of work, especially now that I'm teaching, but I'm up for the challenge."

"I'm sure you are, dear." She smiled. "Let's get you settled, then we can catch up before dinner."

I followed her through the living room to a short hallway

where three doors stood open. Two bedrooms and one baby-blue-tiled bathroom. Aunt Mae led me to the room on the left. A quilt-covered bed, nightstand, and an old cabinet-encased sewing machine, complete with a wide foot pedal, were the only furnishings. The walls were bare.

"I don't have much company stay overnight." She glanced around the sparse room. "Harris is the only one who sleeps in here these days."

A flash of memory surfaced when I approached the sewing machine, positioned under a window where late afternoon sunshine spilled through lacey curtains. "I remember you used to make clothes for my sisters and me. Matching dresses. Nightgowns. Even things for our dolls."

Her mouth lifted in a wistful smile. "I enjoyed sewing for you girls."

Another wave of guilt washed over me. I couldn't recall ever thanking her for the handmade gifts.

"Make yourself at home." She turned to exit the room. "We'll eat around six."

"Thank you, Aunt Mae," I hurried to say before she got away. "For everything. I'm happy we can spend some time together."

The wrinkles on her face softened. "I'm glad you're here."

After she left, I retrieved my suitcase from the back seat of the car. The neighbor next door—a woman about the same age as my aunt, I guessed—gave a friendly wave from her place on her porch.

"Hello," she called across the space, her voice and expression curious.

I returned the gesture and the greeting but continued to the house. While I did hope to talk to people in town about their time in Oak Ridge, especially if they were here during the war, right now I just wanted to take off my shoes and relax.

After I unpacked, made a collect call to Mom from the wall

phone in the kitchen, and freshened up in the bathroom, I found Aunt Mae in the living room, seated in a comfy-looking overstuffed chair near the front window. She worked a pile of buttery yellow yarn with a crochet hook.

"I don't see well enough to sew anymore." She squinted at me as I landed on the same sofa I'd slept on years ago. "But my fingers have crocheted so many blankets over the years, they seem to know what to do on their own. A young couple down the street are expecting a new baby any day, but I'm behind schedule. I hope the little one doesn't arrive until I have this finished."

"I don't recall Dad mentioning you were having issues with your eyesight."

"I probably didn't tell him." She shrugged. "I don't want Harris worrying about me more than he already does. Every time he stops by for a visit or we chat on the telephone, he tries to convince me to move to Boston."

"That would be great," I said. "I know Dad would love to have you nearby."

She looked thoughtful. "It would be nice to be closer to my family, but . . ." Her gaze swept the small room. "This is my home. I've lived in Oak Ridge since I was a young woman in my twenties."

Her comment was exactly the opening I needed to broach the reason I'd come.

"I was hoping to talk to you about that. Dad said you came to Oak Ridge during the war to work at the plant where they enriched uranium for the atomic bomb. I have to admit I didn't know anything about the role Oak Ridge played in the war until recently." I smiled. "I've decided to write my dissertation on the people, especially the women, who worked on the Manhattan Project. What it was like to live and work in a city no one knew about, and how they felt after they learned the secret. I'm particularly interested to know if it still affects them today."

I thought my announcement would please Aunt Mae, but her face paled.

Her brow tugged into a deep frown. "No one wants to talk about those days. The past is the past. Best to leave it there."

Dad had warned me his sister was closemouthed about her time in Oak Ridge during the war. She hadn't moved back to Kentucky after Japan surrendered, and never spoke to him about her job. If she had interesting stories regarding what took place behind the high fences and guarded gates of Oak Ridge, I had a feeling it was going to take some real effort to pry them out of her.

"But don't you think it's important for people of my generation and younger to know how your generation gave everything you had to the war effort?" I leaned forward, elbows on my knees. "The war in Vietnam is what we're familiar with, but it was different from World War II. People responded differently to it because of the politics involved. The respect that came from helping defeat Germany and Japan wasn't there when soldiers came home from Vietnam. It's people like you, Aunt Mae, whose stories we need to learn from. What you and your generation did was heroic."

Her frown deepened. "I'm no hero. Far from it."

I pressed on, hoping she'd see my genuine interest. "I wasn't aware Oak Ridge was a 'secret city' like Los Alamos until I saw a news story about a woman in London who was arrested for being a spy. It said she passed information about the British atomic program to the Russians. One of the history professors at the school where I teach had to explain it to me. I feel foolish for not knowing about Oak Ridge's history. Dad showed me a book about the Manhattan Project, and it said the bomb that was dropped on Japan wouldn't have existed without the work done at Oak Ridge." I paused, my next words sincere. "I'd very much like to hear your story, Aunt Mae. Not just for my research, but because it's part of your life. Your history."

After long moments, she faced me. "Just as nothing good came from talking about what went on in Oak Ridge back when the war was raging, nothing good can come from talking about it now. What we did, what we saw, the confidential things everyone kept to themselves. None of that matters now." She took a shaky breath. "Not every secret needs to be told. Some just need to be forgotten."

Her forceful words and the strong emotions behind them caught me off guard. I couldn't begin to guess what she meant. Yet wasn't that the reason I'd come to Oak Ridge? To discover how the secrets involved with the Manhattan Project affected people, including my own aunt? I'd drop the subject for now, but I hoped to prove to her in the coming days that she could trust me. Her story, along with everyone else's who worked on the Manhattan Project, was important, whether she recognized it or not.

"I understand, Aunt Mae." I reached across the small space between us to grasp her hand. I found it frigid despite warm air coming through the open window. Her fingers closed over mine, and she gave a single nod. We didn't say another word about it.

Together we prepared a simple dinner of baked chicken and mashed potatoes and settled at the green 1950s-style Formica table shoved against the wall. Aunt Mae said grace, asking God to bless our family, my studies, and someone named Velvet who was suffering from gout. Over the meal, I told her about Mom's art projects and caught her up on my sisters' busy lives. We discussed the history-making election of England's first female prime minister and agreed it would be interesting to see what changes Margaret Thatcher brought to the stuffy British parliament.

Yet Aunt Mae's life in Oak Ridge during the war was never far from my mind.

Why keep secrets about things that happened over thirty years ago? From what I'd read, the world learned about Oak Ridge and the role it played in ending the war soon after Little Boy, the first atomic weapon ever used in wartime, was dropped on Hiroshima. While few of the thousands of workers in Oak Ridge knew of their involvement in creating the bomb while the war continued, the truth came out with President Truman's announcement on August 6, 1945, exposing shocking secrets and irrevocably changing the world.

So why was Aunt Mae adamant about keeping her silence? What was it that made her hesitant to revisit those extraordinary days? Young women like her had been so eager to do their part to end the war, they'd left home and family to come to a secret city that didn't exist on any map. I very much wanted to learn more about their stories, including my aunt's.

She seemed more relaxed by the time we bid each other goodnight. Night sounds came through the window screen as I crawled beneath the cool sheet and turned out the light. Exhaustion rolled over me, and I let my body sink into the soft mattress. My mind, however, mulled over the problem of how to get Aunt Mae to share her story. Although I hoped to interview other wartime residents of Oak Ridge while I was in town, my aunt was the main reason I was here.

I let out a drowsy chuckle.

My friends tended to label me as *driven*. Whether or not it was a compliment depended on the situation. When it came to working hard to earn my degrees, the moniker fit well. But I also recognized I could come on a bit strong when something fired up my passions. I'd need to take things slowly with Aunt Mae and build our relationship to the point of trust.

However, I was determined to learn what happened in Oak Ridge during World War II. Not only did my dissertation depend upon it, but my curiosity was now piqued to the point I couldn't let it go, even if I tried.

My eyes drifted closed.

Images from photographs I'd seen of the Secret City floated across my mind as sleep crept in, but it was the fresh face of twenty-one-year-old Maebelle Willett that filled my dreams.

CHAPTER TWO
MAE

OAK RIDGE, TENNESSEE
CLINTON ENGINEER WORKS

APRIL 1944

The first thing I noticed about Clinton Engineer Works was the armed guards. Uniformed men stood at a gate flanked by guardhouses, guns holstered at their hips, faces unsmiling. Barbed wire fencing extended out of sight in both directions from the gate, whether to keep people in or out, I wasn't certain.

The sight was unexpected and unsettling.

Our bus, full of young women my age who'd all boarded in Knoxville, stopped at the entrance. Soldiers, their armbands indicating they were military police, searched every inch of the vehicle and checked each woman's ID. When they were finally satisfied, we were allowed to enter what was oddly referred to as *the Reservation* by one of the guards, tucked in a valley of tree-covered hills somewhere in East Tennessee.

After we passed through the gate and wound our way along a

dirt road to a small town, the second thing I noticed was the mud. Acres and acres of thick, reddish-brown mud filled the landscape as far as I could see. It gave one the impression that once-fertile farmland had been plowed over by a giant tractor and was left devoid of all manner of vegetation. Miles and miles of wooden walkways led to dozens and dozens of simple, unattractive buildings and hordes of structures under construction, eventually disappearing into woods at the edges of the red-brown mud. A spring rain shower had erupted over us as we made our way west from Knoxville, intensifying the already uncomfortable humidity, but upon seeing the squishy, saturated ground here on the Reservation, I gathered it had rained quite a bit lately.

The third and most baffling thing I saw were large billboards and signs meant to catch our attention. One depicted three monkeys, each with their hands over eyes, ears, or mouth, that read *What You See Here, What You Do Here, What You Hear Here, When You Leave Here, Let It Stay Here.* Another read *Loose Talk Helps Our Enemy* with a picture of a German soldier and a swastika.

I couldn't begin to guess their meaning.

The brave driver slowly navigated the muddy path as best he could and eventually came to a stop in front of a large, two-story building. A cluster of people stood outside, ostensibly waiting for us to arrive.

With my old suitcase clutched to my chest, I disembarked with the other women. I did my best to follow the foot impressions of those who'd gone before me, hoping to keep my brand-new saddle oxfords from being completely ruined on the first day. Mama had sewn two dresses for me—one made over from her Sunday-go-to-meetin' best, and another from piecing together two I'd outgrown—but she'd splurged to purchase the sturdy shoes and white socks from the coal company store. She'd saved our shoe ration coupon for a special occasion, but I was familiar enough with the greedy practices of the company-owned store to know the exorbitant price would be added to the already enormous debt Pa owed. I'd protested the extravagance, but Mama wouldn't hear of me going off to a new and exciting job in Tennessee with worn-out footwear passed on from a kindly lady at church.

I fell into line with the women who'd traveled on the bus with me, all headed to the same destination, with the same questions on our minds: Where are we going, and what will we do once we arrive?

No one, it seemed, knew the answers.

I thought back to the day a man approached me while I worked behind the counter of Wagner hardware store in our small Kentucky town. He introduced himself as a recruiter for Clinton Engineer Works, a Tennessee company involved in "war work." Ever since President Roosevelt announced that the United States had declared war on Japan, Germany, and Italy, factories all over the country changed course and were converted to produce things the military required to defeat our enemies. Automakers built trucks, tanks, aircraft engines, guns and munitions. Clothing factories put out thousands of uniforms and boots. Even the Lionel toy train company got involved and began making items for the war effort, including compasses and compass cases for ships.

The recruiter was impressed with my knowledge of plumbing parts and tools and declared that kind of experience could be useful to the company he worked for. He guaranteed I would earn three times the salary I was making now if I came to Tennessee.

That got my attention.

"I can't tell you exactly where Clinton Engineer Works is located or what they're producing there," he said, seemingly sincere, "but I promise it will help win the war. And isn't that what we all want? To end the fighting and bring our boys home?"

He'd given me a pamphlet to take home to my folks and talk over the job offer. Pa, who'd gone back to work at the coal mine despite his failing health and Mama's pleading to stay home, had heard companies with military contracts were recruiting women. With most of the country's young men off fighting in Europe or the Pacific, it fell to the female population to roll up their sleeves and work in the factories.

Pa's face came to mind.

Last year the coal company owner warned we'd lose our housing if Pa didn't come back to work. I'd cried silent tears watching my frail, bone-thin father pull on his blackened helmet and carry his lunch bucket out the door. It was the very reason I stood in ankle-deep mud somewhere in Tennessee, ready to accept a job I knew nothing about. The money I hoped to send home would surely be enough to pay off the store debt and allow Pa to quit his job in the mines.

"Ladies," a woman's voice rose above all the others, bringing me back to the present. Everyone fell silent. "Welcome to Clinton Engineer Works. I'm sure you have many questions, but I'll need you to keep them to yourselves for the time being. When you hear your name, come forward."

She called us in alphabetical order, so it would take time before she got to me.

The pretty blonde woman in front of me turned and offered a friendly smile. "Ain't this excitin'?"

I nodded. "I've never seen anything like it."

"Me neither. I can't imagine what we'll be doing in a place this far from the city, but I don't guess it matters as long as it helps end the war. My brother Joe is in Europe fightin' Hitler, and Mama worries every day something bad is gonna happen to him." She stuck out her hand. "I'm Sylvia Galloway, but everyone back home calls me Sissy."

I shifted the case to my left hand and shook hers with my right. "Maebelle Willett, but most folks call me Mae."

We chatted about the small town in Georgia where she grew up, and I told her about Kentucky. It wasn't long before she was called forward and we bid each other goodbye.

There were only two of us left in line by the time I heard my name.

After quizzing me on how I learned about the job at CEW and what type of experience I had, the woman handed me a piece of paper with typed information on it. "Take this and go through that door." She indicated one of the entrances. "Someone inside will give you further instructions."

I accepted the paper. It bore my name at the top, along with a five-digit number. "Thank you," I said. She nodded and called for the remaining woman.

I made my way to the door she'd indicated. It opened into a room where ladies sat behind desks, the clickety-clack of typewriters and voices echoing off bare wooden walls. Women I'd watched go through the door ahead of me sat in chairs opposite the typists.

"Over here." A lady seated toward the back of the room waved to me.

I hurried in her direction.

She didn't introduce herself once I was seated but immediately began to ask dozens of questions—my birth date, where I was born, and more—then typed out my answers. She wanted to know what I did at my job at the hardware store and if I could drive a vehicle.

Then she inquired about personal things that made me uneasy.

Are you a drinker? Do you have a boyfriend? Would you turn in a family member if they did something illegal? Would you ever belong to an organization that wished to overthrow the government?

I didn't have anything to hide, but I wondered what my answers had to do with the job I'd been hired for.

When the questioning came to an end, she took my photograph, made ink impressions of all ten of my fingertips, had me sign some official-looking documents that emphasized the need for confidentiality, and handed me a carbon copy of the form she'd filled out. "You've been assigned to the maintenance shop at K-25. Your security clearance will take a few days but be ready to start work as soon as you're notified. Go through there"—she pointed at yet another door—"to continue the process."

I didn't know what K-25 was, but now didn't seem the time for questions.

I did as I was told and found myself in a large room filled with rows of chairs, occupied by women I'd seen in the first line, including Sissy. She motioned me to the empty seat next to her.

"What'd you think about all those questions they asked?" she whispered once I was seated.

"I suppose they have to be thorough before they can hire us and know what we'll be good at."

"I ain't good at anything useful," she said. "I just finished school in May. Been helpin' Pa on the farm since my brother left for Europe, but I don't guess these folks'll need a hand with hogs 'n' chickens."

We shared a laugh.

"Mama wasn't too keen on me coming to Tennessee," she confided, "but Pa said I needed to experience the world outside of Georgia. I'm to work at someplace called Y-12."

"I'll be at K-25."

"What do you s'pose those letters and numbers mean?"

I shrugged. I honestly had no idea. Everything about Clinton Engineer Works seemed shrouded in mystery and speculation.

An older man wearing a suit made his way to the front of the room.

"Ladies," he said, his voice commanding silence. "Congratulations on joining Clinton Engineer Works. The job each of you will perform here is vital to the war effort, but as you may have guessed already, it is not something you're allowed to talk about. To anyone. Each of you signed an agreement that states you will follow the rules we've established and will do your utmost to protect your fellow workers by keeping quiet about everything you see and do. Signs are posted throughout the Reservation to remind you to stay mum about what goes on here."

A woman in the center of the room put her hand in the air. "Why is that, sir?"

He wore a grave expression as his gaze traveled over the audience. "Because we don't want our enemies to know about this place or what might be happening here. It's as simple as that." He paused. "What I'm about to tell you may come as a shock, but it's the truth. Someone in this very room could be a spy."

An audible gasp went through the women, followed by murmuring and suspicious glances. Sissy and I exchanged a wide-eyed look.

The man called for silence. "It's true," he said when he had our full attention once again. "Spies are not always sinister-looking men wearing dark suits. They can be handsome gentlemen or amiable young women. They come in all shapes, sizes, and ages. You might work with a spy or even live with a spy and never be aware of it. That is why it is *imperative*"—he emphasized the word—"that you do not talk to anyone about the job you do here. Not to your coworker. Not to your roommate. Not to your boyfriend or your husband if you have one. Not even to the mother who brought you into this world. No one must know what you do. If anyone asks, tell them you make lights for lightning bugs or holes for donuts."

Although his comment received a smattering of chuckles, I didn't think he meant it as a joke. Whatever was happening at CEW was important enough to the war effort that the enemy had an interest in it.

When the room quieted, he read something called the Espionage Act of 1917. It defined what a disloyal American citizen might do and the punishment one would receive for such acts, including imprisonment and even death. As I listened, I couldn't imagine why anyone born in America would do something to bring harm to their country. Surely it was foreigners, people with roots in a distant land, that would do such things.

I cast an uneasy glance around the room, wondering if the man exaggerated. Surely none of these women—normal-looking women—could possibly be a spy.

I peeked at Sissy out of the corner of my eye. She sat on the edge of her seat, listening intently as the man told the tale of an employee who was fired for writing a letter home that listed the number of dormitories at CEW. Sissy came across as a simple farm girl from Georgia, but was it a charade? Could someone as innocent looking as she was be a spy? The very thought seemed absurd. But what about the others, I wondered, studying the unfamiliar faces around me? Was someone even now gathering information to pass on to . . .

To whom? The Germans?

Surely not.

That anyone would betray their country by giving aid to Hitler wasn't something I'd ever considered. Yet if the man speaking could be believed, it must happen often enough that precautions were put into place to prevent information from being leaked. The realization that I'd left home and traveled to Tennessee to work for a company mired in mud and secrets left me unsettled. Had I made a mistake by accepting the job?

"All mail—outgoing and incoming—is censored," the man went on. "You will use a PO box in Oak Ridge as your return address. When you receive mail, military personnel will read it first, then it will be delivered to your residence. When you write to someone, you'll leave the envelope unsealed for censoring, then it will be mailed. At no time are you allowed to write about what you see, what you hear, to describe the area, or divulge our proximity to Knoxville. It is vital the location of the Reservation remains confidential. My advice is to keep your correspondences with friends and family short and sweet. Tell them about the weather or the latest movie you saw at the theater—all without mentioning where you are and who you're with. Remember, your pen and your tongue can be used as enemy weapons."

There were rules against taking photographs, owning binoculars, or using a telescope. We couldn't enter or leave the Reservation except through one of the highly guarded gates. We would each receive an identification badge with our photograph, name, and physical description that must be worn at all times, no matter where you were or what you were doing. If you were caught without your badge, you could lose your job.

"I hope I've answered many of the questions you arrived with," he said in closing, "but the truth of the matter is, we cannot tell you everything. We can train you how to do the job assigned to you, but we can't tell you what you're doing. I can only assure you that if our enemies discover what we hope to achieve here and beat us to it, God have mercy on us all."

The ominous words echoed in the silent room.

After watching a short film about the perils of loose lips, we were directed outside into afternoon sunshine. An information station was set up in the shade of the building where employees offered assistance regarding housing, cafeterias, buses and transportation, security badges, and more. It was overwhelming, but Sissy and I stuck together and eventually found ourselves assigned as roommates in one of the many two-story dormitories not far from the administration area. We would each pay ten dollars a month for the room, maid service, linens, towels, and soap. Because there was no cooking in the dorms, we'd take our meals at the nearby cafeteria, open twenty-four hours a day.

Wooden walkways led across fields of mud to our new home. Mrs. Kepple, the pleasant housemother charged with keeping track of dozens of young women, handed us keys and emphasized the importance of observing the ten o'clock curfew and the rule regarding no men in our rooms. Housing on the Reservation was limited, she warned before leaving us alone, so the eviction of a rule breaker was swift and final.

Left on our own, Sissy and I stood silent and glanced about the sparse room we were to share. Two single beds, a night table between them, and two dressers filled the space.

The enormity of what I'd done began to sink in.

I was far from my family, surrounded by strangers I might not be able to trust, hired to do a job I knew nothing about and couldn't explain to anyone even if I did. Was I cut out for all this secrecy and uncertainty? If it weren't for the promised salary, I'd be tempted to catch the next bus back to Kentucky.

"I ain't never slept anyplace other than home," Sissy said, her voice small and shaky.

I glanced over and found her blue eyes wide as she perused the stark room. I guessed she felt as anxious as I did about it all. "Me neither."

After several seconds ticked by, she added, "Don't reckon I'll miss Pa's snorin' though."

When she met my gaze, she grinned.

We burst into laughter.

CHAPTER THREE
LAUREL

AUNT MAE WAS UP at the crack of dawn. I knew this because the bathroom was across from my room, and the old pipes sang an earsplitting song while she bathed and readied for the day. By the time I got up, showered, and dressed, the aroma of fried bacon drew me to the kitchen like a magnet.

"Good morning." Aunt Mae stood at the stove, tending a big cast-iron skillet with enough bacon to feed an army. Peggy sat at her feet, as though waiting for some morsel to float down like manna from heaven. "How did you sleep?"

"Like a rock. I guess the drive wore me out."

She nodded toward the counter. "There's coffee. Cream and sugar if you take it."

I poured myself a cup and loaded it with cream but left out the sugar. "I wasn't much of a coffee drinker until I started working at the community college. Teaching Psychology 101 at seven o'clock in the morning to a group of uninterested freshmen required something stronger than chocolate milk."

She chuckled. "I remember visiting when you girls were young. Your dad would have a cup of chocolate milk and a piece of toast ready in the mornings before you went to school." She used a fork to lift bacon from the pan onto a plate overlaid with a paper towel, then cracked eggs into the hot skillet. "Sallie isn't the typical homemaker. I can't recall her doing much cooking. It was always Harris at the stove, loading the washing machine, running you girls to your activities."

I felt the need to defend my mother, even though Aunt Mae's observations were mostly true. "Dad always said Mom's talents are better suited elsewhere. He fully supported her art classes and the time she spends in her backyard studio."

"Your mother is definitely a talented artist."

I beamed. "One of the galleries in downtown Boston is showing her work, and she's hoping to get a commission soon. Some bigwig dude with a ton of money is building an enormous mansion and wants to hire local artists to paint murals of scenes from around Boston. According to the gallery owner, the man has taken an interest in Mom's style."

"That's wonderful." Aunt Mae's face took on a wistful expression. "I'm proud of all that Harris, Sallie, and you girls have accomplished. Mama and Pa would have been proud, too."

"I wish I could have known them," I said as I settled at the table.

Both of my grandparents passed before I was born. Dad often declared he learned his work ethic from his father, who was the hardest-working man in the world according to his son. Grandpa died from lung disease after slaving away in a Kentucky coal mine from the time he was twelve years old. Dad had been a teenager at the time, and he and Grandma moved to Oak Ridge to live with Aunt Mae while he finished school. He'd received an academic scholarship to Boston University, met Mom, and started a life far away from the hills and hollers of Appalachia.

"Our parents were good, God-fearing, hardworking people." Aunt Mae had a faraway look. "I always wanted to make them proud too, but . . ."

Her voice faded and a pained expression filled her face before she shook her head, as though flinging off whatever melancholy thought tried to take hold.

We ate an enormous breakfast of biscuits, gravy, bacon, and fried eggs, then lingered at the table, sipping coffee.

"I need to go to the market, but I confess my eyes have been giving me trouble this week." Aunt Mae rubbed her temple. "The doctor prescribed some drops, but I haven't noticed any improvement. Things are still a bit out of focus, and now I'm getting headaches."

This news was troubling.

"I'm happy to take you wherever you need to go, Aunt Mae. I was hoping to do a little sightseeing anyway." I bit my lip. "But I'm concerned about you. Should you call the doctor?"

She shook her head. "I've talked to him about it. The drops are supposed to help, and he wants me to get more vitamins. But, as he says, I'm getting older. Things are bound to quit working the way they did when I was younger."

We cleaned up the kitchen, with me washing dishes and her putting them away. I'd forgotten she didn't have an automatic dishwasher—something my mother considered vital to any household. An hour later we left the house and got into my Camaro.

"Harris was so tickled to surprise you with this car," she said, smoothing the vinyl seat and admiring the black interior. "I wish I'd been there to see the look on your face when you realized you didn't have to drive that big ol' station wagon any longer."

I laughed. "I'm not sure who was more excited that day—me or Dad. My college friends dubbed the wagon *the brown bus*, so it was very satisfying to leave it behind."

As I steered the car onto Illinois Avenue, following her instructions to Winn Dixie, Aunt Mae asked questions about my college days. After I chattered on about fascinating classes and crazy escapades, she grew thoughtful.

"When I was a girl, I'd hoped to go to college. I'd wanted to be a teacher, like you."

"Dad didn't give us much choice. He drilled it into us that getting an education was imperative. Amanda plans to get her MBA soon, and Eliza is finishing her nursing degree at Columbia." I glanced at my aunt. "Why didn't you go to college after the war ended?"

She stared out the window. "Things were different when I was your age," she finally said. "The war changed everything for me."

I didn't pursue the conversation. It was becoming clear the war years were hard on Aunt Mae. I knew her father had been ill and eventually passed, leaving her mother and younger brother without a place to live. That's when they'd moved to Oak Ridge. I hoped in the coming days she'd open up and tell me more about her life back then, but I'd need to tread carefully. I didn't want to upset her like I'd done yesterday.

When we reached the shopping center, we parked and went inside. Along with milk, butter, and eggs, we purchased ingredients for cookies and her special lemon cake. While a teenage boy loaded our groceries into the trunk of the Camaro, a nicely dressed woman approached, carrying a single paper bag.

"Hi, Mae. I thought that was you I saw over in the produce section." Her curious gaze shifted to me, and I recognized her as Aunt Mae's neighbor. The one who'd waved at me the previous day.

Aunt Mae tipped the boy a quarter and sent him on his way. "Good morning, Georgeanne. This is my niece, Laurel. Laurel, this is my neighbor, Georgeanne Stokes."

We shook hands. "It's nice to meet you, Mrs. Stokes."

"I wondered who came to visit Mae. *It must be one of Harris's girls,* I said to myself. And I was right. How long are you in town, Laurel? I hope you and Mae will come over for tea some afternoon before you leave."

I glanced at Aunt Mae, who wore a patient expression on her face. She didn't indicate whether she would enjoy tea with her neighbor or not.

"That would be nice," I said. "I'm not sure how long I'll stay. I'm hoping to get some work done while I'm here."

"What kind of work could bring you to sleepy Oak Ridge?" Georgeanne asked with a friendly laugh. "The most exciting thing going on here is the opening of a home for senior citizens and the long lines at Fiesta Cantina, the new Mexican food restaurant out on the turnpike." She smiled at Aunt Mae. "There's torn-up ground, mounds of red clay, and stacks of two-by-fours all over town. Reminds me of how Oak Ridge looked back when we first came to work here in the forties, don't you agree, Mae?"

Aunt Mae nodded, but she didn't elaborate.

"That's actually why I'm here." I cast a quick sideways glance at Aunt Mae. I hoped I wasn't stepping out of line. Even though Aunt Mae didn't want to discuss the early years after she came to Oak Ridge, I needed to interview other residents for my dissertation. "I'm writing a paper about the history of Oak Ridge. I hope to meet people—women, in particular—who lived and worked here during the war and hear their stories. Would you be interested in answering some questions for me at some point? It shouldn't take more than an hour or so."

"My, that sounds interesting. Do you work for a newspaper or magazine?" Georgeanne asked.

"No, ma'am. I'm working on my dissertation. I hope to get a doctorate in psychology."

The woman's brow rose. "A doctorate?" She glanced at Aunt Mae. "You must be brimming with pride."

Aunt Mae didn't smile. "I am, but I also told her no one wants to talk about those days. What's past is past and should stay there. The things we did and saw aren't anyone's business."

Her hard tone seemed to surprise Georgeanne. "Why, Mae, I don't see the harm in talking about what went on in the Secret City all those years ago." She met my gaze. "People give all the credit for the bombs to those who worked at Los Alamos, but we here in Oak Ridge played an important role too. Without us, Oppenheimer and General Groves wouldn't have had the uranium required to make Little Boy. Same goes for the folks who worked in Hanford. They produced the plutonium that fueled Fat Man."

I'd only recently delved into the history of how the atomic bomb was developed. I found myself awed that Georgeanne threw out the names of the famous scientist and of the two bombs that were dropped on Japan as if they were common, everyday conversation topics. Here was a woman who knew her stuff. I had a feeling she and I would get along splendidly.

My gaze ping-ponged between the two women. I didn't want to hurt Aunt Mae's feelings, but I was pleased to find her neighbor more vocal on the subject.

"Maybe I can come over and chat with you later this afternoon," I said. It wouldn't do to invite her to Aunt Mae's.

Georgeanne beamed. "That would be lovely, dear. You're welcome to come too, Mae. I know we worked in different areas of Oak Ridge during the war, but I've never heard your story. We can compare notes, as they say."

Aunt Mae's lips pinched. "Thank you all the same, but I'd rather not remember those days. Like I said, nothing good can come from it." She opened the passenger door of the car. "Goodbye, Georgeanne."

With that, she climbed in and closed the door with a bit more force than necessary.

Georgeanne and I looked at each other.

"I'm sorry." I felt awful for having upset Aunt Mae again. "Maybe I shouldn't come over today."

"Nonsense." The woman lowered her voice. "Mae's always been secretive about what she did during the war. I can't tell you how many times I've tried to worm it out of her. Why, if I didn't know any better, I might think she'd been one of the people who actually knew what was going on back then. I've heard that those who were in the know are still hesitant to talk about it all. You come on over around three o'clock and I'll tell you about my time as a cubicle operator."

"A what?"

She grinned. "See you at three." She turned and climbed into a dark blue Ford Lincoln Continental parked next to us. With a wave, she drove off.

When I got back into the Camaro, Aunt Mae stared out the passenger-side window.

"I didn't mean to upset you, Aunt Mae," I said. "But if I'm going to write my dissertation, I have to talk to the people who were here during the war. What they experienced—what you all experienced—is historic and important." I decided I needed to be completely transparent. "I would love to know about your time here in Oak Ridge. I've read about how people, especially young women, came from all over the country to work in the Secret City. Dad remembers when you left Kentucky, but he doesn't recall ever hearing you talk about your work."

"There's a reason for that." Her brow knit. "We weren't allowed to talk about it then, and I don't want to talk about it now."

"But the secret isn't a secret anymore," I said gently. "Everyone knows about the atomic bomb."

After a long moment, she turned to face me. "You probably think I'm just a foolish old woman, but there's a reason I can't—won't—relive those days. That reason is no one's business."

I reached to grasp her hand. "I don't think you're foolish. I don't know what you experienced during the war. If it is truly something you don't wish to discuss, I will respect your privacy." I squeezed her fingers. "Is it okay if I stay with you a little longer? I promise not to bring up the subject again."

She tightened her grip on me. "Of course you can stay. I'm glad you're here." She paused. "And I am proud of you, Laurel. Proud of your hard work and determination. I know you mean well, but I'm not going to be able to help with your project. I'm very sorry, but I just can't."

"It's okay, Aunt Mae."

We made our way back to the house. After lunch, we baked a batch of chocolate chip cookies, then Aunt Mae went to her room to lie down. As three o'clock neared, I gathered a notebook and two pencils, ready to jot down Georgeanne's remembrances of bygone days.

She was waiting on her porch when I arrived.

"I can't recall the last time anyone was interested in hearing my stories about working in Oak Ridge during the war." She led the way into the house. "My kids and grands aren't interested. They'll humor me every now and again and let me tell a tale or two, but we might as well be back in the days of the war, keeping secrets, for all I get to talk about it."

I settled on a floral sofa with my notebook and pencils while she got comfortable in a plaid armchair. Although her home and Aunt Mae's were identical in their layout, the similarities ended there. Unlike my aunt's sparse décor, Georgeanne's house brimmed with furniture, knickknacks, framed photographs, and books. Lots and lots of books.

When I remarked on the similar floor plans, Georgeanne filled in the details.

"Housing was always a problem in Oak Ridge during the war. The Army built different sizes of homes, dormitories, apartments, and barracks as fast as they could, but it was never fast enough. They even brought in thousands of tiny trailers and simple wooden shelters they called hutments." She glanced around the room. "These little two-bedroom houses were classified as Type A Cemestos, named after the building material used to construct them. There were others that were larger—types B, C, D, and so on. Only married couples with children were allowed to live in them back then. Stanley and I bought this one in 1962. Mae moved into hers the following summer."

I noticed a wedding photograph on the mantel. Georgeanne's gaze followed mine.

"We spent many happy years in Oak Ridge and raised our daughters here. Stanley passed away five years ago. I miss him every day."

"Did you meet him here in Oak Ridge?"

She nodded. "He worked at X-10, the graphite reactor. I hadn't been here but a couple days when my shoes got stuck in the never-ending mud on the way to my first dance. I tell you, it felt like I was in quicksand. I was nearly in tears when this handsome fellow slogged out to me, scooped me up in his arms, and carried me to one of the wooden walkways. Then he went back and retrieved my shoes. I knew I'd found my knight in shining, albeit muddy, armor."

She picked up a plate with blueberry-filled pastries from where it sat next to a pitcher of iced tea on the low table between us. I was stuffed with tuna salad and cookies but didn't turn down the delicious-looking treat.

"I appreciate your willingness to tell me about your experiences.

Last week I had the opportunity to interview a gentleman who was one of the mathematicians in Los Alamos. He lives in New York City now. His stories were fascinating, although I'm sure he didn't tell me even half of what really went on. I hope to travel to New Mexico and Washington next summer to visit those locations and meet with people who still reside in the area."

Georgeanne looked thoughtful. "I imagine those who held important jobs—the scientists and people who knew the truth about the Manhattan Project from the beginning—would be a bit reticent about divulging certain information. Both Los Alamos and Oak Ridge have laboratories that are still in operation, working on all kinds of top secret jobs for the government. Secrecy was drummed into us back in those days, and I suspect that is still true today."

She asked questions about my studies, about psychology in general, and what I hoped to achieve after I received my doctorate. Then we dove into the reason I was there.

"I'm writing my dissertation on the people who worked for the Manhattan Project during the war. How the secrecy and pressure affected them, short term and long term. I'm especially interested in learning more about women like you and Aunt Mae. I want to understand why you were willing to come to a place you'd never heard of and do a job you knew nothing about." I picked up my notebook. "I'd like to ask a series of questions about your time at Oak Ridge. Would that be all right?"

"Of course, dear. Like I said, I don't get to talk about those days much, and unlike your aunt, I believe there's value in telling our stories. After all, no one on the planet experienced what we did. Our role to help win the war was as unique as the bomb itself."

I jotted down her words. "That's exactly how I feel. My generation and the generations to come need to hear those stories. We can't change the historical facts or the outcomes, but we can learn from them." My aunt's worried face came to mind. "I know there are people like Aunt Mae who would rather not go back and relive those days, and I respect that. But I'm also grateful for people like you who are willing to share with the world about the important work you did back then."

Georgeanne chuckled. "My, you make me sound like a heroine in a novel. The reality, however, was far less dramatic. I was a country girl looking for some excitement. My papa owned a farm in Clinton, not far from here. When the government started snatching up thousands of acres of land near the Black Oak Ridge, he feared they'd take ours too. They didn't, of course, but back then we didn't know what was going on over here. Communities like Wheat and Elza, Scarboro and Robertsville—places where we'd had friends and family—all but disappeared in just a matter of weeks."

"That must've been frightening. I can only imagine what it must have been like for people who were forced off their land. You said you knew some of them?"

"Oh, sure, we knew a number of folks who had to move. Some families had lived on their land for generations." She shook her head. "They'd receive a letter in the mail or tacked to the door, telling them they had so many days to vacate the premises. Some of the school children even heard about it from their teachers or principal and ran home to tell their folks. The whole thing was upsetting, but people didn't have any choice. If the government said they had to go, they had to go. The officials eventually acquired sixty thousand acres. I don't know how many families had to move, but it was a lot. Most of them didn't get a fair price, either. We were awfully glad the suited men didn't come to Clinton."

"When did you first realize a large government facility was being built here?"

"Rumors and speculations flew from the moment folks heard

about the land acquisitions. Lots of companies in those days were making things for the war effort. Tanks, guns, munitions, that sort of thing. We figured some big manufacturing plant was comin' in, considering all the acres of land they'd bought. Once we got over our initial touchiness about how the properties were taken, excitement about what was being built settled in. Jobs in those days were scarce. The depression still had its grip on most of us, so the prospect of a big employer comin' to the area was good news." She shrugged. "Funny thing is, no one could figure what was being manufactured here. Trainloads of something came in at all hours of the day and night, but nothing ever went out. No tanks. No Jeeps. No nothing."

"How old were you when you began working at Oak Ridge?"

"I was nineteen, as naive as the day I was born, almost. I was hired to work for a company called Clinton Engineer Works. Papa couldn't believe it when I told him how much money they were willing to pay me. If my memory is correct, I made seventy-five dollars every two weeks, which was a fortune for a country girl like me."

"What was your job?"

"I was what they called a cubicle operator. I didn't have a clue what that meant back then. I'm still not certain I fully understand what I did all day, but I'll try to describe it to you." She sat forward. "You see, I worked at the plant known as Y-12. All the buildings at CEW were given code names—a letter, followed by a number—and thousands of us girls were assigned to Y-12. The plant ran twenty-four hours a day, seven days a week, so we worked in shifts. Even though the job was tedious and boring most of the time, I took pride in my position. I tried never to miss a day or call in sick, because every job was important to the overall project. What I did, all day long, was sit on a high stool and monitor knobs and dials on a big machine we called a cubicle."

I tried to visualize what she meant. "Can you describe it? What did the cubicle look like?"

"It was a tall, wide, metal boxlike machine, and it had all kinds of needle gauges and meters across the front of it. There were handles and knobs to turn, too. We were given some training, and they told us, 'If this dial went over too far on that gauge, you get busy and get it back where it's supposed to be.' The same thing would happen on this gauge or that gauge, and we would have to twist and turn instruments lickety-split until it was right again. I got the hang of it after a while and knew which knobs to turn to get everything back to normal."

"What happened if you couldn't get them—the dials—back to where they should be?"

"We had a supervisor, and he'd come over to help."

I tapped the pencil on the notebook. "But you didn't know what you were doing at the time? You didn't have any idea what the dials and meters were for?"

She shook her head. "Not a clue. We learned about the atomic bomb the day they dropped it on Hiroshima. Someone later told me Y-12 was where the uranium was enriched using giant magnets, and that the cubicles we worked on had something to do with the process." She gave a slow nod. "That's when it all began to make sense."

CHAPTER FOUR

MAE

MY FIRST WEEK at Clinton Engineer Works was uneventful. I couldn't start my job at K-25 until my security clearance was approved, so I filled the days becoming familiar with Townsite.

Townsite, or Oak Ridge, as it had officially been named last summer, had most everything any other American city offered. Grocery markets, drug stores, department stores, shoe shops, barbers, restaurants. There was a movie theater, tennis courts where dances were held in the evenings, and a bowling alley. The difference was every business in Oak Ridge was brand-new and stayed open twenty-four hours a day. Even the cafeteria where we took our meals never closed. Because everyone at CEW worked in shifts, Townsite remained a bustling place day and night. Only on Sundays were things a bit quieter.

Although Sissy and I had fun exploring our new home and getting to know the girls in our dormitory, I was anxious to begin work and find out what all the secrecy was about. Many of the young women I'd arrived with were assigned to Y-12, like Sissy, who'd started her new job the previous day but hadn't come home that evening with any information she was willing to share. Some of the other girls from our group were hired to work as clerks, telephone operators, teachers, and other jobs I couldn't remember. But according to Prudence Thorpe, a girl from the dorm whom Sissy and I dubbed "the knower of all things," I was the only newbie assigned to K-25.

Prudence worked at the main administration building, nicknamed Castle on the Hill, where we'd gone that first day for our orientation. She had a way of revealing information that led you to believe you were simply sharing an innocent conversation with the chatty redhead, rather than treading into dangerous gossip-infested waters where you ought not go. She'd been at CEW for six months, which made her an old-timer compared to the rest of us. I had a suspicion I'd need to keep on my toes whenever she was around. I wouldn't want to be caught talking about things that were off-limits.

When my security clearance was finally approved, I was required to have a physical examination and a blood test at the medical clinic. The results were apparently acceptable, because I was given a schedule and told to be at the plant the following morning. It surprised me to learn I had to travel eleven miles outside of town by bus to get to K-25. The plant where Sissy worked was only three or so miles away.

Like everything else in town, buses ran twenty-four hours a day. The terminal, a fair trek along wooden walkways and muddy streets from our dormitory, was a madhouse of people and bulky vehicles, but I'd managed to find a bus going to K-25. I'd enjoyed the thirty-minute drive, taking me west out of town into the green, tree-covered hills that reminded me of Kentucky.

However, the first time I saw the enormous structure where I was to work, my mouth gaped. Rising up from rich Tennessee farmland like an ancient behemoth, the giant creature Job writes about in the Old Testament, K-25 was like nothing I'd ever seen or even imagined. It was impossible to believe construction on the massive four-story, U-shaped building had begun just two years prior, a fact I'd learned from Prudence.

Upon arrival at the enormous complex, the guard at the entrance portal checked my ID badge, then directed me to K-1024, the maintenance shop, a building located in the open U area of the plant, known as the courtyard. Once there, I met Mr. Colby, the foreman. He informed me my main job would be as a maintenance clerk, but I would also run errands throughout the plant that included transporting tools and small parts to crews making repairs. He handed me a thick instruction and operations manual and told me to familiarize myself with thousands and thousands of mechanical parts and tools listed within the pages.

That was three days ago. I hadn't seen Mr. Colby again until he appeared in the doorway to the small office where I sat.

"Miss Willett, are you ready to get to work?"

I stood, nervous excitement swirling through my belly. "Yes, sir."

He led the way outside where we crossed a sort of alley between the primary maintenance shop and the main building. As we went through a door and entered the behemoth, I found myself in a world as foreign to me as Wonderland was to Alice.

Mr. Colby offered a running monologue of what I was seeing while we toured the huge building. The first level housed auxiliary equipment such as transformers, switch gears, and air handling systems. The second floor contained hundreds of what he referred to as converters and compressors. The third level was filled with thousands of pipes, big and small, where groups of women worked, doing what, I couldn't say. The operating floor on the fourth level housed rows of instrument panels, as well as a control room where operators monitored hordes of gauges and dials. I couldn't fathom what any of it was for, especially since Mr. Colby neglected to show me the product that was being manufactured at the plant.

Back at the maintenance shop, he gave me a tour of it too, introducing me to men and women along the way. The whole thing was overwhelming, and I felt utterly inadequate when we returned to the small office where we'd started. I wasn't sure why I'd been hired to work in such a place, and I feared I'd be fired before I had a chance to send any money home to my family.

"I imagine you have questions about what you just saw," Mr. Colby said, "but for now, keep them to yourself. As you become accustomed to your job and the layout of the plant, many of them will be answered."

I must have looked like a frightened squirrel, frozen as I was, because he offered a sympathetic smile. "Don't worry, Miss Willett. I'm sure you'll get the hang of things quickly."

He was about my pa's age and had a fatherly way about him. I hoped he was right in saying I'd get used to things.

"Can you ride a bicycle?"

The question seemed odd. "Yes, sir."

"Good. You'll use a bicycle to get around. K-25 is one mile long, from end to end, with four levels. That's a lot of walking."

He instructed me to utilize a map of the facility tacked to the wall in his office to help find my way around. Because some areas of the plant were restricted, I was given special security clearance on my badge to access them on an as-needed basis.

"But," Mr. Colby said, a firmness to his tone, "you are only allowed in areas where you've been assigned. And remember, what happens at K-25 needs to stay at K-25."

Cleanliness, he went on, was of utmost importance at the plant. I was to take care not to track in mud and dust, two of the most available and bothersome commodities on the Reservation.

He recommended I purchase a pair of rubber galoshes from one of the shops in town. I didn't tell him I couldn't afford such an extravagance, at least not until I received my first paycheck. I would need to remember to clean my shoes before entering the plant every morning.

The most surprising advice he gave, however, was regarding my attire.

"It would be best if you wore trousers rather than a skirt," he said, indicating Mama's made-over dress I'd worn. "You'll be riding a bicycle and sometimes carrying machine parts that may be greasy. If you don't own any trousers, we can put in a requisition with Union Carbide for some coveralls. You'll notice many of the women wearing them."

I couldn't help but grin. I'd never worn trousers before. The prospect seemed quite daring.

Within an hour, I found myself on a bike equipped with a basket, zipping around what surely must be the biggest building on the planet. It surprised me to see that many other employees utilized bicycles to get around too. I became lost multiple times, but people were kind and offered directions. By lunchtime my legs were tired, but I found I'd enjoyed the experience.

The cafeteria was a lengthy walk from the main building. A long line of hungry employees was already there when I arrived. The sight was nothing new at CEW. Everywhere you went—market, movie theater, dormitory bathroom—you were likely to encounter lines. Just yesterday I'd seen a string of people that stretched half a block near Town Center Number 1, the main shopping area. Someone said they were waiting to purchase cigarettes from a newly arrived shipment. As I skirted around them, I was very glad I'd never taken up the habit.

I stood outside the cafeteria waiting my turn. A second line formed on the opposite side of the building, but it consisted only of Black employees. I'd grown up in a small Kentucky town that had as many Black families as white, but we were all poor coal mining people, living in company-owned shanties. Other than segregated bathrooms at the local café, I hadn't paid much attention to the separation of races that was common in other parts of the country.

A woman about my age met my gaze across the space between us. I'd seen her in the pipe area that morning, polishing giant pipes. It seemed an odd thing to do, since everything in the plant looked pristine, including the concrete floors, but then I remembered what Mr. Colby said about the importance of cleanliness. I didn't know what was being manufactured at K-25—I hadn't seen any military tanks, guns, or things soldiers would use to fight the enemy as I biked around—but whatever the product was, the powers that be didn't want it coated in dirt.

The woman offered a slight nod, then disappeared into a separate dining area.

I quickly downed a ham sandwich with a glass of water, then returned to the maintenance shop. By the end of my shift, I was exhausted. Along with hundreds of other employees, I left the building through Clock Alley, where we clocked in and out, then took a shuttle across the complex to the security portal and bus terminal. When it was finally my turn, I presented my badge to the armed guard and exited the secure area through a turnstile.

While I waited at the bus stop with a crowd of noisy people, I noticed the same woman I'd seen at the cafeteria standing on the fringe of the group. Other Black women stood with her. Again, we made eye contact. This time I gave a friendly nod. She inclined her head, a hint of a smile at the edges of her eyes.

A bus arrived and we piled on as many as would fit. I squeezed onto a bench seat with two other women, hoping I didn't fall off the edge if we hit a bump. I glanced to the back of the bus and found the Black woman sitting alone, with a bench to herself. I wished I could move to join her, but even in Kentucky that wasn't allowed.

Instead of going directly to Townsite, as the buses I'd ridden thus far had done, this one went in a different direction. I feared I'd made a mistake and would need to ask for a transfer if it didn't go to town.

The first stop was Happy Valley, a sprawling residential area not far from the plant, made up of small houses and khaki-colored trailer homes, the likes of which I'd never seen before. Hundreds of the miniature, bullet-shaped residences lined the streets, making me curious about what they looked like inside.

People poured off the bus, including the two women I'd shared the seat with. Others boarded but none asked to sit with me.

After another stop in Happy Valley, we drove to a separate housing area. Here, the dwellings were different. Instead of trailers or typical houses, dozens and dozens of identical, square huts filled the view. A fence and a ditch divided it into two sections, with a guard stationed at a gate to one of them. Wooden walkways and electrical poles with wires ran throughout, although there wasn't much space between the huts. I was surprised to see that each one had wooden shutters instead of glass windowpanes, most of which were propped open to let in a breeze. The dwellings were even smaller than the shanties the coal company provided back home, and I couldn't imagine who lived in such crude conditions.

It was then that I noticed every Black person—men and women alike—got off the bus.

As the bus pulled away, I saw the woman from the cafeteria. With her back straight and her chin held high, she walked with other women to the guarded entrance of the sad-looking housing area, while the men went in the opposite direction.

The driver announced the next stop was Townsite, and I settled back in the seat. However, some of the excitement I'd felt that day faded as I thought about the comfortable dorm room that awaited me.

My days were filled with office tasks and running errands for Mr. Colby. I enjoyed biking throughout the cavernous plant, carrying parts and tools used on enormous machines, huge holding tanks, and millions of miles of pipe, all located within the main building. There were smaller structures throughout the K-25 complex, too, and errands to them allowed me to go outside and get some fresh air. K-1101 housed big cylinders and smaller tubes. K-1201 held air compressors that powered many of the tools used in the machine shop. There was K this and K that, and I had to learn each of their locations. By the end of the week, however, I had no more knowledge of what was happening at K-25 than I'd had on my first day, a fact that annoyed my naturally curious nature.

Sissy was in the same boat as far as her job at Y-12.

"I know we aren't s'posed to talk about what we do to anyone," she said that night as we prepared for bed, "but I can't figure how telling you that I sit in a chair all day long, turning dials and knobs, is gonna hurt a thing."

I agreed. "I feel the same way. All I do is file papers or ride a bicycle here and there, delivering parts and tools. Whatever the big secret is that everyone is trying to keep, it hasn't got anything to do with me."

We settled on our beds, separated by a nightstand.

Sissy had her pale-yellow hair in rollers, ready to style in the morning. She was a pretty thing, with her deep-blue eyes and curvy figure, but I'd happily found her unassuming and sweet. We'd had tons of fun that evening at the tennis court, dancing with one fellow after the other. With so many single men and women working at CEW, flirting and romances were in abundance. I, however, was determined not to let myself get carried away by every charming man who asked for a dance. Even the military boys, looking so handsome in their uniforms, couldn't sway me to take a walk in the woods with them, no doubt a place where more than one kiss was stolen.

Sissy fluffed her pillow. "Did you notice that older fella who kept asking me to dance?"

"Was he bothering you?" I was two years older than my roommate and already felt like a protective big sister.

"Oh no, he was very polite." She giggled. "He's kind of tall and skinny, with wire-rimmed glasses, but," she paused, growing serious, "he's nice."

"What's his name?"

"Clive. Clive Morrison. He works at K-25, like you."

I frowned. "He shouldn't have told you that. You just met."

"I don't see how it could make a difference. Besides, we talked about a lot of things that had nothin' to do with this place. He's from Massachusetts. His ancestors came over on the Mayflower." Her wide eyes told me this tidbit of information had made an impression.

I scoffed. "I doubt that. I'm sure he was just trying to sound important so you'd go on a date with him."

Her brow puckered. "He seemed like a respectable gentleman, Mae. I like him."

It was clear I'd need to tread carefully on the subject of Clive Morrison, at least until another boy caught her attention. "I'm sorry. I don't mean to imply he lied to you. I just think it's best to get better acquainted with him, that's all."

"I know I'm young and don't have much experience with fellas." Her slim shoulders lifted in a shrug. "Mama wouldn't let me date any of the boys back home. She said I was destined for somethin' bigger and better than being a farmer's wife in rural Georgia." A sheepish look crossed her face. "Mama says I'm pretty enough to be in movies, but I don't know about that."

"I would have to agree with your mother," I said. "But pretty girls can do anything they put their minds to, same as anyone else. Look at you now." I waved my hands in a dramatic way to indicate our austere dorm room. "Here you are in *exciting* Nowhere, Tennessee, sitting in a chair all day long, turning knobs and dials at a plant where they don't make anything we can name. You stand in long lines, ride in crowded buses, and walk through mud every day. I don't see how being in a Hollywood movie can even compare to this, do you?"

We laughed so hard, the girls in the room next door banged on the wall.

CHAPTER FIVE

LAUREL

I SPENT AN ENJOYABLE AFTERNOON with Georgeanne. Her stories were fascinating and brought wartime Oak Ridge to life in my imagination. Those unforgettable days would have been something to experience, to be sure. The most important question I asked her, and the answer she gave, played over in my mind as I walked back to Aunt Mae's.

"How did you feel after you learned your work at Oak Ridge had a role in making the atomic bomb that killed over one hundred thousand people when it fell on Hiroshima?"

Georgeanne had sat silent for a long time, staring out the window, before she answered.

"Like everyone else, I was elated the war came to an end. Some people wished we'd had the bomb years earlier, because it might have stopped Hitler and prevented the loss of millions of lives. When we heard that we'd helped enrich the uranium that was used to make it, we were proud. Proud that our work helped bring our boys home. Proud that President Truman mentioned us in his speech to the nation."

Her eyes had taken on a troubled look. "But once things settled down and I had time to think about it, I wasn't as proud as I'd been when I first heard the news."

"Why is that?"

"Because so many innocent people in Japan were killed by that bomb. By Little Boy. It wasn't just enemy soldiers. It was men, women, children. All gone in a matter of seconds. Three days later when the military dropped Fat Man on Nagasaki . . . Well, it was too much. Too much death. Too much destruction."

The sorrow in her voice was unmistakable.

"I was happy, then I was sad. There were days when I couldn't stop thinking that I had a part in killing all those people. It bothered me. It bothered me for a long time afterwards, but there wasn't anything I could do about it. I ultimately had to stop thinking about it and move on, so that's what I did. That's what we all did."

We'd sat in silence for a time, letting the truth of her words linger in our minds.

I'd had one last question.

"Knowing what you know now, would you do anything differently? Would you still accept a job at Oak Ridge, knowing that what was being produced here would change the world irrevocably?"

She'd met my gaze straight on. "I would. It brought the war to an end."

I found Aunt Mae in the backyard, watering a patch of flowers in a bed beneath the kitchen window. Weeds sprouted up, nearly as tall as the plants themselves. Peggy wandered through the vegetation, her pug nose close to the ground.

Aunt Mae glanced up as I approached. "How did it go with Georgeanne? I imagine she has all kinds of interesting stories about living and working in Oak Ridge in the early years."

I appreciated Aunt Mae's inquiry, considering her resistance to discussing anything about those days. "I learned a lot and got some good information I'll use in my dissertation."

She moved to the faucet and turned off the water to the hose. A heavy sigh followed.

"I feel bad that I've been so adamant about not wanting to talk about my time at Oak Ridge." When I gave her a hopeful look, she said, "I haven't changed my mind. Those are days I'd rather not think about. But I also don't want to be the only one who didn't help you with your research. You're *my* niece, and I'm very proud of you, Laurel. I brought out a box of things I kept from back then. Old newspapers. A handful of mementos and such. You're welcome to look through it."

Her offer was surprising and much appreciated. "Thank you, Aunt Mae." I hugged her. "I'll go through it after dinner."

Wanting to continue to build on the connection we were slowly forming, I volunteered to weed the bed while Aunt Mae cut flowers for the table.

"I haven't spent much time out of doors this spring. My poor eyesight makes it hard to get around. I wouldn't want to take a tumble in the yard and hurt myself. I've even had to hire a high school boy to come mow the grass." She glanced to the overgrown plot in the corner. "I won't try to plant a garden this year, although I'll miss my homegrown tomatoes."

I followed her gaze. What should've been a well-tended garden with new growth was instead overrun with weeds. It would take some elbow grease to get it ready for planting. I didn't have much of a green thumb, but I did have a strong desire to do something nice for my aunt.

"If you'd like, I could help get the garden planted. Some tomatoes and whatever else you might enjoy that wouldn't take too much tending."

Her brow rose. "You wouldn't mind? It's a lot of work, getting the ground prepared and all."

"I've never planted a garden, so this will be a learning experience."

She chuckled. "That it will. We can go to the hardware store tomorrow and buy some seeds and starter plants." The look of pleasure on her face was my reward.

Over a dinner of homemade pot pie made with the leftover chicken from last night, we began a list of what to purchase the next day. I suggested we buy an extra hose and sprinkler so Aunt Mae wouldn't have to cross the uneven lawn every time the garden needed watering. She could just step out the back door and turn on the faucet.

"Mama always had a garden when we were growing up," she said as we lingered at the table once our bellies were full. "Pa worked in the coal mines and money was scarce. The company store charged outrageously inflated prices for everything, so Mama did her best to supplement our diet with homegrown vegetables. She'd save seeds all winter and barter with neighbors for this one or that one. If she could scrape up enough money, she'd order some from a catalog."

"Dad said Grandma was an excellent cook." I smiled. "You certainly inherited her skills."

"Our mama could make the most delicious meals out of the simplest ingredients. I was glad when she and Harris came to live with me after Pa died. I hope I was able to make her last years a little easier."

After we tidied the kitchen, I was anxious to look through Aunt Mae's Oak Ridge memorabilia. As we moved into the living room, my eyes fell on the plain, medium-sized wooden box where it sat on the coffee table. I hated to abandon her and carry it to my room, but I also didn't know if it was a good idea to look through them in her presence.

She must've sensed my dilemma. "Why don't we go through the box together." She settled on the sofa. "It's been ages since I opened it. I can't recall what I might have saved."

Thrilled with her change of heart, I sat next to her.

I read the words stamped on the lid. "Union Carbide Company."

"That was the name of the company in charge of K-25, the plant where I worked. They still run things today."

"I thought everyone was employed by Clinton Engineer Works."

"We were," she stated matter-of-factly, "but Clinton Engineer Works was just a code name for the Manhattan Project at Oak Ridge. Of course we didn't know that at the time. There were different companies under CEW's umbrella, I guess you'd say. Tennessee Eastman operated Y-12, where Georgeanne worked. DuPont was involved with X-10, which was the graphite reactor."

It was extraordinary to hear my aunt share her knowledge of the history of Oak Ridge. She'd seen and experienced things I'd only read about in history books.

"I didn't know you worked at K-25. Do you mind if I ask what you did there?"

She hesitated before answering. "It's not very exciting. I was with the maintenance department and worked as a clerk and an errand girl. I rode a bicycle around the plant because it was so big, and carried parts and tools to the various areas where machinery was housed."

"I saw an aerial photograph of K-25 in a book at the university library. The caption said the U-shaped building was the world's largest structure at the time. Bigger than the Pentagon, which had recently been built."

She nodded. "General Leslie Groves oversaw the construction of both buildings. President Roosevelt handpicked him to head up the Manhattan Project, although we didn't hear his name or the official project name until everyone knew about the bomb."

I couldn't imagine working for a company without knowing what its purpose was or what was being made. Yet that is exactly what over seventy thousand people did every day in Oak Ridge during the war.

She seemed to warm to the subject. "General Groves was given the monumental task of finding people—scientists, physicists, and the like—smart enough to figure out how to construct an atomic bomb before the Nazis beat us to it. Then he had to build the facilities to make it. No one had ever done anything like this before. Years later I read that even some of the scientists who worked on the project weren't sure the bomb would work once it was built."

To prepare for writing my dissertation, I'd done quite a bit of research on General Groves, J. Robert Oppenheimer, Los Alamos, and the making of the atomic bomb. Yet it was utterly fascinating to hear the story from Aunt Mae's point of view. Like Georgeanne and the others, she'd witnessed it all unfold and had a unique, personal perspective that doesn't carry over in written historical accounts of the event.

Those were the stories I was after.

I lifted the lid to the box. A yellowed newspaper lay on top. *The Knoxville Journal's* bold headline announced, "War Ends."

"Wow," I breathed, carefully removing it from the box. "I've seen microfilm of newspapers from August 1945, but to actually hold one is really cool."

Aunt Mae leaned in to get a closer look, squinting behind her thick glasses. "Newspapers generally cost five cents in those days, but after the bomb fell, the price went up to a dollar because there was such a demand. We didn't have television back then, so newsprint and radio were how we heard about everything."

Two more newspapers followed. One front-page headline read "Oak Ridge Attacks Japanese" and another proclaimed "Atomic Super-Bomb, Made in Oak Ridge, Strikes Japan."

Aunt Mae rubbed her eyes and leaned her head against the back of the sofa. "As you can imagine, the atomic bomb and the role Oak Ridgers played in its creation was the talk of the town for weeks."

I longed to ask her all sorts of questions—the same ones I'd asked Georgeanne earlier—but I didn't want to spoil things. Aunt Mae seemed willing enough to share general information about the history of Oak Ridge and her experiences, so I didn't want to push. Hopefully she'd see that talking about the past wasn't as unpleasant as she believed.

I set the newspapers aside with a plan to read them later that night after I turned in. Beneath lay a hodgepodge of items. A bound security manual. Ticket stubs to a movie theater. A booklet that once held ration stamps. A man's yellowed handkerchief.

At the very bottom lay two identification badges.

I picked up the one that had a black-and-white photograph of a younger Aunt Mae and held it where we both could see it. A five-digit number was printed beneath her picture, followed by *Oak Ridge Resident*.

She didn't lean forward as she'd done before but fixed her gaze on the badge. "We couldn't go anywhere on the Reservation without that."

"The Reservation?"

"That's what everyone called Oak Ridge back then. Sometimes people used its code name, Site X, or Townsite. Oak Ridge as a city didn't exist on any map. It sprang up out of the ground nearly overnight after General Groves decided this was the location where he wanted to build the plants to enrich the uranium. It's said that by the end of the war there were over seventy-five thousand people living and working on the Reservation, yet the world didn't know we were here until the bomb was dropped on Japan."

"It truly was a secret city," I said.

She nodded but didn't elaborate.

I removed the second badge. A pretty blonde woman looked into the camera, her lips lifted in a slight smile. "Who is this?" I handed it to her.

Aunt Mae squinted at the badge, then gasped. "I'd forgotten this was inside that box." She stared at the photograph, clearly distressed by the image.

My question went unanswered. Without knowing who the woman was, I couldn't begin to guess why seeing her pleasant face upset my aunt. It seemed best to end this trip down memory lane.

I gently took the badge out of her grasp. "We can put these things away now, Aunt Mae."

She let me take it from her, but her face had drained of color. "I knew it was a mistake to revisit the past," she whispered, shaking her head. "I'm sorry, Laurel. This is all a big mistake."

Without waiting for a reply, she stood and hurried down the hall. Peggy trotted after her. The door to her bedroom clicked shut a moment later. Muffled sobs followed.

I huffed out a breath, loaded with frustration and regret. Even though it had been her idea to look through the contents of the box, I felt guilty. Curious, I studied the picture of the blonde woman, then turned the badge over and found printed information.

Bearer: Sylvia Jean Galloway.

I'd never heard the name before. It listed her height, weight, hair and eye color. It also bore her signature and that of an Identification Officer.

Her hair was styled in the fashion many young women wore in the 1940s, with a large roll of hair in the center of her head and bouncy waves of golden locks to her shoulders. Her rounded cheeks and bright eyes gave the appearance of innocence.

"Who are you?" I wondered aloud. "And why did seeing your picture hurt Aunt Mae?"

The answers to those questions may never come.

I picked up Aunt Mae's badge. "Maebelle Ann Willett." It too gave her physical description. When I turned it over again, twenty-something-year-old Aunt Mae looked at me. She was young, pretty, full of dreams, I suspected.

I thought back to the day before I left for Tennessee. I'd gone to my parents' house for dinner, hoping for some inside information on Aunt Mae. Dad said his sister was beyond excited to leave Kentucky on what she'd called a grand adventure.

"Mae was always curious about the world," he'd said. "Always had her head in a book she'd borrowed from her teachers. She'd wanted to go to college and do something with her life, but she was different after the war."

"How so?" I'd asked.

"It was as though the light in her had been snuffed out. She'd lost her zest for life. Whether that was due to the war or the atomic bomb, I couldn't say. She stayed in Oak Ridge and worked at K-25 until it shut down in 1964. Funny thing, though. Mae never wanted to talk about her job or anything to do with Oak Ridge's big secret."

I repacked the box, put the lid on it, and carried it to my room. Reading through the newspapers tonight, however, no longer appealed. Clearly Aunt Mae's memories of life in Oak Ridge during the war held an unpleasantness she had no desire to revisit. Research for my dissertation wasn't important enough to cause distress to my aging aunt.

As I readied for bed, I came to a conclusion.

I'd simply need to find other Oak Ridge residents like Georgeanne willing to share their stories and leave dear Aunt Mae's in the past.

CHAPTER SIX

MAE

DAYS TURNED INTO WEEKS. Weeks turned into months.

By the end of September, I felt like an old-timer at CEW, especially when new, wide-eyed employees arrived, which happened on a regular basis. I'd become used to mud, buses, and long lines, but I'd also experienced more fun than I ever had in Kentucky.

Sissy and I joined a bowling league, played bridge in the recreation room, and saw two movies I'd heard about but hadn't had the opportunity or the money to see back home. There were dances at the tennis court or one of the rec centers, sporting games to attend, Sunday church services at Chapel on the Hill, and gab sessions in the dormitory after curfew with girls who'd quickly become friends. The first day we visited the community swimming pool, a young photographer—Ed Westcott, the only person authorized to document life in Oak Ridge through photographs—asked permission to take our picture. We felt like movie stars as we posed beside the pool's edge.

Life on the Reservation suited me just fine.

A maintenance request came in after lunch. Although there were other clerical girls employed at the shop, I was the only one currently in the office. A large compressor on the second level required repairs. I loaded the basket on my bike with tools the crew may not have in their tool kits and arrived to find a group of men gathered around the gigantic machine. Three employees from the maintenance crew were adamant about what the problem was, but another young man I didn't recognize calmly disagreed.

While I waited, I noticed the fellow doing the talking wore trousers and a white short-sleeved button-down shirt like the guys I'd seen in the control room upstairs. Most of the maintenance crew and other employees who worked on the plant floor opted to wear coveralls, since much of what they did every day required getting their hands dirty. Wearing regular street clothes was only done by those whose jobs kept them away from grease and grime.

The argument ended when a supervisor arrived. Much to the obvious chagrin of the maintenance crew, he agreed with the young man. I saw frustration in their eyes as they unloaded my basket, adding the tools I'd brought to those they already had, and got to work.

The young man stepped away to let them do their job.

When he glanced at me, he smiled. "Hi. I'm Garlyn Young." He stuck out his hand.

I offered mine. "Maebelle Willett."

He nodded as we shook hands. "I know. I've seen you around."

When my brow rose, he hurried to add, "Your boss, Mr. Colby, and I work together sometimes. He mentioned your name."

An awkward silence sat between us. I couldn't escape, since I had to wait in case the repair crew needed additional tools or something from the maintenance shop. Garlyn didn't appear to be in a hurry to leave either.

"How long have you been in Oak Ridge?" he asked after a time.

"I arrived a few months ago. You?"

A wry grin inched up his face. "I arrived last year."

"Wow, you're really an old-timer."

He chuckled. "That I am."

The crew boss asked me to retrieve some parts from the shop, so I moved in the direction of where I'd parked my bicycle.

Garlyn followed. "May I ask you a question?"

"That depends." I glanced at him. "If you want to know what I do at K-25, what we make here, or how many people are employed at CEW, then the answer is no."

That made him laugh. "Your secrets are safe. I was wondering if you'd like to have dinner with me tonight. We could go to the snack bar in town. Have you tried their milkshakes yet?"

My mouth fairly watered at the mention of the sweet treat, but I was determined not to form any romantic attachments. When the war ended and I was no longer employed at CEW, I would return to Kentucky.

Sissy, on the other hand, had gone on a number of dates with Clive Morrison. His job gave him access to an Army sedan, making him one of the few people we knew with a vehicle. She said they'd park near the river and talk for hours. Although she didn't gush about the young man, I could tell she was smitten. I'd only met Clive once, but there was something about his demeanor that felt phony to me. Like he was putting on airs, wanting to impress people, which seemed silly. We lived in a secret city in the hills of East Tennessee. No one cared what school you graduated from or how far back your lineage went.

But Garlyn Young seemed polite and obviously had a good position at K-25. He was also nice-looking, with sandy-colored hair and warm brown eyes. Maybe I should consider—

"Get going, Willett," the crew boss bellowed.

I startled.

Turning, I found his angry glare aimed at me. "Yes, sir."

I hurried to climb onto the bicycle, embarrassed. When I peeked at Garlyn, his scowl was directed at the other man, not at me.

He moved alongside me as I began to pedal. "Dinner?" he said, his voice lowered.

I nodded and whispered, "Yes, I'll have dinner with you."

He grinned as I pedaled away.

By the time I returned with the requested parts, Garlyn was nowhere in sight. I worried how I would find him after my shift ended, but I would have to figure that out later.

The repair wasn't going well. I sat on the concrete floor to wait it out. I wished I'd brought *The Long Winter* with me to fill the time. I'd borrowed the book by Laura Ingalls Wilder from the Reservation library and found the tale of blizzards, farmwork, and life on the Dakota Territory prairie fascinating. I couldn't wait to read what happened next.

"Ma'am?"

I looked up to find the Black woman from the cafeteria a short distance from me. I hadn't seen her again after that first day and figured she'd been put on a different shift. She carried a big bucket filled with rags and bottles of liquid in one hand and a broom with a dustpan in the other.

I scrambled to my feet. "Yes?"

She gave a polite nod. "I was told to come clean up once the repair is finished." Her soft voice held a light Southern accent.

I glanced at the crew, who seemed to be wrapping things up. A pool of some type of oil or dirty water spread over the concrete beneath the compressor.

When I faced her again, I introduced myself. "I'm Mae Willett."

"Pleasure makin' your acquaintance, Miss Willett. I'm Velvet Maxwell."

"Velvet. What a lovely name."

A soft smile lifted her lips. "My mama was a seamstress for a wealthy woman in Montgomery. She took a likin' to the velvet that woman had a particular fondness for. When I come along, Mama said my skin felt like velvet."

"I don't think I've ever heard such a sweet story of how someone got their name."

"My husband, Roonie, bought me a piece of velvet after Mama passed on to her glory a few years back. I keep a square of it in my pocket and rub its softness when I'm missin' her."

"Willett," the crew boss called, interrupting our conversation. I gave Velvet a look of apology and hurried over.

"Take this to the shop." He handed me a metal machine part. A long crack ran across its length. Then he glanced at Velvet. "Get over here and get this cleaned up."

His hard tone didn't sit well, but I was in no position to chastise him.

As Velvet and I passed each other, I whispered, "It was nice meeting you, Velvet."

The slight squint of her eyes told me she agreed.

At the end of the day, I clocked out and made my way to the security portal. Garlyn was waiting for me when I arrived.

"I'm really sorry I got you in trouble," he said after greeting me, his words sincere.

"It's okay. Mr. Ross doesn't seem to like any of us office girls."

"Don't feel bad. He and some of the other maintenance guys don't like us engineers either. I guess they think we're know-it-alls or something."

"But you were right," I offered. "The supervisor said the compressor might have blown had the crew not followed your instructions."

He rammed his hands into his trouser pockets and gave a slight shrug. "I helped build the plant, so I do know what I'm talking about. Most of the time, anyway."

The bus to Townsite arrived. We shared a seat, with me by the window. He asked questions about where I was from and what it was like growing up in Kentucky. After we arrived in town and settled at the snack bar with grilled cheese sandwiches, french fries, and chocolate shakes, I turned the questions around, inquiring about his family.

"I grew up in Scranton, Pennsylvania. Dad worked for the railroad and fought in the Great War. After everything he experienced in Europe, he didn't want me or my younger brother to join the military. Instead, he worked like a dog to put William and me through Penn State. When Japan bombed Pearl Harbor, William quit and became a B-17 pilot. He's stationed in Italy."

I couldn't imagine Harris going off to war. "That must be hard on your parents. I'm sure they're thankful you took your dad's advice and didn't join up."

An odd expression filled his face. "Well," he said, dunking two fries in a dollop of ketchup, over and over. "That's not exactly true." He glanced around, as though to make sure no one else was listening. When he spoke again, it was in a hushed tone. "I'm in the Army, but I'm part of a group of soldiers called the Special Engineer Detachment. I've been assigned to K-25."

"But you don't wear a uniform like the other soldiers at CEW."

"They want us to blend in." He paused. "What I just told you isn't necessarily a secret, but like everything else around here, we're not supposed to talk about what we do. I can trust you, can't I, Maebelle?"

I nodded. "Of course. I'm certainly not one of those spies they warned us about when I first came to the Reservation, handing secrets over to the Germans."

"Those aren't the spies I'm worried about," he whispered.

When I offered a confused look, he said, "A lot of people on the Reservation are watching and listening to everything around them. If they hear anyone discussing information they shouldn't—like what I just told you about the SEDs—they report it."

My eyes widened. "Who do they report it to?"

"The FBI, if rumors can be believed."

I didn't know what the FBI was, but his revelation unnerved me. Sissy and I agreed we didn't know anything of importance to share with anyone, but Garlyn's words served as a reminder I needed to watch what I said and to whom I said it.

"What happens to someone if they speak out of turn?"

"Most of them lose their job and are immediately escorted off the Reservation. Sometimes not even their friends or coworkers know what happened to them."

The seriousness of his tone told me he wasn't jesting.

I couldn't afford to lose this job. Mama confessed in her last letter that Pa wasn't doing well, so the money I sent home was vital to my family's well-being. More than anything, I wanted to make it possible for Pa to quit working in the mines.

"Mr. Colby says you're one of his best employees," Garlyn said, "so I don't think you have anything to worry about. Just be careful."

We finished our meal and walked outside into a humid evening. The scent of rain hung in the air, and clouds over the hills on the southern horizon looked dark.

"I hope we don't get another storm," I bemoaned as we made our way along the wooden walkway, heading in the direction of my dormitory. "I haven't been able to buy a pair of galoshes yet. Every time the stores get a shipment, they're snapped up before I can get there. My shoes won't last much longer if I have to keep walking through mud. Without a shoe ration card, I can't get another pair."

A look of empathy crossed his face. "It's crazy how quickly things fly off the shelves."

We reached the entrance to the dormitory just as light rain began to fall. "Thank you for dinner. That was a real treat."

"My pleasure." After a beat, he added, "I hope we can do it again."

Suddenly shy but pleased, I smiled. "That would be nice."

The rain fell harder.

"I better go before I get soaked."

"Do you live in the men's dormitory?" I asked, indicating the group of buildings not far from the women's dorms.

"No. The SEDs are housed in barracks in Happy Valley."

This news surprised me. "You came all the way to town just to have dinner with me?"

The look he gave me sent a shiver racing up my arms that had nothing to do with the turn in the weather. "I did, and I'd be happy to do it a lot more. Goodnight, Maebelle."

"Goodnight."

I watched him jog down the wooden walkway toward the bus stop. He'd be drenched when he finally got home.

I turned and went upstairs. I hadn't wanted to date anyone at CEW. Romance was the last thing on my mind. Sending money home to my family was the sole reason I was here.

But spending time with Garlyn tonight had been more than pleasant. I looked forward to doing it again.

I giggled as I reached my room.

It seems I may have changed my mind about romance.

CHAPTER SEVEN

LAUREL

AUNT MAE DIDN'T FEEL WELL the next morning. A headache kept her awake most of the night. I couldn't help but wonder if it had something to do with the contents of the box and my desire to know more about her life during the war. I wasn't sure what exactly upset her last night, but I felt responsible, nonetheless.

"Don't worry about me." She spoke from her bed when I peeked in to check on her. "I just need to rest. You go on to town and do some of that sightseeing you were talking about."

We'd planned to purchase seeds and plants for the garden today, but it looked as if that was on hold for the time being.

"Can I get you anything before I go? Some hot tea or cocoa?"

She sank into the pillow. "No, thank you, dear. I think I'll take a little nap. If I feel better, perhaps we'll work on the garden later this afternoon."

I kissed her forehead, grabbed my purse, and left the house. Georgeanne was in her yard, watering a plethora of multicolored flowers growing haphazardly throughout the small space.

"Good morning, Laurel." She waved me over. "I've got news."

I changed course and made my way to the low picket fence that separated the yards. "Good morning. Your flowers are gorgeous."

"Thank you. They make me happy."

"You have news?"

"You mentioned that you'd like to interview other residents of Oak Ridge who were here during the war, so I made some inquiries. I hope you don't mind."

"Not at all. Talking to a varied group of individuals will provide a good range of thoughts and opinions about the secret work that took place here."

She seemed pleased. "Some of my friends would be happy to share their stories with you. Elliot was especially interested in your research. He was in the Army and came to work at Oak Ridge as a young soldier. He's still employed at the labs."

This news intrigued me. "I haven't spoken with anyone who still works at Los Alamos or Oak Ridge. His perspective could be really interesting."

Georgeanne left me with the water hose while she went inside and returned with a handwritten list of five names, addresses, and telephone numbers.

"I know they'll be thrilled to chat with you."

I accepted the list, thanked her, and handed back the hose. While it would be easier to call the potential interviewees from Aunt Mae's telephone, I didn't want to go inside and disturb her. I'd find a pay phone in town.

Armed with a plan, I drove to Jackson Square, which seemed the best place to begin. Georgeanne said it was known as Town Center when she first arrived and was the main shopping area. She'd also informed me the dormitories and administrative offices, often referred to as Castle on the Hill, had been located nearby, but I hadn't thought to ask if any of them still existed. Happily, the Guest House, where Manhattan Project VIPs stayed—now the

Alexander Motor Inn—and Chapel on the Hill, a small, white-painted church, still stood where they'd been built, a short walk from the shopping center. As soon as I made my phone calls, I'd poke around the World War II-era buildings.

I parked in front of the movie theater and found a pay phone nearby. I dialed the first number on Georgeanne's list. A man answered.

"Hi, is this Elliot Tyson?"

"This is his son, Jonas. May I help you?"

"Is Elliot available? Georgeanne Stokes gave me his number. My name is Laurel Willett, Mae Willett's niece. I'm doing some research into the history of Oak Ridge, and Georgeanne said Elliot was interested in speaking with me."

Seconds ticked by. "Just a moment." A loud rustling noise sounded, as though he put his hand over the mouthpiece. Murmured voices in the background followed.

When the noise cleared, his deep voice filled the receiver. "Miss Willett, my father says if you're available now, you're welcome to come over. He's home with a sprained ankle and bored out of his mind. He'd love to talk to someone new."

I thought I detected a hint of humor in the comment. "Perfect. I'm currently at Jackson Square. Is your home nearby?"

He gave me directions to the house, located along the Black Oak Ridge on West Outer Drive, and we hung up.

I walked back to where I'd parked the car. I'd have to explore the town later.

Jonas Tyson answered the door when I arrived at the two-story brick home on a spacious lot. The house looked similar to those I'd seen around town, but the darkhaired man wasn't at all what I expected.

Tall, good-looking, and maybe a few years older than me, he wore a police uniform, with a gun holstered on his hip.

"Miss Willett, come in."

I stepped inside, slightly unnerved. While I held no personal grievances with police officers, the unrest in the United States during the Vietnam War caused many people to mistrust government officials, including the police. When I was a student, we heard reports of false arrests, brutality, and other unpleasantness that took place at protest rallies on college campuses throughout the country. Although I knew there were two sides to every story, it all served to make me wary of cops.

"Dad's in the den." He led the way down a hallway.

I followed, noting the house was neat and tidy. Framed photographs lined the walls, and I recognized Jonas in many of them.

Elliot Tyson sat in a recliner with his bandaged leg propped up on the footrest, a middle-aged version of his son.

"So, you're Mae Willett's niece. I've heard a lot about you." He reached to shake my hand. "She's mighty proud of you and your sisters. Talks about y'all every time I see her at church."

"It's nice to meet you, Mr. Tyson. I appreciate your willingness to see me on such short notice."

He motioned for me to take a seat on the sofa. I did, but Jonas remained standing sentry near his dad, his steady gaze on me, which caused my nervousness to return. I'd never even received a parking citation, so I didn't know what type of behavior to expect from a cop.

"Georgeanne says you're working on your doctorate," Elliot said. "You're too young to be a professor."

I hid a smile. "I hope to become a psychologist rather than teach. I'd like to use what I learn to help people achieve a deeper level of contentment in their lives. Sometimes speaking with a psychologist can help unlock issues that keep us from achieving happiness on our own."

He pondered that for a moment. "A psychologist. Well, I

suppose we need some of those too. I'm curious about your research. What does the history of Oak Ridge have to do with becoming a psychologist?"

Out of the corner of my eye, I saw Jonas shift his stance and cross his arms, as though waiting for my reply.

"I'm studying the long-term effects on residents of the Secret City and how they felt after the atomic bomb was dropped on Japan. Those of you who worked on the project experienced something completely unique that can't be duplicated. I've spoken with people who worked in Los Alamos, and I hope to travel to Washington at some point as well. I came to visit Aunt Mae and learn more about her life as a young woman in Oak Ridge, but I also wanted to talk to others who were here during the war. I'd love to hear your story."

Elliot's eyes narrowed as he gave a slow nod. "Life in the Secret City was different. Different from anywhere else in the world, except maybe Los Alamos and Hanford. The town sprang up overnight and was run by the Army. The average age of Oak Ridgers was twenty-five, which was fun and strange all at the same time."

"Why was it strange?"

"The town didn't have any elders. No grandparents or mature folks to offer wisdom. No one had grown up here or had kin who'd always lived here. Everything was brand new. There were older men in charge of the military personnel, but most of the engineers, scientists, and administrators weren't much older than me."

His answer triggered a memory. "I read a quote from someone who worked in New Mexico who said something similar. Although the work they were doing was intense, the off-duty atmosphere was very party-like at times."

Elliot glanced at his son. "Do you remember when we took a trip out west and stopped in Los Alamos? I guess you were about eleven years old and your sister was six."

Jonas nodded. "I do, although I mostly remember the Rocky Mountains, not the history." His attention returned to me. "May I ask what kind of information you hope to get from my dad, Miss Willett? Even though some data on the Manhattan Project has been declassified and made available to the public, there are still many topics that aren't up for general discussion."

His stern tone surprised me, considering we'd just met.

"Officer Tyson," I began, only to have him interrupt.

"Detective Tyson."

"Pardon me. Detective Tyson." I didn't know why Jonas took the defensive so quickly, but I hoped he would see I wasn't there to take advantage of his father in any way.

"I'm well aware certain information remains classified." My gaze took in both men. "I have no interest in the confidential details of what went on here during the war. My interest is in the people. How they coped with the secrecy and the hardships everyone experienced. About day-to-day life in Oak Ridge. However, the main focus of my dissertation will be on how employees of the Manhattan Project felt when they learned about their role in the making of an atomic bomb. How did it affect them then and does it affect them now."

Jonas seemed to evaluate my words.

"You'll have to excuse my son, Miss Willett." Elliot wore a mischievous grin. "Those of us in law enforcement tend to have suspicious minds. Jonas comes by it naturally, I'm sorry to say."

His comment confused me. "I didn't realize you were in law enforcement."

"I enlisted in the Army after Pearl Harbor." He settled back in his chair as though preparing for a lengthy chat. "Thought they'd send me overseas, but instead I got shipped to Tennessee. I wasn't allowed to tell anyone where I was or what I was doing. Fact is, I didn't know anything *to* tell. I just knew I was an MP assigned to guard duty at Elza Gate, one of the seven entrances into Oak Ridge, a place that wasn't on any maps."

"How old were you, if you don't mind my asking?" I opened the notebook I'd brought with me and began to jot down notes.

"I was still in school when Pearl was bombed. The day I turned eighteen, I quit and enlisted."

"What did your job at Oak Ridge involve?" I glanced at Jonas. "Is it all right to ask that question, Detective?"

The corners of his mouth twitched before he gave in and grinned. It completely transformed his face.

"Yes, Miss Willett. I'm convinced you're not here to steal national secrets." He turned to his father. "Tucker's wife went into labor last night, so I worked his shift. I'm going home to get cleaned up. Do you need anything before I leave?"

"Not a thing. We'll enjoy a nice chat without you hovering and scaring Miss Willett with your sour face." Elliot winked at me, making Jonas laugh. It was obvious the two had a healthy father-son relationship. "I'd like to show Laurel the town, but I'm laid up with this doggone ankle. Hey, I have an idea." He glanced between Jonas and me, landing on Jonas again. "Since you have the rest of the day off, you can take our guest on a tour. You know all the interesting places as well as I do. Then you can have lunch at Big Ed's and bring me a slice of pizza when you come back." He seemed quite pleased with the plan.

Jonas, on the other hand, had a look of annoyance in his hazel eyes. Probably as annoyed as I'd be if my dad tried to force me to spend time with someone I'd just met. While a tour of the town by someone knowledgeable would be fantastic, I wouldn't inflict myself on the detective.

"I can't ask you to do that," I said, giving him an out. "Especially if you've worked all night. I'm sure I can find things on my own."

Just as Jonas seemed about to respond, Elliot scoffed. "Nonsense.

You need a good guide, and he needs to stop playing nursemaid to his old man. My wife is out of town. Gone to Chicago to visit her sister for a couple weeks. She isn't aware I sprained my ankle. Jonas is taking good care of me, but he needs a break."

I stole a peek at Jonas.

After a moment, he put his hands up in surrender. "All right." Facing me, he said, "It would be my pleasure to show you around town, Miss Willett. If you're interested, that is. Don't let my father bully you into doing anything you don't want to do."

Elliot let out a loud guffaw.

What a pair.

"If you're sure," I said, "I'd love to see the town through the eyes of someone who grew up here."

It was decided I would stay and visit with Elliot while Jonas went home to freshen up. We bid him goodbye.

"He's a good son." Elliot's eyes shone with parental pride. "A good cop, too. He's one of the youngest to make detective."

"I didn't think detectives wore a uniform. At least, they usually don't in the movies."

"Our police department is modest," he said, "so Jonas still does patrol work from time to time. If there's an active investigation going on, he'll wear street clothes. The uniform tends to make some people nervous."

He told me about his daughter, Ashley, an elementary school teacher in Chattanooga. "She and her fella got engaged on New Year's Eve. They're planning a fall wedding. That's why Charlotte went to Chicago. She and her sister are making Ashley's wedding dress."

"Did you meet Charlotte here in Oak Ridge?" I asked.

"Sure did. She was a cubicle operator, like Georgeanne. In fact, I met both of them at a dance in the rec center. Georgeanne was more outgoing, but I took a shine to Charlotte's quiet nature."

I smiled. "It sounds like you've had a good life here in Oak Ridge."

"Yes, ma'am. After the war I was discharged from the Army, but I continued to work for the laboratory on the security force. The town opened to the public in 1949, and the population gradually decreased. Things became more normal. It was a great place to raise a family. Still is."

"I'd like to ask some questions about your work as a military police officer," I said, glad that Jonas wasn't around for this part of the interview. "What was your day-to-day job like? What did you do?"

"I started out guarding the gates. There were seven main gates on the Reservation, plus some inside the fence that led to secure areas. Everyone who entered or exited was required to have a badge with their name and photograph, ID number, and color codes indicating what areas they were authorized to be in. We checked every badge on every person, coming and going, all day and all night."

"I found Aunt Mae's badge in a box of mementos." I didn't mention the badge belonging to the pretty blonde woman. It didn't seem right to talk about things that Aunt Mae might not want known.

A sudden thought spilled through my mind.

Was this how it felt to live and work at Oak Ridge during the war? Keeping secrets about everything, all the time?

"Each vehicle that came through the gates had to be inspected," Elliot continued. "Some guards patrolled on horseback, mostly down by the river. At times I was assigned to the rail yard where we had to search railroad cars. Some contained building supplies, and some had components used to build the equipment that produced the enriched uranium. Lots of them were loaded with coal. But every few weeks or so, a shipment of containers would arrive that were heavily guarded.

"Did you know what was going on at the plants? Did you know uranium was being enriched?"

He looked pensive. "Not at first. But as time went by, things started to add up."

"How so?"

"Well, for one thing, the railroad cars arrived full, but they always left empty. Made me wonder what was being manufactured inside those massive buildings, and why nothing was ever shipped out. Most people who worked in Oak Ridge weren't allowed in different areas of the Reservation, but my job as an MP gave me access to the whole place. I'd pick up information here and there and sort of piece it together, like a big ol' puzzle." A smug look crossed his face. "By early 1945, I'd figured things out. At least, as much as I could. I didn't know about Los Alamos, of course, and I didn't understand about fission and isotopes and all that scientific stuff, but I had a suspicion we were working on some kind of new bomb."

"Then you must not have been surprised when you heard the news about Little Boy being dropped on Japan."

He slowly shook his head. "No, I wasn't surprised."

"What did you think about it? About the role Oak Ridge played in its development?"

He pressed his lips together and didn't answer right away. "War is a terrible thing. Millions of people had been killed in Europe before the US even got involved. Then Pearl Harbor was attacked, which meant Americans were dying now. When would it stop? No one knew the answer. By May of '45, we'd defeated Hitler and Germany, but Japan refused to surrender. President Truman and those in power had to consider what would happen if we *didn't* use the bomb on Japan. How long would the war continue? How many more Americans would die before it ended?"

He paused, then faced me.

"I know there are people who don't think we should have used the bomb, especially after learning that most of the Japanese citizens killed in Hiroshima and Nagasaki were women and children. That is a terrible, heartbreaking fact. It's easy to look back on history and make judgement calls about what should or shouldn't have been done. We can debate the decision to use the bomb from now until eternity, but it won't change things. All we can do is learn from it and pray a weapon like that is never used again."

His eyes narrowed in thought. "But to answer your question, I believe using the atomic bomb was a dreadful but necessary wartime decision that ultimately brought an end to the fighting. Japan refused to surrender unconditionally. After the bombings, that is exactly what they did. I don't think anyone who worked at Oak Ridge should ever feel guilty about what he or she did, especially since the vast majority were unaware of their role in it all."

I appreciated his honest answer.

We moved on to more general questions about Oak Ridge during and after the war. It wasn't long before Jonas returned. His transformation left me a bit speechless.

Gone was the intimidating police detective. No longer wearing his uniform, he'd changed into jeans, a bright orange University of Tennessee T-shirt that showed off his muscles, and sneakers.

"I'm ready whenever you are, Miss Willett."

I stood and thanked Elliot for his time. "It was a pleasure meeting you."

"Come back anytime. I have lots more stories."

Jonas and I left the house. He approached the Camaro.

"This is a really nice car," he said, appreciation in his eyes. When his gaze returned to me, he seemed to hold back a grin. "Not exactly the kind of car I would've guessed you drove."

I didn't take offense. "What kind of car would you put me in?"

He angled his head, as though sizing me up. "Maybe a VW or a Honda. Something small and economical."

I had to laugh. He was spot-on. "I confess if it had been up to me to purchase my own ride, those would have been in the running. But my dad bought this for me when I graduated from college. I think he loves it as much as I do."

"Ah, now it makes sense." He indicated the black Ford Bronco parked at the curb. "But if you don't mind, we'll leave it here and take mine."

He opened the passenger door and I climbed in. After he'd settled behind the wheel, he met my gaze.

"Are you ready to discover the mysteries of the Secret City, Miss Willett?"

A thrill rushed through me. "Lead the way, Detective Tyson."

CHAPTER EIGHT

MAE

A LARGE PACKAGE wrapped in brown paper waited for me when I returned to the dormitory after my shift. It had been a long day of biking miles upon miles throughout the K-25 complex. Between the unseasonably warm weather outside and machinery running nonstop on the inside, the temperatures throughout the enormous building soared. I was beat.

"This came for you." The front desk attendant wore a curious expression when she handed the parcel to me. "Feels heavy."

She was right. I couldn't guess who'd sent something to me or what might be inside. Only my name and dorm number were written on the front. Mama had mailed a tin of molasses cookies three weeks ago, but I'd had to go to the post office to pick them up. The package had been opened, no doubt by military censors who checked every article of mail that entered the Reservation, and I was certain a few cookies were missing.

The curious attendant looked disappointed when I didn't open the package right then and instead hurried upstairs. Sissy wasn't in our room. I guessed she was out with Clive again.

With excitement, I tore off the paper and gasped when I lifted the lid of the box.

A pair of brand-new rubber galoshes met my eyes.

All I could do was stare at them, confused.

Where had they come from? There surely had been a mistake. They must've been delivered to the wrong person. Was there another Maebelle Willett in Oak Ridge? I hadn't heard of someone with the same name.

I took a boot out of the box, inhaling the strong aroma of new rubber. I couldn't help but admire it. The waterproof footwear was exactly what I needed to conquer Oak Ridge's never-ending mud. But disappointment immediately followed such a thought, knowing I had to return them to whomever made the mistake.

For a brief moment I considered keeping the galoshes. I desperately needed them. No one could fault me if I kept them for myself. My name was on the box, after all. It wasn't as if I'd stolen them.

Guilt washed through me even thinking such a thing.

God and Mama would both be disappointed in me. The sender would no doubt realize their mistake when the other Maebelle Willett didn't receive the package. They would come looking for the boots. The right thing to do would be to try and track that person down and alert them to the error. Perhaps the girl at the front desk would remember who delivered them.

I gazed at the footwear with longing.

Couldn't I at least try them on? Just to know if they fit? When I was finally able to purchase a pair from the store, I'd know what size to get.

Unfortunately for me, the boots were a perfect fit, making it even harder to think about returning them. I tromped around the room, imagining how it would feel to trudge through the mud without fear of ruining my shoes. Rain would no longer be a despised visitor.

With a heavy sigh, I took off the boots. As I started to return them to the box, I noticed a folded piece of paper at the bottom.

Maebelle,
　I hope these fit. I saw them at the PX and thought you could use them.
　Would you like to have dinner with me tomorrow night?

Garlyn

I stared at the note, then at the boots.

Garlyn bought me a pair of galoshes?

I hadn't seen him today, but then most of my errands took me to areas of the complex away from the main building. I studied the footwear, their Army-green color a clue I should have noticed when I first opened the box.

According to Prudence, military personnel shopped at a PX, a place where they had access to many hard-to-find items the general population of Oak Ridge was unable to get their hands on. The lucky girls in the dorm who were dating GIs proudly paraded around in nylons and lipstick that were impossible to obtain for anyone not in the military.

I wasn't sure what to think.

While Garlyn's kindness was thoughtful, I hoped he didn't expect something in return. We'd only shared one dinner, and although I found him amiable, I didn't know him any more than he knew me. With all the secrecy and spying that went on at CEW, I was fast learning not everyone could be trusted.

I returned the boots to the box, torn about what to do.

I needed the galoshes. There was no doubt about that. But I also couldn't accept such an extravagant gift from a man I barely knew.

Decision made, I closed the lid.

Tomorrow, I'd find Garlyn and return the boots.

The box of galoshes rode in the basket of my bicycle the next day, but I never saw Garlyn. I didn't inquire if anyone knew his whereabouts, because asking questions drew attention to oneself. I wasn't certain what area of the plant he worked in, since his job as an engineer often took him all over the enormous building. I'd simply leave the boots in the locker in the maintenance building assigned to me and hope I saw Garlyn tomorrow. The sooner I returned them to him, the better.

Thunder rolled across the gray sky as I exited the building at the end of my shift. I hurried to catch a shuttle while fat drops of rain began to pelt the earth.

I groaned. I didn't have my umbrella to keep me from getting drenched. With dozens of other employees, I ran from the shuttle to the security portal. The line inched forward while rain fell harder. By the time I passed through the turnstile, any dry space beneath the covered waiting area was occupied. I hovered on the edge, soaked to the bone. A chill in the air only made things worse.

"Maebelle."

I squinted through the downpour to see Garlyn hurrying toward me, an umbrella in hand. He drew up close and positioned the small shelter over me.

"I was afraid I'd missed you," he said.

I shivered but didn't reply.

"Here." He handed me the umbrella, then proceeded to remove his jacket. "You'll catch cold."

He draped the outerwear over my shoulders. It felt wonderfully warm, but again, I wasn't sure what to think about his attentiveness. "Thank you."

"I didn't see you today," he said, glancing down at my feet. "I wasn't sure you received the note and package I sent you yesterday."

People darted around us, rushing to and from buses that came and went.

I bit my lip. "It arrived."

Confusion crossed his face as he glanced at my wet shoes again. "Did you not like the boots? Were they the wrong size? There weren't many options, so I just guessed."

I'd rehearsed what I would say all day, but now the words failed me.

"I . . . I can't accept them. I'll return them to you tomorrow."

Disappointment shone in his eyes. "I don't understand."

Someone bumped into me in their mad dash to the bus, nearly toppling me.

"Let's get out of the rain." He led the way to a bus going to Townsite. We boarded, but there was only one vacant seat. Garlyn remained standing as the bus pulled away. The lack of privacy kept us from continuing our conversation.

The drive to town took longer in the rain. We passed a bus that had become stuck in the mud, with passengers waving out the window for us to stop. Thankfully our driver kept going, otherwise we may have become bogged down ourselves. He assured us he'd have the dispatcher send a bus to pick them up.

By the time we reached the terminal, the rain had stopped. We disembarked and maneuvered through the crowd to a quieter area away from the ticket windows.

"I'm sorry, Maebelle," Garlyn said, an earnestness in his voice.

"I didn't mean to offend you by purchasing the boots. I see now that, well, that it may have seemed rather forward, and that isn't what I intended at all."

His sincerity eased the tension I'd felt all day. "It was a very nice thing to do. I have to admit they fit perfectly."

A small smile crinkled his eyes. "The only other pair was a size eleven, and I didn't think your feet were quite that big."

I grinned, grateful he wasn't angry. "Not quite, but I really can't accept them."

He nodded, then said, "Instead of me returning them to the PX, how about you purchase them from me? You still need galoshes, don't you? I'll even charge you a little extra if you want. For my trouble and all."

That made me laugh. "It's a deal."

He glanced in the direction of the cafeteria down the street. "Would you like to join me for dinner? I hear they're serving fried chicken." When he faced me again, he said, "I'll understand if you'd rather not."

The honesty in his brown eyes convinced me I'd been silly to think he was anything but a gentleman. That he'd bought me a pair of galoshes simply because he knew I needed them warmed me down to the wet soles of my feet.

"If you'll give me a minute to stop by the dorm and change out of these wet things, I'd be happy to join you for fried chicken."

He extended his arm. "Shall we?"

I happily accepted.

My schedule changed the following week, which meant Sissy and I were now on different shifts. She was usually asleep when I arrived back at the dorm, and I slept soundly while she readied for work in the morning. I wasn't a night owl, so these odd hours would take some getting used to, that's for certain.

I quietly changed into my nightgown. I wasn't sleepy, but I didn't want to wake Sissy by stirring around the room. I crawled into bed, thinking about Garlyn. We'd met at the K-25 cafeteria on my dinner break earlier this evening. His work hours hadn't changed, but he'd figured out that I ate an hour after his shift ended. With a twinkle in his eye, he said he didn't mind waiting for me. I wasn't sure where our friendship was headed, but after the galoshes, I'd come to the conclusion I wanted to find out.

I reached to switch off the lamp on the bedside table when I noticed a small, leather-bound book. The cover was plain, with no title or author's name. Thinking it might be something interesting I could read for a while, I reached for it.

I was surprised to find neat handwriting filled the page instead of printed words.

It was dated the day we arrived on the Reservation.

Dear Diary,

I'm in Tennessee! Mama thought it'd be fun for me to write down my experiences and share them with her later, so she bought me this diary. But the man who gave us a stern talking-to today said keeping diaries and journals was discouraged. I can't figure why, considering I ain't got nothing interesting to write about yet. I figure I'll just jot down some things here and there for Mama so's she'll be pleased I used the diary.

My roommate Maebelle is a nice gal from Kentucky and . . .

I quickly closed the book.

I hadn't known Sissy was keeping a diary. I vaguely recalled being told not to maintain journals and such, mainly due to the threat of them being found by enemy spies.

I stifled a laugh.

Anyone who stole Sissy's diary would surely be disappointed with the contents. She didn't know any more than I did about why we were in Oak Ridge or what was going on here. I imagine her most recent entries were about Clive, but whatever she wrote, it wasn't any of my business.

I returned the book to the bedside table and shut off the light. My thoughts, however, wouldn't settle. Just yesterday Mr. Colby informed me one of the clerks I'd worked with at K-25 was fired because she spoke out of turn. A *creep*, the nickname Oak Ridgers used for someone who worked as an informant for the FBI, overheard the young woman share information about the layout of the massive plant. I hadn't known the girl well, but she'd seemed as nice and normal as anyone else. That she'd been fired because she talked about the building where I worked every day left me feeling anxious. One slipup to the wrong person and I could lose my job too.

It was easy to forget everything on the Reservation was classified information. It wasn't just the buildings and the equipment inside, either. We were never to discuss the number of employees we worked with, the neighborhood or dorm where we lived, even the food at the cafeteria or the shortages at the local market.

Everything—*everything!*—was to be kept secret.

I mulled that over for a minute.

I still didn't know what was being manufactured within the walls of K-25. Since I'd begun working there, I'd become familiar with the various buildings that housed different machines, storage tanks, and pipes, yet I hadn't seen even one product come out the doors. It became obvious in my first days that military tanks, guns, and weapons for the Army weren't being assembled in the enormous building. Because that was as near to the truth as I could determine, it seemed more likely the machines processed something, but what, I couldn't imagine. I had a suspicion Garlyn knew the answer to the mystery, but asking him wasn't something I considered doing. Even if we continued to see each other, I wouldn't let my curiosity risk putting him in jeopardy of losing his job.

I rolled onto my side and looked out to the night sky.

The window faced north, toward Kentucky. Mama came to mind, and I whispered a prayer for her, Pa, and Harris. I missed them, but I had to admit I enjoyed living in Oak Ridge. I may not know exactly what was happening on the Reservation or even what my part in the whole thing was, but I knew we were doing something important. The government wouldn't've spent millions of dollars to build Oak Ridge if it wasn't vital to the war effort. Enemy spies wouldn't be interested in the work taking place behind the fence if it wasn't essential to us winning the war. I was convinced that whatever was going on here would allow us to defeat our enemies and bring our boys home.

Bits of President Roosevelt's speech from December 1941 trickled through my mind. I couldn't recall everything he'd said in the radio address, but his passion and confidence in Americans had stirred something deep inside me that day. Something patriotic. The president needed each of us to do our part. I hadn't known what I could do from my tiny corner of the universe, tucked in a holler of Kentucky, far from Europe or Japan, but I was determined to do *something*.

I could have never imagined that *something* would take me to a secret city in the hills of Tennessee, hidden away from the world, working on a project that promised to help bring the war to an end.

I pressed my lips.

Pride was something Mama declared vain and wicked, but the

feeling of it welled up within me anyway. Me, little ol' Maebelle Willett, would have a part in bringing Hitler and Mussolini to their knees.

President Roosevelt himself would commend me if he could.

CHAPTER NINE
LAUREL

JONAS TURNED OUT to be a knowledgeable tour guide.

He first drove through town, pointing out interesting landmarks and World War II-era buildings that had been repurposed into offices and other uses.

"Growing up here," he said, "I didn't fully appreciate the history that surrounded me every day."

We sat in rocking chairs on the long front porch of what was once the Guest House during the war. Now the Alexander Motor Inn, I couldn't help but imagine the various Manhattan Project VIPs who'd stayed in the two-story lodge, sitting on this very porch, looking out over the secret town. People like General Groves, Secretary of War Henry Stimson, and famous physicist and project scientist J. Robert Oppenheimer, none of whom used their real names when they signed the guest register. Even physicist Enrico Fermi, the man credited with building the first nuclear reactor, went by the alias "Mr. Farmer" during his stay at the Guest House.

"I imagine most of us take for granted what we see every day. The familiar doesn't usually leave a lasting impression on us." I pointed to the tennis courts just down the hill from the inn. "I read that dances were held there when the courts weren't being used for tennis. That sounds fun, dancing under the stars of a summer sky to Big Band music."

His brow rose. "So, you're a romantic, not just an academic."

I chuckled. "Maybe. I do appreciate the fact that young people like Aunt Mae, Georgeanne, and your parents had opportunities to relax and enjoy themselves despite the important work that was going on here. That must have helped them cope with being so far away from family."

"Isolation and secrecy were both hard to deal with, according to Mom," he said. "She tells the story about a letter she received from her parents after she'd been in Oak Ridge a few months. My grandmother told her not to write to them anymore, because all of Mom's letters were full of blacked-out words and sentences. Grandma couldn't make sense out of anything Mom had written. The people who censored the mail took their jobs seriously."

"Your dad said he met your mom at a dance."

He nodded. "Would you like to walk over to Chapel on the Hill? That's where they were married in 1946."

We stepped off the front porch and made our way around to the back of the inn. A small, white chapel with a steeple sat at the top of a hill, overlooking the town.

"In the early days of Oak Ridge," Jonas said, "there wasn't any place for people to hold a church service. Some congregations met in the cafeteria or rec centers until this chapel was built."

We climbed the steps to a covered entry. Jonas tried the door and found it unlocked, and we went inside. The stillness of the place felt peaceful.

"It's a standard military chapel." Jonas's voice echoed in the small building. "All denominations used it. Baptists, Methodists, Catholics. Mom says a good number of couples were married here during the war."

I moved up the aisle while Jonas remained near the door.

Wooden pews sat in rows on either side of me, and warm sunshine spilled through windows that lined the room. I closed my eyes and could almost hear the old-timey hymns and sermons that filled this quaint church back in the 1940s. I wondered if Aunt Mae ever attended services here. According to Dad, she was quite active in her church nowadays.

We left the chapel and got back into the Bronco. Our next tour stop was the Y-12 plant site where Georgeanne and Jonas's mother worked, but because it was still in operation as a national laboratory, we didn't try to enter through the highly guarded gate.

"If you're interested, we can grab lunch at Big Ed's." Jonas grinned. "They're known for having the best pizza pies in town."

I glanced at my watch. It was already after one o'clock. "I really should get back and check on Aunt Mae. She wasn't feeling well this morning."

He seemed a little disappointed, which surprised me. "I'm sorry to hear that. I thought we could drive out to K-25 after lunch. We can't go inside, but I can get us onto the site. You really should see how gigantic the building is." The corner of his mouth lifted. "Besides, I've enjoyed being your tour guide today."

I'd liked his company too. "I do want to see the plant where Aunt Mae worked."

"Are you free tomorrow afternoon, say around three o'clock?"

"I hate to take up more of your time."

He gave a nonchalant shrug. "Like I said, it was nice revisiting Oak Ridge's history with you today. I'm reminded of why our little town is so special."

"Then I'll take you up on your offer," I said, unexpectedly

pleased with the prospect of being with him again the following day.

When we arrived at Elliot's house, I declined Jonas's invitation to come inside. "Thank you for taking time to show me around. If you ever decide to leave the police department, you could give tours of Oak Ridge."

He laughed. "I think I'd rather catch bad guys, but I'll keep it in mind."

He waited while I climbed into my car and backed out of the driveway. With a wave, I headed to Aunt Mae's, quite satisfied with how things had turned out. Jonas was easy to talk to once he let down his police detective persona. I'd learned many interesting things about Oak Ridge that weren't found in the history books.

Aunt Mae sat in the shade of the porch when I pulled into the driveway. Another woman was with her. They both stood when I exited the car and approached.

"Laurel, come meet my friend Velvet Maxwell."

The older Black woman offered a gentle smile. "It's good to finally meet you, Laurel. Your Aunt Mae has spoken of you and your family so often through the years, I feel as though I already know you."

We shook hands. "It's nice to meet you. It's a beautiful afternoon to sit outside." I turned to my aunt. "Are you feeling better?"

"I am." She cast a mock glare at Velvet. "But I made the mistake of mentioning my headache to Velvet when she called earlier. She hustled right over with a chicken casserole and some chamomile tea."

The other woman chuckled before she met my gaze. "Your aunt is as stubborn a woman as I've ever met. Never wants help with anything."

I grinned. "It must run in the family. My dad is stubborn too."

"I remember when Harris and your grandmother came to live

in Oak Ridge." Velvet glanced back to Aunt Mae. "You had a time gettin' that young man to obey all your rules."

"He was fifteen and had a mind of his own," Aunt Mae said.

"How long have you and Aunt Mae been friends?" I asked.

Velvet smiled. "We met in 1944 at K-25. We both worked there. I understand you're here gathering information about Oak Ridge for your dissertation."

"Yes, ma'am. I've already interviewed Georgeanne, and this morning I met with Elliot Tyson."

"Elliot?" Aunt Mae's brow arched in surprise. "How did you know to get in touch with him?"

"Georgeanne gave me a list of people who might be interested in sharing their stories," I said.

She huffed. "I should've known it was Georgeanne's doing. Always meddling in business that doesn't concern her."

"Now Mae," Velvet said, gentle rebuke in her voice, "you want Laurel's trip to Oak Ridge to be successful, don't you?"

I bit my bottom lip. The last thing I wanted was to cause trouble between friends. I was about to take Aunt Mae's side in the conversation when she heaved a sigh.

"Of course I want Laurel to get the information she needs." Her shoulders eased when our eyes met. "It was thoughtful of Georgeanne to provide names of people interested in talking to you. I should have done that myself." She glanced at her friend, a slight smile inching up her lips to replace the frown. "How about Velvet? She and her husband Roonie both worked in Oak Ridge during the war."

Velvet's warm laughter told me after thirty-five years of friendship, she was used to dealing with my aunt. "I doubt Laurel wants to hear about how I cleaned miles of concrete floors at the plant, or how Roonie worked on a railroad crew. I'm sure there are others who had important jobs whose stories would be far more interesting."

"I'd very much like to hear about your time at K-25," I hurried to say. "And your husband's job if he wouldn't mind talking to me. Everyone who lived and worked in Oak Ridge had different experiences. I'm interested in hearing as many as I can."

She studied me for a long moment before she gave a single nod. "All right. If you'd like, you can come by the church in the morning."

At what must have been a puzzled expression on my face, she explained. "Roonie is a pastor these days. I work in the church office on Saturday mornings, helpin' him get things ready for Sunday. It'll be nice and quiet so we can talk."

I took a pen from my purse and jotted down the address on the paper Georgeanne had given me earlier. "Thank you. I look forward to chatting with you both."

Velvet took her leave then, giving Aunt Mae a hug, along with a reminder to rest.

After she drove away, we stayed on the porch, gently rocking in rockers that reminded me of those on the porch at the Guest House. I told Aunt Mae about Jonas giving me a tour of the town and his invitation to continue tomorrow afternoon. I didn't mention he planned to take me to see K-25. Hopefully Aunt Mae would be willing to answer some questions after I saw where she'd worked during the war. It would help me fill in the blanks of her life in Oak Ridge.

We enjoyed Velvet's delicious casserole for supper, then watched an old movie on television. Before we readied for bed, I remembered my promise to help Aunt Mae with the garden. But when I suggested I could change my plans with Velvet and Jonas tomorrow and instead take her to the nursery to purchase seeds and plants, she declined.

"Let's wait until next week," she said, followed by a yawn. "You keep working on your research. There's plenty of time to get some things planted. And if we don't, it isn't the end of the world. Oak Ridge has always had farmers markets in the summer. Even back during the war, farmers brought their fresh produce to town. Some sold chickens and milk outside the gates."

After we bid each other goodnight, I thought over the events of the day.

Thanks to Jonas, Elliot, and Georgeanne, I was well on my way to gathering the information I needed to write my dissertation. When I'd asked Georgeanne and Elliot about how they felt after they learned of Oak Ridge's role in making the bomb, their answers were similar to the mathematician from Los Alamos whom I'd interviewed. They each expressed sadness about the devastation in Japan, but they were grateful the war came to an end.

So far no one expressed shame over anything they'd done at Oak Ridge. Georgeanne admitted to feeling troubled and sorrowful that the atomic weapon killed so many innocent people, but she hadn't felt personal guilt. From what I'd read in my research, not even President Truman had second thoughts about his decision to use the bomb against Japan, despite learning of the devastation left in its wake.

Tomorrow promised to be another productive day.

While I looked forward to chatting with Velvet and Roonie, the unexpected opportunity to spend more time with Jonas sent a slight flutter through my belly.

CHAPTER TEN

MAE

MIDMORNING SUNLIGHT spilled through the window, yet I lounged in bed in my nightgown, glad for a day off. Sissy's schedule had changed too. We were now on the same shift, except her day off was tomorrow. Clive was out of town, and Garlyn had to work late last night, so Sissy and I saw the midnight showing of *Since You Went Away* at the theater. The story of a family in small-town America, holding things together while their men are away at war, hit home for a lot of people. I'd heard sniffles from the audience, especially when Jane learns Bill was killed in action.

"Wasn't Claudette Colbert wonderful in her role as Anne Hilton? Very believable, I thought." I glanced to where Sissy stood at the small mirror we'd hung on the wall near the door, combing her hair and readying for work. "And boy oh boy, Shirley Temple sure has grown up, hasn't she?"

Sissy continued to fuss with a curl in the center of her head. I'd never mastered the popular "victory rolls" hairstyle and simply chose to let my wavy locks do whatever they wanted.

"It was a good movie," she said, "but I thought the story had too many sad parts. I didn't like seein' the wounded boys in the hospital."

"Well," I said with a shrug, "it is about the war. My favorite part was the dog, Soda. What a hoot, especially when he kept annoying the grumpy colonel who comes to board with the Hilton family."

I thought my reminder about the show-stealing English bulldog would bring back Sissy's easy smile, but it didn't.

"I kept thinking about my brother." Sadness filled her voice. "Mama worries somethin' terrible will happen to Joe over there, fighting the Germans. I don't like to imagine her getting one of those telegrams with bad news. I'm gonna write to her and tell her not to see the movie. At least not until Joe is home safe."

I hadn't considered how the movie might make her feel when I suggested we see it. "I'm sorry, Sissy. I guess I focused on the happy ending, but you're right. There were a lot of depressing scenes too."

She moved to sit on the edge of my bed. I scooted over to make room. Sissy was as bright as sunshine most days, so it was unusual to observe this subdued side to her.

"I'm glad I saw it. It reminded me that people all over the world have loved ones in the military that they're worried about. After I came here and met you and Clive and the others . . . well, I tried to forget about the war. Isn't that awful? I tried to forget that my brother is somewhere in Europe, fighting for his life. I don't like to think on it." She met my gaze. "I feel so selfish at times, Mae. Why should I be here, safe and having a good time, going to the movies and such, when so many of our boys won't be comin' home? If I fret over it too much, I get sick inside with worry. Forgetting about it is easier."

We hadn't talked much about her brother in the months we'd shared a room. Other than a comment here and there about him,

I too tended to forget she had a loved one in harm's way. It made me consider how I would feel if Harris was old enough to join the military and what I'd do if something terrible happened to him. How would Mama and Pa cope?

I reached for her hand. "It's not selfish to enjoy your life. You're doing your part to help win the war, same as Joe is doing his. I remember when Pa was real sick a few years back. Black lung is a terrible thing, and we weren't sure he was going to make it. Mama asked our preacher to come to the house and pray over him."

The memories of that dark day flooded my mind. The paralyzing fear. Anger at the owner of the coal mine. Even anger at God for letting Pa get sick.

"I don't remember much of what that preacher man said that day, but what I do recall is his confidence that God can be trusted. He said the Bible tells us we've got to trust the Father with everything, including the people we love. The hard part is letting go of control."

Tears swam in her eyes. "I hardly pray for Joe anymore, because when I do, I start to cry. I want God to promise that Joe will come home and live to be an old man, but that promise never comes."

I folded her into my arms. Her slim shoulders shook as she wept.

When she'd quieted, I said, "Mama made me memorize a Scripture after the preacher left that day. It's from the Book of Matthew. *Take therefore no thought for the morrow: for the morrow shall take thought for the things of itself. Sufficient unto the day is the evil thereof.*"

She sniffled and pulled away. "What does it mean?"

I dug a clean hankie from beneath my pillow and handed it to her. "Mama says Jesus is telling us we shouldn't worry about what may or may not happen tomorrow, because today has enough trouble of its own. He was teaching his disciples, reminding them that the Father takes care of the birds of the air and the flowers of the fields. If he'll do that, why not trust God to know what we and our loved ones need?"

She blew her nose with a dainty toot. "I'll try to remember that."

"Do you want me to pray for Joe with you now?"

She nodded.

We held hands as I offered a simple prayer, asking God to protect Joe from harm, but also admitting that we know he has plans for Joe's life that are a mystery to us. I asked the Father to give peace to Sissy and her parents, and to help them trust him more. Finally, I beseeched the Almighty to please bring an end to the war soon.

Sissy gave me a hug. "I'm glad we met that first day, Mae. I wouldn't want to share a room with anyone else."

I agreed. "Will Clive return to Oak Ridge today?"

She instantly brightened. "Yes. He promised to bring me somethin' special from Nashville. I can't wait to see what it is."

I still hadn't warmed to Clive Morrison. There was something about him that didn't seem genuine. Granted, I hadn't spent much time in the man's presence, usually in passing when he came to pick up Sissy in his Army sedan. Last week I mentioned him to Garlyn. He said he knew Clive. Not well, but they were both SEDs, although Clive's position as a health physics officer put him in different work areas throughout the Reservation. Oddly, he said, Clive somehow wrangled special permission to bunk in one of the trailers in Happy Valley rather than share the crowded barracks with the rest of the SEDs—a show of favoritism that didn't sit well with the group of soldiers required to live in the rough-and-ready military quarters.

"Did Clive say why he had to go to Nashville?" I asked Sissy.

Her expression answered my question before she even opened her mouth. "He said it was top secret, but . . ."

"But?"

She dropped her voice to a whisper when she spoke again. "It has to do with somethin' called 'orange oxide' and what happens to it when it gets to Y-12."

I frowned. "I don't like that he shares that kind of information with you. You know what all the signs say around here. 'Loose talk helps our enemy, so let's keep our trap shut.'"

She giggled. "Now, Mae, how can Clive telling his own girlfriend about his job help the enemy?"

I hadn't heard her refer to herself that way before. "You're getting serious about him, aren't you?"

A pretty flush filled her cheeks. "I think I'm in love with him, Mae. I ain't never been in love, but this feelin' is . . . I don't know how to explain it, but it's like nothing I've ever felt for a boy before."

I wasn't sure what to say. Even though I was two years older, I'd never been in love either. I knew I had a crush on Garlyn, but we were still a long way from getting serious. We were just having fun.

I could see that wasn't the case with Sissy. "Have you told your mama about Clive?"

Guilt shone in her eyes when she shook her head. "She wouldn't like it. She told me not to get mixed up with anyone. Clive thinks it's best to wait and tell my family about us once the war is over."

I stared at her. "Has he asked you to marry him?"

"Not in so many words." Her eyes gleamed. "But the way he talks sometimes makes me believe he will soon. I think it'd be grand to have a spring wedding in Chapel on the Hill, don't you?"

I didn't answer. We'd attended the wedding of one of our friends a couple weeks ago. Colleen came to work at CEW last year and met her future husband on the very first day. They were a swell couple, and I was happy for them. But the thought of Sissy marrying Clive didn't elicit the same feelings. He was too old for her. Too odd. Too . . . everything.

"I best get going. Mr. Howell doesn't take kindly to us girls being tardy. Enjoy your day off, Mae." She donned a sweater and walked out the door.

I stewed over her revelation after she left for Y-12.

It wasn't any of my business if Sissy wanted to marry Clive. Yet I felt a sense of responsibility for her, considering her youthful age and inexperience. Now that I knew her mama hadn't wanted her to date while she was at Oak Ridge, I was even more concerned.

Should I write a letter to Sissy's mother and let her know her daughter was contemplating marrying a man she'd only known a short time? Sissy kept the letters she received from her family in the same drawer in the nightstand where I kept mine. It wouldn't be difficult to find their address.

Yet how would Sissy feel when she found out what I'd done? Her mama would no doubt tell her who ratted her out. I didn't want to ruin our friendship, no matter how uneasy I was about her relationship with Clive. Besides, would I want someone to stick their nose into my personal business?

I huffed out a sigh.

I'd simply have to hope Sissy soon tired of the fellow and found someone more amiable. Maybe I should ask Garlyn if he had a friend we could introduce to Sissy. It couldn't hurt.

Just about anyone would be better suited for my sweet roommate than Clive Morrison.

CHAPTER ELEVEN
LAUREL

THE WHITE BRICK CHURCH sat on a corner, not far from the Scarboro Community Center. Across the street were long, narrow houses that looked like they'd been there a while. Jonas had pointed out similar structures during our tour yesterday, indicating the multifamily units had been built by the Army Corps of Engineers during the war. I wondered if I was now looking at homes where workers of the Manhattan Project once lived.

I parked the Camaro next to the only vehicle in the lot. A glance at my wristwatch told me I was a little early for my meeting with Velvet and Roonie, but I was anxious to hear what the couple had to say about their time in Oak Ridge.

Last night over supper, Aunt Mae told me life was different in Oak Ridge for Black employees during the war.

"It was the 1940s. Everything was segregated," she'd said, a frown creasing her brow. "Housing, cafeterias, recreation areas. Legal racism prevented Velvet, Roonie, and the others from having access to the same goods, services, and work opportunities available to the rest of us." She'd shaken her head. "It wasn't right."

I'd sat silent, letting the truth of her words sink in.

I hadn't considered that the wrongs done under mandated segregation extended to the Secret City during the war. Surely Black citizens willing to work under the unusual circumstances the Manhattan Project forced upon its employees deserved the same treatment as their white counterparts. Their work contributed to the success of the mission too.

Yet Aunt Mae's disclosure revealed that hadn't been the case.

As I studied the church's plain exterior, I thought back to the civil rights rallies I'd attended at Boston University when I was a student. Although I believed in liberty and freedom for everyone, I didn't have firsthand experience with the prejudices people in the South dealt with. Growing up in Massachusetts, segregation and its lasting effects was known as a *Southern issue*. Most of my Black friends never even spoke about it.

Yet hearing that the *Southern issue* had been prevalent in Oak Ridge during World War II made me wonder if segregation had taken place at the other Manhattan Project facilities as well. Had Black employees been treated differently at Los Alamos and Hanford?

I entered the church through a set of double doors. Everything was quiet. After some moments, however, the murmur of voices came from an open doorway at the front of the sanctuary. I quietly walked in that direction.

I'd just reached the entrance when a man with short, graying hair exited. We were both startled.

"Land sakes, you 'bout gave me a heart attack." He chuckled. "You must be Mae's niece. I'm Roonie, Velvet's better half."

As we shook hands, Velvet herself appeared in the entryway. "I heard that. Don't go telling falsehoods to Laurel from the very beginning. She won't believe a word you say later on."

I smiled, enjoying the teasing banter between the couple. "I appreciate you both being willing to talk with me today."

"I'm always glad to hear of young folks furthering their education," Roonie said, "'specially if they intend to do good in the world with all that book learnin'. If our stories about those long-ago days in Oak Ridge can help you, I'm happy to tell 'em."

"Let's sit in the sanctuary." Velvet motioned to the rows of wooden benches I'd passed. "This office is barely big enough for the two of us."

We moved to the front pew, although Roonie sat on the step to the platform, facing Velvet and me.

"Thing is," Velvet said as I readied my notebook and pencil, "we don't talk much about our early years here."

"That's actually not unusual, from what I've learned." I glanced between the two. "Many of the people I've interviewed admit they don't revisit those days very often. Whether that's due to the secrecy that was a constant concern or simply a result of passing time is something I'm interested in discovering."

Roonie gave a slow nod. "I suspect it's a bit of both. From the moment we stepped a toe on the Reservation, keepin' our mouths shut about everything we saw and heard was drilled into us."

"Daily," added Velvet. "Everywhere you went in Oak Ridge, there were signs posted about keeping mum about this or that. The enemy was always watchin', they said. I didn't figure I had much to talk about, but I still never spoke out of turn to anyone. Roonie"—she glanced his way—"is the only person I trusted."

"Did you meet here in Oak Ridge?" I asked.

Roonie grinned and looked at his wife. "I saw her for the first time when she was seventeen years old, workin' behind the counter at a drugstore as a soda jerk in Montgomery, Alabama. Prettiest thing I ever did see, I tell ya. I knew right then I'd marry that gal."

I stifled a chuckle when Velvet snorted and rolled her eyes.

"As I recall, there were quite a few 'prettiest things' you were interested in back then."

"Now, that ain't true and you know it." He met my gaze. "I haven't looked at another woman since I met Vel. Been married thirty-seven years next month. Raised five children and started this church. I thank the good Lord every day for blessing me with the perfect helpmate."

Velvet sent her husband a warm look, then said to me, "We've had a good life here in Oak Ridge. Lots of friends and family live here. Your aunt is one of my oldest and dearest friends."

I was certain Velvet knew of Aunt Mae's reticence to talk about her life at Oak Ridge during the war. I hoped she would be able to help me understand the reasoning behind it.

"You mentioned that you both worked at K-25."

"We did. For the maintenance department but doing different things."

"How did you first learn about Oak Ridge?"

Roonie spoke before Velvet could answer. "I'd tried to join the Army but wasn't allowed to, as they said I had a heart murmur. I needed work. My brother heard there were construction jobs up in Tennessee, workin' for the government. Said they were payin' good money. I figured I'd go up and see what's what—"

"And leave me in Montgomery alone," Velvet added, giving him a mock scowl.

"But my *wife* wouldn't hear of me going without her," Roonie continued as though she hadn't spoken. "So, we packed up my brother's car and drove to Knoxville."

"When was that?"

"October of 1943," they said in unison.

It was becoming clear this interview would be entertaining as well as enlightening.

"I remember it well," Velvet said, "because the leaves were turning, and everywhere I looked was something beautiful. Hills covered with gold, red, and orange. God's handiwork was sure on display." Then she grimaced. "Except for the mud. I never could get used to traipsing through that red, mushy mess."

"Georgeanne mentioned that too. Why was it so muddy all the time?"

"Because," Roonie said, "the government bought up sixty thousand acres of farmland and then proceeded to scrape every livin' thing off it to make room for what they intended to build. All that was left was dirt. Every time it rained, even light showers that didn't last long left fields of mud to slog through."

I jotted some notes, then asked, "What kind of work did each of you do when you arrived in Oak Ridge?"

Roonie nodded to Velvet to go first.

"As I said, I worked in maintenance at K-25. My job was simple: keep the place clean. Me and dozens of other gals swept, mopped, and polished all day, every day. The only jobs available to Black women on the Reservation—we were called *colored* back then—were janitorial, kitchen, or maid service."

She went on to give a description of the massive plant, giving me a good idea of what it was like to work there.

"One day I was called to where there'd been a leak that needed cleaning." A soft smile parted her lips. "That's the day I met your aunt."

Here was an opening to learn more about Aunt Mae's work, but I wasn't sure it was right to question Velvet. She must've read my mind.

"I know Mae doesn't like to talk about those days. She probably hasn't spoken much about what she did back then."

I shook my head. "I'd love to hear about her life as a young woman, but she isn't willing to share about it. The only thing I know is that she worked at K-25 as an errand girl and had to ride a bicycle around the plant because it was so big."

"She was such an outgoing gal when we first met. Treated me

like an equal. We formed a friendship despite our differences." Her face took on a serious look then. "But sometime around the end of '44, somethin' changed. She changed."

"How so?"

"She started keeping to herself, I guess you'd say."

"But you don't know why?"

Velvet shook her head. "Even though we'd become friendly, there were still rules—spoken and unspoken—about how Black people could interact with white people. Prying into her personal business wasn't somethin' I felt I could do."

Aunt Mae's words from last night filtered through my mind. "She told me about segregation in Oak Ridge during the war."

"It wasn't any different here than it had been in Alabama," Roonie said matter-of-factly. "Jim Crow laws followed us, no matter where we went."

They took turns sharing the various ways those laws affected them, from separate drinking fountains and riding in the back of the bus, to poor quality food in the cafeterias that served Black residents. However, I wasn't prepared when I learned about their living conditions on the Reservation.

"All the Black folks lived in what they called 'hutments'," Velvet said, "but they weren't real houses. I'd describe them as sixteen-by-sixteen shacks made from the cheapest plywood the government could find. They didn't even have glass in the windows. Just an opening with a wooden shutter that let in the heat in the summer and the cold in the winter. We had a potbellied stove in the center for warmth, but we weren't allowed to cook on it. The gals I shared a hut with were nice enough, but I would've rather lived with my husband."

I glanced between her and Roonie, confused. "You didn't live together?"

They both shook their heads.

"It was against the rules for a colored man and woman to live in the same hut in Oak Ridge," Roonie said, his voice taking on a hard note, "despite them bein' married."

I sat silent, dumbfounded.

It had never occurred to me that a legally married couple, no matter the color of their skin, would not be allowed to live together. I couldn't begin to imagine how the inadequate housing and outrageous regulations made Roonie, Velvet, and the others feel.

"We ladies lived in what we called 'the pen' because it was fenced off from the men's area," Velvet continued. "A guard stood watch at the gate and checked our badges when we'd come and go. Sometimes he even checked inside our huts after curfew to make sure we were all there, usually without knocking on the door first. I'd visit Roonie's hut after work, but come curfew, I had to be in my own hut. The gals I roomed with weren't married, so it didn't affect them same as it did me."

She paused before adding, "But at least I didn't have any babies yet. Black children weren't allowed to live on the Reservation when we first arrived. I knew one gal who left three young ones with her mama in Mississippi. She and her man took the bus down there every so often to visit them."

Roonie described the housing area, with public bathhouses and wooden boardwalks snaking throughout. "Rumor had it there was a slave cemetery not far from our hutments. There we were, livin' on the same patch of dirt where enslaved folks worked a hundred years before, yet not all that much had changed for us. We still weren't free. Not completely."

His words were sobering. They told the shameful story of prejudice and racial inequality in our country. Issues that continued today, in one form or another.

"Were those the conditions you had to deal with throughout the war?" I asked.

Roonie nodded. "When Scarboro Village opened up in 1950, we were able to purchase a real house."

"We started having Bible study sessions soon as we moved in." Velvet smiled. "Had over forty people packed into that little ol' house at times. It wasn't long before folks started asking Roonie to start a church."

They went on to tell about their family, mentioning their children took part in the integration of Oak Ridge schools in the mid-1950s, and how two of their daughters are now teaching in those same schools.

Roonie revealed that Black men, like their female counterparts, were relegated to mostly menial jobs like janitors and laborers, regardless of their education or experience. After the war ended, he heard that a renowned Black scientist from Chicago was denied a job at Oak Ridge, simply because of the color of his skin.

"I mostly worked on a railroad crew," he said. "I'd often puzzle over all that equipment and the tons of coal comin' onto the Reservation, yet the trains always left empty. *What was it used for?* I'd wonder. That information was so hush-hush, even the engineers employed by the railroad company weren't allowed on the Reservation. They had to stop at the boundary and disembark, then engineers for the Manhattan Project took over and brought the train in."

He paused. "Only recently did I learn that most of the uranium being enriched in Oak Ridge had been mined in the Congo. Kinda makes me feel a connection to those African miners."

When I asked the same question I'd asked each of my interviewees—*How did you feel when you learned about Hiroshima and the role people in Oak Ridge had in it?*—they both expressed sorrow over the enormous loss of life. Roonie's words, however, seemed to sum things up.

"We didn't know the work we were doing here would lead to

a weapon of such terrible destruction. I believe God in his mercy doesn't hold folks accountable for what they don't know. As for those who did know, like the generals, the president, and the scientists, they were tryin' their best to end the war. It's hard to say what would've happened if they hadn't used the bomb. All we can do is seek God's forgiveness for things known and unknown, and trust in his grace to cover it all."

By the time I reluctantly acknowledged the need to let them get back to their work, I had a much greater appreciation for all that the Black residents of Oak Ridge endured during and after the war, most of which I hadn't found in my research. My mind was alive with ideas of how to include the information in my dissertation in a meaningful way.

After I bid Roonie goodbye, Velvet walked me to my car and gave me a warm hug. She promised to stop by Aunt Mae's next week and bring some photographs Roonie took of Oak Ridge after the gates were opened to the public in 1949, when the Secret City was no longer restricted. Up until then, a man named Ed Westcott had been the official photographer for the Manhattan Project.

As I drove back to Aunt Mae's, I couldn't help but see Oak Ridge a little differently now that I'd heard Velvet and Roonie's perspective. Despite the important scientific work that took place here—cutting-edge work that would one day help end the war—Black residents had endured the age-old ills of segregation and injustice.

Aunt Mae's words from last night echoed in my heart.

It wasn't right.

CHAPTER TWELVE

MAE

THANKSGIVING DAY ARRIVED on a cold wind.

Despite the holiday, work in Oak Ridge continued nonstop. Luckily, Sissy and I were both scheduled for the early shift and made plans to enjoy roasted turkey and all the fixings that evening at the cafeteria. I invited Garlyn to join us, but Clive declined Sissy's invitation, claiming he had to work. For some reason, I didn't believe his story. It was more likely he'd rather not dine with Garlyn and me.

I pedaled my bicycle down the long truck alley on the second floor of K-25, passing through an area where operators processed a mystery product called C-616. Mr. Colby had sent me on an errand, but my mind was on Sissy. She'd been quieter than usual lately. When I asked if something was bothering her, she'd declared herself fine. Maybe a little tired but nothing I should concern myself with. Still, I wondered if perhaps things with Clive weren't going so well. They continued to see each other on a regular basis, but Sissy was more closemouthed about what they did on their dates than she had been in the beginning of their relationship. I certainly wouldn't be sad if things between them cooled, but I also didn't want Sissy to end up with a broken heart.

I parked the bike and made my way up metal stairs, first to a catwalk in the pipe gallery, then to the operating floor, located on the fourth level. I couldn't count the number of women who worked on this floor, monitoring instruments on large machines. Even though I'd been told K-25 was not up to full capacity yet—doing what, I still didn't know—the place was a beehive of activity.

The large envelope Mr. Colby asked me to deliver to one of the engineers in the control room was sealed and had the words *Restricted Data* stamped on it in red ink. This wasn't the first time I'd handled confidential documents. Not long after I began working at the plant, Mr. Colby informed me I'd been cleared for access to the control room, operating floor, administration building, and other areas off-limits to general employees. That very day he'd handed me a thick, sealed package and directed me to take it to the incinerator in one of the outbuildings. I was to make sure the contents were completely destroyed before I returned. I never knew what was inside the envelopes and packages, but since I had no understanding of the work that took place inside the massive plant, it didn't matter. From that point on, I'd repeated the task multiple times, as well as delivering envelopes like the one I now held to various employees throughout the plant.

The control room was a fascinating place. Instead of the miles of pipes, holding tanks, and loud machinery that filled a good portion of K-25, the walls of this room were lined with metal panels covered with lights, knobs, gauges, and dials. Desks sat in the center, occupied by men and a couple women.

When I arrived, I handed the envelope to Frank, a new engineer who'd begun work at K-25 two weeks prior. I'd just turned to leave the room when the door opened. Clive Morrison stood there, taking me by surprise. In the months I'd been at the plant, we had never crossed paths.

He appeared just as shocked to see me. "Mae? What are you doing here?"

His unfriendly tone rankled. "I work here, same as you."

Frank looked up from the document I'd brought him, which appeared to be some sort of technical drawing. "Is there a problem?"

Clive immediately offered a false smile. "No, Mae is a friend. I was just surprised to see her, is all."

Frank nodded and went back to work.

I moved around Clive and exited the room. He followed me out, closing the door behind him. As I made my way to the stairs, his voice stopped me.

"Sissy told me you worked at K-25, but I didn't know your position. I wasn't aware you had access to the control room."

I faced him and crossed my arms. "Sissy shouldn't be talking about me or my job. It isn't anyone's business what I do or where I go. And you shouldn't share information that could get her into trouble. Three girls from the dorm have been fired for talking about things they shouldn't."

His eyes narrowed. "What has she told you?"

"Only that you work here at K-25."

"Nothing else?"

I didn't like being interrogated. "You'll have to ask her, but I assure you if she had, it wasn't anything I would repeat."

He studied me, as though determining if I told the truth or not. After a moment, he said, "I need to get back to work."

When he turned to leave, I decided to test my theory regarding his story about tonight. "It's a shame you have to miss the big Thanksgiving dinner. You must have an odd schedule, being that you're here now and yet you have to work tonight too."

He stiffened. "As you said about yourself, what I do isn't

anyone's business. My schedule doesn't concern you." He didn't wait for my reply and disappeared into the control room without a backwards glance.

I stewed over the exchange all the way back to the maintenance shop.

What does Sissy see in him? I wondered. He wasn't terribly handsome, but then outward appearances had never been important to me either. Garlyn was certainly nice-looking, but it was his friendly personality and kindness that drew me the first day we met. Clive, on the other hand, never smiled, never offered pleasant conversation, never acted as though he thought me worthy of his time.

By the end of the workday, I'd decided not to tell Sissy I saw Clive. Like me, she would surely wonder why he was working the day shift as well as the night shift. His loss was my gain, as I saw it. I'd make sure she had a wonderful evening with Garlyn and me and our other friends, proving to my roommate she didn't need sour-faced Clive Morrison.

I bundled in the warm coat I'd purchased last week and made my way to the bus terminal. It had been a splurge, but the hand-me-down coat I'd brought to Tennessee stood out among the nicer garments the girls in the dorm wore. Even Sissy's wardrobe was of better quality than the meager dresses I owned. While I didn't usually pay mind to things like that, now that I was seeing Garlyn and attending social gatherings on a regular basis, I didn't want to look like a girl from a Kentucky coal mining camp.

Sissy sat on her bed when I arrived, her diary in her lap. She hurried to tuck it beneath her pillow before she greeted me.

"Is Garlyn meeting us at the cafeteria?" she asked a bit too brightly.

I felt the question was more for distraction than information, since we'd discussed what time we would have dinner before we left for work that morning. Recently, I'd noticed she was careful not to leave the small writing book on the bedside table as she'd done in the early days of keeping a journal. No doubt she'd begun to include private things about her relationship with Clive, but I hoped she knew I wouldn't read it.

"Garlyn said he'd be there at seven o'clock sharp."

"I wish Clive could join us." A frown marred her face as she gazed out the window to the darkening sky. "Whatever he's working on must be important, because his supervisor insisted he stay at the plant tonight."

I remained silent while I changed into the dress I considered my best. I would need to purchase something new at Miller's department store soon, but I figured I'd wait until after Christmas. Mama hinted in her last letter she'd send a special package for the holiday, and I couldn't help but wonder if she might've sewed some things for me. She'd also written that she, Pa, and Harris were invited to the pastor's home for the Thanksgiving meal. I was glad to hear it. Pa wasn't well enough to go hunting for a wild turkey, and Harris was still too young to go on his own.

We left the dormitory a short time later. Delicious aromas and a smiling Garlyn greeted us when we arrived at the cafeteria. While Sissy walked on ahead to join some of our dorm mates in line, I linked arms with Garlyn.

"Happy Thanksgiving, Mae." He handed me a bar of chocolate, the kind I knew was sold only in the PX. I'd seen some of the SEDs and other military guys munching on the hard-to-get treat from time to time. "It's not much, but I just wanted you to know . . . I'm thankful I met you."

His warm words and earnest expression caused a tingle to run through me. "I'm thankful I met you, too."

We hadn't kissed yet, but I'd recently decided I wouldn't stop him if he tried. I liked Garlyn. A lot. He talked about returning to Scranton after the war, and I had to admit the idea of going with him crossed my mind more than once. But, I chided myself as we joined Sissy and the others, I was getting ahead of things. A chocolate bar was not a proposal of marriage. It was simply a nice gesture to let me know he appreciated our friendship. With the war continuing to rage in Europe and in the Pacific, with no end in sight, we had plenty of time to see where our relationship might take us.

Today, I would simply be grateful for Garlyn's easy company, a dear friend and roommate in Sissy, and delicious food—all of which reminded me of God's goodness and faithfulness.

I couldn't ask for anything more.

Saturday morning found me loading dirty laundry and a container of soap into a large wicker basket. I would rather skip this particular task, being that this was my only day off for a while. Yet if I didn't attend to my growing pile of laundry today, I'd regret it later.

I'd lingered in bed long after the sun rose in a clear sky. There was no point rushing. Long lines at each of the four laundry and ironing rooms formed every hour of the day, every day of the week. From time to time I used Sissy's handheld washboard to rinse underthings or a blouse, but today required use of an electric washing machine, especially since I'd volunteered to do Sissy's laundry as well.

I tossed a bath towel on top of the pile and thought of poor Mama. She did laundry on an old wringer-style washer—for our family as well as dozens of other people in town—working backbreaking hours, six days a week. Wouldn't it be something if I could save enough money and buy her an electric washer? Although the main reason I'd come to Tennessee was to do my part to help win the war, I also wanted to help my family. Mama said the money I sent home every week had already eased some of the worry Pa carried.

I plopped down on my bed and glanced at Sissy where she stood in front of our small wall mirror. "Where are you and Clive going today?"

She continued to dab on bright red lipstick from the cardboard container it came in these days. All metals went to the war effort, forcing beauty product manufacturers to find alternative materials to use for lipsticks, powders, and other items deemed necessary to the girls in the dorm. I'd brightened my lips with Sissy's makeup a couple times when I had plans with Garlyn, but mostly I used petroleum jelly. It was inexpensive and easily obtained at the market.

"There's a Judy Garland movie showing at the theater in Knoxville," she said. "It isn't playin' in Oak Ridge, and Clive knows how much I love her movies."

"That sounds nice." I struggled to evoke cheerfulness. Although a trip to the larger town twenty miles away would be fun, her companion was the problem.

She reached for the thin gold chain and heart-shaped locket she always wore. The small case contained a cloudy miniature of her parents on their wedding day. It had once belonged to her grandmother and passed to Sissy when the woman went on to glory. I often thought it would be nice to have a sentimental family keepsake, but neither Pa, Mama, nor their families had ever had money for extravagances. Every dime earned went to more important things, like food and shelter.

Once the necklace was in place, she met my gaze in the mirror, a serious look in her blue eyes. "Clive says there's something important he wants to talk to me about."

We stared at one another through the reflection.

"I think he might be planning to propose," she whispered.

My heart sank. "What will you tell him if he does?"

She turned and gave a slight shrug. "I don't know, Mae. I thought I was in love with Clive and wanted to marry him. Lately, though . . ." Her voice trailed.

I didn't want to hurt Sissy. She was a dear girl, although a bit naive. If she had doubts about Clive, maybe now was the time to voice my own reservations about the odd fellow.

"Sissy, if you're having second thoughts about Clive, just cancel. You don't have to go today. You're under no obligation to continue seeing him."

She gave a half-hearted nod. "I know. I do like him. Love him, I think. He's smart and knows so many interesting things about the world. But I . . . I'm not sure I can . . . trust him."

Her faltering words alarmed me. "What do you mean? Has he tried to make you do things you shouldn't?"

"I don't mean that." Her cheeks turned pink. "He's always a perfect gentleman when we're together. It's probably nothin'. I promised him I wouldn't mention it to anyone."

Concern swirled through me. "You can tell me, Sissy. I give you my word I won't say anything to anyone else. Not even Garlyn."

She hesitated a long moment before she sat on the edge of her bed and faced me. "A few weeks ago, he took me to the trailer where he lives."

At my widening eyes, she hurried to say, "Nothin' improper happened. He had a bottle of bootleg rum he'd snuck onto the Reservation, and we drank some. A little later, he walked down to the men's restroom. While he was gone, I poked around, just looking at this or that."

She paused, her brow furrowed. "I knocked over a box that was sitting on the counter. Papers fell out. When I picked them up, I noticed some had 'Confidential' or 'Secret' stamped on them in red ink. I thought it was strange that he'd brought them home, being that everythin' around here is so hush-hush."

I couldn't agree more.

"When I picked up the last paper, I saw it was handwritten, but I couldn't read the words. I don't think they were English." Distress washed over her face. "Clive walked in while I was tidying up the mess I'd made. He got real angry, Mae. Angrier than I've ever seen him. He grabbed me by the arm and hauled me outside. It . . . it scared me," she said, ending on a shaky whisper.

I didn't know what to make of the strange story. As far as I knew, Clive's job allowed him access to restricted areas throughout the Reservation. It made sense that he'd have access to classified documents too. But why become angry with Sissy for simply seeing them?

"He gave you no explanation about the papers?"

She shook her head. "He drove me straight home. We didn't speak the whole way back to town. I've been too afraid to bring it up again."

My alarm deepened. "I don't think you should go to Knoxville with him, Sissy. I don't have a good feeling about this. About Clive."

"I know he can be a little peculiar, Mae," she said, her brow knotted, "but I really do care for him. He's not like the farm boys back home, all rough and rowdy. He's smart and has tons of book learning. I like listening to him talk, even if I don't always know what he's talkin' about. It was my fault he got upset. If I hadn't been snooping, I wouldn't have knocked the box over. He has an important job, and I wouldn't want to do anything to mess that up for him."

I didn't like where this was going. "He didn't need to get angry about an accident, and he shouldn't have grabbed you. It's not like you were trying to discover the big secret by looking at the papers. You said yourself he scared you, Sissy. That isn't good."

She opened her mouth to reply, but a knock on the door interrupted us. Prudence Thorpe appeared in the opening.

"Clive is downstairs, Sissy." The nosey young woman's eyes traveled the length of my roommate, who looked lovely in a new dress, with her golden hair fashioned in a becoming style. "Gracious, Clive looks like he's dressed for a hike in the woods, but you're ready for a party. What gives?"

Sissy stood. "Would you please tell him I'll be right down?"

Prudence pouted, clearly miffed she didn't get an answer to her inquiry. "Sorry, hon, I'm not going downstairs." She exited the room without closing the door behind her.

Sissy picked up her purse and coat. Now that the weather had turned cold, her identification badge was pinned to the lapel of the outer garment instead of her dress.

"Sissy, please reconsider—" I began, only to be stopped by her raised hand.

"I'm going to Knoxville with Clive, Mae. I probably shouldn't have said anything to you. I'm sure I'm just being silly. He's very sweet, and . . . I love him."

Was she trying to convince herself or me?

"Clive said we'd have dinner in town, so it may be late when we get back. Oh, and thank you for offering to do my laundry, Mae. You're the best."

I stood and gave her a tight embrace. "I hope you have a fun day," I said, pulling away to look her in the eye, "but will you do something for me?"

"What's that?"

"Call Mrs. Kepple if Clive does anything that makes you uncomfortable. She has a car, and we'll come get you."

She nodded, her blonde curls bouncing. "I will, Mae. I promise."

The door clicked closed behind her.

CHAPTER THIRTEEN
LAUREL

JONAS ARRIVED at Aunt Mae's promptly at three o'clock.

"How's your father doing?" Aunt Mae asked after he greeted us. "I heard your mother was out of town when he injured himself."

The corner of his mouth tipped. "He's as ornery as ever. You know how he hates being idle. Mom isn't going to be happy when she finds out he sprained his ankle, but he didn't want her to cut her trip short."

Aunt Mae chuckled. "I wouldn't be surprised if she hears about it anyway. Gossip can travel all the way to Chicago." She glanced between Jonas and me. "Where are you two going today? It sounded as though you had the full tour of Oak Ridge yesterday."

"I'm taking Laurel out to K-25," he said. "Even though we won't be able to go inside, one needs to see it to understand how big it is."

Aunt Mae seemed surprised. "I didn't know you were able to get onto the site."

As Jonas explained his access to the restricted area, I noted

Aunt Mae seemed less agitated talking about the wartime plant with Jonas than she had with me.

"It's been years since I've been out there," she said. "Last I heard, the buildings were starting to show their age. There's no telling how many miles I traveled inside those walls, riding my bicycle up and down the long corridors."

"Would you like to come with us, Aunt Mae?" It would be fantastic to hear her reminisce about her time in the enormous building.

A shadow crossed her face. "No, dear, but thank you. I'll stay here and read. You children have a nice time. I wasn't planning anything special for supper, so feel free to grab a bite in town."

If I didn't know any better, I'd think she was encouraging us to go on a date. I hoped Jonas didn't get that impression. It occurred to me I didn't know his relationship status, but in the brief time I'd known him, he didn't seem like the type of guy to spend time with a single woman if he wasn't single himself.

We left the house and climbed into Jonas's Bronco. As we drove west through town on the turnpike, I told him about my visit with Velvet and Roonie.

"I admit I was shocked—and still am—to learn how segregated Oak Ridge was during the war. I guess I didn't expect the government to make distinctions like skin color while fighting for freedom and equality around the world. I realize pro-segregation laws had been on the books for decades, but it seems like wartime practices should have been different."

Jonas agreed. He said he'd been friends with the Maxwells' son since junior high school and had played basketball on the same team.

After we left town, we passed a small white building on the north side of the road. An even smaller structure sat directly across the highway from it.

"That's the Oak Ridge Turnpike Checking Station," Jonas said. "The station was built after the war and controlled access to K-25 during the late forties and early fifties. Even though the town itself opened to the public in 1949, the plants remained restricted. By then, the Atomic Energy Commission was in charge of things."

He went on to describe his father's job as an MP during the war, charged with keeping the secret and the Reservation safe.

"Dad tells the funniest story about a woman who tried to smuggle bootleg moonshine into Oak Ridge. She had it hidden under her skirt, but the jar had a crack in it. As you can imagine, a puddle started to form at her feet." He chuckled. "Rather than let everyone think she was . . . you know . . . having an accident, she fessed up."

I laughed. "Bootleg moonshine? That's crazy."

"People attempting to sneak alcohol into town was a regular problem for the guards. It was banned, but that didn't stop folks from trying to bring it through the gates. They'd hide it under their hat or behind the hubcap of an automobile. Dad says he and the other MPs had to search every bus, every vehicle, every day, and every night. Rules and regulations were tight if you wanted to live and work behind the fence."

We traveled past the abandoned guard house, with thick forests and hills all around. "How far is K-25 from town?" I asked.

"It's about eleven miles one way."

"Wow. I hadn't realized it was located such a distance from the main area. Why did they build it so far away?"

He looked thoughtful. "The men in charge of the Manhattan Project had never worked on anything like this before. No one had. Atomic science was brand new and untested. If something catastrophic were to happen during the process to enrich the uranium, they hoped the hills and distance from town would save lives. It's the same reason General Groves chose the remote location of Los

Alamos in New Mexico and Hanford in Washington. Neither of those areas were densely populated."

His explanation was sobering. "I'd never considered it could have been dangerous to simply live and work in Oak Ridge. It's a bit alarming to think that most of the residents had no idea they might be putting themselves and their family's safety in jeopardy by coming to work here."

"That's one of the complexities of Oak Ridge's history. The vast majority of people, like my folks and your aunt, had no idea what was going on. They simply needed jobs, and the Manhattan Project provided them. I don't believe the government could get away with something like that nowadays."

It wasn't long before Jonas steered the vehicle off the main road into a complex of buildings, paved streets, and crisscrossing railroad tracks. We passed through a checkpoint where Jonas flashed his police badge, assured the guard we wouldn't be long, and drove slowly through the industrial-looking area.

"All of the buildings you see are part of the Oak Ridge Gaseous Diffusion Plant. Some were built after the Manhattan Project ended, and they each have their own code name." Jonas glanced at me. "Your aunt would be a well of information about all of this. It's a shame she seems hesitant to revisit those days."

I nodded. "I've thought the same thing."

"Any idea why she doesn't like to talk about the early years of Oak Ridge? Once Dad gets on a roll reminiscing, it's hard to get him to stop."

"Not a clue. My dad says she never talked about it. The only time his mother mentioned Aunt Mae's work on the Manhattan Project was right after the war ended. They'd been as shocked as the rest of the world to learn that the work Aunt Mae and the others did had helped to create an atomic bomb."

He pointed out a number of interesting sites before he turned a corner. There in front of us was an enormous building. The largest I'd ever seen.

"K-25!"

Jonas grinned. "There she is. All two million square feet, about the equivalent of thirty-five football fields. The whole thing is a mile long, from one end to the other, with four levels. It was designed in a U shape to make it somewhat easier for employees to get around."

My mouth gaped. "It's gigantic. No wonder Aunt Mae had to ride a bicycle to do her job."

"I've been inside a couple times. It's overwhelming. I can't imagine what your aunt's first impression was when she saw it. Wasn't she from a small town in Kentucky before she moved here?"

I nodded. "My grandfather was a coal miner. Dad says they lived in a tiny shack owned by the coal company. Aunt Mae had never been anywhere before she came here."

"That's a common story for most of the young women who worked in Oak Ridge. Mom was from Hot Springs, Arkansas. She'd never even ridden on a bus until she came to Tennessee."

He parked the Bronco in a paved area near the massive structure and cut the engine. We exited the vehicle and stared up at the four-story giant. Windows were sporadic, and shafts as tall as the building jutted every so often, making me think they were stairwells.

"I still don't fully understand the purpose of K-25," I said. "I read it was used for enriching uranium, but I confess the science is way over my head."

Jonas chuckled. "I couldn't begin to explain the science of it, but I'll tell you what I do know. There were three main facilities in Oak Ridge whose purpose was to enrich, or purify, the uranium that would later be used in the nuclear bomb. K-25, a gaseous diffusion plant, Y-12, the electromagnetic plant, and X-10, the graphite reactor. They all had the same goal, which was separating the isotopes—the atoms found in uranium known as 235 and 238—but each plant used a different method to accomplish it. Later, a liquid thermal diffusion plant, S-50, was added to the Reservation as a sort of *helper* facility, but it was too costly to run and used too much power. The Manhattan Project scientists figured they only needed a hundred pounds or so of the stuff to make the bomb, but it took many months and millions of dollars to achieve. It's said that during the war, Oak Ridge used more electricity than New York City."

I studied the huge building. "I wish I'd paid more attention in high school science class when we were studying atoms. I had no idea what the teacher was talking about, although I do remember a phrase he used over and over: *Atoms are the building blocks of matter.* Wasn't it German scientists who eventually figured out how to split uranium atoms?"

"It was," Jonas said, "which is what made the world nervous, considering Hitler ruled over Germany at the time. An interesting fact is, Oak Ridge might not exist if it wasn't for Albert Einstein."

"That's right," I said, recalling something I'd read in my research. "Einstein was Jewish and was born in Germany but fled in the early 1930s because of Hitler's rise to power and the Nazis' antisemitism. He sent a letter to President Roosevelt that started the ball rolling toward developing an atomic bomb."

Jonas leaned against the vehicle, clearly enjoying our back-and-forth history lesson as much as I was.

"Einstein and others feared Germany would develop an atomic bomb with their newly found knowledge. At the urging of Leo Szilard, the Hungarian physicist who first came up with nuclear reaction, they wrote a letter to the president basically saying if America doesn't catch up to Germany, we could find ourselves facing a powerful weapon in the hands of a madman."

A shiver raced up my spine. "Can you imagine what the world would be like if that had happened?"

"Would there still be a world, is the question."

We stood in silence, pondering the terrible realities of nuclear war. It was, of course, still a possibility. Although Germany ceased being a threat when World War II ended, the Cold War with the Soviet Union continued today. I clearly remembered how terrified we all were during the Cuban Missile Crisis that took place when I was in grade school. We'd had drills about what to do should the emergency sirens sound. With everything I'd read recently about the power of an atomic bomb, it seemed ridiculous that we were told to get under our desks for protection.

My eyes traveled up and down the vast building. "So the machines and pipes and everything Aunt Mae saw every day were part of a process to enrich uranium using . . . What did you call it?"

"Gaseous diffusion, which is different from the process used at Y-12. Over there, hundreds of enormous magnets were situated on something called a *racetrack* to separate the isotopes. The work Mom, Georgeanne, and thousands of other young women known as cubicle operators did was part of that process. But General Groves didn't know which method would be the fastest or produce the most product, so he convinced the president they needed to try them both."

"I imagine that cost a pretty penny."

He smirked. "K-25 alone cost five hundred million dollars back in the 1940s."

I whistled. "I don't think I want to know what that would be in today's dollars."

Jonas shared what he knew about each level of the huge building, including the operating floor where a control room was located. I wished I could peek inside and see where Aunt Mae had worked, but although the other plants in the area continued to produce uranium for nuclear power, K-25 itself had been shut down in 1964.

"From what I understand," Jonas said, a serious note in his voice, "there's a growing concern about health risks associated with radioactive materials and the chemicals used in the enrichment process. Not just for former employees, but for those who continue to work at the plants, as well as the surrounding community. I suspect there will be future investigations, maybe even some lawsuits, if it turns out to be true."

I thought about Aunt Mae's failing eyesight. Did it have anything to do with her time working at the plant?

We climbed back into the Bronco. "Thank you for bringing me out here. I've seen pictures of K-25, but it's completely different to see it in person."

"I'm glad to be of service."

On our way back to town, Jonas pointed out the area that had once been a residential neighborhood called Happy Valley, now overgrown with vegetation. The houses and other structures were torn down shortly after the war ended, but during the height of the Manhattan Project, thousands of workers resided there in simple homes, trailers, and the infamous hutments Velvet and Roonie lived in.

"You should check out the library," Jonas said. "They have a great section on Oak Ridge's history, plus there's microfilm of old newspapers from back then. They might be a good resource for your research."

I immediately made a mental plan to do exactly that Monday morning.

Taking Aunt Mae's suggestion, Jonas declared I couldn't return to Boston until I'd eaten a slice of Big Ed's pizza. Big Ed himself delivered our pie to the table, joking that Jonas, a regular customer, usually ate a large pizza by himself. I had to admit the handmade dough and fresh vegetables were delicious, but the sauce . . . Oh my. Perfection. Over dinner, we undertook more historical discussions about K-25, the war, as well as the aftermath of the atomic bombs dropped on Japan. By the time we returned to Aunt Mae's, the sun had already dipped below the hills.

"I had a great time," I said when we pulled into the driveway. "It was incredible to see where Aunt Mae worked. I understand a little more about what her life was like when she was a young woman here."

"I had a good time too." His attention fixed on me. "I don't know how long you're in town, but maybe we could have dinner again."

A warm flutter tickled my belly. "I'm not on any kind of schedule. Dinner sounds nice."

He seemed pleased. "I'm working late tomorrow, but I'll call and see when you're free."

I nodded and opened the passenger door. "Goodnight, Jonas," I said, suddenly feeling like a shy teenager talking to the boy she had a crush on.

"Goodnight, Laurel."

I returned his wave as he drove away, a smile firmly in place. Aunt Mae sat in the living room when I entered the house, the television tuned to an episode of *The Love Boat*.

"I thought I heard a car door." She stood and clicked off the set. "Did you have a nice evening?"

"I did," I said. "I'm stuffed with pepperoni and mushrooms from Big Ed's."

She chuckled, then sobered. "And what did you think about my former workplace?"

I met her gaze. "It was amazing to see it in person and learn about the work that took place there. You, Velvet, Roonie, Georgeanne, and Jonas's parents were all part of something big and important, and it has such far-reaching significance. I'm proud of you, Aunt Mae."

She exhaled and returned to her seat. I settled on the sofa, hoping my comment hadn't stirred up the dark memories that kept her from sharing about her early years in Oak Ridge.

"Sometimes I'm not so sure what we did was a good thing."

"What do you mean?"

"Years after the war ended, I read that many of the scientists who worked on the atomic bomb urged President Truman not to use it. Hitler was dead and Germany had surrendered. Some say the Japanese weren't far behind." She paused. "One can't help but wonder what President Roosevelt would have done had he still been alive. Truman had only been president a handful of months when he made the decision to use this new atomic weapon. He hadn't even known the bomb existed while he was vice president. I just don't know if it was the right thing to do."

I heard uncertainty in her words. The same uncertainty I'd heard before in the voices of others who'd participated in the Manhattan Project, especially when I asked about Hiroshima and Nagasaki. I had to admit the situation was a lot more complex than I'd ever realized. Yes, I was proud of Aunt Mae and the others. What they accomplished, knowing so little of the big picture, was truly remarkable. But at the same time, they unknowingly contributed to the creation of a devastating weapon, the use of which on innocent civilians was still questioned to this day.

"The thing is, no one could predict the future." I hoped my words would bring a measure of comfort to her. "Not President Truman, and not the scientists. Elliot thinks the war in the Pacific could have gone on for years if we hadn't used the bomb. What a terrible choice our leaders had to make."

After a quiet moment, she sighed. "I know the work we did for the project here in Oak Ridge was meant to end the suffering, but it also brought suffering to so many. I just wish the war had never happened. It cost too many innocent lives."

I didn't have to wonder who she meant.

Millions of military personnel from all over the world had died in the war. The Nazis murdered millions of Jews. Tens of thousands of Japanese citizens were killed and maimed when the atomic bomb, fueled with uranium enriched right here in Oak Ridge, fell on Hiroshima. More perished three days later when the plutonium bomb Fat Man dropped on Nagasaki.

No, it wasn't necessary to ask who she meant.

Every life lost was a tragedy.

CHAPTER FOURTEEN
MAE

SISSY'S BED WAS EMPTY when I awoke Sunday morning.

With a yawn, I sat up and stretched. Groggily, I scanned the room, trying to remember if she was scheduled to work. With rotating shifts, it was hard to keep track sometimes.

I'd gone to bed early last night, exhausted. The chore of doing laundry had become a frustrating, all-day affair. In mid-cycle, the washing machine broke down. Mrs. Kepple called maintenance, but they couldn't come right away. I'd had to wring out sopping, soapy clothes, only to discover the wait for another washer was twice as long. My patience had evaporated. I'd hauled the wet laundry upstairs to the bathroom and hand rinsed everything in the tub. Then I'd lugged it back down and found an empty clothesline outside in between the dormitories. By the time everything was dry and I'd ironed out the wrinkles on two of Sissy's dresses, I was bone-tired.

A glance at my wristwatch on the nightstand told me it was a little after seven o'clock. I remembered that Sissy and I planned to attend services at Chapel on the Hill before I started my shift at noon. Maybe she rose early and was in the shower, although the fact that her bed was already made was unusual. Neither of us put much effort into housekeeping. Someone routinely cleaned floors and bathrooms throughout the dorm, otherwise we'd be living among mounds of dust bunnies and dried mud.

I changed into Mama's Sunday-go-to-meetin'-made-over dress, added a sweater, and walked down the hall to the bathroom. Chattering girls stood in line for the showers, but Sissy was not among them.

I returned to our room, sat on my unmade bed, and studied her neat coverlet.

Had she gone to work earlier than usual? It wasn't outside of the realm of possibilities. A nasty virus was going around, with many employees at each of the plants unable to attend to their duties. Perhaps she'd received word she was needed.

I stood and walked to the closet we shared. Her coat and the new dress she'd worn yesterday on her outing with Clive weren't hanging up, so she must still be wearing them. Like many of the women who worked at Y-12 monitoring cubicles, Sissy changed into coveralls once she was at the plant, then changed back into her street clothes when her shift ended. If she'd gone directly to work after she returned from Knoxville, that would account for why nothing in her closet had been disturbed.

I donned my coat and made my way to the cafeteria, hoping she'd be there.

She wasn't.

I ate a hasty breakfast and returned to the dorm.

No Sissy.

At a quarter to ten, I walked up the hill, past Jackson Square and the Guest House, to the chapel. Services in the small church were well attended, no matter the time of day or the denomination, and I squeezed onto a bench near the back. A search of the room, however, told me my roommate was not there.

Worry began to creep into the edges of my mind, and I couldn't focus on what the preacher was saying. Where was Sissy? Yes, she could be at work already, but it seemed odd that she hadn't mentioned anything about the need to go in earlier. We didn't often leave notes for one another, but we had on occasions when we knew we wouldn't cross paths.

When the service ended, I hurried back to our room. Still empty.

After I readied for work, I scribbled a note to Sissy and left it on her bed. I didn't admonish her for not coming home last night, but I did tell her I'd been worried when she didn't meet me at the church service as planned.

The bus ride to K-25 took twice as long due to a flat tire, requiring riders to transfer to a second bus. Mr. Colby wasn't happy when I finally arrived, late.

"A dozen people are out sick," he said, unusually gruff. "We'll be busy today."

He was right.

I don't know how many miles I traveled on my bicycle, but I was beat when it was finally time to clock out for the day. Yet even though I'd constantly been on the go, Sissy's absence was never far from my mind. I felt an urgency to get back to the dorm and make sure all was well with her.

Garlyn was waiting for me at the security portal.

"I thought we could have dinner at the snack bar," he said once we were seated on the bus. "They have a new cook and everyone is raving about the hamburgers."

"Sure." I gave a distracted nod.

His keen gaze traveled over my face. "What's wrong?"

Exhaustion and worry crashed over me at the genuine concern

in his voice. My vision blurred with tears. "I don't think Sissy came home last night," I whispered.

I hadn't wanted to admit it at first, assuming she'd simply gone to work early. But the more I thought about it, the more I realized I didn't believe that scenario.

My gut twisted.

The only logical explanation was that she'd spent the night with Clive.

Garlyn's brow tugged into a frown. "That's not like her."

"I know." I sniffled. Garlyn took a handkerchief from his pocket and handed it to me. "Thank you," I said and blew my nose.

Over the din of passengers' voices and the bus's noisy engine, I told him about Sissy's trip to Knoxville with Clive. I didn't say anything about their relationship or her concerns, even though I knew I could trust Garlyn. I was still hopeful she would break up with Clive soon. Yet if she'd spent the night with him, that wasn't likely to happen now.

"Did you see Clive today?" I'd looked for him all afternoon but hadn't run into him.

Garlyn shook his head. "I was in meetings in the admin building most of the day."

I mulled over the situation. I needed to know more about the odd fellow my roommate may have compromised herself with. Especially if there were consequences—the kind that would arrive in nine months. Would he stand by her?

"What do you know about Clive?"

I'd avoided that question until now. I never wanted to put Garlyn in the awkward position of divulging—or withholding—information he didn't feel comfortable sharing with me. But after Sissy's admission regarding her confused feelings for Clive, coupled with his strange behavior, I needed to know as much as I could about Clive Morrison. I was determined to convince Sissy he wasn't the man for her.

He checked to make sure no one was listening, lowered his voice, and said, "I know he joined the Army while he was in engineering school somewhere up north. He was assigned to the SEDs and came to Oak Ridge about the same time I did. He's part of the health physics department. He's a smart guy. Not real friendly. Does his job well. Never causes trouble. Captain Barger seems to like him, since he approved Clive's request to bunk in a trailer instead of the barracks."

"Why would the captain grant his request?" I asked. "It doesn't seem fair to the rest of you."

"I heard it was because Clive is allergic to something in the barracks. He claimed it was making him sick." Garlyn gave a shrug. "Seems kinda lame to me. The guys think he just wanted his own place."

I appreciated the trust Garlyn showed by sharing this information. He could find himself in a world of trouble if someone found out. How I wished I could tell him about the top secret documents Sissy found in Clive's trailer. It may not mean anything, since I didn't know if Clive's clearance as a health physics officer included authorization to remove confidential papers from K-25 and other restricted areas. The fact that he became angry when Sissy saw them could simply be due to the air of secrecy we all lived and worked under every day.

But I couldn't tell Garlyn. I'd made a promise to Sissy not to share that information with anyone, so I kept it to myself.

We exited the bus at the terminal in town and made our way to my dormitory. While he waited in the lobby, I hurried upstairs. The door to our room was locked, a sure sign Sissy wasn't inside. My shoulders slumped when I found everything exactly how I'd left it that morning. The note I'd written still lay on her bed, unread. Nothing had been removed from her closet that I could tell. Her purse wasn't on the shelf, and her laundry hamper was empty.

Clearly, Sissy had not been back to our room while I was at work.

A knot of fear began to form in my belly. When I returned downstairs, Garlyn's brow tugged into a frown when our eyes met.

"She isn't here?"

I shook my head and met his gaze. "I'm starting to get worried, Garlyn. This isn't like Sissy at all. What if there's been an accident? Would anyone know to contact me?"

"Maybe you should talk to your housemother. She might know something since you were at work all day."

I agreed.

Mrs. Kepple's smile of greeting fled when I inquired if the woman had a message for me from Sissy. When she questioned me further, I had to confess that my roommate hadn't returned to the dorm last night, although I didn't mention the trip to Knoxville with Clive. Rumors spread like wildfire, especially if they were juicy. If word reached Prudence Thorpe that Sissy may have spent the night with a man, the entire Reservation would know about it, and my roommate's reputation would be forever sullied.

"I'm sure she must've had to work a double shift at Y-12," I said, hoping that was indeed the explanation for her absence. "So many girls are down with the virus. Quite a lot of people were out from K-25, too."

Mrs. Kepple didn't appear convinced, but she agreed that was a possibility.

"I want to be informed when Sissy returns." Her stern voice reminded me of Mama's when I'd done something wrong. "We have rules we must abide by. If Sissy's work schedule changes and she'll be out past curfew, she needs to let you or me know."

Garlyn was in the lobby waiting for me after I exited Mrs. Kepple's small office, located behind the dormitory attendant's desk. A group of women stood at the counter, chatting with the attendant while she shoved letters and messages into mailboxes behind her.

"Mrs. Kepple hasn't heard from Sissy," I whispered once we were out of their earshot. "I fear I may have caused a problem for my roommate. Our housemother wants to speak with her as soon as she returns."

He gave a sympathetic look. "It's not your fault, Mae. Sissy should have let you know she wouldn't be back. It's not as if you reported her. You're concerned, as any good roommate would be. She'll understand."

I appreciated his encouragement. "I hope you're right. I'd hate for Mrs. Kepple to evict Sissy because of this. Last week, a girl down the hall was told to pack her bags and move out because she kept missing curfew."

By the time we reached the snack bar, a line of hungry patrons extended out the door. It appeared most of Oak Ridge had heard about the new cook's juicy burgers. Garlyn offered to take me to the cafeteria instead, but I didn't mind the wait. I wasn't looking forward to returning to an empty room.

Garlyn walked me back to the dorm just before curfew. We both agreed the burger was tasty, but I hadn't been able to enjoy it. My mind was on Sissy.

"I'm sorry I wasn't very good company tonight," I said as we stood outside on the sidewalk, holding hands.

"I bet Sissy's upstairs right now. She'll have a whopper of a story, too."

I knew his grin was meant to cheer me up. "Mrs. Kepple will no doubt give her a lecture. I may give her one too."

Garlyn gave my fingers a gentle squeeze. "I'll see you tomorrow after work, Mae."

Despite my reluctance to confront Sissy, I rushed upstairs. I needed to know she was safe and sound.

My heart sank when I walked into a darkened room.

I simply stood in the open doorway, my feet anchored to the floor. Light from the hallway illuminated Sissy's empty bed and my note. I didn't know what to think or feel.

Where was she?

If she and Clive had car trouble and were forced to remain in Knoxville until it was repaired, she would have sent word to me. Or even if there hadn't been car trouble but they'd decided to stay in Knoxville another day, she could have let me know so I wouldn't worry.

A shocking thought suddenly sprang to my mind, and I practically choked on it.

Had Sissy and Clive eloped?

That awful possibility hadn't occurred to me until this very moment, but it made complete sense. Sissy had confessed that Clive wanted to talk to her about something important. Maybe he'd planned the whole thing as a surprise. I could well imagine sweet Sissy unable to say no. My roommate could at this very moment be Mrs. Clive Morrison, basking in newly wedded bliss, without a care for me or Mrs. Kepple. I wouldn't be surprised if Knoxville hadn't been their destination at all. They could've driven to Nashville for a honeymoon, for all I knew.

Aggravation quickly replaced my earlier concern. I flicked on the light and closed the door with more force than necessary. Here I'd been worried about Sissy, anxious to know if everything was well, while she and Clive may have snuck off and gotten married without telling anyone. It was the only logical explanation for her continued absence.

I fumed as I readied for bed, muttering about Sissy's foolishness. What would her mama say when Sissy confessed what she'd done? I could imagine my own mama's reaction to such news. I didn't envy Sissy having to write a letter to her family with the stunning announcement.

Sleep fought to claim me after I crawled under cold sheets, and my heavy eyelids closed. My last coherent thought, however, nearly made me cry.

When Sissy returned to Oak Ridge and moved into Clive's trailer, I'd have to get a new roommate. I'd miss late night chats and giggles with my friend.

CHAPTER FIFTEEN
LAUREL

FIRST THING MONDAY MORNING, I took Jonas's advice and headed to the Oak Ridge library. I hoped to spend a good chunk of time digging through old newspapers and other historical records that might help me get a feel for what life was like in Oak Ridge during the war.

Aunt Mae left the house too, assuring me she didn't have far to go when I expressed concern about her eyesight impairing her driving. I'd helped her load the back seat of her car with colorful Tupperware containers filled with the six dozen cookies we'd baked yesterday afternoon when we returned from the church service. While I'd rolled out dough for sugar cookies and she mixed up a batch of snickerdoodles, Aunt Mae filled me in on her volunteer work.

On Mondays she helped in the church nursery while a group of young mothers met for Bible study in the fellowship hall. Moms, children, and even the pastor were treated to home-baked goodies. When she left there, she spent the afternoon at the nursing home where she wrote letters, washed hair, or simply played cards with the residents, leaving the remaining cookies for them to enjoy. On Wednesdays she helped at the elementary school, and on Fridays she visited church members who were under the weather, often taking them a casserole or soup. Before her eyesight became an issue, she'd also sewed and knit items to send to missionaries overseas.

"Dad told me you kept busy with volunteer work," I'd said, impressed by her full schedule, "but I had no idea how much you accomplished each week. You must have more energy than most people half your age, including me."

Her face had remained serious despite my offhanded joke. "I admit I'm worn out by the end of the week, but," she'd paused, her brow tugged, "it's my responsibility."

Her choice of words puzzled me. "I'm sure they all appreciate your hard work, Aunt Mae, but you don't want to overdo it. It wouldn't hurt to cut back somewhere."

She'd shaken her head. "I don't want to let anyone down. You mustn't worry about me, dear. I'm fine."

I didn't pursue the subject further. If she was happy with her volunteer work, who was I to say otherwise? We agreed we'd have a simple dinner of grilled cheese sandwiches and tomato soup that evening, since we both planned to be away from the house most of the day. I'd stuffed an apple in my purse to tide me over.

Now, after obtaining assistance from a very helpful librarian, I was parked in front of a microfilm machine loaded with images from the *Oak Ridge Journal*, beginning in 1943.

Anticipation swirled through me.

Although I didn't know exactly what I hoped to discover by reading the old newspapers, I couldn't help but feel they would lead me to a better understanding of life in Oak Ridge during the days of the Manhattan Project. Because I'd gotten to know some of the people who actually lived through the war, I found myself interested in them and what they experienced on a personal level that had nothing to do with research for my dissertation. Reading through old news articles was an opportunity to go back in time through the written words of people living behind the fences of the Secret City, experiencing day-to-day life there and not just retelling about events that took place many years ago. I would especially like to find new information that hadn't already been shared by the residents I'd interviewed. Some nugget of historical significance that was fresh and exciting.

While the machine warmed up, I couldn't help but smile, thinking back to the telephone conversation I'd had with Jonas yesterday evening. He'd called, just as he'd promised, to see if I'd like to join him for dinner tomorrow night. Of course I'd said yes, and he offered to pick me up at six o'clock. After I hung up the telephone, I decided a trip to the department store downtown was in order. The clothes I'd packed for the trip weren't first-date worthy.

I tapped the table with my index finger, a bad habit whenever I became nervous.

It had been a while since I'd gone on a date. Scotty Gurley and I had been sweet on each other since the seventh grade, but once he became a game-winning high school quarterback, he dropped me for the head cheerleader. Although I hadn't been heartbroken, my hurt feelings were assuaged when I heard she dumped him right after graduation. She was bound for New York City, with dreams of breaking into modeling, and didn't want a boyfriend to spoil her plans. I'd thrown myself into my studies in college, much to the dismay of friends who continually tried to set me up with guys they thought would pique my interest.

What about Jonas? I wondered. Did he date much? I was only in town for a week, two at the most, so there wasn't any fear of things turning serious. We'd simply connected over the history of Oak Ridge. We would have a nice meal and share some laughs. Nothing to be nervous about.

Images of the *Journal* soon filled the small screen in front of me. All thoughts of boys and dating gave way to life during the Manhattan Project and World War II.

The first issues were typed and printed on what appeared to be regular sheets of typewriter paper, beginning with a letter from Lieutenant Colonel Crenshaw of the Corps of Engineers dated September 4, 1943. He encouraged residents of the new community of Oak Ridge to put their best foot forward so that "the war effort may go on at full pace." Considering the extraordinary secret work that would take place in Oak Ridge—work that eventually resulted in an atomic bomb—it seemed a bit dishonest of the area engineer to refer to it simply as "the project." Folks like Aunt Mae could never have imagined what the project truly entailed.

I clicked to the next page, a letter from Town Manager Captain Samuel Baxter, repeating the previous encouragement to residents to give their best and have a bit of a "Pollyanna" attitude regarding the limitations of a brand-new town still under construction.

By January 1944, issues of the *Oak Ridge Journal* included a line at the top that read "Published for Oak Ridge – keep it here, please." Obviously, secrecy was of utmost importance. While I didn't think the newspaper would be allowed to print information the enemy could use to discover the secret work taking place, Oak Ridge remained hidden from the world in 1944. A newspaper from a town that didn't exist on any map could alert a savvy spy that something was amiss.

I paused as I considered the reality of life in Oak Ridge back then.

What crazy times those were. The world at war. Hitler and Mussolini determined to spread their evil. The Allies just as determined to stop them. That was the sole reason the Manhattan Project was created. The reason Oak Ridge existed.

I spent the next hours reading news articles and taking notes. While everything I read fascinated the history nerd in me, I didn't find anything revelatory. I did notice that sometime in 1944 the newspaper switched from being printed on regular paper to what looked like actual newsprint. Articles were arranged in columns with headlines, and the warning on the front page changed to "Keep this copy here please."

At noon, I took a short break and went outside to eat my apple. The air was warm but clouds filled the sky. It appeared we were in for a rain shower soon. I hoped Aunt Mae made it home before the storm broke. Now that I was aware of her eye problems, I worried about her driving around town.

Back at the microfilm machine, I whipped through pages filled with stories about town events, upcoming dances, and building and construction updates. In June 1944, the front page held news about the successful D-Day bond drive, complete with a black-and-white photograph of dozens of young women gathered around a table where bonds were sold.

By August 1944, the warning at the top had changed yet again, this time reading "Not to be taken or mailed from the area." Stories followed the same pattern you'd find in any newspaper across the country, with local tales as well as updates on the war. Photographs of recent high school graduates, summaries of town hall meetings, and even a story about a group of nurses' aides receiving their caps found their way onto the pages.

As though Oak Ridge was simply a town like any other.

As though the secret made no difference in the lives of the residents.

I considered their unique situation. Despite the vital, clandestine work of enriching uranium for a bomb that took place right under their noses, most of the residents of Oak Ridge had no idea why the town existed. Why they'd been brought in from across the country to live in a place founded on and embroiled in secrecy. Held together by that very secrecy, even. If not for the project, none of the people I'd read about today would have been in Oak Ridge, because Oak Ridge would not have existed. The East Tennessee land General Groves appropriated for the enormous plants and the quaint town would still be farmland. The communities of Wheat, Scarboro, Edgemoor, and others would've remained where they'd been for decades. Farmhouses commandeered for residents of the Reservation would instead be passed down through the generations, as had happened long before buildings with names like K-25 and Y-12 sprang up instead of crops.

The story of Oak Ridge got even stranger when I came across an article that told the bizarre tale about a man named John Hendrix and a prophecy he made decades before the Manhattan Project came to Tennessee. According to the newspaper, Hendrix was born in 1865 and died in 1915, twenty-eight years before General Groves began buying up land with the intention of building an enormous uranium enrichment facility. An odd fellow, Hendrix often disappeared into the woods where he remained for weeks. Once, after spending forty nights in the hills, he returned with a wild prediction. "A huge factory will be built in Bear Creek Valley," he told folks at the general store, "that will help win the greatest war there will ever be." He predicted there would be a city on Black Oak Ridge, railroads, and thousands of people running to and fro.

No one believed him.

It was a little after three o'clock when the headline of a small article in the corner of the third page caught my attention. The date of this issue was from the second week in December 1944.

M. Willett Requests Information on Missing Roommate

M. Willett? Could that be Mae Willett, my aunt? I enlarged the article so I could read the small print.

Maebelle Willett requests your help locating her roommate Sissy Galloway who has not been seen in Oak Ridge since November 25, 1944. If you have information on Miss Galloway's whereabouts, please contact Miss Willett immediately.

The article went on to give the name of a dormitory and a telephone number for Mrs. Kepple, the dorm mother. While I supposed there could have been two Maebelle Willetts in Oak Ridge during the war, how likely was it? The article must be about Aunt Mae.

According to the article, Aunt Mae's roommate had gone missing sometime after Thanksgiving. The fact that Aunt Mae went to the newspaper for help was an indication she was concerned about her roommate.

The image of a pretty blonde woman's face on the security badge I'd seen in Aunt Mae's box of mementos flashed across my memory. I couldn't recall her surname, but I did remember her first name was Sylvia. Was she the Miss Galloway who went missing?

I pressed a button on the microfilm machine. A printed copy of the page on the screen exited from a slot. After tucking it in my purse, I continued to search for more articles about Aunt Mae's roommate, but no mention was ever made of her again that I could find.

At a quarter to five, I turned off the machine, paid for the photocopy, and thanked the helpful librarian for the stack of books she had ready for me to check out. My back and shoulders were stiff from hunching over the microfilm monitor for long hours. A soak in the bathtub sounded divine.

Aunt Mae's car was not in the driveway when I returned. She must still be at the nursing home. My mind went over the limited details of the mystery surrounding Aunt Mae's roommate as I headed for the house, leaving me with questions rather than answers.

What were the circumstances that led to a newspaper article requesting information about Sissy's whereabouts? Communication back then wasn't as easy as today, with telephones and pagers offering people around the world a way to stay connected. Not everyone had a phone in the 1940s, as strange as that seemed compared to our modern world nowadays. The fact that I hadn't found a follow-up article about Sissy's continued absence made me think she'd most likely been located, thus eliminating the need for a story in the newspaper. The mystery may not be a mystery at all.

Entering through the front door Aunt Mae left unlocked, Peggy greeted me. I let her outside, leaving the door open for her return, then went to my room. With my aunt out of the house, now was the perfect opportunity to compare the name on the security badge to the name of the missing roommate mentioned in the article. I laid the page I'd printed at the library on the bed, then retrieved the wooden memory box I'd tucked in the corner next to the dresser. After removing the old newspapers I had yet to read, I dug around and found the security badge I was looking for.

Sylvia Jean Galloway.

Although the article referred to her as Sissy Galloway, I was certain it was the same woman. And now that I knew she was indeed Aunt Mae's roommate, I felt a sense of urgency to know what happened to her. Had she ever returned to Oak Ridge? Where had she been and why hadn't she contacted Aunt Mae?

One last question circled my mind as I studied Sissy's pretty face.

Why did Aunt Mae have her roommate's security badge?

I retrieved the second ID from the box. Aunt Mae had been a pretty young woman too, even if her hair wasn't fashioned in a popular style like Sissy wore. I could imagine the two of them having fun together, living in a town where the women outnumbered the men. After reading through *Oak Ridge Journal* articles today, I'd learned the town planners had done their best to provide all the amenities and entertainment opportunities one would find in any other town. Black-and-white photographs documented sporting events, dances, plays at the theater, and other activities that were available to keep employees of the Manhattan Project happy and on the job. I felt certain Aunt Mae and Sissy took full advantage of the entertainment offerings, especially knowing my aunt had grown up poor in a small coal mining community in Kentucky. Oak Ridge would have been an exciting place for twenty-something-year-old Maebelle Willett.

An ache in my lower back reminded me I'd wanted to soak in the tub before dinner. Setting the badges and article on the bed, I walked across the hall to the bathroom and turned on the faucet. The noisy pipes sang their loud song while I sat on the closed commode and waited for hot water to arrive, which usually took at least a full minute. Once the flow was warm, I plugged the drain with a rubber stopper and watched the water level rise until the tub was half full. A couple drops of Aunt Mae's rose oil filled the air with a sweet aroma before I turned the knob to the off position.

I returned to the bedroom to change out of my clothes but stopped short in the doorway.

Aunt Mae stood next to the bed, Peggy at her feet. The printed page from the *Oak Ridge Journal* and Sissy's badge were in her hands. Her face had drained of all color.

When our eyes met, tangible fear shone in hers, intensified by the thick glasses she wore.

"Where did you get this copy of the *Journal*?" she hissed, her body trembling.

Peggy let out a whimper and hurried out of the room.

"At the library," I said, hoping the gentle tone in my voice would help to calm her. "Remember? I went there today to go through old newspapers to learn more about Oak Ridge during the war. When I saw the headline with your name, I got curious."

Her breath came heavy. "You shouldn't be poking your nose where it doesn't belong. I told you nothing good can come from bringing up the past."

I didn't take her angry words personally. I had a feeling her reaction was more about whatever it was that kept her from wanting to remember bygone days than it was about me.

"Aunt Mae, I'd like to understand what it is about the past that upsets you. Does it have to do with Sissy? The article says she was missing. You must have been worried about her. Was she okay?"

Her hands shook when she looked at the badge, then to the printed page. I thought she might give an explanation, but in the next instant, she threw the items on the bed and bolted from the room. The small house shook when she slammed her bedroom door closed.

I stood in shocked silence.

Something was terribly wrong, but I had no clue what. Remorse washed over me as I put the badge and the article in the box. I'd really done it this time. I felt horrible, yet I didn't know how to make things better.

I didn't linger in the tub. When I came out of the bathroom, her door was still closed. I ate a peanut butter sandwich, then retired to my room and read over the notes I'd taken at the library, all the while hoping she'd come out and we could talk things over. But she remained closeted in her room. At my knock and offer to bring her a sandwich, she declared she wanted to be left alone.

While I readied for bed, I mulled over the situation. If Sissy had truly gone missing, wouldn't there be a police report? Even back in the 1940s, things like that were investigated.

I crawled into bed, my back complaining as I stretched out.

Maybe Jonas could help. He was an Oak Ridge police detective, after all. But should I involve him? I wouldn't want Aunt Mae to think I was discussing her personal matters with everyone in town.

I yawned and turned out the light.

It wouldn't hurt to ask him about police records from the 1940s. If he indicated they still existed, I'd see if he could look for information on Sissy Galloway without divulging the connection to Aunt Mae. I could tell him about the article I found but leave out my aunt's name. That would protect her privacy but would also hopefully yield answers as to what happened to her roommate.

I made a silent promise to Aunt Mae before sleep claimed me.

If Jonas couldn't find anything on Sissy, I'd drop the matter entirely. I didn't want my visit to Aunt Mae's to end with a severed relationship because I'd become too nosey.

CHAPTER SIXTEEN
MAE

BY WEDNESDAY EVENING, I was beyond worried about Sissy.

I told myself every morning I awoke to an empty bed across from mine that she and Clive were living it up as newlyweds, without a care in the world. Yet somewhere deep inside me, I didn't believe it. Sissy wasn't the type of person to run off and get married without telling anyone, especially me. Even if they had eloped, wouldn't she have called or sent word, knowing I'd be concerned when she didn't return from Knoxville?

But if they hadn't run off together, where were they?

I'd spoken with Mrs. Kepple again yesterday morning. The dorm mother had stopped me in the lobby when I came downstairs and asked if Sissy had returned. She'd frowned at my negative answer.

"I must tell you this is most unusual," she said, clearly vexed. "I will have to report her absence to the administration if she doesn't return soon. They'll need to terminate her employment at Y-12."

Thursday morning I boarded the bus to K-25 with one

objective: to discover if Clive Morrison had returned from Knoxville. I'd gone to Mr. Colby's office yesterday and asked in a roundabout way if he'd seen Clive, pretending I needed to speak to him about something related to the job, but my boss, busy looking over technical drawings of the pipe gallery, had offered an impatient shake of his head.

"Why would I know anything about Morrison? Ask his supervisor, Captain Barger."

I'd never met the captain, but I was determined to locate the military officer today and find out once and for all what was going on. Surely he would know if Clive and Sissy had eloped, especially if Clive had taken time off for an impromptu honeymoon.

My plotting, however, came to a screeching halt shortly after lunchtime when I nearly ran Clive down with my bicycle. Mr. Colby had sent me on an errand, but I was so distracted with my personal mission that I didn't notice him when I turned a corner. I dodged around him, slammed on the brakes, and skidded to a stop.

"Hello, Mae." He gave me his usual pasted-on smile. "You're in a hurry."

My mouth hung open while I stared at him, catching flies as Mama would say.

"Where have you been?" I blurted, ignoring pleasantries. "I've been worried sick about Sissy. She should have called me or Mrs. Kepple to let us know the two of you wouldn't be back right away. Did you elope? Has she moved into your trailer already?"

Accusation laced my words, but I didn't care. He'd kept my roommate away from her friends with no consideration as to how concerned we would be when she didn't return home. His feelings were of little consequence to me at this point. I'd be even more furious if he said they weren't married. Sissy's reputation would be forever ruined when word got out she'd spent the past four days with him without the benefit of marriage.

Yet instead of the guilt his face should have worn, Clive gave me a puzzled look. "Elope? What are you talking about, Mae? Sissy and I broke up Saturday."

The floor seemed to tilt, and I stumbled backwards.

I studied him, struggling to figure out if he was jesting or not. "No, that's not true. You took her to Knoxville with the intention of proposing to her. When she didn't come home that night, I assumed the two of you had eloped."

His brow shot up. "Good grief, Mae. Who told you that wild tale? Sissy?"

I could only stare at him.

What was going on? Why was Clive acting as though he hadn't seen Sissy lately?

"If you didn't elope with Sissy, then where is she?"

It took a moment for him to answer. My heart nearly stopped as his expression grew serious.

"Are you telling me she didn't return to the dorm Saturday afternoon?"

Tangible fear poured over me with the implications that came with his question.

"Sissy is missing, Clive." Panic tightened my throat. "I haven't seen her since you picked her up for your outing to Knoxville."

"Whoa, now." He raised his hand. "I didn't take her to Knoxville. I'd told her I needed to talk to her about something, which was that I didn't think we should see each other anymore."

I gasped in disbelief. "*You* broke up with *her*?"

He nodded. "I realized we didn't have much in common. She's a swell girl, and we had some fun times, but I knew she wasn't the one for me." He paused. "She took it kind of hard. Cried and begged me to reconsider, but I told her she'd find the right guy soon. I'm sure it won't be long before she's dating someone else."

My mind spun, completely bewildered. "If you didn't take her to Knoxville, then where is she?"

He seemed genuinely confused. "I don't know. I didn't want to break up with her in public, so we drove to the river and parked like we usually do. We were there a couple hours before she was ready to return to the dorm. I dropped her off sometime in the afternoon because I had to work the late shift."

While I attempted to sort through the information he'd shared, he glanced at his watch. "I have a meeting in ten minutes I can't miss." He put his hand on my shoulder. It felt clammy through my coveralls. "I'm worried about Sissy, Mae. I wish I'd known earlier that she didn't make it back to the dorm. The only thing I can think of is she was too embarrassed to face everyone and took a bus home to Georgia."

I watched him walk away, stunned by everything I'd just heard.

Clive and Sissy hadn't eloped. They hadn't even gone to Knoxville to see a movie and have dinner. They hadn't left Oak Ridge, according to Clive. And contrary to what Sissy said before she left, he had not proposed but had instead broken off their relationship.

I don't know how long I stood there, my mind reeling. I didn't know who or what to believe. Had Sissy lied to me? Had she suspected Clive was going to break things off and told me a story to cover her embarrassment?

I thought back to our last conversation Saturday morning. *Clive says there's something important he wants to talk about. I think he might be planning to propose.*

Had she made it all up?

Then I remembered her next words. *A few weeks ago, I thought I was in love with Clive and wanted to marry him. Lately, though . . .* She hadn't finished her thought nor had she come right out and said she'd changed her mind, but that's what I understood her to mean.

I went back to work, but all the while my mind labored to unravel the mystery of what happened between Sissy and Clive. What was true and what wasn't. Who was lying and who'd told me the truth. By the time I met Garlyn at the portal, I was an emotional mess.

"I don't know what to think," I said after filling him in on my conversation with Clive.

He held my hand in his. "Maybe you didn't know Sissy as well as you thought you did. You just met her in August, after all. She may have guessed Clive was about to break off with her and lied to cover it. It sounds like she didn't want to face everyone and just went home."

I heaved a sigh. "I suppose you could be right, but she's never given me reason to doubt she was anything but an honest, unpretentious young woman. We've shared lots of things with each other, and she always seemed sincere."

By the time we reached town, I wasn't hungry. I just wanted to go to sleep and wake up tomorrow to a new day.

Garlyn walked me to the dorm and gave me a long hug. "Get some rest, Mae," he said, tucking a loose strand of hair behind my ear. "Sissy is no doubt safe at home with her family, so you don't need to worry anymore."

I sniffled. "I hope you're right. Maybe I should write a letter to her and send it in care of her parents' address."

"That's a good idea. I bet she'll write back with an apology."

I bid Garlyn goodnight and headed for the stairs. However, Prudence Thorpe waylaid me as I passed through the lobby.

"Mae, you're just the gal I've been lookin' for," she said, drawing out her words in an exaggerated manner. "Rumor has it Sissy didn't come back from Knoxville. I declare, I would have never guessed our sweet Sissy was the type of woman who would stay overnight with a man." Her big blue eyes grew wide with feigned shock.

My blood boiled with her insinuation. As aggravated as I was with Sissy, I wouldn't let her reputation be sullied by wild gossip, whether she returned to Oak Ridge or not. "You're mistaken, Prudence. Sissy went home to Georgia. Her mother is ill," I said, not flinching at the bold-faced lie.

Disappointment filled Prudence's face. No doubt she'd relished spreading the juicy gossip about my roommate. "Well, we'll miss her sunshiny personality," she said, her sugary-sweet words as false as her smile.

Once in my room, I closed the door and leaned against it. Guilt washed over me. I'd lied to Prudence about Sissy going home. God and Mama didn't approve of telling falsehoods, but I couldn't stand by and let the meddlesome young woman badmouth my roommate. Besides, even Garlyn seemed to believe Sissy had gone back to Georgia. It hurt my feelings to think she left without saying goodbye. On the other hand, I was relieved my fears about Sissy eloping with Clive had been unfounded.

I changed into my nightgown, brushed my teeth in the bathroom, then fell into bed, exhausted from the upheaval of the past few days. My mind, however, raced with everything that had happened. From Sissy's confession about her feelings for Clive on Saturday, to his shocked expression when I told him she hadn't come home.

I tossed and turned until midnight before I finally sat up and clicked on the light.

The entire situation was driving me crazy. I wouldn't be able to sleep until I figured things out. One question seemed to hold the key.

Did Sissy know Clive intended to break up with her?

From everything she'd told me Saturday morning, she was convinced he planned to propose marriage, not break up. Yet if Clive were to be believed, he'd seen how incompatible they were and knew it wasn't going to work out. If I were honest, I had to admit it was rather honorable of him to end their relationship. Sissy had taken it hard, according to Clive, which I found believable. At one time, she had wanted to marry the guy.

But hadn't she also indicated her feelings had changed?

"Oh, Sissy," I whispered, frustrated. "I wish you would've confided in me more."

My gaze swept the room, searching for clues to the mystery. Some indication she'd had no intention of returning. Nothing in her closet or drawers held much value, so leaving them wouldn't have been too difficult, especially if she was as upset as Clive claimed. The morning she walked out of our room, she took her purse, her new coat, and her security badge. Anything else she left behind was easily replaceable.

A sudden thought brought me up straight.

What about her diary? Had she taken it with her? She'd stopped leaving it in the bedside table drawer, but I had a suspicion about where she'd hidden it.

I threw back the bedcovers, knelt on the cold floor beside Sissy's bed, and slid my hand beneath her mattress.

My fingers met something hard.

I pulled the diary from its hiding place and stared at the cover.

It didn't feel right to read Sissy's personal thoughts and feelings. Even if she had gone back to Georgia, the words she'd recorded in the small journal were none of my business.

But what if something in the entries held answers to the questions I'd asked since she hadn't returned from Knoxville? People who kept diaries often included details they didn't want anyone else to know. Wrote things they wouldn't speak aloud. If reading her private musings helped me understand what happened to my friend, then it was worth breaching the boundaries of trust that were normally in place between roommates.

I crawled beneath the warm covers of my bed, and with a deep breath, opened the book.

Dear Diary,
  I'm in Tennessee! Mama thought it'd be fun for me to write down my experiences and share them with her later, so she bought me this diary.

I recalled reading this entry the day I discovered the journal on the table. But unlike the last time I'd held the book, I continued to read the remaining words, which were all about me.

Sissy wrote that she had a feeling we were going to be good friends. I was pleased by the compliments she gave me, expressing how she'd never had an older sister before but hoped she'd found one in me. I too had felt a sisterly connection from the beginning, although we'd never spoken about it. When I saw her again, I'd be sure to tell her how much I'd enjoyed rooming with her.

I turned the page.

The next entries were all about Oak Ridge. The mud. The long lines. The people she met. She described the scenery surrounding the town, using flowery words like *emerald hills* and *cornflower blue skies*. By the end of the first week, however, Sissy confessed to feeling homesick and expressed her hope that she would receive a letter from her mama soon.

I wonder if I made a mistake coming here. It's so far away from Georgia. I miss my family, she'd written. *If I still feel like this next week, I might get on a bus and go home.*

I drew an imaginary line with my finger, underscoring her words. *I might get on a bus and go home.*

Is this the answer I was looking for? Sissy admitted to having thoughts of leaving Oak Ridge, even before Clive broke things off with her. She'd felt loneliness for her family and wondered if she'd made a mistake moving so far away from them. If Clive's rejection left her emotions raw and her spirit broken, she very well could've shaken the dust of our secret town off her shoes and hightailed it back to Georgia. Although it hurt that she hadn't said goodbye, I couldn't blame her for not wanting to face the likes of Prudence Thorpe and others whose favorite form of entertainment was spreading gossip throughout the Reservation.

I skimmed the next two pages, which were mostly about her new job at Y-12. I wasn't interested in the needle gauges, knobs, and dials she adjusted on her cubicle all day. She didn't know the purpose for any of it, and neither did I.

I was about to conclude the diary was of no help when I came to the entry she'd written after her first date with Clive.

Dear Diary,

I met a man named Clive Morrison at a dance the other night. He said I was the prettiest thing he'd ever seen and asked me to dinner. Tonight we ate at one of the restaurants in town instead of the cafeteria. After that we took his car to the river and talked for hours. He's awfully smart. He's nice-looking too, but not in a Clark Gable way. More like Jimmy Stewart, I guess. But there's something about him I really like. I can hardly wait to see him again.

"I wish you'd never met Clive Morrison," I muttered.

If Sissy hadn't gone out with the odd fellow, she'd still be here with me. With a pang of regret, I realized I'd have to let Mrs. Kepple know that I needed a new roommate. I'd have to pack up Sissy's things and send them to her in Georgia.

A number of entries about Clive followed. I sped through icky, gushy comments, claiming him wonderful, considerate, and romantic. I was convinced my naive roommate had been fooled by the man. I'd sure never seen those qualities in him.

Although the thought didn't bring me satisfaction, I'd bet Sissy's opinion of Clive Morrison changed considerably after he broke things off with her. I just wish she would've recognized how ill matched she and the serious, unfriendly engineer were and had broken up with him first. Plenty of fun, amiable fellows had been interested in Sissy, but she'd only had eyes for Clive.

My own eyes began to grow heavy. I let out a noisy yawn.

I flipped ahead and saw there were only a half dozen or so entries left. Maybe I should wait and finish reading them tomorrow. I had work in the morning, and I'd be sorry if I didn't get some sleep. Biking around K-25 all day was hard enough when I was fully rested. Mr. Colby wouldn't be pleased if he found me napping on the job.

I was about to close the book when my gaze landed on the final entry, dated two days before Sissy disappeared.

I fear Clive is a spy. In fact, I'm sure of it. I don't know what to do. He warned me not to tell a soul about the papers I saw or the secrets he's shared with me. He said if I did, I'd be sorry, and so would whoever I told. I'm scared, Diary. So very, very frightened.

My hands shook as words leaped off the page.

Spy. Secrets. Frightened.

I stared at Sissy's shaky handwriting.

Could it be true? The man who'd given us the introduction speech the day we arrived in Oak Ridge warned that anyone could be a spy. To discover that Sissy believed Clive was one sent a cold chill racing through me.

One question demanded an answer.

If Clive was indeed a spy, did he have something to do with the reason why Sissy was no longer in Oak Ridge?

CHAPTER SEVENTEEN
LAUREL

AUNT MAE WAS UP EARLY Tuesday morning. She greeted me with a smile when I entered the kitchen and acted as though nothing out of the ordinary had occurred the previous day. I thought it best to play along. Despite a powerful need to know what happened to her roommate thirty-five years ago, I didn't want to spoil things with a repeat of yesterday.

"I thought we could go to the hardware store and pick up some tomato plants," she said, scraping fluffy scrambled eggs onto my plate once I was seated at the table. "Maybe a couple squash plants, too."

I grinned, thrilled she seemed her usual self. "That sounds great. Mom tried gardening when the girls and I were little, but none of us has your green thumb. After the excitement of planting a garden wore off, we usually forgot to water it. It's amazing how much a garden *doesn't* grow without water."

She set a plate of yummy-looking biscuits in the center of the table, along with fresh butter and homemade strawberry jam, then took a seat across from me.

After the blessing, she said, "Mama taught me all about growing vegetables and how to can them. Pa's meager salary at the coal mine barely covered rent and things like flour, coffee, and sugar, so we relied on what we could grow and what Pa could shoot when he went hunting. When we did purchase necessities, we had to shop at the store owned by the coal mining company. They charged exorbitant prices, so Pa mostly had to use credit. The problem is, once you were in debt to the store, you had no choice but to do business with them. It was robbery, pure and simple, but there wasn't anything anyone could do about it."

"How long did Grandpa work at the mines?"

Her brow tugged. "He started mining coal when he was thirteen. His pa before him mined coal, too. That's what most men did in that part of Kentucky. And like many miners, my pa and his pa died from black lung."

The sobering reality of coal mining.

"I wish he and great grandpa could have had an easier life," I said.

She sighed and set her fork down. "I did too. The reason I came to Oak Ridge was because the salaries offered here were higher than what I could get in Kentucky. I sent money home every chance I could so Pa could quit the mines."

I reached across the table to place my hand over hers. "I'm sure your parents appreciated everything you did to help them."

"Pa passed away soon after the war ended. That's when Mama and Harris came to live with me."

"In this house?" I asked, trying to envision my father as a teenager in Oak Ridge.

"No," she said, "I hadn't bought this place yet. I lived in a dormitory, but when Mama agreed to move, I rented a small house in town. Harris wasn't too happy about leaving his friends. As soon as he graduated from high school, he moved to the big city."

"You never wanted to move away? Go someplace more exciting?" I wriggled my eyebrows.

Aunt Mae didn't smile. "I couldn't leave Oak Ridge. I had to stay."

Once again her choice of words intrigued me, but I let it go.

We finished breakfast, with me volunteering to clean up while she changed clothes for our outing. Within the hour, we were seated in the Z28. Once we arrived at the hardware store, Aunt Mae took hold of a small, wheeled shopping buggy and off we went.

I followed her around like a little kid. I couldn't recall ever being inside a hardware store and found it new and interesting. She chuckled each time I stopped and asked about this item or that. Who knew replacement toilet seats came in so many different styles and colors.

"I see we need to get your nose out of those psychology books more often," Aunt Mae teased.

I stood before a rack of colorful gardening gloves, trying to decide which pair to purchase, when Jonas and his father appeared at the end of the aisle. A warm flutter tightened my belly. Jonas wore his police uniform, looking official but devastatingly handsome.

"Well, fancy meeting you ladies here," Elliot said. I noticed he walked with a cane, but his limp wasn't too bad. "Getting ready to do some gardening, I see." He indicated the small pots of plants and bag of potting soil in the buggy.

"Yes," Aunt Mae and I said at the same time.

"Nothing like homegrown tomatoes," she added.

Aunt Mae asked Elliot how he was doing. While he updated her on his accident and healing process, Jonas stepped closer to me.

"I'm looking forward to our dinner tonight." His lowered voice was only for my ears.

I smiled. "Me too."

"Do you like Mexican food? There's a new place out on the turnpike that's pretty good."

"I love it."

Elliot's voice drew our attention. "I hear you were understandably impressed with K-25 when Jonas took you out to see it the other day." His curious gaze was on me.

"It's amazing," I said. "I've seen pictures of the building in books, but they don't do it justice. There's no way to truly comprehend how enormous it is until you see it in person."

He chuckled. "Just think what all of us country folks thought when we first saw it back in the forties." He turned to Aunt Mae. "I guess you'd know all about that, seein' as you worked there for years."

She nodded but didn't add to the conversation.

"I worked at the K-25 security checkpoint some," Elliot continued, unaffected by Aunt Mae's silence. "That post was easier than manning the main gates in and out of town. People were always trying to smuggle things in or enter without an ID or proper pass. It could get tedious. At K-25, there was just one rule: you didn't get in or out unless you had your badge."

"Was there much crime in Oak Ridge back then?" I asked. While I was thinking about the disappearance of Aunt Mae's roommate, I was also curious how crimes were handled in a city that didn't exist on any map.

Elliot seemed to ponder the question before answering. "There was the usual. Petty theft. Domestic disturbances. Teenagers causin' trouble. Seems like I recall a murder that took place sometime in '44, but that was closer to Union County. One of the fellas accused worked in Oak Ridge, so the MPs got involved."

I was about to ask a question regarding the storage of old records when Aunt Mae abruptly began to walk away.

"It was nice to see you, Elliot, Jonas," she said over her shoulder, already several steps away, "but Laurel and I need to get home if we're to have these plants in the garden before sundown." She didn't wait for their reply and hurried around the corner.

Her rudeness left me embarrassed, but neither man seemed offended. "It was good to see you again, Mr. Tyson."

"Call me Elliot." He glanced between Jonas and me. "You two kids have fun tonight."

Jonas shot me a grin. "I'm sure we will."

I bid them goodbye and hurried to join Aunt Mae at the checkout. A college-age young man carried her purchases to the car for us, and we were soon back at the house. After a quick lunch, we went to work in the garden. By the time we put away our hats, gloves, and tools, we were hot and sticky but satisfied with the fruits of our labor.

"You get cleaned up first," she said from her place seated at the table in the kitchen, sipping from a tall glass of cold lemonade that matched my own. She studied me before adding, "Jonas is a fine young man. Comes from a good family. I'm sure your parents would approve of you seeing him."

"We're just friends." I gave a small shrug. "Even if I were interested in dating someone, which I'm not, it wouldn't work out with Jonas. He lives here, and I live in Boston. Besides, getting my doctorate is my priority right now. It could take several years, plus an internship. That's way too long to try to maintain a relationship over the telephone."

She considered my declaration for a time before she spoke, a hint of sadness in her eyes. "Getting your doctorate is a fine goal, Laurel, but don't let it cause you to miss out on an opportunity to love and be loved. You don't want to end up alone, like me."

I sat in the chair opposite her. "Were you never in love with anyone?"

She stared off into space. "I don't know that I was in love, but there was a young man here in Oak Ridge when I first came to the Reservation. We both worked at K-25."

"What was his name?"

A soft smile played on her lips. "Garlyn. Garlyn Young. He was an engineer with the Army. We became friends." The smile faded as quickly as it had come. "But that was a long time ago. You run on now and get bathed. I think I'll lie down for a while."

While I readied for my date with Jonas, I wondered what had happened between Garlyn and Aunt Mae. Bit by tiny bit, I was piecing together what her life in Oak Ridge was like during the war. Her work at K-25. Her desire to send money back home to her family. Then there was her roommate Sissy, and the mystery surrounding her. Yet each time I thought Aunt Mae might open up about her time on the Reservation, she'd grow tense and refuse to talk about it. As though she wanted to forget the past in order to avoid having to deal with it.

My Psychology 101 teacher persona kicked in.

We called what Aunt Mae was doing a *defense mechanism*, a key concept of psychoanalysis. People often use repression, usually unconsciously, to protect themselves from anxiety-producing thoughts and feelings related to internal conflicts and outer stressors. In Aunt Mae's case, I had a growing suspicion something took place during the war that left her emotionally wounded or irreversibly frightened. Maybe both. But until she was willing to trust me enough to share her story, whatever it was would likely remain locked away in her psyche, just like the secret work she did for the Manhattan Project.

At six o'clock, I heard Jonas's Bronco pull into the driveway.

"You look lovely," Aunt Mae said, her voice startling me when she arrived in the open doorway to my bedroom and found me peeking out the window curtain.

"Thank you. I didn't have time to shop for anything new." I'd chosen the simple dress I wore to church on Sunday. There wasn't anything fancy about the pale-yellow outfit with daisies printed on the material. I'd added some dangly earrings and a bangle bracelet, hoping to create a casual yet slightly dressy look.

Jonas's knock and Peggy's barking interrupted us. I went to greet him then turned to Aunt Mae, who stood watching from the hall doorway.

"Can we bring you something from the restaurant?"

"Don't worry about me. There are plenty of leftovers in the refrigerator. Have a good time." She waved as we exited the house.

Jonas opened the passenger door to his vehicle. "You look really nice," he said as I climbed in.

"You do too." He wore khaki slacks and a light-blue button-down shirt, the cuffs rolled to mid-forearm.

On the drive to the restaurant, he asked about our afternoon gardening project, and I filled him in on the details.

"What brought you and your dad to the hardware store?" I asked as we pulled into a parking space. The number of cars in front of Fiesta Cantina told me the food must be good.

"Mom's been after him to fix the leaky kitchen faucet for weeks," he said with a chuckle. "He thought it best to get it done before she gets home tomorrow since he'll be in the doghouse for not letting her know about his injury. He still can't drive, so I gave him a ride."

Luckily we didn't have long to wait for a table. The Mexican-themed décor and mariachi music created a fun atmosphere. A handful of customers greeted Jonas as we made our way to a table near a window. He offered polite greetings but didn't stop to chat.

"This place is great," I said once we were seated. "We need a good, authentic Mexican-food restaurant in Boston. Don Jose's is as close as we can get, but I think the owner and chef is Irish."

Jonas laughed, then pointed to the menu. "So far everything I've eaten here is fantastic."

After the waitress took our order—beef enchiladas for both of us—we settled into easy conversation. Jonas asked about my studies, and I quizzed him on being a cop.

"I have to confess, I've never been too keen on cops."

Instead of looking offended, he grinned. "You're not alone. I suspect most of the general public feels the same way."

"Doesn't that bother you? I mean, they don't know you personally but make assumptions based on the uniform and the position of authority."

He squinted in thought. "I think most people appreciate police presence when something goes wrong, like a crime or a car accident, but they don't like it when we enforce the law, especially laws they would rather not obey."

"I've never been pulled over for speeding, but I admit to going faster than I should when I'm in a hurry."

"I'm sure we're all guilty of that," he said. "I wish people understood that most cops join the force to protect and help the public, not to make life more difficult. There are some bad apples in the barrel, of course, but I'd wager that most every police officer would do everything he or she could to keep people safe."

I couldn't help but feel proud of him, even though I hadn't known him long. I raised my glass of water. "Thank you, Detective Tyson. For being willing to do the hard things."

He clinked his glass with mine. "My dad's the one who inspired me. He was an MP during the war, then transitioned to the AEC Security Patrol. Here's to Dad."

After our food arrived, he asked about my work and why I went into psychology.

"I've always had an interest in what makes people do the things they do," I said. "Dad calls me a fixer, because even as a little girl, I wanted to fix people. If a schoolmate was angry, I wanted to figure out what was wrong and how to make it better. If someone was sad, I did my best to make them happy again. While I understand fixing people isn't exactly what psychologists do, I'd like to spend my life offering whatever I can to help them find happiness."

"That's an admirable goal," he said, his voice sincere.

"It'll take me a while to finish my doctorate, but I'm excited about the process. The information I'm gathering here in Oak Ridge is fascinating, and I can't wait to get started on my dissertation."

Over coffee, I broached the subject of crime and police records during the Manhattan Project.

"I took your advice and spent some time at the library reading old newspapers," I said.

"That's great. I'm sure you learned a lot."

"I did." I kept my voice casual, even as anticipation rose up within me. I was determined to discover what happened to Sissy Galloway, but I needed to tread carefully. Aunt Mae wouldn't want me discussing her private life or my suspicions that she was holding something back. "There was an article . . . well, more like a notice . . . about a young woman who went missing in November 1944. It made me curious about how things like that would have been handled back then, considering all the secrecy that surrounded Oak Ridge."

He looked thoughtful. "I imagine cases would have gone through a process in the forties similar to what we use today. We have more technology than they had, but procedures wouldn't have changed that much. After I joined the force, Dad told me about the times he had to make arrests and the paperwork he had to fill out. But you're right. Secrecy was always a priority. I doubt information would have been shared with departments from other communities about a crime that took place in Oak Ridge. Were there any details in the article about the case of the missing woman? Where she disappeared or who she was with the last time anyone saw her?"

"It just says she hadn't been seen in a couple weeks, which was unusual according to her roommate. The notice was basically a request for information." I paused, feeling a bit deceptive by leaving out Aunt Mae's connection. I could at least bring some truth to the subject. "The focus of my research is on how keeping secrets affected people, then and now. It would be interesting to know the outcome of this case."

He gave a slow nod. "There are boxes of old records in a storeroom at the police station that came from the basement of the Security Forces headquarters over on Bus Terminal Road. If you give me the name of the missing woman, I can poke around and see if there's a file or some kind of report about her."

I held in my excitement. "That would be great, if you have time, of course." I wrote Sissy's full name on a scrap of paper I found in my purse and handed it to him.

We finished our meal—everything was as delicious as Jonas predicted—and walked outside to a warm evening.

"Are you up for a little drive?" he asked once we were seated in his Bronco. "I promise it will be worth it."

"Sure. Are you going to tell me where we're going?"

He steered the vehicle east on the turnpike, in the opposite direction of Aunt Mae's house, and answered my question with one of his own. "Do you like ice cream?"

I chuckled. "Yes."

"Good. There's this great little drugstore in Clinton called Hoskins. It's been in business since before the Manhattan Project. They run an old-fashioned soda fountain and make the best ice cream sundaes."

"Sounds perfect."

We followed the winding Clinch River out of town. While

Jonas told me about fishing trips when he was a Boy Scout, I enjoyed the beautiful scenery beyond the window. Tennessee sure was pretty this time of year, with green hills, forests, and crystal-blue skies. Living in a big city was exciting, but I had to admit there wasn't anything this beautiful in Boston.

It was dark when we finally returned to Aunt Mae's.

"I'm so full, I don't think I can walk," I said, laughing. "That sundae was huge."

"I'm not gonna lie. I didn't think you'd be able to finish it. In fact," he grinned, "I was kind of hoping you wouldn't so I could swoop in and devour what was left."

"You looked pretty busy with your own sundae, Detective. Next time we'll have to try a cheeseburger and onion rings. They looked amazing."

A pleased expression filled his face. "Are you asking me out on a date, Miss Willett?"

Heat filled my cheeks. "I guess I am."

"I accept." He exited the vehicle and came around to open the passenger door for me. "After my shift tomorrow, I'll poke around the boxes of old files and see if I can find anything on . . . What did you say the missing woman's name was?" He pulled the scrap of paper from his pocket. "Sylvia Galloway."

"Thank you, Jonas," I said as he walked me to the front door. "But if you have other pressing matters, please don't feel obligated to look into a thirty-five-year-old case. I don't know if it was even an actual case of a missing person or just a misunderstanding."

"Welcome to my world. You just summed up my job. Digging into the details, solving the mystery. That's what I love about what I do."

Jonas promised he'd call me the next day to make plans for our burger date, then bid me goodnight.

A happy sigh escaped my lips as I watched him drive away.

We lived a thousand miles away from one another. We each had dreams and goals for the future. I had no idea where our friendship would lead, but sometime over ice cream and easy laughter, I'd come to a conclusion.

I wanted to find out.

CHAPTER EIGHTEEN
MAE

THE NEWSPAPER NOTICE I'd placed in the *Oak Ridge Journal* last week hadn't yielded any information on Sissy's whereabouts so far. It had, however, stirred up a hornet's nest of gossip about my roommate, led by Prudence Thorpe. The meddlesome young woman had waylaid me in the hallway on the way to the bathroom the morning after the article appeared.

"Maebelle Willett, you told me Sissy went home." She'd planted her fists on her hips, shrouded in a fuzzy blue bathrobe that matched her eyes. Her glare had held me hostage. "Why would you feed me a tall tale like that if you knew it wasn't true?"

I'd groaned inwardly. In my concern to locate Sissy, I'd forgotten all about the false story I'd given Prudence.

I'd offered a helpless shrug. "I'm sorry, Prudence. I just didn't want anyone spreading rumors about Sissy and Clive. I spoke with him, and he assures me they didn't spend the night together. In fact, he says they broke up, and it was he who suggested she'd gone home."

Prudence's scowl had eased some with my explanation. "Well, I suppose that's a possibility. But I must tell you, people are indeed talkin' about Sissy and how she up and disappeared." She'd glanced up and down the hallway before whispering, "One gal claims she saw Sissy with a fella at the tennis courts late that night, drinkin' tainted moonshine. There's no telling what could'a happened to poor Sissy if that's true."

It had taken every ounce of restraint I possessed to keep from grabbing Prudence and giving her a good shake. "That is exactly why I didn't want to tell anyone about Sissy until I had more information. Whoever thinks they saw her is wrong. Besides, how could they know the moonshine was tainted?"

Prudence's face revealed she hadn't thought of that. "You needn't get huffy about it, Mae. We're all quite worried about Sissy."

I was too, but it had nothing to do with gossip and tainted moonshine. Ever since I read Sissy's last diary entry about Clive possibly being a spy, her words had kept me up at night.

I'm scared, Diary. So very, very frightened.

I'd gone over every line in the journal multiple times, searching for clues. She'd written about the top secret papers she'd discovered in his trailer and his anger that followed, but I already knew about that. She'd told me about the incident herself, although she hadn't used the word *spy* or expressed her suspicions about him.

Was it true?

I'd asked myself that question at least a hundred times. I'd only seen Clive once since the day he told me about his breakup with Sissy. He'd been with his superiors and barely acknowledged me as I rode past. I thought he might seek me out later, anxious to know if I had any news, but he didn't, which seemed odd, considering he'd appeared quite concerned upon learning Sissy hadn't returned to the dormitory. I kept my eye out for him in the days afterwards, but we hadn't crossed paths again.

I had a hard time focusing on my job after Sissy left Oak Ridge. Even on my days off, my mind constantly worked the problem, never coming up with a credible solution as to her whereabouts or whose story to believe. It was nearly impossible to imagine dull Clive Morrison as a spy. Didn't spies come from other countries, like Germany or maybe Japan? Clive was as American as apple pie. He was in the United States military, same as Garlyn, and claimed his people arrived on the Mayflower. The documents Sissy saw in his possession did give me concern, but without knowing exactly what they were, I couldn't be certain how important they were. Clive's job as a health physics officer might be such that he took paperwork home. It was more likely he was nervous after Sissy looked through them rather than being angry that she'd simply seen them in his house. Secrecy, after all, was drilled into us every single day.

But according to one of the last entries in the diary, Sissy had been shaken up by the incident. Enough so to cast a shadow on her future relationship with Clive.

Clive treats me like a child sometimes, she'd written the week before she disappeared. *I may not be as smart as he is, but I'm a full-grown woman. I'm starting to learn things about him that make me unsure if I should keep seeing him or break things off.*

Had Clive sensed her change of affections and called it quits first? That's what he claimed. But if Sissy truly had second thoughts about him, wouldn't she have been relieved when he ended their relationship? It didn't seem likely she'd be so heartbroken that she'd leave Oak Ridge without taking her personal belongings or telling anyone goodbye. Each time I contemplated writing to her family, something held me back. What if she wasn't in Georgia? My letter could make matters worse. Yet if she hadn't gone home, where was she?

I groaned.

"Oh, Sissy," I whispered, although no one in the noisy plant could hear me over the constant hum of machinery. "I wish you had confided in me right then and there instead of telling your diary. I sure as shootin' would've given you a mouthful of advice."

I continued to hope she would write to me. I checked the mail daily, looking for a letter from Georgia that assured me all was well. I'd already decided I wouldn't scold her when I sent a reply. As long as she was with her family, where she was loved by people who would help heal the hurt Clive caused, that's all that mattered.

But a letter from Sissy had yet to arrive.

I hopped off my bike and walked it through a doorway that led to the outdoor courtyard, the U-shaped area of K-25, where the maintenance building was located. All the while my mind played over the details of the past weeks. Maybe I should—

"Willett."

I jumped at the sound of Mr. Colby's voice behind me. Earlier, he'd asked me to take a thick packet of confidential documents to the incinerator. I'd had to wait for the attendant to return from his lunch break before I could complete the task, so I was delayed in my own return to the office.

"Yes, sir?"

He scrutinized me a long moment. "You haven't been yourself lately. Anything I should know?"

My stomach flipped.

I couldn't lose my job, no matter how worried I was about Sissy. Mama had confided in her last letter that Pa was sick again and hadn't been able to go down into the mines. She thanked me for the money I sent, telling me she didn't know what they'd do without it.

"No, sir. I just have some things on my mind. I'll do better, I promise."

His features softened. "I'm not firing you, Willett, but if there's something going on that you want to talk about, I'm all ears. It's not easy working in a place like Oak Ridge, with all the secrecy and whatnot. It can get to some people." He paused. "You know there's a doctor at the clinic in town, as well as dorm counselors, you can talk to about things. I've never met Dr. Clarke, but I'm told he's a fine psychiatrist. Nothing but the best for Oak Ridge."

I wasn't sure what a psychiatrist was, but I didn't need a doctor. I just needed to know Sissy's whereabouts.

"I appreciate that, sir. I'm fine. Just a little problem with my roommate, but nothing to concern you about. I'm sure everything will work itself out."

"Ah, I see. If you need a recommendation to move to a different dorm, let me know. Although, I hear housing is at capacity, in Townsite as well as Happy Valley. You'd do well to stay where you are."

I thanked him and we parted ways.

I felt a bit deceptive, allowing him to think Sissy and I weren't getting along. I hadn't lied though. There was indeed a problem with my roommate, but I couldn't reveal the details to my boss. Not yet anyway. Not until I discovered Sissy's whereabouts.

To accomplish that, a plan had begun to form in my mind early this morning as I lay in bed mulling over the situation. My instincts told me it was reckless, insane, and potentially illegal, but the more I thought about it, the more it seemed my only option.

I needed to search Clive's trailer.

Even thinking such a thought made my heart race. I'd never broken the law before, but that's exactly what I'd be doing if I went forward with this crazy scheme. Yet it was increasingly imperative I locate the documents Sissy had seen and somehow determine if they were evidence of espionage or simply part of his job.

I spent the afternoon filing paperwork in Mr. Colby's office, yet it was Sissy's suspicions about Clive possibly being a spy that held my focus. Her words, although brief and unsubstantiated, were written with obvious fear. If Clive was indeed a spy and had threatened Sissy in some way, forcing her to leave Oak Ridge, he should be held accountable.

But if I was going to put the plan into motion, some things had to fall into place.

First, it could only happen on my day off, which was tomorrow. Second, I had to confirm Clive wouldn't be home. Obtaining that information hadn't been as difficult as I'd thought. Earlier, I'd mentioned to one of the fellows working in the control room that I was supposed to deliver some documents to Clive later that week and needed to know his schedule. The unsuspecting SED took a sheet of paper from a file, looked it over, then assured me Clive was scheduled to work the next four days.

The final obstacle, however, could prevent the mission from even getting off the ground.

I didn't know where Clive lived. Sissy only mentioned going to his trailer in Happy Valley once in her diary, but she didn't include an address. There were thousands of trailers in the housing community not far from K-25. If I couldn't discover the name of the street where he lived, I'd have to resort to canvassing neighborhoods, knocking on doors, asking if anyone knew Clive Morrison. That could draw a lot of unwanted attention.

My brain was as exhausted as my body by the end of the day. Garlyn was working the late shift, so he wouldn't be at the portal waiting for me. I had to confess I was glad. I hadn't shared Sissy's fears or my plans with him. He wouldn't approve of my idea, and I couldn't sit across from him at the cafeteria and pretend all was well. If I went through with my scheme and discovered anything incriminating in Clive's trailer, I'd tell Garlyn as well as Mr. Colby.

On weary feet, I made my way to the bus stop amid a nippy

breeze, glad for the headscarf that kept my ears somewhat protected against the biting air. Instead of joining the group of employees waiting for a bus to take them to Townsite, I walked toward the larger group of people going to Happy Valley. I wanted to see the neighborhood again and get my bearings before tomorrow.

More people joined the throng, and I was pleased to find Velvet near the back. It had been weeks since I'd last spoken to her.

I wound my way to her. "Hello."

"Mae," she said, a genuine smile on her face. "It's nice to see you."

"And you. How have you been?"

"Busy." She chuckled. "But I guess we can all say that, can't we? The Lord has been good to me, so I can't complain."

We chatted about the chilly weather and the upcoming Christmas holiday, all the while inching forward in line to board the next available bus.

"Are you visiting someone in Happy Valley?" she asked.

I bit the inside of my lip. What story should I give her?

"A coworker lives there." I forced my voice to remain normal. "I need to pick something up from him, but I didn't write down his address. Maybe you know where he lives. Clive Morrison. He's staying in one of the trailers and drives an Army sedan."

She looked thoughtful. "I'm not familiar with the name, but it seems like I've seen military vehicles parked along Wheat Avenue. The bus sometimes takes that route, dependin' on the driver."

A full bus pulled away, making room for an empty one. People ahead of us began to board, and we followed.

"See you later, Mae."

I bid her goodbye and watched as she moved toward the back of the bus where other Black people sat. I was tempted to join her, but I didn't need the unnecessary attention it would bring. Other than Velvet, no one on the transport knew me, so no suspicions would be raised when I got off on Wheat Avenue, the street Velvet mentioned. It seemed the best place to begin my search.

Velvet sent me a small smile when she passed down the aisle and exited the bus at the hutment residential area. It bothered me that she and the others lived in such crude conditions, but there wasn't anything I could do about it. Jim Crow laws were still in place, which meant legal segregation. From living areas, to dining options, to schools. It seemed ludicrous to me, especially considering we were fighting a war in Freedom's name.

The bus started up again and made a left turn, away from the hutments.

Soon, a vast sea of small trailer homes filled the view, all looking nearly identical, with very little to distinguish one from its neighbor. Some residents had attempted to make the fabricated house a home, with planters that no doubt held flowers in the warmer months. Some had awnings over the windows and front door, and others had wooden porches added to the exterior, but mostly they appeared tiny, dreary, and impossible to tell apart.

My shoulders slumped the farther we went into the housing area.

How would I ever find Clive's trailer without an address?

The driver soon announced Wheat Avenue. I disembarked with two women at a four-way stop. They chatted as they walked down the street, completely ignoring me. I contemplated which way to go, ultimately deciding in the opposite direction of the women. The road wasn't paved, and the yards of each trailer were dirt with dead weeds. Long wooden walkways ran behind the homes and led to community bathhouses that appeared to service a full block of trailers or more. While the privacy that came with having your own place would be nice, I was glad I lived in a dormitory and didn't have to go outside to get to the restroom, especially in inclement weather.

I passed dozens and dozens of trailer homes lining both sides of the road. Numbers were stamped on the outside of each one, but I wasn't certain if they were addresses or manufacturing information. Each had a wooden walkway leading from the street to the front door. Those situated on slopes included wooden stairs. Clothes flapped in the chilly breeze on lines behind many homes, and children's toys lay in the yards of others. A handful of cars were parked in front of various trailers, but none were the vehicle I'd seen Clive in when he picked Sissy up for their dates.

When I reached the end of the street, I huffed out a breath. It was going to be impossible to discover which trailer was Clive's. They all looked the same. Only those with feminine touches or children's items could be ruled out.

I hunkered down into the collar of my coat and started up the opposite side of the street just as the sun dipped behind the hills. It was getting late and would be dark soon. I didn't want to be in the unfamiliar neighborhood at night. I knew Clive worked the following day, although I wasn't certain which shift he was on. If I couldn't determine which trailer was his, I'd have to take a bus back to Happy Valley late tomorrow morning and continue my search.

I'd just turned a corner, going toward the nearest bus stop, when headlights approached from behind. I didn't turn to look but kept moving forward. As the car went by, I peeked up.

An Army sedan.

I couldn't see who was driving, but it appeared he or she was alone.

The vehicle continued down the street and crested a rise.

Without thought, I took off running. I had no idea if Clive was driving the vehicle, but I needed to know where the sedan ended up. Even if it wasn't Clive's, I'd have one less trailer to investigate.

Cold air stung my throat by the time I topped the rise.

My heart skidded to a stop, or so it seemed, when I found the vehicle parked on the road in front of a trailer in the middle of the block. The headlights were still on, indicating the driver remained inside the car.

I dropped to my knees. There wasn't anywhere to hide, no trees or shrubs to conceal me should anyone look in my direction. I held my breath, hoping the owner of the home I crouched in front of didn't peer out the window and mistake me for a thief.

After long moments, the engine cut off. Everything went still. Muffled voices from the trailer behind me rose and fell. An owl hooted from woods at the end of the neighborhood.

The driver opened the car door and exited the vehicle. I felt certain the person was a man, because he had on the customary hat, trousers, and long coat most men on the Reservation wore. Whether it was Clive or not, I couldn't tell.

Yellow light soon shone through a tiny window on the front of the trailer he'd entered.

What should I do now? Sneak to the house and peek inside? It seemed bold and dangerous, yet I had to know if the man was Clive. I had to know if this was his trailer.

My legs felt like jelly when I rose and quickly made my way down the street. A car passed by, but it wasn't military issue and kept going. I crossed to the opposite side of the road down from where the Army sedan was parked. Should the man look outside, I didn't think he'd be able to see my features in the waning evening glow.

When I was directly across from the trailer in question, I ducked into the shadows. No light came through the windows of the trailer where I hid, giving me hope the residents weren't home. My brown coat and military-green rubber boots blended in with the darkness, offering protection.

Minutes ticked by. The smell of woodsmoke filled the chilly air. Another car drove past.

My tense muscles began to cramp. How long would I have to stand here, waiting for the driver of the car to show himself in the window? The thought of peeking through the glass made my stomach flip with nervousness, but I couldn't wait all night. The owner of the home where I hid could arrive at any moment. Besides, the temperature continued to drop, and my fingers, toes, and nose were starting to tingle from the cold.

I squinted at my wristwatch, but it was too dark to make out the hands. I resorted to counting to sixty in my head, repeating it five times. I'd give him five more minutes, then I'd have to make a decision about what to do. Peek in the window or return in the morning and hope I could determine if the home was Clive's or not.

I'd just begun counting again when a small light outside the trailer's only door blinked on. I held my breath. A moment later, the door opened.

Clive Morrison stepped out.

I pressed my lips to keep from making any noise.

He glanced up and down the street, then leaned against the trailer before striking a match to light a cigarette. Minutes passed while he smoked, something I hadn't known he was in the habit of doing. At one point, he looked across the street in my direction. I stood completely still, not even breathing, until he looked away. After one last puff, he squashed the cigarette on the ground with his shoe and went inside.

As soon as I heard the door click shut, I bolted down the street. A dog barked from somewhere nearby, but I didn't slow until I reached the bus stop. Thankfully no one else was there.

I bent to catch my breath. Nervous laughter bubbled up.

Good gracious, what would Mama say if she could see me now? Wandering around a strange neighborhood at night, spying on a man? But it worked. I'd found Clive. I hadn't been able to read the number on his trailer in the dim light, but I remembered the number of the one across the street where I'd hidden.

A bus soon arrived, and I boarded. Even at night, most of the seats were occupied. As we traveled the eleven miles to Townsite, I stared out the window into darkness. Stars blinked in the cloudless sky. The moon was nowhere in sight.

A sense of purpose replaced the anxiety I'd felt since Sissy disappeared.

Tomorrow's the day, I silently declared, my chin lifted in stubborn resolve.

Tomorrow I would discover the truth. Sissy had clearly been afraid of something. Whether it was Clive himself or the knowledge that he could possibly be working for the enemy, I wasn't certain. Like me, she'd been inundated with instructions from the moment we set foot on the Reservation about what to do if someone spoke out of turn or acted suspicious. Informants lurked everywhere, from the dorms to the cafeterias, to K-25 and beyond. Everyone knew they were to report odd behaviors and shady suspects. Sissy had been infatuated with the fellow in question, which seemed to act as an obstacle for her good sense.

I had no such qualms.

If I found out Clive was indeed involved in espionage, I would report him immediately.

And if I discovered he had threatened Sissy in some way, forcing her to leave Oak Ridge, he'd be sorry he ever met Maebelle Willett.

CHAPTER NINETEEN
MAE

MY HEART POUNDED in my chest, making it hard to breathe as I walked along the dirt road in Happy Valley. Sunshine glinted off the roofs of rows and rows of trailers, exposing the dreariness of the fabricated dwellings. I'd stayed awake most of the night trying to figure out what I intended to do once I arrived at the home I knew to be Clive's. The answer continued to elude me.

I glanced behind me for the umpteenth time, nervousness tightening my belly.

What if someone saw me approach Clive's trailer and asked what I was doing? A nosy neighbor could get suspicious and call the authorities if they noticed me lingering outside, especially with Clive's car gone. I'd told Velvet I needed to collect something from my coworker, and while that statement was factually correct in the minutest way, Clive would unreservedly disagree should I get caught red-handed snooping through his home.

The neighborhood was quiet, exactly what I'd wanted. My watch told me it was a little after ten o'clock. Morning shifts at

K-25 had begun earlier, as did the school day for the children of Happy Valley. Most people who worked the late shift would be home in bed, asleep by now. A few housewives with young children might notice me walk past their home, but otherwise I felt now was the most opportune time to search Clive's trailer.

I clutched my purse to my side.

I'd stuffed several items into it that would hopefully help me gain access to the small home. A knife I'd borrowed from the cafeteria. A pair of scissors, tweezers, and two bobby pins. I'd never picked a lock before, but my brother Harris was an expert at it.

I thought back to the time he broke into the shed where Granny Woods, an elderly woman who'd lived in our small Kentucky community for decades, kept her most valuable possession: a hundred-pound bag of sugar. No one knew how she'd come by it, but with sugar being one of the first items rationed in the United States once the war began, Granny's sugar became famous. When folks couldn't get the sweetener at the company store, they'd go to Granny and buy some from her. Being a savvy businesswoman, Granny never sold more than a few ounces to anyone, and only on certain days of the week. It would cost them a pretty penny, too, because Granny's sugar wasn't cheap. But it didn't require a ration card, and as Mama often said, the money Granny made from selling her sugar kept food on her table now that her husband had died from black lung.

Harris, however, had learned how to pick the lock on the small sugar shed. Mama would've taken a switch to him if she knew he was stealing from Granny. I'd gone with him once just to see if he was telling the truth and was shocked when he had the lock open in a matter of seconds, using an ice pick and a nail.

"You best not ever get caught," I'd said on our way home while he licked sugar from his lips. Once he'd opened the door, he dipped his fingers into the bag, claiming he only took a pinch whenever he snuck into the shed. "You won't be able to sit for a month of Sundays if Mama finds out what you've been doing. Stealing is wrong, Harris. Especially from an old widow woman."

I'd advised him to quit his wayward practices and instead volunteer to help Granny with her garden to make amends. Whether he took my advice or not, I didn't know, because I left for Oak Ridge soon afterwards.

It wasn't lost upon me that I was planning to break into someone's house—a far worse crime than sneaking into an old woman's shed for a taste of sugar—but I wasn't doing this for selfish motives. I needed to know what Sissy had seen in Clive's trailer that frightened her. And the only way to accomplish that was to search it while he was away.

When I reached the trailer with the number I recalled from last night, I slowed and glanced across the street.

All seemed quiet.

Clive's car was not parked on the street. Nothing looked out of the ordinary.

I continued walking for another block before I crossed and started back up the opposite side. As I came closer to Clive's trailer, uncertainties assailed me.

"This is insane," I whispered to myself. Completely and utterly insane. And illegal. I couldn't forget about that.

I moistened my dry lips.

Could I go through with this?

I felt like an entire day had passed since I'd crawled out of bed. The sky had still been black when I rose, without even a hint of pale pink along the eastern horizon, but I couldn't sleep. Yesterday, my bravado convinced me I would do whatever it took to discover the truth about Clive and the role he played in Sissy's leaving Oak Ridge so suddenly. But here in the daylight, boldness was nowhere to be found. Doubts and fears consumed me. If I got caught, I'd be arrested and lose my job. What would Mama and Pa do if I couldn't send money to them anymore?

I drew even with Clive's trailer. My feet slowed on their own.

I looked around. No one was out and about.

"If you're gonna do this, it's now or never," I hissed.

Decision made, I darted up the wooden walkway to the front door. Unlike the trailers that had awnings or a porch, Clive's barren home left me fully exposed. I tried the knob, but the door was locked. Petty theft was a problem in Oak Ridge, even in the dormitories. Everyone took care with their belongings if they didn't want them to go missing.

My hands shook as I hurriedly dug out the tools of my crime from my purse. Should a neighbor happen to be watching, I hoped it would appear I was searching for keys.

I tried the knife first, but the tip was too big to fit into the keyhole. Next I used the tweezers. When Harris picked Granny's lock, he'd used two instruments at the same time, seeming to work in tandem. I held the tweezers still and poked one end of the bobby pin in next to it. I had no idea what to do next, so I simply wiggled and jiggled the two, up and down, sideways and back.

A feather could have knocked me down when I heard a click.

Swallowing hard, I reached for the knob. The door swung open.

With one last look to be certain no one was around, I stepped inside and closed the door.

A shiver raced through me.

I'd just committed my first—and hopefully last—crime. How much time does a person spend in jail for the offense of breaking and entering? Months? Years?

The thought was sobering. But if my criminal efforts helped locate Sissy and brought her back to Oak Ridge, then breaking the law would be worth it.

I looked around to get my bearings. The first thing I noticed was how orderly and clean the confined space appeared. A cushioned bench ran along the front end of the trailer on my right, with built-in cabinets above the tiny window I'd seen from the outside. Across from where I stood was a small stove and a narrow refrigerator, with a shelf above that contained salt, pepper, and a tin of coffee. The sink and more cabinets that went from floor to ceiling were on my left. Past them, at the far end of the trailer, was a neatly made bed.

I gulped.

It felt wrong—so very, very wrong—to be inside Clive's private home. He may be odd, and I may not like him much, but I wasn't sure he deserved to have me break into his trailer, looking for something to prove he was a spy. What if Sissy had been mistaken about the documents she'd seen in his possession? What if her fears had been unjustified? Had I broken into the home of an innocent man?

I exhaled a long breath.

The deed was done. I might as well move forward with the reason I'd come. The sooner I found the documents and determined whether they were worrisome or not, the sooner I could get out of here. My stomach was in knots with nervousness. What would I do if Clive returned home while I was inside his trailer? That was a scenario I refused to dwell on.

Unfortunately I didn't see any papers lying about. That meant I would need to open cabinets and look under furnishings. Over the next minutes, I poked around the tiny kitchen and sitting area, but I didn't find anything out of the ordinary. Dishware and glassware occupied one of the cabinets above the sink, while pots and pans filled the other. I even peeked inside the refrigerator, but only a half-full glass jar of milk and a hunk of cheese sat on a wire shelf. The tiny icebox above was empty.

The last place left to search was the area where Clive slept and kept his personal belongings. Dread washed through me at the mere thought of handling his things, but what else could I do?

I did a hasty search, opening drawers but not touching anything. I peeked in the storage beneath the bed and came up empty-handed. Disappointed, I returned to the entry. My eyes traveled the entire home. Had I missed something? If I were a spy, where would I hide items I didn't want anyone to know about?

I ticked off what I'd seen in each of the kitchen cabinets. When I came to the door beneath the sink, I remembered seeing a wastebasket. But, I realized, I hadn't looked behind it.

I knelt and opened the small door. When I removed the empty basket, I discovered a cardboard box with a lid, pushed all the way against the back wall. If I hadn't been on my knees, I wouldn't have seen it.

A bad feeling gnawed my gut as I removed the lid.

My breath came out in a rush at seeing the contents.

Documents. Dozens and dozens of documents, all stamped with *Secret* or *Confidential* in red ink. When I got over the shock of seeing them, I lifted the stack and thumbed through them. Some were memos. Others were technical drawings. Some had what appeared to be math equations, with symbols and numbers whose meanings I couldn't begin to guess.

All I could do was stare at them, my brain racing.

"Sissy was right." The words echoed in the small space.

Clive had to be a spy. Why else would he have all these confidential papers hidden in his house behind a container for garbage? Yet, I reminded myself, being in the possession of secret documents could be part of his job as a health physics officer. If I was going to report my suspicions to Mr. Colby, I had to have more proof. I'd be in a world of trouble for breaking into Clive's trailer if it turned out he brought work home on a regular basis with the approval of his superiors. I knew SEDs worked long hours at times. Garlyn occasionally had to stay past the end of his shift to solve a problem or supervise a repair. It wouldn't be so far-fetched if Clive brought paperwork home to work on instead of remaining at the plant after hours.

What would convince Mr. Colby and the authorities that Clive was potentially a spy?

A sealed manila envelope lay at the bottom of the box. I took it out, but there wasn't anything written on it. Something small but slightly weighty was inside. I ran my fingers over the unseen contents. It felt flat, hard, and rectangular.

I chewed my lip.

The fact that it was in the box with the secret documents led me to believe it was important. That it was in a sealed, nondescript envelope convinced me Clive didn't want anyone to know what was inside.

Should I open it? I doubted that something this small was the evidence I sought to prove Clive's involvement in espionage, but my curiosity was on high alert. I wanted to know what was inside.

However, if I opened it, Clive would certainly know someone had been in his trailer and had gone through the box. He would never suspect me though. Why should he? If whatever the envelope contained proved he was a spy and I reported him, he would be arrested and taken far away from Oak Ridge. Even if he later learned I was the one who'd notified the authorities, there wouldn't be anything he could do about it by then.

I stared at the envelope, vacillating between tearing it open or simply returning it and the documents to the box and calling the whole thing done. Yet I'd come this far. I needed to turn over every stone, as the saying goes.

I took the knife from my purse and attempted to run it beneath the sealed flap, but the glue held fast. If I had the time, I would steam the envelope open, but I needed to get out of here soon. With a flick of my wrist, the knife sliced through the paper flap. It wasn't a ragged tear, but there was no way to seal it again.

I set the knife on the linoleum floor and peered into the envelope.

An ID badge lay at the bottom.

My shoulders slumped. It was probably one of Clive's old badges. When an employee obtained new security clearances, we were issued an updated, color-coded ID. I'd received a new badge when Mr. Colby approved my clearance so I could handle classified documents bound for the incinerator, as well as carry them to personnel in the control room and other offices.

With little interest, I tipped the envelope, and the badge slid into my hand.

My breath stilled.

The face in the black-and-white photograph was not Clive's.

Sissy's sparkling eyes stared back at me.

CHAPTER TWENTY
LAUREL

AUNT MAE'S TELEPHONE rang in the kitchen, startling me where I sat at the table, the books I'd borrowed from the library about Oak Ridge's history spread across the surface. Aunt Mae had gone to visit the couple down the street whose baby was due to arrive any day, so I stood to answer the call.

"Hi, Laurel," Jonas said. "I'm glad you answered." His voice sounded tense.

"Is everything okay?"

"Are you free right now? Could you come down to the station? I found something I think you need to see."

Surprise surged through me. "About Sylvia Galloway? That was fast. Can't you just tell me about it over the phone?"

"It's actually about your aunt," he said, his voice lowered. "I'd rather talk about it in person."

That didn't sound good. "Of course, I can be there in twenty minutes."

I hurried to freshen up and change from shorts to jeans, then scribbled a note to Aunt Mae, letting her know I would be out for a while. The fact that Jonas had found something he wasn't willing to discuss over the telephone stirred up an anxious feeling inside me.

He met me in the front lobby of the police station, his expression sober.

"Thanks for coming."

I nodded, my concern growing. "I confess you have me worried."

He led the way down a hall to a small room with a table and three chairs. A file lay on the tabletop. "We'll have some privacy in here," he said as he closed the door.

"Jonas, what's going on?"

He motioned me to a chair while he settled in the one opposite from me.

"After you told me about Sylvia Galloway and the article asking for information on her whereabouts, I did some digging. Records from the 1940s are stored in cardboard boxes, so locating a specific case file is no easy task."

"But you found something?"

He nodded. "I found the box that held records from the last half of 1944. There's not a file on Sylvia. At least, not about her specifically."

My brow tugged. "I don't understand."

He reached for the folder that lay on the tabletop between us, opened it, and took out a single sheet of paper. "This is a report from December 1944. It was filed with the MP's office by someone named Clive Morrison." He met my confused gaze. "It's a complaint against your aunt, Maebelle Willett."

"A complaint? For what?"

"Mr. Morrison claims your aunt broke into his home."

I stared at him, my mind spinning. "That's absurd. Aunt Mae is not a thief."

"It says nothing of value was stolen, but—"

"Then why file a report?"

A look of remorse filled his face. "Because Mr. Morrison claims your aunt was his scorned lover, and she wanted to discredit him in some way."

It felt like the air evaporated from the room with his words.

I shook my head. "That can't be. Aunt Mae wouldn't . . ." Whatever else I was going to say faded in disbelief. I simply shook my head again. "She wouldn't."

Jonas glanced at the report. "Mr. Morrison's statement goes on to say that Mae was jealous when he broke things off with her and started to date her roommate." He paused. "Sylvia Galloway."

When I didn't appear surprised by the revelation, he studied me a long moment. "You knew Sylvia was Mae's roommate." It wasn't a question.

"I did. I'm sorry," I said. "The notice in the newspaper about Sylvia was posted by Aunt Mae. I didn't want to tell you because . . . well, I suppose I wanted to protect her privacy. But this," I indicated the report, "kind of blows privacy out of the water."

He offered a compassionate nod. "I understand."

"Is there any information on the man who filed the complaint?"

"Some." He referred to the paper in his hand. "It says Morrison was in the Army and lists his rank. His job in Oak Ridge was something called a health physics officer." He shot me a look that told me there was more and handed the paper to me. "He claims Mae's jealousy drove Sylvia to leave town."

He handed the paper to me. I read over the typed report, dumbfounded that Aunt Mae had been accused of breaking into someone's home. That the complaint also described her as the man's scorned lover was beyond comprehension.

"I just can't believe this," I said, setting the document on the table. "Aunt Mae might be a little eccentric, but it's impossible for me to accept what this report says about her." I leaned forward to look at the date below the signature of the MP who took the statement. "This report was filed after the article in the newspaper ran."

I took the printed copy of the article from my purse and showed it to Jonas, who read it aloud.

"Maebelle Willett requests your help regarding her roommate Sissy Galloway who has not been seen in Oak Ridge since November 25, 1944. If you have information on Miss Galloway's whereabouts, please contact Miss Willett immediately." He looked up. "How did you know her roommate's name was Sylvia? This refers to her as Sissy."

I told him about the two security badges in the box of Aunt Mae's mementos. "I figured an official report would use her given name rather than a nickname."

"Let's get the timeline down," Jonas said.

"The article says Aunt Mae last saw Sissy on November 25." I watched as he jotted some notes. "I wish we had a calendar from 1944."

He tapped his pen on the table. "Mr. Morrison said Mae was jealous of his relationship with Sissy, yet it was Mae who posted the newspaper notice."

"That seems odd."

"You also said your aunt has Sissy's security badge. I've often heard Dad mention that people who lived in Oak Ridge during the war couldn't go anywhere without their ID badge. Not the cafeteria. Not the grocery store. You couldn't pass through the gates to come into town without it, and you also couldn't leave if you weren't wearing it. If someone was caught without their badge on a regular basis, they'd lose their job. So that begs the question, why does Mae have Sissy's badge?"

I shrugged. "The only person who knows the answer is Aunt Mae, and she isn't talking."

"The complaint Morrison filed may have something to do with that." Jonas frowned. "I hate to say this, but when someone is guilty of breaking the law, they usually clam up. They don't want their friends and family to know what they've done."

I knew he was right. "Some of the coursework I've done for my doctorate involved studying guilt complexes. Feelings and emotions resulting from guilt or remorse can consume a person. While guilt is a normal emotion, guilt complexes can cause long-term psychological harm, such as depression, anxiety, and low self-esteem. In the short time I've been in Oak Ridge, I've observed all of those in Aunt Mae's behavior."

"But even if she did break into Morrison's home, she was never charged that I can see. Why carry so much guilt over something relatively minor?"

I heaved a sigh. "It seems we have more questions than answers."

"I'll keep looking through the old files. There may be something from 1945 that can help us figure this out."

His generosity warmed me. "I appreciate the offer, Jonas, but I can't ask you to waste any more of your valuable time on this. Besides, I don't have a valid reason to pursue it other than my burning curiosity."

He smiled. "I don't mind. One of my hobbies is digging into old unsolved case files. It gives a new perspective on crimes that happened decades in the past. The exercise has even helped me work current cases with new eyes."

"I admit I really want to know what happened to Sissy and why Aunt Mae has her ID badge. I'd also like to hear her side of the story regarding Clive Morrison. I've never been close to Aunt Mae, but I can't imagine her being so angry at an ex-boyfriend that she'd break into his home to . . . What did the report say? Discredit him?"

Jonas agreed. "It does seem uncharacteristic for the woman I've known for years, but domestic issues like this aren't uncommon."

We stood and exited the small room. Jonas walked with me to my car.

"Thank you," I said. "I have a feeling that all of this has something to do with Aunt Mae's reticence regarding her past. I'd love to help her get over whatever it is that's keeping her from letting it go."

"I'd be honored to help, too. She's a wonderful lady." He met my gaze. "So is her niece."

I'm sure my face revealed my pleasure at his words. "Thank you."

On the way back to Aunt Mae's, I passed the library. Maybe I should follow Jonas's lead and continue the search for information in old issues of the *Oak Ridge Journal*. I'd stumbled upon the notice about Sissy, so maybe I'd missed something about Aunt Mae and the break-in. It was worth a try, anyway. I turned the car around.

The same librarian I'd met before greeted me when I came through the door. She was happy to help pull up the microfilm I sought. I was soon seated in front of the familiar screen, anxious to dive back into stories written in the Secret City during World War II. What had started out as a research trip for my dissertation had become so much more personal.

"Aunt Mae," I whispered. "Please let me help you. No matter what's in your past. Nothing is so terrible that you can't put it behind you and move on."

With that, I settled in for a long afternoon.

CHAPTER TWENTY-ONE
MAE

MR. COLBY DIDN'T SMILE when he found me cleaning tools in the maintenance shop. I usually enjoyed my work at K-25, but this particular task was not one of my favorites. Dirt, oil, and grunge covered my hands and coveralls.

"Willett," he said, an unexpected firmness to his voice. "Get cleaned up and come to my office. Now."

My stomach dropped to my feet. "Yes, sir."

I hurried to the restroom to wash my hands, leaving a ring of grime on the small porcelain sink, all the while trying to figure out what caused my boss's anger. Had I broken something? Misplaced an important instrument? Nothing stood out in my memory, but obviously whatever slipup I'd committed was serious enough that Mr. Colby was not pleased. I hoped I wasn't about to lose my job.

The door to his office was closed when I arrived. Knots twisted my gut. Surely whatever I'd done could be handled with a stern reprimand and instructions to never do it again.

Inhaling a deep breath, I knocked.

"Come in."

I pressed my lips together and entered.

Mr. Colby sat at his desk, but he wasn't alone. An MP stood next to him, his eyes fixed on me.

Alarm stilled my feet.

"Sit down, Willett. This officer has some questions for you." Mr. Colby's normally pleasant face displayed a deep scowl.

My entire body shook as I moved to the straight-backed chair against the wall.

This could only be about one thing.

Somehow, some way, they knew about Clive's trailer. That I'd broken in and taken something. Was the MP here to arrest me?

"We've had a complaint registered against you, Miss Willett," the MP said. He couldn't be much older than me, yet he had an air of authority that surpassed his age.

When I didn't respond, he continued. "Where were you yesterday?"

"In the dorm. It was my day off." My wobbly voice gave away my nervousness. Although I told the truth, it wasn't complete.

"Can anyone vouch for you?"

I swallowed. "I'm sure any number of girls saw me, although I mostly stayed in my room to read."

"What about your roommate? Where was she?"

My gaze slid to Mr. Colby, who sat listening intently. Our conversation from two days ago played in my mind. I'd let him believe I'd had a disagreement with Sissy. Now, it seemed best to answer the question honestly.

I met the MPs gaze once again. "I don't know where Sissy is. I haven't seen her since the Saturday after Thanksgiving."

The guard's eyes narrowed. "Did you and she have an argument? Say, over a man?"

The question stumped me. "No, we never argued. Over anything."

"The person who registered the complaint against you says otherwise. He states that you were jealous of his relationship with Miss Galloway and that you broke into his home at some point yesterday while he was away. Is that true?"

My body trembled uncontrollably.

Not only had my crime been discovered, but it had been reported to the authorities. If I said too much, I had no doubt they'd put me in jail.

The men waited for an answer.

"I don't know what you're talking about. Sissy and I are best friends. She confided that she was thinking about breaking up with Clive Morrison—I assume that's who filed the complaint against me—but after she didn't return from an outing with him, he told me it was his idea to break up. He also claims Sissy left Oak Ridge and went home to Georgia because of it."

"Did you post the notice in the *Journal* about Miss Galloway?"

I nodded. "I did."

"Have you had any response?"

I shook my head.

The MP studied me a long moment before turning to Mr. Colby. "That's all I need for now. Our office won't take action against Miss Willett at this time, however"—he pinned me with a hard look—"should more evidence surface that places you at Mr. Morrison's home, you will be taken into custody. Until this is resolved, do not attempt to leave Oak Ridge. You will be arrested if you do."

The man didn't wait for a reply and exited the room. The door banged behind him.

I sat frozen in the chair. What a mess. Would Mr. Colby fire me on the spot?

After an excruciating period of silence, he heaved a sigh. "What in tarnation is going on, Willett? I asked you if something was wrong, since you'd been acting strange. Now I have an MP in my office, asking questions and nosing around. Care to explain?"

I couldn't tell him about the documents I'd seen in Clive's trailer, nor could I tell him about my suspicions that Clive was a spy. I didn't have enough evidence yet, and now the authorities wouldn't believe me even if I did come forward. They'd think I was some crazy jealous woman who breaks into homes to get even with a man. No, if I told any of this to Mr. Colby, he'd call the MP back as soon as the words passed my lips.

My hand moved to the deep pocket of my overalls.

I also couldn't tell him about the security badge I concealed. A badge that belonged to Sissy. The moment it fell out of the envelope and into my hands, a terrible feeling had begun in the pit of my stomach. Why did Clive have Sissy's badge? Had she given it to him as a memento, a keepsake of their supposed love? Did she want him to remember her after she was gone? I had to discover the answers to those questions before I could tell the whole story to anyone.

I swallowed. "I've been worried about Sissy. What I told the MP about her and Clive is the truth. The Saturday after Thanksgiving, she said they were going to Knoxville to see a movie and have dinner, but when she didn't return by the next day, I asked Clive about it. He told me they never left Oak Ridge. He said he broke up with her and that she was so upset, she got on a bus and went home."

Mr. Colby's gaze narrowed. "But you don't believe him?"

Tears sprang to my eyes unbidden. "I don't know what to think. She didn't take any of her belongings or tell anyone goodbye. I thought she might write and let me know where she is, but I haven't heard from her."

It felt good to share that part of my burden with my boss.

How I wished I could spill the whole story, but until I had solid proof that Clive was involved in espionage, I had to keep quiet. Otherwise it would be me behind bars instead of him.

Mr. Colby leaned back in his chair. "You should have told me all this when I asked about it. Why would Morrison say you were jealous of his relationship with your roommate? It doesn't sound as though he cared much about her."

"I most definitely was not jealous, sir," I said, emphatically. "I—"

I'd been about to say I didn't trust Clive, but that might get back to the MPs. "I never thought he was the right fellow for Sissy. She's sweet and fun to be around, while he's so serious." I wanted to include *odd* but thought better of it.

Mr. Colby stared at me, as though trying to decide if I told the truth or not. I could beg him to let me keep my job, but I remained silent. I wouldn't want to make him feel guilty for doing what he thought was best.

"Here's the deal, Willett." He sat forward, leaned his elbows on the desk, and tented his fingers. "I like you. You've been a good worker, and I've never had any problems with you until now. I hope you're being on the up-and-up with me, and this situation with Morrison goes away." His unyielding gaze held me. "But if it doesn't and I have more MPs in my office, I'll have no other choice but to terminate your employment at K-25. Do you understand?"

I offered a shaky nod. "Thank you, sir."

I left his office and closed the door with a soft click. My body trembled as I stood there wanting to cry but not allowing myself to do so. Tears could wait until I was in the privacy of my dorm room. Here at the plant, I needed to act as though everything was fine. As though nothing out of the ordinary had occurred. I couldn't let anyone see my guilt. Or my fear.

Waves of it, however, crashed through me as I walked back to the shop. Clive knew I'd broken into his trailer. He knew I had Sissy's ID badge. Did he also know I'd taken two of the documents from the box?

I pictured the papers, now hidden beneath my mattress.

The first was a memo from a chemist who worked in the K-1004 laboratory complex. The official communication had something to do with a component called UF_6 and a firm named Harshaw Chemical Company. I'd never heard of either, but the document seemed like a good one to keep should I need to turn it over to the authorities to help prove Clive was up to no good.

The second document was a technical drawing. It reminded me of a plumbing part. Words were written off to the side, with arrows pointing to different sections. Nickel pipe. Copper pipe. Iron pipe. Steam. Again, the unfamiliar code UF_6 appeared. I was clueless what it all meant, but the stolen papers would remain hidden until I could figure out the next step I needed to take in order to prove Clive couldn't be trusted. If the MPs moved forward with my arrest, I would spill everything I knew about Clive, including Sissy's fear of him. I would even use her diary to convince them I wasn't making things up out of jealousy.

A dreadful thought sped through my brain as I returned to work.

What if Garlyn heard about the MPs report? What would he think if Clive spread rumors among the other SEDs, claiming I was jealous of Sissy? I didn't think Garlyn would believe it, but what man would want to spend time with a girl mixed up in something like this? Hopefully I would have a chance to explain things before Clive's lies reached Garlyn's ears.

I was emotionally and physically exhausted when it was finally time to go home. My brain had continuously worked the problem throughout the long afternoon hours until it was all I could think of.

What would Clive do now that he knew I'd broken into his home? For that matter, what would the MPs do if he pursued charges against me? He didn't have proof of my crime, but Clive was a respected military man. They'd believe his word over mine.

For a brief moment I considered leaving Oak Ridge and disappearing like Sissy had done. People were always coming and going from the Reservation. No one would think twice if I up and left. I could catch the bus to Knoxville as soon as I packed my meager belongings. Once I arrived in the larger town, I'd purchase a ticket home to Kentucky. It seemed unlikely the authorities would go to the trouble of tracking me down, considering the crime I'd committed was relatively minor. I didn't want to leave Oak Ridge though. I enjoyed my independence and my job, plus it allowed me to send much-needed money to Mama and Pa. No job in our small mining community paid what I was making at K-25.

Yet it was risky to stay. Should Clive change his mind about pressing charges, Mr. Colby would immediately fire me. I might even end up in jail. Then there was Sissy. I felt an urgent need to remain in Oak Ridge in case she wrote to me. I couldn't leave until I knew she was safe. I also couldn't let Clive get away with espionage, if that's what he was doing. I'd be letting our country, our soldiers, and President Roosevelt down if I did.

With slow movements, I gathered my things and joined the throng headed to Clock Alley. I'd grab a sandwich from the cafeteria in town and eat in my dorm room. I had no desire to sit in the noisy dining hall and make idle conversation with anyone tonight.

Lost in my own thoughts, I followed the person in front of me, each step taking me to the bus terminal. I could barely put one foot in front of the other, I was so weary. A good night's sleep was what I needed. Tomorrow I'd figure out what to do about the MP's report.

"Hello, Mae."

A man's low voice near my shoulder brought my head up. Clive fell into step beside me.

Anger rushed forward and spilled from my mouth. "How dare you show your face here," I hissed.

The woman ahead of us turned, glanced at me and then at Clive, before facing forward again. I slowed, letting some distance separate us from her. The last thing I needed was for someone to overhear harsh words and assume we were a couple having a spat. That tale would only feed the lie Clive told the MPs about my supposed jealousy over his relationship with Sissy.

"We need to talk." When he reached for my elbow, I jerked out of his grip.

"Don't touch me," I whispered. "I have nothing to say to you."

"Then perhaps I'll have another chat with the MPs." His upper lip curled as he whispered the threat. "I suspect Mr. Colby won't be too pleased when they show up in his office again. I'm sure the authorities will understand when I suddenly realize I am indeed missing valuable items from my home. What the items might be, well, I'll leave that to my imagination. Money? A watch? Perhaps a token given to me by Sissy? Hmm, that rings true. You may find yourself behind bars by nightfall. Either that or you'll be on a bus bound for Kentucky because you are no longer employed in Oak Ridge. The Army doesn't take kindly to thievery."

His bullying hit its mark.

"What do you want?" I didn't bother to lower my voice.

"To talk. That's all."

I stared at him, contempt for the man burning through me. "Fine."

He reached for my elbow again. This time I allowed him to steer me out of line toward his car, parked a short distance away. Once we reached it, he opened the passenger door.

A warning sounded in my head. "I don't want to go anywhere with you. We can talk here."

While his lips curved in a smile, his voice grew hard. "Get in the car, Mae."

Something told me not to cross him. Was this how Sissy felt when he'd caught her with the documents?

Against my better judgement, I climbed into the military sedan. He closed the door and went around to the driver's seat. A chill coursed through me that had nothing to do with the frosty December weather.

"Let's take a little drive, then we'll discuss why you were in my trailer and what you took."

The ominous words echoed in the quiet vehicle.

He started the engine and drove west, away from the crowded bus terminal. A couple turns and we were soon traveling a road I'd never been on before. Thick forest hedged us in on either side. Fear mounted in my belly with each turn of the wheels. If Clive tried to hurt me, no one would hear me scream way out here.

I suddenly remembered the knife in my purse. I'd forgotten to return it to the cafeteria yesterday. "Where are we going?" I forced calmness into the words as I shifted the small bag on my lap so the flap opening faced me. If I felt threatened at any point, I'd use the weapon without hesitation. The man wouldn't know what hit him if he tried anything nefarious.

He glanced over at me. "Do you know about S-50?"

I shook my head, playing along, yet all the while keeping alert to our surroundings in case I needed to walk back to the plant.

"S-50 was completed this past July. It's a liquid thermal diffusion plant, unlike K-25, which is a gaseous diffusion plant." He laughed when he found what was certainly a blank look on my face. "You don't have any idea what's happening here on the Reservation, do you? Oak Ridge is one of the biggest secrets of the war. The world doesn't know it exists. Even the employees who work here every day don't know what's going on."

I didn't respond.

"I'll let you in on the mystery," he continued, clearly enjoying himself. "Every hour of every day, uranium is being enriched in little ol' Oak Ridge, Tennessee."

My ignorance must have shown. He emitted a sound of disgust.

"Let me guess. You've never heard of uranium. Don't they teach you anything useful in those backwoods schools in Kentucky?" Disdain practically dripped from every word. "Uranium is a heavy metal. It's found in rocks. Here in Oak Ridge, we're working to enrich enough uranium to fuel a bomb. A big bomb. After the uranium is ready, it's shipped to a secret location in New Mexico where the actual bomb is being built. Y-12, K-25, and the X-10 reactor all have the same purpose, just different methods to accomplish it. S-50 is the newest cog in the wheel. General Groves and the other top dogs hope it will speed up the enrichment process, because beating Hitler to the bomb is imperative. Unfortunately that hasn't been the case. The plant is using more energy than expected, not to mention a plethora of problems that came with its hasty construction."

My mind reeled even as I fought to keep a straight face.

Uranium? Bombs? Another secret location? Was he telling the truth, or was this some elaborate story he'd concocted to make himself sound important, like his lie about his ancestors arriving on the Mayflower? Sissy had written in her diary multiple times about Clive's vast intelligence, which to me meant the fellow had done his best to impress her. I, on the other hand, wasn't impressed by him at all.

I was about to declare his ramblings bogus when we broke free of the trees. The wide Clinch River ran along the road to our left, but on our right stood a dozen or more buildings clustered together. While the site wasn't as sprawling as K-25, I couldn't believe my eyes.

There was another plant on the Reservation? A plant I'd never heard of?

I stared in dumbfounded silence.

The tallest structure was topped with three towering smokestacks where puffs of white escaped into the late afternoon sky. A smaller building with no windows had a long, elevated conveyor running from railroad cars, their cargo being off-loaded by a crew of workers, to the top of the building. A different conveyor carried the mysterious load to the structure with the smokestacks. More buildings of various sizes were arranged in neat order.

Clive slowed the car. "Behold, I give you S-50. Believe it or not, the whole thing was built in sixty-nine days."

I practically pressed my face to the window. As my eyes traveled over the site, I couldn't imagine how I hadn't known this place existed. I'd never heard anyone talk about it nor had I seen any buses with a destination sign for S-50. But, I reasoned, I hadn't been looking for them either. Watching a railroad crew off-load something from a string of railcars, I wondered how many people worked at this plant. With its location so far from town, I guessed most of the employees lived in Happy Valley.

It occurred to me Sissy surely must have been aware of S-50 but hadn't said anything to me about it. I held no doubts that Clive had revealed these same secrets to her. The slogan on one of the newest billboards in town flit through my mind as I gazed out the window. *Hold your tongue. The job's not done.* Sissy may have adhered to the warning, but Clive certainly hadn't.

A new wave of fear rolled through me. "Why are you telling me all of this?" I turned and faced him. "I'm not supposed to be here or have knowledge about these things. I could lose my job if someone found out."

He continued to look straight ahead. "Insurance, plain and simple. The more you know, the less you'll say."

Is this what had frightened Sissy? Knowing too much? Maybe she had gone back to Georgia because of it.

We sped past the buildings and followed the river around a bend. Twelve or more enormous storage tanks appeared, but Clive didn't comment on their purpose as we went by. The dirt road eventually came to an end. Piles of unused building materials sat here and there.

Clive stopped the car and shut off the engine. We sat in the stillness, not moving, not speaking. The scenery was beautiful, with the Clinch River meandering along, surrounded by woods ready for a long winter's slumber. Clive's presence, however, spoiled the tranquility. I had no desire to remain here a moment longer than necessary. The sun was on its westerly descent, and I wanted to be safely back at K-25 long before it dipped behind the hills. His security clearance obviously gave him permission to be here, but if someone found us, I could be in serious trouble.

With unhurried movements, Clive removed his glasses, then took a small cloth from his jacket pocket and wiped the round circles of glass. After he returned them to the bridge of his nose, he faced me. "I want it back." His words were measured but firm.

There was no reason to pretend I didn't understand what he meant. "No."

The muscle in his jaw ticked. "You don't know what you're dealing with, Mae. For your own safety, give me the badge."

I shook my head and stubbornly crossed my arms. "Where is Sissy? Why do you have her ID? You answer those questions and I'll consider giving you what you want."

I wasn't sure where this bravado came from, but I wasn't leaving until I knew why Sissy left Oak Ridge so suddenly.

"I told you, she went home after I informed her I didn't want to see her anymore. She was upset and embarrassed. She said everyone assumed I was going to propose, which was the furthest thing from the truth." He gave a nonchalant shrug. "I guess she didn't want to face you and the others, so she got on the first bus to Georgia."

I didn't believe him. "She wouldn't have gone home without saying goodbye. She didn't take any of her belongings. Even if she planned to leave Oak Ridge, she wouldn't have just vanished."

"You can believe what you want, but the facts say otherwise."

"The facts? The facts don't make any sense. I think you threatened her. I think she discovered you're a spy and you forced her to leave."

There. I'd said it out loud. What would he do now?

We stared at each other, neither willing to look away. I wouldn't let him intimidate me another moment. He was the one doing wrong, not me. If he truly was a spy, he was a traitor to the United States of America. A traitor to his fellow soldiers.

In an instant, his demeanor changed.

His eyes narrowed on me, and his breathing grew hard. "You're a little fool, you know it? You've messed with the wrong person, Mae. Would you like me to tell you what happened to Sissy?"

A tremor raced through my body, but I nodded. "Where is she?"

He glanced out the window. "This was our favorite place to come. We'd neck, right here in this car."

I grimaced, repulsed by his crudeness. "Where is she?" I repeated.

He took his time answering. "We were supposed to go to Knoxville that day, but Sissy wanted to talk. We came here instead. She said she was confused about our relationship and wasn't certain we should continue seeing each other. When I asked why, she said she couldn't trust me." He gave a humorless laugh. "That was the wrong thing to say."

When he turned to face me, his expression held its usual bland look. "I took her back to the dorm. That's the last I saw of her."

Even though parts of his story rang true, it didn't explain why Sissy disappeared. "If she broke things off with you, why would she go home? She loved being here in Oak Ridge."

"Because of you."

I stared at him, confused. "What do you mean? Sissy and I are friends."

"*Were* friends, up until I told her I hadn't been in love with her at all." He paused. "I told her I was actually in love with you and had used her to get close to you."

I reared back, as though he'd struck me. "What? Why would you say something like that?"

"I wanted to hurt her, the same way she'd hurt me. I didn't expect her to fly into a rage. She was furious with you. You'd said negative things about me the entire time she and I were dating, but now she believed you were just jealous. She took off her badge and threw it at me." He shrugged. "My guess is she got on a bus that very day and went home."

I didn't know what to believe.

Had Sissy truly thought I was interested in Clive? It was an absurd idea, yet it would explain why she left in such a rush and why she hadn't written to let me know she was safe. *Oh, Sissy.* As soon as I returned to the dorm, I'd write to her and tell her that everything Clive said was a lie. Hopefully she could get her job at Y-12 back and we could put all of this behind us.

I glanced at Clive. The self-satisfied look on his face made me sick.

"Even if Sissy went home because she was angry, she was right about you, wasn't she? You're some kind of spy. That's why you have all those papers. She didn't want to continue seeing you because she didn't trust you. Neither do I."

He smirked. "That's rich, considering you're the one who broke into my house. But as for me being a spy, that is a figment of Sissy's naive imagination. My security clearance gives me access to everything about the project, including top secret documents. Anyone who reported that wild tale to the MPs would look ridiculous, including you. Do you really think anyone would believe a well-respected soldier in the Army is a spy?"

Some of my bluster seeped out with his logical explanation. Wasn't that what I'd thought all along?

"We're done here. I have something in my trailer that belongs to Sissy. We'll go by there and get it, then you can take the bus home."

I was more than happy to leave this place. The sun had dropped behind the hills, and it would be pitch-dark soon.

We drove back to K-25 in silence. He continued past the plant's entrance and turned into Happy Valley. Lights shone in many of the trailer windows, including those on either side of his, as well as the one across the street.

He parked in front of his small house. "Wait here. I won't be long."

Minutes passed. Laughter floated on the cold air, and I saw a couple walking up the street, holding hands, coming straight toward me. I sank down into the seat so they wouldn't see me. Thankfully they were too occupied with one another to notice anything else. If Clive didn't come out of his trailer soon, I'd leave without seeing whatever it was he thought so important.

A short time later, he exited, carrying a box in one hand and a suitcase in the other. Instead of putting them in the back seat of the car, he opened the trunk and stored the items. Then he came around to my side of the sedan and opened the passenger door.

"Get out."

I was happy to comply. "It's late. Show me whatever it is you want me to see so I can go home."

He closed the car door. "I've changed my mind. We'll talk more tomorrow." He took a step away, then stopped. "Don't even think about discussing any of this with anyone. One word from me, and the MPs will arrest you. This time the crime will be far worse than a simple robbery."

I stood in the road, fuming, and watched him climb into the driver's seat and drive away. If he thought his empty threats would rattle me, he was wrong. He was as strange as ever, even more so now that I'd spent time with him. What had sweet Sissy seen in the guy?

I shook my head, exasperated. "Good riddance."

I made a decision right then.

First thing tomorrow morning, I would go to Mr. Colby and tell him everything. The two documents, as well as Sissy's diary and her ID, were enough evidence to cast a shadow of doubt on Clive. I'd let the authorities decide if they should investigate.

I tugged up the collar of my coat and started toward the bus stop. It had been a long day, and I was ready to get back to the dorm.

I hadn't gone far when a scream broke into the night air.

"Fire! There's a fire!"

I whirled around and gasped.

Flames shot out the window of Clive's trailer. People ran into the street, some with buckets of water, everyone shouting. I stood, dumbfounded, trying to process what was happening. How had his trailer caught fire so quickly? Had Clive dropped a cigarette or match in his haste and accidentally set his home ablaze?

This time the crime will be far worse than a simple robbery, he'd warned before he sped away.

My body began to tremble as I stared at the shooting flames. Cold dread stole my breath.

He'd set the fire on purpose.

He'd brought me here and left me standing in front of his home so everyone would see me. So I wouldn't have an alibi when the MPs came to accuse me of arson.

So I would keep my mouth shut.

About my suspicions. About the bomb. About Sissy.

About everything.

CHAPTER TWENTY-TWO

LAUREL

I STARED AT THE BOLD HEADLINE on the screen of the microfilm machine.

Fire Destroys Trailer in Happy Valley

The old issue of the *Oak Ridge Journal* was from December 1944. I would have passed over the article had it not been for the familiar name that practically jumped off the page as I skimmed the printed words.

"A fire destroyed the trailer home of Clive Morrison last night," I read quietly. The Oak Ridge Fire Department attempted to put out the blaze, but the house could not be saved. The article went on to say that Mr. Morrison had been away at the time of the emergency and was uninjured. Neighbors reported no suspicious activity, but the military police would investigate, nonetheless.

I drummed a beat on the desk with my fingernails.

I wouldn't have an interest in a story about the fire if the house hadn't belonged to Clive Morrison, the same man who'd filed a complaint against Aunt Mae. Curious, I backed up the film reel to view the first page of the issue and reread the date.

Unease swam in the pit of my stomach.

The fire took place the day after Mr. Morrison claimed Aunt Mae broke into his home. A home that burned to the ground less than twenty-four hours later.

It couldn't be simple coincidence.

A terrible question took root in my mind as I stared at the black-and-white print.

Did Aunt Mae have something to do with the fire? The very idea seemed ludicrous, but the timing could not be ignored. It seemed impossible the two incidents were unrelated. Yet without knowing Aunt Mae's side of the story, I couldn't be certain.

As I'd done before, I printed the page and tucked it into my purse. I'd share my findings with Jonas the next time I saw him. I spent the next two hours searching articles from January through August 1945. News of the bombings in Japan, the end of the war, and Oak Ridge's shocking role in the enrichment of uranium filled each issue, but there were no other references to the fire, Mr. Morrison, Sissy, or Aunt Mae that I could find.

I'd just turned off the machine when I saw Jonas come through the library entrance, looking handsome in dark slacks and a white shirt. The librarian greeted him with a friendly smile. After they chatted, she looked in my direction. Jonas nodded when he saw me.

"Hi there," he said when he approached. "I saw your car in the parking lot. I hope I'm not interrupting."

"Not at all." I held back a grin. I was quite pleased he'd sought me out. "I was just finishing up."

"Did you find anything interesting?" He pulled up a chair from a nearby table and sat down.

I removed the printed page from my purse and handed it to him. "Check out the article about the fire."

After he finished reading, he took a folded sheet of paper from his pocket and gave it to me. "I found something too."

"What?" I asked.

He simply pointed to the paper.

A half dozen handwritten, dated entries from December 1944 filled the lined page.

5 p.m. Mrs. Fenlor wants her husband removed as he had been drinking again. John Fenlor, age 42, locked up overnight to help him recuperate. I looked at Jonas. "What is this?"

"It's a copy of a police log. We have something similar down at the station, although ours are typed these days. Calls, arrests, disturbances. Everything is recorded in the log. This one," he indicated the document I held, "is from the 1944 Oak Ridge Police Department. Keep reading."

I did.

The next entry was about a barking dog. Then I came to the third incident.

6 p.m. Fire department called to burning trailer on Wheat Ave., MP on duty took over investigation. Resident Clive Morrison unharmed.

I met Jonas's gaze. "I guess you came to the same conclusion I did when I read the article about the fire."

He gave a slow nod. "The timing can't be a fluke."

"I agree," I whispered, trying to keep my voice down. "But it also doesn't mean Aunt Mae is guilty of anything. Especially not arson. I searched the old newspapers through August 1945 but didn't find any other articles about her, Morrison, or the fire."

"Same." He handed back the printed news article. "I went through records and logs for the entire year of 1945. This is the only thing I found with Morrison's name. There wasn't anything about your aunt, which is good news. That means they never charged her with starting the fire."

"That's a relief." I held the two documents side by side. "I wish I could ask Aunt Mae about all of this, but I don't want to upset her. It's probably nothing, especially if the military police didn't pursue it. Besides, it happened over thirty years ago. It has no relevance to anyone today."

"You're right, but . . ." His voice trailed.

"But what?"

"The cop in me suspects there's more to the story. What that might be, I don't know. But you're right. It happened a long time ago."

I gathered my things and we made our way outside. Brilliant sunshine and temperatures in the low eighties created a perfect summer day. His police cruiser was parked next to my Camaro in the parking lot, the windows down, something you wouldn't see in Boston. Delinquents had no qualms about filching from an unattended vehicle, including a police car.

"My mom got home last night," he said with a grin. "She wasn't happy when she found out about dad's injury. He's doing everything he can to appease her. She loves entertaining, so Dad's going to fire up the barbeque grill tomorrow and invite some folks over. I was hoping you could join us. Your aunt, too, if she'd like to come."

"That sounds fun. I'll check with Aunt Mae to see if she has any plans and let you know."

A male voice came over the radio from inside the police car, interrupting us. "I've got a 10-52 at the intersection of Illinois Avenue and Oak Ridge Turnpike. Fifty-six-year-old driver. Name is Maebelle Willett."

I gasped. "Jonas, that's Aunt Mae. What does he mean by a 10-52?"

He didn't answer as he reached into the police car through the open window and grabbed the radio microphone.

"10-4. This is Tyson. What's the situation?"

Static sounded, then the man on the other end said, "We have a 10-50 in progress, blocking the intersection."

Sirens sounded before he cut off.

"10-4. I'm on my way."

I didn't wait for him to explain. "What's going on, Jonas? Is Aunt Mae all right?"

When he faced me, he wore a look of concern. "She's been involved in a car accident. They've called for an ambulance."

I sucked in a breath and covered my mouth.

"Why don't you come with me? I can get you there faster."

We jumped into his vehicle. Jonas flipped a switch that turned on flashing lights and a siren, then tore out of the library parking lot. Cars pulled over to let us by, and I was grateful he'd volunteered to take me to the scene. All the while, I prayed Aunt Mae wasn't seriously injured.

Two other police cars and an ambulance were on scene when we arrived.

"Let me find out what's going on before you get out of the car, okay?" Jonas reached a hand to touch my shoulder. "I'll be right back."

He didn't wait for an answer and exited the vehicle. I watched him stride over to where the ambulance was parked. From where I sat, I couldn't tell if anyone was inside the emergency transport or not.

Not far from the ambulance, I saw Aunt Mae's car, stopped in the middle of the intersection. It faced away from me and looked perfectly fine from this vantage point. However, another car sat across from it, the damage obvious. While I couldn't be certain, it looked like Aunt Mae had broadsided the vehicle on the passenger side. A man stood a few paces from it with a uniformed police officer, his hands motioning as he spoke.

Jonas soon returned and slid into the driver's seat.

"Is she okay?" I asked, my voice wavering.

He pressed his lips. "She's pretty banged up, but the paramedic is hopeful her injuries aren't life-threatening."

Tears sprang to my eyes. "Can I see her?"

"They're transporting her to the hospital now. We'll follow."

We drove behind the ambulance, lights flashing on both emergency vehicles. When we reached the hospital, Jonas pulled into a parking space while the ambulance headed for the ER entrance. We rushed over as the attendants brought Aunt Mae into the building on a wheeled gurney, with one of them explaining her condition to the doctor on duty as they sped down the hall. A blanket covered her up to her neck, and her head was swathed in a bandage. Her eyes were closed and her face had no color, causing my heart to race with fear.

Jonas and I hung back as they took her to a private, curtained area. Nurses immediately hovered over her, calling out medical terms, working in tandem. One hooked up an IV while another carefully lifted Aunt Mae's arm to examine her bandaged wrist.

The doctor used a small flashlight to check the pupils in both of her eyes. "Ms. Willett?" He spoke close to Aunt Mae's ear. "Can you hear me, Ms. Willett?"

Aunt Mae mumbled but didn't open her eyes.

"You've been in a car accident," the doctor said. "You're in the hospital."

She didn't respond.

"This is Miss Willett's niece, Laurel Willett," Jonas said, gaining the doctor's attention.

"Were you in the vehicle with your aunt?" the man asked, giving me a once-over.

I shook my head, unable to speak.

He seemed to assess my emotional state. "We'll take good care of her. She sustained a pretty bad blow to the head. I suspect she has a concussion. We also believe she has a fractured wrist, but we'll confirm that with an X-ray. Once we get her settled in a room, you can see her. For now, why don't you go out to the waiting room." His gaze shifted to Jonas. "Maybe you could get her a soda or something cool to drink. She looks a little pale."

Jonas gently led me away. Instead of stopping in the crowded ER waiting room, we continued down a hallway to a quieter area. Chairs sat against the wall, and I practically fell into one. He used his walkie-talkie to let dispatch know where he was, then joined me.

"Do you want something to drink?" he asked. "I saw a soda machine."

My stomach rebelled at the thought. "I just need to know she's going to be okay."

He reached for my hand. The warmth of his fingers wrapped around mine was comforting. "They'll take good care of her."

I nodded, then frowned. "Was the accident Aunt Mae's fault?"

His face gave me the answer before he said a word. "I spoke with the officer who arrived on scene first. It does appear that Mae ran the red light."

My heart sank. "I was afraid of that. I've been concerned about her driving. She's had some vision issues lately."

Compassion filled his face. "If she is at fault, she'll receive a citation, but there won't be any charges against her. She wasn't drinking alcohol and didn't intentionally cause harm."

A new thought brought me up. "I need to call Dad. He'll want to come down."

"That's a good idea. Maybe you should wait until you know more about her injuries."

His suggestion made sense. "Thank you for being here with me." My throat tightened. "I've never been close to Aunt Mae, but being in Oak Ridge with her has been really special. I don't want to lose her."

His grip on my hand tightened. "I know."

We sat in the hallway for nearly an hour before the doctor found us.

"The good news is, your aunt doesn't appear to have any internal injuries," he said when Jonas and I stood. "She does, however, have a concussion and a broken wrist. We'll keep her in the hospital overnight. She's been moved to a room. You're welcome to see her now."

My legs felt wobbly as the doctor led the way. I'd never been in a situation where someone I cared about was seriously injured. The intense emotions swirling inside of me were unlike anything I'd ever felt before.

The hospital room had two beds, but thankfully the second was unoccupied. I immediately went to Aunt Mae's side.

"Aunt Mae?" I said softly. Bruising on her face was beginning to appear. She must have slammed into the steering wheel when she hit the other vehicle.

Her eyes fluttered before partially opening. "Who's there?"

I realized she wasn't wearing her eyeglasses. Her left hand was in a cast, so I grasped her right hand where it lay on her chest. "It's me, Aunt Mae. Laurel."

"Laurel," she repeated. A groan escaped her lips. "I don't know . . . what happened. I can't . . ." Her words became incoherent, and her eyes drifted closed.

"Shhh. You don't need to worry about that right now. Just rest."

There was no response.

The doctor came around to the opposite side of the bed. "She's had a low dose of pain medication, but with a concussion, we're cautious about administering anything that can increase the risk of bleeding. People with head injuries are often confused, agitated, and can even experience hallucinations. We'll watch her for the next twenty-four to forty-eight hours. As her relative, we'll need you to fill out some paperwork."

I remembered Dad. "My father—her brother—will want to be involved in her care. I planned to call him as soon as I knew more."

"That's fine. We just need someone to give us basic information. Name, age, address. That sort of thing."

A young nurse brought in a clipboard and pen. While I sat in a hard metal chair and filled out the forms, Jonas and the doctor spoke in low tones in the hallway. After I handed the paperwork back to the nurse, Jonas returned alone.

"The doctor said Mae's glasses were broken in the accident. They'll have the ophthalmologist examine her to make sure her eyes weren't damaged, then get a new prescription going."

Worry tightened my throat. "This is just awful. What will we do if she isn't able to see well enough to drive or live alone? I need to call Dad."

"There's a pay phone in the waiting room. I'll stay with Mae."

Again, appreciation for Jonas welled up. Tears formed in my eyes. "Thank you."

I hurried to the public phone and made a collect call to Dad's office.

"Hi, honey," he said after accepting the charges. "You never call me at the office. Is everything okay?"

A sob escaped. "No, Daddy, it's not. Aunt Mae's been in a car accident. She's in the hospital." I filled him in on Aunt Mae's injuries and everything I could remember of what the doctor had said, adding, "The accident was her fault, Dad."

"Poor Mae. Hold on, Laurel." I heard him speak to someone, although I couldn't make out the words. Moments later he said,

"My secretary is working on getting me a flight. I'll get there as soon as I can, honey. Are you okay? Were you in the car with Mae?"

"No, I was at the library. We were supposed to have dinner together later. I don't know where she was going." Tears ran down my cheeks. "I'm sorry, Dad. I should've been with her. I should've been driving."

"This isn't your fault, Laurel. I've been concerned about my sister living alone, fearing something like this might happen. I'm sorry you're having to deal with everything, but I'm glad you're with her. Hang in there, sweetheart. I love you."

"I love you, too, Dad."

I hung up the phone receiver, letting tears flow.

"God," I whispered, a sob choking me. "Please let Aunt Mae be okay. I'm just getting to know her. I promise to be a better niece."

When I returned to Aunt Mae's room, I found Jonas speaking to Velvet and Roonie in the hallway.

"Laurel," Velvet said, her voice motherly, "we came as soon as we heard."

At my questioning look, Roonie had a sheepish look. "It's a small town. Word travels fast. Someone saw the accident and called someone else. You know how that goes."

Being from Boston, I didn't. "Thank you for coming. I spoke to my dad. He'll get here as quickly as he can."

"I'm glad to hear that." Velvet glanced into the room, worry on her face. "Poor Mae, I just hate that this happened. Everyone is prayin' for her, you can be assured of that."

I nodded, unable to speak past the tears welling again.

"I should get back to work." Jonas's eyes held an apology. "I'll come by to check on you and Mae a little later. Is there anything I can bring you? Do you need anything from the house?"

My brain felt so foggy, I couldn't think of a thing. "I'm sure there is, but at the moment I couldn't tell you what."

After he left, Velvet said, "I'm going to stay with you until Harris gets here."

"I can't ask you to do that. It could be late when he finally arrives."

She gave a single nod. "All the more reason for me to stay. You don't need to be alone. Besides, we came in separate cars for this very purpose."

The kindness of these people meant more than they would ever know.

Roonie left us a short time later. A nurse brought in a second metal chair, not the most comfortable furnishings, but Velvet and I settled in for a long night after the doctor gave us permission to stay beyond normal visiting hours. Nurses came and went, checking Aunt Mae's vitals, adjusting tubes.

"I haven't spent much time in a hospital," I said, my voice low. "A friend from high school had a baby last year, and I visited her. But this," I indicated Aunt Mae, "is completely different. This is . . . frightening."

"As a pastor's wife, I've spent many hours in hospitals. What I've learned is that while it can be overwhelming, especially when someone you care about is injured or sick, this is also a place of healing, filled with good people who have dedicated their lives to helping others."

I glanced at Aunt Mae's still form. "I should have been home so I could've driven her where she needed to go. Just yesterday I admitted I was concerned about her eyesight, but she assured me she was okay to drive. I should've listened to my instincts."

Velvet offered an understanding look. "Mae is a stubborn woman. She's also one of the most unselfish people I know. Always giving and doing for others. She doesn't like to be on the receiving end of things though. I tell you, sometimes she wears herself out volunteering here or giving a hand there."

"What was she like when you first met her?"

A soft smile lifted her lips as her eyes fastened on Aunt Mae. "Kind. Friendly. Full of curiosity. She'd left home to come to Oak Ridge all by herself, and I always thought she was so courageous. Of course, that was true of most of the young women who worked on the project. Young people always seem to be more adventurous than us old folks. If Roonie and I hadn't been married already, I don't believe I would have been brave enough to come here by myself."

I thought back to the day I'd interviewed Velvet and Roonie. She'd mentioned that Aunt Mae changed, becoming withdrawn. Wasn't it the fall of 1944 when that happened? The same time period Clive Morrison filed a complaint against Aunt Mae, followed by the fire that destroyed his trailer the next day. I had a strong feeling all of it was somehow connected.

Before I could question Velvet about it, a pretty blonde nurse came in. After taking Aunt Mae's vitals, she attempted to rouse her.

"Ms. Willett? Can you hear me? Try to open your eyes."

Moments passed. Aunt Mae took a deep breath, and her eyelids fluttered open.

"Good job," the nurse said, pleased. "Do you know where you are?"

Aunt Mae glanced around the room, then back to the nurse. "Hospital?"

"Yes, ma'am. You have a concussion." She turned to me. "I'm sure she'd love to see you."

I hurried to the opposite side of the bed. "Aunt Mae? It's Laurel."

Her head moved slightly on the pillow, and she turned toward me. "Laurel, I didn't know you were here." Her words were slow and slurred. "What are you doing in Tennessee?"

I shot a concerned look at the nurse. "Is she okay?"

The nurse frowned. "I'll get the doctor."

After she left the room, Velvet joined me. She leaned down so Aunt Mae could see her.

"Hi, Mae." Warmth and caring radiated from her voice.

Aunt Mae's eyes focused on the woman. "Velvet, what . . . doing . . . here?" The slurring continued.

Velvet reached to put her hand on Aunt Mae's. "I had to come see about my friend. You gave us a bit of a scare."

The nurse returned. "The doctor will be in shortly." She moved to Aunt Mae's bedside. "Ms. Willett, I'm going to ask you some questions."

Aunt Mae's attention moved to the nurse. Suddenly her eyes widened and a look of fright filled her features. "Sissy? Is that you, Sissy? I thought you were . . . I thought you were . . ." She panted, her hands grasping the air. "Where? I don't understand . . ." Aunt Mae tried to sit up, but the nurse gently pushed her back against the pillow.

"Calm down, Ms. Willett," the nurse said. "We don't want you to injure yourself."

Aunt Mae continued to fight and mumble unintelligibly.

The doctor arrived in the middle of the commotion. "What's going on?" He came up behind the nurse.

Before she could answer, Aunt Mae let out a piercing scream.

"Leave her alone. Don't hurt her. Don't hurt her. Oh, Sissy, Sissy. He hurt you. He hurt you."

CHAPTER TWENTY-THREE
MAE

THE DAY AFTER THE FIRE, I went to work as usual and acted as though nothing out of the ordinary had occurred. As though I hadn't a care in the world. As though the living, breathing fear that swirled through me like a twister every waking moment didn't exist. Although Clive had not verbally threatened me, the fire was a dangerously clear warning. If I said anything to anyone about my suspicions regarding him being a spy, I would find myself behind bars.

So I biked around K-25 as I'd done every day since I arrived last summer. I carried tools to work crews and transported parts to the maintenance shop. I filed papers, wrote work orders, and ate lunch at the cafeteria, even laughing at the silly joke a coworker told. Mr. Colby seemed to keep a close eye on me, and it was exhausting to go about my work without showing the raw terror I carried inside of me.

By the time my shift ended and I made my way to the bus stop, my emotions were on the brink of spilling onto the pavement.

While I waited at the back of the crowd, Velvet arrived and smiled as she approached. It faded when our eyes met.

"Mae, is somethin' wrong?"

The compassion in her voice was my undoing. Tears escaped, and my chin trembled. "I just feel so alone," I whispered. I hadn't meant to say anything, but the despair-filled words left my mouth on their own.

She touched my arm. "Is there anything I can do?"

I shook my head. There wasn't anything anyone could do.

"Would you like to come to my house for a cup o' coffee?"

Her offer took me by surprise. "I . . . I don't know."

"My roommates are working the late shift, so they won't be around. It's always nice to have the place to myself. It can get crowded and noisy when all four of us are home."

I had dreaded going back to the dorm. Sissy's absence and Prudence Thorpe's meddling made me want to crawl into a hole and never come out. Velvet's invitation offered me time to get control of myself. "Yes," I finally said. "I'd like to come to your house."

A warm smile filled her milk-chocolate-colored eyes. "I'm glad."

We boarded the bus. As I made to follow her to the seats in the back, she gave her head a small shake. "We'll meet up again when it's time to get off."

The journey from K-25 to the area of Happy Valley made up of hutments didn't take long. I disembarked with Velvet and other men and women, all Black. If anyone wondered why I'd joined them, they kept it to themselves. When we passed through the gate, the guard eyed me and scrutinized my badge, but he ultimately waved me through.

I followed Velvet as we wound our way through rows of lookalike dwellings. All were tiny, square, and made from plywood. A pipe stuck out the middle of each pitched roof, smoke curling from some of them, and plywood-shuttered windows kept out the cold weather as well as the warm sunshine. Clotheslines stretched between houses, where stiff items flapped in the December breeze.

"How long have you lived here?" I asked.

"Roonie and I came to Tennessee in 1943." Velvet led the way up a wooden walkway to the front door of a hut. "He lives over in the men's section."

Her comment puzzled me. "Who is Roonie?"

"My husband," she said over her shoulder as she entered the house. "Come on in."

I hesitated on the stoop.

I'd never been inside the home of a Black person before. The Black families in our small mining community in Kentucky kept to themselves, yet Mama'd always taught Harris and me that everyone was created in God's image. There weren't any differences between the races that should ever make anyone think themselves better or more deserving than the others.

When Velvet turned a welcoming smile to me, my shoulders relaxed. "Thank you," I said as I crossed the threshold.

Every inch of the confined space appeared occupied by something. Four narrow beds along the four walls; four straight-backed wooden chairs; a coal-burning stove in the center; clothes on pegs; personal items scattered about. There was just enough room to walk a circle around the stove and back.

"It ain't much, but it keeps the rain off our heads."

I tried not to stare. It wasn't Velvet's fault there weren't better living accommodations provided for her and the others. Her earlier comment rolled through my head. "You said your husband lives in a different area. Why is that?"

"Because," she said, matter-of-factly, "colored men and women aren't allowed to live together, even if they're married." She didn't meet my gaze but moved to the stove to get a fire started. "Have a seat." She indicated the chair next to one of the beds.

I did, noticing a well-worn Bible lay on the pillow of the neatly made bed.

"My mama gave that to me when Roonie and I married up." She reached to pick up the black book and smoothed the rough cover lovingly. "It belonged to her daddy. He was born a slave on an Alabama cotton plantation. After the Civil War ended and he was free, he saved enough money to buy this Bible. He didn't know how to read yet, but he was determined to have the Word of God in his home." She carefully returned the book to its spot.

As I watched her fill a kettle with water from a bucket and set it on the stove to heat, it occurred to me I had no idea the depth of suffering Velvet and her family had endured because of hatred and ignorance. Like most white people, I'd learned about slavery in school. I knew about segregation and laws I didn't agree with, like the one preventing Velvet from living with her husband. But other than being an aggravating nuisance, they didn't affect me. At least, not in the way they affected Velvet.

"I'm sorry."

I wasn't exactly sure why I felt the need to apologize, but I did. Not for being white, but for not being able to do anything about the prejudice and harm she and her loved ones had to endure every single day.

She seemed to understand. "Me too."

We spent the next hour chatting over coffee and graham crackers. She told me how she met Roonie and about their hope to start a family as soon as the war was over. I told her about Mama, Pa, and Harris. She shared about the time she and Roonie saw the Gulf of Mexico, and I described the beauty of the Appalachian Mountains of east Kentucky. Never once did our jobs at K-25 come up for discussion, nor did I mention anything about the situation with Sissy and Clive. In fact, some of the heaviness I'd carried all day evaporated in the warm, relaxing atmosphere. It was nice to simply enjoy easy conversation with a friend.

As the sun dipped below the hills, Velvet walked me to the gate. A Black man stood on the other side of the fence. He looked surprised as we approached.

"Mae, this is my husband, Roonie. Roonie, this is my friend, Mae."

He blinked, then nodded politely. "Ma'am. It's a pleasure meetin' you."

"And you."

"Men aren't allowed in the women's area," Velvet explained. "Roonie comes to get me when it's time for supper." She faced me. "I enjoyed visiting with you, Mae. Thank you for doing me the honor of coming to my home."

"Thank you for inviting me." I wanted to give her a hug, but the guard waved me forward.

I boarded a bus bound for town a few minutes later while Velvet and her husband walked in the direction of the unfenced hutment area. As I settled in the seat for the thirty-minute ride, I whispered a prayer of thanks for my new friend.

Garlyn was waiting for me when I arrived at the maintenance shop the following morning.

His eyes sparkled when he saw me. "Hi, stranger."

I attempted a smile, but I hadn't slept much all night. Worries about Clive, Sissy, and MPs kept me awake, fretting until I was ill.

"Hi, yourself. I figured you'd be home, fast asleep by now after working the late shift."

He followed me into the shop office. Thankfully Mr. Colby

wasn't there, nor was the supervisor who took over when Mr. Colby was off duty.

"There was an emergency just before my shift ended. We finished fixing it a little while ago, so I decided I might as well hang around and say hello to you." He grinned. "Hello."

I couldn't help but chuckle. "Hello. Is the emergency anything I need to know about?"

He shook his head. "Nah. Just the usual."

I studied Garlyn. Now that I knew about the top secret project and how the work being done here in Oak Ridge would eventually lead to a bomb, I wondered how much Garlyn knew about it. Like Clive, he was an SED with the Army. I didn't know his clearance level, but he seemed to have access to every area of K-25, including all of the smaller buildings scattered throughout the complex.

How I wished I could tell Garlyn everything that had happened, but I couldn't say a word. A lowly errand girl like me wasn't supposed to know about uranium and the location of yet another secret city. I had no solid proof Clive was a spy or that the papers I'd seen in his trailer were important. I didn't even know if his story about Sissy returning to Georgia was true or not. If I spilled the wild tale now, I would sound crazy.

"I heard there's a Christmas concert at the Grove Recreation Hall at eight o'clock tonight." He closed the distance between us. "I thought, if you're interested, we could have dinner and then go to the concert together."

Warmth filled my face at his intense look. "I'd like that."

He seemed pleased. "The newspaper said other musical events are lined up in the coming days. The brass and woodwind choir is playing at the high school. Traditional carols will be sung at the Robertsville School. There's even a performance of Handel's *Messiah* at Chapel on the Hill. That's one of my favorites."

"I guess everyone is getting into the holiday spirit. It's hard to believe Christmas is almost here."

"There's also a dance on the twenty-third, as well as one on New Year's Eve." His gaze held mine. "I'd sure like to ring in the new year with you, Mae."

I was about to respond when Mr. Colby appeared in the doorway. He glanced between us. "Can I help you, Mr. Young? I thought the repair was finished."

"It is, sir." Garlyn stepped away from me. "Miss Willett and I were just talking about the upcoming holiday."

My face was on fire, and I didn't look at either man.

After a moment, Mr. Colby chuckled, then said, "Miss Willett, I believe you've got work to do."

"Yes, sir." I hurried to where my bike was parked. I peeked at Garlyn. He wore a silly grin and didn't seem at all flustered at being caught fraternizing.

"See ya, Mae. Mr. Colby. Have a good day." He walked out the door, but not before tossing me a wink.

Mr. Colby didn't question me about Garlyn's presence and went on with his business. Requests for tools and parts awaited me, so I loaded my basket and set off into the cavernous belly of K-25. When I passed through the pipe gallery, I waved to Velvet where she sat atop an enormous pipe, polishing it. I'd enjoyed my time at her humble home and hoped she'd invite me again. I doubted it was appropriate for me to invite her to the dorm, but I would check with Mrs. Kepple just the same.

By the time my shift was over, my mood was much improved from when I'd first arrived that morning. The normalcy of work. The friendships of Garlyn and Velvet. Even Mr. Colby's steady leadership. All served to remind me I had a good life here in Oak Ridge. A life I wanted to continue, despite the troubles with Sissy and Clive.

While I made my way to the bus terminal, I came to a decision.

I wouldn't spend another moment trying to figure out what to do about Clive Morrison. Even though I was certain he was a spy and was up to no good, someone else would have to report him to the authorities. He'd proven himself dangerous when he set his own trailer on fire. I couldn't jeopardize my job or my freedom, no matter how much I wanted to see him stopped.

I also decided to wait until after Christmas to write to Sissy. My letter might cause her further hurt, and I didn't want to spoil her holiday with her family. But as soon as the new year arrived, I would tell her everything, assuring her that I had not betrayed her and had no feelings for Clive. If she chose not to return to Oak Ridge, I still hoped we could remain friends.

The line for the buses moved at a snail's pace. It seemed one of the big vehicles had broken down right there at the stop and was causing a backup. While I waited, my mind wandered back to my conversation with Garlyn. Warmth spread up my arms despite the chilly breeze, remembering the way he'd looked at me when he invited me to dinner and a concert. When I saw him on the operating floor later, he said he'd pick me up at my dorm. Maybe I should purchase a small Christmas gift for him. He'd already shown himself to be a generous sort of fellow by surprising me with the rubber galoshes and a candy bar. We weren't officially dating, but I had a feeling that might change soon.

The blare of a car horn interrupted my sweet train of thought.

Everyone turned toward the sound.

My stomach dropped to the ground when I saw Clive standing next to his Army sedan, parked a short distance away. He stared right at me. With a smirk, he waved me over.

I quickly turned away. I didn't know what he wanted, but I wouldn't play along.

The horn sounded again. This time, a long, shrill blast.

"Who is that jerk?" the woman behind me said.

"What's he want?" another woman asked.

I peeked in Clive's direction. His glare told me he wasn't going to give up and leave. He lay on the horn again, and again.

"Idiot," I finally muttered and stepped out of line.

"You tell him, honey," a woman called after me.

I practically stomped toward him. "What are you doing? Everyone is watching."

"Don't. Ever. Ignore me. Again."

The barely controlled rage in his voice sent a chill racing up my spine.

"Get in the car."

I swallowed and took a step backwards. "No. I'm not going anywhere with you. You need to leave me alone."

His eyes narrowed on me. "Get in the car, Mae. *Now.*"

I turned to leave. He wouldn't dare touch me in front of all these people.

"Do you see that MP over there?" he said. "The one watching us?"

On their own, my eyes found the military man. He stood outside the portal guardhouse, arms akimbo, his gaze fixed in our direction.

"All I have to do is walk over to him, tell him you set my trailer on fire in a jealous rage, and your life is over."

I stood frozen, heart thundering.

His words were not a ploy. He'd made certain I was at the scene of the fire. Someone was bound to remember me. It was as though Clive had read my happy thoughts from minutes ago. He knew he had the power to destroy everything good in my life in an instant. To ruin my present and my future.

I turned to face him, panic racing through me. "I swear I won't tell anyone about you. I don't even care what it is you're doing. Just leave me alone."

Tense moments ticked by before he spoke. "The thing is, Mae, I need you."

Revulsion swept through me. It must have shown on my face, because he gave a humorless laugh.

"Not like that. Trust me, I have no romantic feelings for you whatsoever. What I need is practical help." He came around to the passenger side of the car and opened the door. "Get in. I'll tell you about it while I drive you home."

I didn't move. I glanced at the guard, at the crowd nearby, finally starting to board the buses. Every one of them a witness to what would no doubt appear to be a lovers' quarrel. Once again, Clive had made sure I was seen with him. If I walked away now and went to the authorities with my wild story of suspected espionage, arson, and threats, would anyone believe me?

I knew the answer.

I climbed into the car.

Clive shut the door and returned to the driver's seat. He didn't steer the car toward the river as he'd done before but pointed it in the direction of town.

"You've made things difficult for me," he said after we'd gone several miles in silence.

I shot him a look. "You've made things difficult for yourself. I don't want any part of this. I told you I wouldn't tell anyone, and I mean it. Just leave me alone."

He gave me a patient look. "You're not listening, Mae. This isn't about you or how you feel. This is bigger than either of us. My work is important to the entire world. But now that I've been forced to move back into the barracks, I'm going to need to do things differently."

I didn't respond. I didn't care about his so-called difficulties. His inflated ego clearly prevented rational thinking.

"For obvious reasons, I can't keep important documents in the barracks or in the trunk of my car. A nosy guard could easily find them. They must be kept in a location where no one will think to look." He glanced at me. "I need you to take them to your dorm room and hide them."

I gasped. "I won't do it." I shook my head and crossed my arms. "I won't put myself in jeopardy like that. Whatever it is you're doing, you need to stop. You're helping the enemy. Why would you do that? Don't you want the war to end? Don't you want to see Hitler and the Nazis put in prison where they'll rot for all eternity? How could you betray your country to help them?"

Clive didn't answer. Instead, he pulled the car off to the side of the road and stopped. I feared I'd said too much. I still had the knife in my purse, but I was too afraid to take it out.

"What a little fool you are, Mae. I'm not helping the Nazis." He studied me. "Do you know what communism is?"

"Of course," I said, puzzled by the question. "My pa says communism is a terrible way to run a country. He says everything good about America would come to an end if we let communists take over."

He looked annoyed. "Your pa is wrong. Communism is exactly what America needs. You and your family would benefit from communism. Sissy said your father is a poor coal miner, most likely dying of black lung, and your mother does laundry."

My face heated. I didn't appreciate Sissy talking about me and my family to Clive. "So what? They work hard and are honest, good people."

"I didn't say they weren't, but they and people like them will never have the life they deserve unless things change. Under communism, no one is poor. Everyone has the same income, the same housing, the same rights. Doesn't that sound like a better way of life?"

I answered with a question of my own. "What does communism have to do with you helping the enemy?"

"I told you, I'm not helping the enemy." A self-satisfied look settled on his face. "I work for the Russian government."

I stared at him. Had he lost his mind?

"I see you think I'm crazy." He chuckled, then sobered. "You remember what I told you about the work we're doing here in Oak Ridge? About the bomb we're trying to create?"

I gave a tiny nod, but my mind reeled. He was nuts. Positively insane. I should have seen it before, especially after he set his own home on fire.

"Germany is also working on an atomic bomb," he went on, "but my comrades don't think they'll be successful. Too many of their top scientists were Jews who fled the country or aren't allowed to work. Mark my words. We *will* be successful in completing the project soon. That means the United States would be the only country in the world with such a powerful weapon. Many of us, however, don't think that's a good idea. We don't want Germany to have the bomb, but what if one of our allies did? Wouldn't it level the playing field if Russia also had one? So that's what we're doing. Insuring that the American government doesn't get too power hungry."

My mind spun with his incredible tale. It sounded preposterous. Like something you'd read in a *Flash Gordon* science-fiction comic strip. But what if he wasn't making it up? I'd seen the S-50 plant with my own eyes. I knew no military products like tanks or guns were produced in Oak Ridge, yet thousands of people spent day and night creating . . . something.

Clive's words from the night he took me to the river echoed in my memory. *Here in Oak Ridge, we're working to enrich enough uranium to fuel a bomb. A big bomb.*

I didn't know anything about bombs or uranium, but even I

was aware that everyone on the Reservation was involved in important work for the war effort. Something the military and the government wanted kept secret.

"When we get to town, I'll give you the documents I need you to hide," he said, drawing my attention. "Don't even think about showing them to anyone. If you do, I'll be forced to reveal that not only did you burn down my trailer, you're also a spy for Germany. While you sit in jail and wait for them to disprove it, I'll be long gone."

I felt like a frightened hare, trapped with no way to escape. If I went along with his plan, I'd be guilty of betraying my country. Yet if I didn't agree to hide the stolen papers, Clive would ruin my life. Not only would I lose my job, but I'd go to prison. Just last week, Prudence excitedly whispered to several of us that a lab technician at K-25 had failed a lie detector test and was taken into custody. I didn't know how those types of tests worked, and I didn't want to find out.

"I'll hide your stupid documents," I spat, not bothering to conceal my fury.

He laughed, clearly enjoying his superiority over me. "Espionage isn't so bad, Mae. What we're doing is going to help a lot of people. You'll see."

We drove the remaining miles in silence. When we reached the dormitory, Clive parked but didn't turn off the engine. He pulled a manila envelope from beneath his seat.

"This envelope is sealed and needs to remain sealed." His gaze narrowed on me. "I'll know if you open it, Mae. I'll get it back from you the day after Christmas." He handed the thick packet across the space between us.

I couldn't move. I just stared at the horrid thing, knowing that the moment I touched those papers, I was as guilty as Clive. It didn't matter that I wasn't the one who'd stolen them or passed them on to whomever Clive was working for. My involvement would be seen as traitorous, a betrayal of the trust President Roosevelt had put in me, a citizen of the United States.

"Take it, Mae."

I refused to look at him. If I had to see his smug face one more time, my fist might end up meeting his nose. I grabbed the packet and exited the car. A light snow had begun to fall, and tiny white flakes landed on the envelope.

"You know the motto around here, Mae. Mum's the word."

I slammed the door while he laughed and marched toward the dormitory without a backwards glance. The sedan roared away. Tears threatened to spill, but I had to keep them in check until I reached my room. The wintery weather had brought people outside, laughing and chasing each other, while others tried to catch the fluffy flakes on their tongues.

"Hi, Mae," Prudence Thorpe called from a short distance away where she and other young women stood chatting. "Come join us."

I begged off. "Sorry. I'm not feeling too well."

Her eyes traveled to the packet in my hands, before returning to my face. "Any word from Sissy?"

I shook my head and continued on my way. The last thing I needed was nosy Prudence asking questions. After I locked myself in my room, I flung the packet onto Sissy's bed.

"This is all your fault," I hissed, imagining Sissy sitting across from me. Tears blurred my vision. "If you hadn't gone on that first date with Clive, he would've moved on to someone else. Now look at the mess I'm in."

I sank to the floor. My shoulders shook with silent sobs. I wanted to scream, yell, lash out at the injustice, but I couldn't let anyone overhear me. I had to give the appearance that everything was fine. That I wasn't hiding confidential documents in my room.

That a spy for Russia hadn't threatened me with dire consequences if I didn't help him.

When I couldn't shed another tear, I turned on the lamp and sat up. The loathsome packet mocked me where it lay on Sissy's bed. Daring me to open it. Daring me to turn it over to the authorities.

Daring me to be brave.

But I wasn't brave. I was a coward. Worse than that, I was a traitor.

I glanced around the room. I needed to find someplace to hide the packet. No one should be in my room if I wasn't home, but Mrs. Kepple had a key and could access it if necessary. When I'd seen her in the hallway yesterday, she mentioned that unless Sissy returned soon, I would have a new roommate assigned to me. I could only hope that didn't happen until after I returned the documents to Clive.

The tiny space had limited options for concealing anything. The closet was too obvious. I ruled out tucking the packet under a mattress for the same reason. I could wrap it in one of Sissy's blouses and put it in the laundry basket, but anyone could easily dump it out and discover the envelope.

My gaze landed on the headboard on Sissy's bed. With only one way to arrange the sparse furnishings in the cramped room, the headboards for each of our beds were anchored to the wall. I moved to sit on her coverlet and studied how the wood was held in place. If I loosened the screw in the upper right corner, I might be able to create a gap wide enough to slip the packet in. The problem was I didn't have any tools. I could borrow something from the shop tomorrow, but that didn't help me right now.

I glanced at my purse. The knife was still hidden within. Thankfully I hadn't had to use it against Clive, but it would come in handy for this project.

I retrieved the utensil and quickly had the screw loosened. The wood gapped just enough for me to push the packet down, out of sight. Unfortunately the screw wouldn't tighten all the way, but it didn't matter. No one would notice.

Exhaustion crawled over me. I wasn't cut out for espionage.

The sooner I returned the documents to Clive and washed my hands of this whole mess, the better.

CHAPTER TWENTY-FOUR
LAUREL

I STOOD IN SILENT HORROR, watching as the doctor and young nurse worked to restrain Aunt Mae. A second nurse arrived to administer a sedative. Moments later, Aunt Mae's distress ended abruptly. Once she quieted, the doctor checked her pupils and heart rate before meeting my gaze. I'm certain my own distress was obvious.

"A person with a concussion can become agitated and confused," he said, his calm voice reassuring. "Rest is vital for the brain to heal from the trauma it suffered. We'll keep her sedated overnight, then evaluate her in the morning. You should go home and get some rest yourself. She won't wake until tomorrow."

He and the nurses exited the room. Velvet moved to stand beside me.

"He's right, Laurel. Mae will need your strength to get through this."

I suddenly felt drained. "I hate to leave her, but I suppose there's nothing I can do until she wakes up." I remembered then that I didn't have my car. "Would it be possible for you to give me a ride to the library? My car is there."

"Of course."

I kissed Aunt Mae's forehead, tears springing to my eyes. "I'll be back in the morning, Aunt Mae. I love you." There was no indication she heard me.

We left the hospital and walked to Velvet's car. Once we were seated, I turned to her. "Do you know what Aunt Mae was talking about? It was as though she thought the nurse was her roommate Sissy, and that the doctor was going to hurt her in some way."

Velvet gave a slow nod. "I wondered about that too." She looked thoughtful. "I never met Sissy. She worked at Y-12, while Mae and I worked at K-25. Roonie and I rarely ventured into Townsite where Mae lived in one of the dormitories. The restaurants and activities in town were for white folks, so there wasn't much need for us to take the bus there often."

"Do you know what happened to Sissy?"

"I don't. The only reason I knew something strange was goin' on was Roonie saw a notice in the newspaper, asking for information about Sissy. He recognized Mae's name and showed it to me."

"I read that notice in an old copy of the *Oak Ridge Journal* at the library. Aunt Mae never mentioned if Sissy returned?"

Velvet shook her head. "We weren't close friends yet, but we'd chat when we saw each other at the bus stop or at the plant. She came to my house once for coffee. I noticed a difference in her not long after that. She'd been pleasant and easy to talk to before, but she grew distant. Guarded, I guess you'd say. Roonie didn't think it was a good idea for me to continue a friendship with Mae."

I frowned. "Why not?"

"In those days, the whole town of Oak Ridge was one big secret from the world. There were people watchin' to make sure it stayed that way. If anyone thought you were telling things you shouldn't tell or knew things you shouldn't know, you could lose your job. One had to be careful with whom they associated."

"When did the two of you reconnect?"

She smiled. "After Oak Ridge opened to the public, I'd see Mae from time to time, usually volunteering here or there in the community. We gradually became friends again."

Velvet dropped me off at my car, waiting until I was inside with the engine running and the doors locked before she drove away. Aunt Mae's house was dark when I pulled into the driveway. A wave of sadness washed over me, and I wiped a tear that rolled down my cheek.

"Lord, please help Aunt Mae get better," I whispered. "We love her."

Barking met my ears when I opened the front door. I'd forgotten all about Peggy. The little dog came forward when I knelt to pet her.

"Hi, girl. I'm sorry, but Aunt Mae isn't coming home. You're stuck with me."

I turned on the porch light and escorted Peggy outside, where she ran to the far end of the yard to do her business. While I waited, Georgeanne's light came on. The older woman appeared a moment later, wearing a bathrobe and slippers.

"Laurel," she called, motioning for me to come her direction. We met at the fence. "I've been waiting for you to get home. How is Mae? I was so shocked to hear about the accident."

I didn't ask how she knew. Roonie's words about news traveling in a small town explained it. "She has a concussion and a broken wrist. They're keeping her in the hospital for observation."

"Bless her heart. I told her just the other day I'd be happy to take her wherever she needed to go, but you know Mae. Obstinate and independent. I probably shouldn't tell tales, but this isn't her first accident."

My mouth gaped. "It isn't?"

Georgeanne shook her head. "She hit a mailbox a few weeks ago. The only reason I know about it is because the homeowner is a friend. Mae volunteered to pay for the damage, so my friend didn't alert the police."

My shoulders slumped at this discouraging revelation. "Thank you for letting me know. My dad should arrive sometime tomorrow, and I'm sure he'll want all the facts before making any decisions regarding Aunt Mae."

"I'd hate to lose Mae as a neighbor, but it may be best if she went to live in Boston near your family."

I didn't reply. While I liked Georgeanne, she was a bit too opinionated and nosey.

I bid her goodnight and moved to the steps. "Peggy, come."

The little dog had just joined me on the porch when a vehicle turned into the driveway, its headlights blinding me when I looked to see who it was. Everything went dark again when the engine cut off, and Jonas stepped out of his Bronco.

"Hi," he said as he approached. Peggy let out a friendly yap before entering the house. "I stopped by the hospital after my shift. The nurse told me you'd gone home."

Even though I was bone weary, I needed to tell Jonas about Aunt Mae's outburst. "Do you want to come in for a cup of coffee or something? There's a new development in the mystery."

He followed me into the house to the tiny kitchen. We both opted for lemonade instead of coffee. Once we were settled at the table with some cookies, I told him what happened at the hospital.

"She was terrified," I said, recalling the fright that filled Aunt Mae's face when the doctor arrived. "It was as though she expected the doctor to attack the nurse right there in her room. Except she didn't see a nurse. She saw Sissy."

Jonas's brow tugged into a frown. "That's not a good sign. Even in a delirious state, I wouldn't think Mae would fear for Sissy's well-being unless somewhere in her subconscious she knew Sissy had been in danger at some point."

I met his gaze, impressed. "You're exactly right. It didn't seem as though she was experiencing a dream or an imaginary event. I think she was reliving something."

We sat in the stillness of the house, ticking from the clock on the wall the only sound.

"You said your aunt has Sissy's security badge. Would you mind if I looked at it?"

"Not at all."

I retrieved the badge from the box in my bedroom, then returned to the kitchen and handed it to him. "She was a pretty girl. The nurse at the hospital has the same coloring and fresh look."

Jonas studied the front, then the back of the badge for a long moment. "My parents still have their security badges. Everyone in Oak Ridge had to have one. Even children. You couldn't come or go without it." He handed it back to me. "It would've been unusual for Sissy to give her badge to Mae, even if she left Oak Ridge for good. She would've needed it to exit the Reservation."

Apprehension knotted my belly. "I believe Aunt Mae is hiding something. At first I assumed she didn't want to talk about the past because of the secrecy involved with the Manhattan Project. She's always been a very private person from what my dad has said. But then you discovered the complaint against her, followed by the trailer fire. Now she's out of her mind with fear and calling out for Sissy. I can't bring myself to believe she was involved in criminal behavior, but . . . what if she was?"

"I admit things look suspicious. Of what, I don't know."

Tears welled in my eyes. "I don't want to mistrust her, Jonas. Besides, everything we're discussing happened over thirty years ago. Does it really matter now? Should I just drop it? Maybe Aunt

Mae is right. Maybe things in the past should stay there. Bringing all of this up has upset her, possibly even to the point of causing her to have a car accident."

He reached across the table and grasped my hand. "I know you want what's best for your aunt. Uncovering long-buried secrets can bring out a lot of pain, but it can also be healing. My instincts tell me that whatever happened all those years ago still has a negative influence on Mae today. I think her outburst at the hospital is linked to it."

I squeezed his hand, then stood to get a tissue. As I dabbed my eyes, I exhaled. "Everything you said is exactly what I would tell someone who came to me with the same kind of dilemma involving a loved one. Dealing with the past is often the key to letting go of feelings of fear and unforgiveness." I gave a slight shrug. "The thing is, when it's your own family member, it's hard to make the choice to hurt them further."

He stood and came to me. "When your dad gets here tomorrow, he may have a better understanding of what's going on. Did you tell him about the MP's report and the fire?"

I shook my head. "Everything happened so quickly following the accident. I'll show him the newspaper articles and MP report before we go to the hospital."

We walked to the front door where he offered a sympathetic smile. "Try to get some rest, Laurel. I'll come by the hospital tomorrow, okay?"

"Thank you. For everything."

After he drove away, I locked the door and readied for bed. I'd just turned out the lamp when I heard Peggy's toenails on the wood floor in the hallway. A moment later, I knew she stood next to the bed. I clicked on the lamp and found her staring up at me.

"I know you don't understand why Aunt Mae isn't here." I reached to pet her. "Hopefully she'll be home in a couple days."

The little animal whined.

I didn't know if Peggy usually slept in Aunt Mae's bed or not, but her big, sad eyes seemed to plead to be let up into mine.

"Just this once."

After the dog was snuggled on the blanket at the foot of the bed, I turned out the light again.

"Help Aunt Mae rest, Lord," I whispered. "If there's anything I can do to bring her peace, please give me wisdom."

Thankfully Dad would be here tomorrow. Maybe between the two of us, we could get down to the bottom of what happened to Sissy and why it still seemed to haunt Aunt Mae.

The aroma of coffee woke me the following morning. I lay in bed, sleepy confusion muddling my brain. Had the car accident only been a dream? Was Aunt Mae in the kitchen, making breakfast as usual?

I sat up and rubbed my face. The clock hands indicated it was nine thirty. Peggy wasn't at the foot of my bed, but the clothes I'd worn yesterday lay on the floor exactly where I'd dropped them before falling into an exhausted sleep.

Sounds from the kitchen drew me down the hall. When I reached the tiny room, I found Dad standing there in his rumpled business clothes, a cup of coffee in his hands. Peggy sat at his feet, but when she spotted me, she stood and barked, as though saying, "Look who's here."

"Daddy." I flew to him, nearly spilling his drink.

"Hi, baby girl." He set the cup on the counter and wrapped his arms around me. How good it felt to know I wasn't alone anymore.

When we parted, I asked, "When did you get here?"

"Just now. I managed to get on a late flight to Atlanta last night, but the commuter flight from Atlanta to Knoxville didn't leave until this morning."

I sat at the kitchen table. "I'm glad to see you. I've been so frightened for Aunt Mae."

He took the seat across from me. "How is she? I want to get to the hospital as soon as possible."

I filled him in on everything the doctor said, then told him about Aunt Mae's outburst.

"It was so strange, Dad. It was like she'd gone back in time and believed her roommate Sissy was right there with her. They sedated her after that, so I came home."

He frowned. "I can't imagine what that was all about. Hopefully it's just a result of her injury and won't affect her long term."

"I have something else to show you." I went to my room and retrieved the MP's report and newspaper articles. As Dad glanced through them, I explained. "While I was searching for information about the bomb and Oak Ridge's history, I found this notice in the newspaper requesting information about Sissy's whereabouts. It was posted by Aunt Mae. Then Jonas—he's a friend and a cop—found a complaint that was filed with the MPs against Aunt Mae by a man named Clive Morrison." I paused. "The troubling part of the story is that Clive Morrison's trailer burned to the ground the day after he filed the complaint. A newspaper article says he wasn't home at the time of the fire and was uninjured. It doesn't mention anything about Aunt Mae, but the timing is worrisome."

I sat back and waited for Dad to process the disturbing information. The frown on his brow grew deeper while he read the articles. When he finally looked up, his expression revealed he was as bewildered as I felt.

"I can't imagine what all of this means." He glanced between me and the papers spread across the table. "You said a policeman helped you track all of this down? Is Mae in legal trouble?"

I explained how I met Jonas and how he'd been such a big help, especially when we learned of Aunt Mae's car accident. "I don't believe Aunt Mae started the fire, but it does seem suspicious that it happened the day after the report was filed. And then there's her odd behavior anytime Sissy's name comes up."

"I'm sure my sister hasn't wanted to talk about any of this. Am I right?"

I nodded. "I made the mistake of pushing a little too hard when I first arrived. I don't want to do that again, but I have to admit I can't help but wonder if part of the reason she doesn't want to talk about the past is linked to all of this."

He studied the MP's report. "This says Mae was accused of breaking into this guy Morrison's house." His eyes widened, and he met my gaze. "He also said they were lovers."

I pressed my lips. "I know. It doesn't sound at all like Aunt Mae."

"I've known her my entire life, and I'm confident she wouldn't break into someone's home. She certainly wouldn't set it on fire."

"Do you think the part about her being romantically involved with Mr. Morrison could be true? He claims Aunt Mae was jealous. Maybe they'd had an argument and he wanted to get back at her by filing the report, although I can't imagine she'd resort to arson."

Dad's shoulders lifted. "I've never heard her mention an interest in anyone, but then I was just a kid when we moved to Oak Ridge. I don't recall our mother ever talking about Mae having a boyfriend. She fretted over Mae's singleness and didn't want her to be alone her whole life."

"I hope now she'll be willing to move to Boston."

"We'll have to wait and see. First she needs to get better."

We made plans to leave for the hospital after we'd both cleaned up. When we arrived at the medical center, the doctor was in attendance at Aunt Mae's bedside. She was sitting up and seemed coherent.

"Harris," she said when she saw Dad. Her eyes lit up like a Christmas tree. "I didn't know you were coming. My goodness, what a lovely surprise."

Her speech was normal. No slurring or confusion.

"How's my big sis?" Dad moved to her bedside. She reached a hand to him, which he clasped. "I don't like finding you in the hospital."

"I don't like it either." She cast a glare at the doctor. "They say I have a concussion, but I feel fine. I want to go home."

Dad turned his attention to the doctor, his brow raised in question.

"Now, Ms. Willett," the doctor said, chiding in his voice. "I've already told you, you need to stay in the hospital until tomorrow. A concussion is a serious injury to the brain. You may feel fine at the moment, but we don't want to take any chances of you losing consciousness or having an emergency of some kind." He met Dad's gaze. "It's my opinion she should remain here for observation for at least another twenty-four hours. I believe her new eyeglasses will take a couple days to arrive since they're coming out of Nashville. Television or reading would be too much of a strain on her brain. Quiet rest is what she requires to make a full recovery."

A scowl tugged Aunt Mae's forehead. "Pssh. I can rest at home better than I can here."

"Mae," Dad said, using the I-won't-take-any-nonsense tone I'd heard every time I got into trouble growing up. "You can come home tomorrow . . . *if* the doctor agrees. Until then, you need to rest. I'm here to keep you company."

A look of pure adoration shone on her face as she gazed at her baby brother. "I'm glad you're here, Harry."

Dad followed the doctor and nurses into the hallway, speaking in low tones. I moved to Aunt Mae's bedside. "I'm happy to see you're feeling better."

A sheepish look crossed her features. "I'm sorry to have caused so much trouble." She shook her head. "I can't imagine how the accident happened. I don't remember the traffic light turning red. My poor car. I'm just grateful the other driver wasn't injured."

I agreed. "I think Peggy was happy to see Dad," I said, changing the subject.

She chuckled. "He claims he doesn't care for her, but they have a special bond."

Dad joined us. "I heard that. I'll admit your dog is cute, but I draw the line at letting her sleep in my bed."

"Uh-oh." I laughed. "She looked so sad last night, I gave in."

We were still discussing Peggy when the pretty blonde nurse arrived with some medication. I braced for another outburst, but Aunt Mae simply accepted the pill.

"Is there anything I can get you, Ms. Willett?" the nurse asked. "You didn't eat much of your breakfast."

Aunt Mae wrinkled her nose. "The oatmeal was stiff and lumpy."

The nurse pursed her lips. "Would you like some fruit? Lunch won't be served for a couple hours."

"No, thank you, dear. I'm not very hungry."

After the nurse left the room, Aunt Mae said, "She's a nice girl. Very attentive."

I waited to see if she'd remark on the girl's resemblance to Sissy or mention her panic from yesterday, but she changed the subject.

"I know what you're going to say, Harris." She scowled at her brother. "You're here to tell me I need to stop driving and move to Boston. Well, I'll save you the trouble. I'm not leaving Oak Ridge. If you take my car away, I'll get a bicycle. I used to ride miles and miles every day when I worked at K-25. I'm sure I can get around on one again."

I glanced at Dad. He wore a bemused look on his face.

"I think a bicycle is a great idea, Sis." He grinned. "Maybe we'll get one of those tandem bikes. You know, the kind that's built for two. Then you can pedal me around town when I come for a visit."

Clearly, she didn't see the humor in his comment. "You may find this situation amusing, Harris Willett, but I don't. I know everyone is thinking I shouldn't be allowed to drive anymore or live alone, but I'm telling you I'm still in charge of my own life. I'll be the one to decide when it's time for me to make a change."

Dad didn't appear offended by her stern words. He grasped her uninjured hand and cradled it with both of his. "Of course you're in charge, Mae. No one is going to force you to do anything you don't want to do. But I've told you many times how much Sallie and I would love for you to move to Boston. With the girls grown and moving on with their own lives, we have plenty of room. We've even talked about renovating the basement and turning it into an apartment. You'd have all the privacy you want."

I remained quiet during their conversation. Although I had a strong opinion regarding Aunt Mae driving again, I wasn't involved in the decision. I especially didn't need to add my two cents about uprooting her from the place where she'd lived for more than thirty years. That discussion would take place between the siblings when the time was right.

Aunt Mae's shoulders soon relaxed against the pillow. "I'm glad you agree it's up to me to decide where I should live. I appreciate your offer, and I promise I'll think about it."

"How long have you been having trouble with your eyesight?" Dad asked.

A look of guilt crossed her face. "Six months or so."

Dad clearly wasn't happy with her answer. "You should have told me, Mae. The accident could have been much worse."

"I know." She sighed. "It's only been recently that my eyesight has gotten worse. But I'm not ready to have my independence taken away from me."

Dad nodded. "Let's focus on getting you home first, then we'll talk about the future."

Aunt Mae's eyes grew heavy. "I think I'll take a nap now, Harry."

Dad leaned down to kiss her cheek. "Rest well, Sis. I'll be here when you wake up."

The touching scene reminded me that their relationship went back to the days when Dad was a little boy and Aunt Mae watched over him while their parents worked. The bond between them was strong, made stronger because of the adversity they'd faced together. Poverty, the death of their father, the loss of their mother. Even long miles that separated them couldn't diminish the love they had for each other.

I smiled.

Grandpa and Grandma Willett would be proud of their children if they could see them now.

CHAPTER TWENTY-FIVE

MAE

MY PARENTS WOULD BE ashamed of me.

That thought kept me awake at night after I agreed to hide Clive's stolen documents. Every time I glanced at Sissy's headboard, a wave of guilt rolled over me. Mama would be so disappointed if she knew what I'd done. Pa, too, although I suspected he would have more sympathy for the predicament I found myself in. The thing is, they were the reason I'd done it. If I wasn't so afraid of losing my job and the salary that helped my family, I would march across the muddy field to Castle on the Hill, find the office of the man in charge of the Reservation, and tell him everything. Even if it came down to my word against Clive's, I'd rather go to jail than be part of his traitorous work.

But I knew I wouldn't tell anyone. Couldn't, in fact. Too much was at stake. If Pa was ever to be free of the enormous debt he owed the coal company, he needed my help.

My guilty conscience, however, hung over me like a dark,

ominous cloud. Garlyn had noticed something was wrong when he came to pick me up for the concert at Grove Hall. Although I'd tried to brush it off as simply being tired, I found his worried gaze on me throughout the night. Would he understand my reasoning for helping Clive, I wondered?

Although I usually enjoyed Christmas carols, I hadn't been able to appreciate the beautiful music or Garlyn's company. Too many worries kept me on edge. By the end of the evening, I'd come to a decision. Until I returned the secret documents to Clive, I would keep my distance from everyone, including Garlyn. If he or someone else noticed I was acting suspiciously or in a way that wasn't typical, I could find myself in a heap of trouble. Then once I handed the sealed envelope to Clive the day after Christmas, I would wash my hands of the entire mess and get on with my life.

My resolve was tested, however, when Garlyn walked me to the front entrance of the dormitory after the concert. He'd hinted he would like to hear Handel's *Messiah* at Chapel on the Hill, hope shining in his eyes. As much as I'd hated to do it, I'd lied and said I was busy with an activity in the dorm that night. Disappointment stole the hope from his eyes, but I didn't change my mind. I'd make it up to him once I was free of the hold Clive had on me.

Mrs. Kepple was in the lobby of the dorm when I arrived home after work.

"Maebelle, would you please come to my office? I have something to discuss with you."

My stomach dropped to the floor. Had she heard about the fire? Did she know I had stolen documents hidden in my room? What if she'd discovered them already? Was there an MP waiting in her office to arrest me?

My knees felt like jelly as I followed her to the small room behind the reception desk. To my relief, there was no one else there.

"This package arrived for Sissy," she said. A brown paper-wrapped parcel sat on the corner of the desk. "It appears to be from her family. I was going to return it, but I decided you may want to do that yourself, being that you know more about her sudden departure than I do."

I accepted the package and noted the return address was from Georgia.

Why would Sissy's family send a package to her if she'd gone home, as Clive claimed?

"You should also be aware that I will assign you another roommate in the new year. We can't hold the space for Sissy any longer. People arrive on the Reservation every week. There's even talk of adding additional beds to some of the larger rooms to accommodate more women." I'm sure my face revealed displeasure, because Mrs. Kepple offered a look of compassion. "I know you're disappointed. From what I saw, you and Sissy got along well." She lowered her voice. "Someone indicated Sissy was having issues with the young man she was seeing, which is unfortunate if that's the reason she left. With so many eligible men in Oak Ridge, a pretty girl like Sissy would have her pick."

I could guess who the *someone* was who'd spread gossip about Sissy. Prudence Thorpe was often in Mrs. Kepple's company, no doubt wagging her tongue about this gal or that guy.

"Thank you for the package, Mrs. Kepple. I'll write to Sissy's mother and see about getting Sissy's belongings returned to her."

I left the office and made my way upstairs. In my room, with the door closed and locked, I set the package on Sissy's bed. My gaze darted to the headboard. I was grateful to find the screw was in the same position as I'd left it.

I stared at the parcel. It appeared to have been opened and resealed by military censors. I couldn't imagine why Sissy's mother would send something to her. Sissy left for home weeks ago.

Perhaps the mail was slow. If the package was posted at the time of Sissy's leaving, it may have crossed paths with her as she traveled home. With the ongoing war, it wasn't unheard of for mailed items to get lost or delayed. There's also the fact that Oak Ridge remained a secret to the outside world. Some postmen may not even know it exists.

I lifted the package. It wasn't heavy. I bit my lip, the dilemma of whether to open it or not tugging me both directions. If I didn't open it and simply returned it, I may never know why Sissy's family sent it in the first place. There could be a letter inside that would help me understand the reason it was here and Sissy wasn't.

Decision made, I tore the brown paper from it. A tin can for saltine crackers was inside. Puzzled, I opened the can and found several small items wrapped in red cloth, tied with string. One by one, I took them out. Judging by the shapes and sizes, I guessed one could be socks or nylons. Another was probably cosmetics of some type.

Clearly these were Christmas gifts.

I looked in the tin can and found a folded note.

December 12, 1944

Dearest Sissy,

How we miss your smiling face. Pa says Christmas won't be the same without you. I hope you're well. We had a letter from Joe. He didn't say where he is, but Pa heard on the radio the Army was making its way into Germany. I pray our boy is safe.

Merry Christmas, my Sissy. I look forward to the day when we are all together again.

Love, Mama

I stared at the date at the top of the note. "December twelfth."

My muddled brain calculated how long it had been since Sissy disappeared to the day her mother wrote the letter. Plenty of time had passed for her to arrive back home in Georgia and be reunited with her family. Why then had Mrs. Galloway written the note, indicating her daughter was still in Oak Ridge? Why mail gifts when she could give them to Sissy on Christmas morning herself?

A chill swept through me. Like a frigid wind that suddenly blew through the room, only the window was closed and no drafts came from beneath the door.

"If Sissy isn't in Georgia, where is she?"

The question echoed in the small space.

My heart drummed as I reread the brief note. Sissy's mama sounded nice. She used words like *dearest* and *my Sissy*. Sissy had always spoken well of her family. It was obvious the woman had not seen Sissy since she'd come to Tennessee last summer.

I exhaled a shaky breath.

None of this made sense. The gifts. The letter. Sissy's disappearance.

My gaze once again landed on the headboard and the loose screw.

Had Clive tried to get Sissy to join him in his traitorous activities? I felt certain he'd told her things he shouldn't have about the secret mission taking place in Oak Ridge. The same things he'd told me. What if Sissy had refused? With her brother overseas fighting Hitler, I couldn't see her willingly betraying him. Could Clive have threatened her and forced her to leave Oak Ridge? Was she even now holed up somewhere, frightened the authorities would arrest her for knowing things she shouldn't?

That scenario, however, didn't add up. Even if she'd left town involuntarily, she would have taken her things with her. She would have told me goodbye. She would have written to her mother with a new address.

I thought back to the morning she left on the outing to Knoxville with Clive. I'd been busy with laundry, dreading the chore. She was putting the finishing touches on her makeup, but she didn't look happy. What was it she'd said?

I closed my eyes, trying to remember.

I'm not sure I can trust him, she'd whispered that day.

What had she meant? Was she talking about Clive being a spy or something else? She'd confessed she was having doubts about Clive, going so far as to admit she wasn't sure she loved him. He'd frightened her when she'd accidentally discovered the stolen documents—no doubt some of the same documents I now had hidden behind her headboard.

We were interrupted after her confession. Prudence Thorpe had poked her head into our room to let Sissy know Clive was downstairs. The nosey redhead had seemed surprised to find Sissy decked out in her nice clothes, being that Clive looked like he was dressed for a walk in the woods according to Prudence.

Another memory forced its way to the forefront.

When Clive drove me to the river and revealed secrets I didn't want to know, he'd talked about the day Sissy disappeared. At the time, I'd been more worried for my own safety and hadn't paid attention to everything he said. But now his words bobbed to the surface like one of the marker buoys Pa used when he'd take me and Harris fishing, warning us of hazards.

We were supposed to go to Knoxville that day, but Sissy said she wanted to talk. We came here instead. She said she was confused about our relationship and wasn't certain we should continue seeing each other. When I asked why, she said she couldn't trust me. I distinctly remembered him giving a humorless laugh, followed by, *That was the wrong thing to say.*

My pulse raced as pieces to the puzzle slowly began to connect, creating a hideous picture.

Clive took Sissy to the river that day. She'd told him she couldn't trust him and had ended their relationship.

Then she'd vanished.

Frantic, my gaze tore around the room, taking in the clues that were right in front of me.

Christmas gifts from her family. Her clothes still hanging in the closet. Her cosmetics in their case. I jumped up and opened the drawer where I'd hidden Sissy's badge. Her sweet face looked back at me. Clive said she threw the badge at him in anger. *She didn't need it anymore,* he'd claimed.

"Oh, Sissy," I whispered, my voice strangled. "What's become of you?"

A cold sweat covered my body as I paced the room. I wrung my hands to keep them from shaking as I went over every piece of evidence, again and again. From the conversation I had with Sissy before she left that day, to the bizarre exchange I had with Clive at the river. I relived each moment of how he'd forced me to hide the stolen documents. His confession to spying for Russia. The fire. The threats.

All of it—every wretched detail—pointed to a truth I'd been too blind to see until now.

Images of the wide Clinch River filled my mind's eye. The secluded area past the new plant where Clive and Sissy spent time was far away from prying eyes. No one would have been around to witness anything that happened. Clive was the last person to see Sissy. The only one who truly knew what happened.

I dropped to my knees as a terrible awareness forced breath from my lungs. I gasped for air as hateful words spun through my mind.

Is Sissy dead? Did Clive kill her?

CHAPTER TWENTY-SIX
LAUREL

DAD SETTLED IN to stay at the hospital with Aunt Mae but said there was no need for me to hang out with them all day.

"She'll probably nap on and off," he said. "There isn't anything pressing to keep you here if you have other things to do. I brought my briefcase to keep me busy. Why don't you go on to the library? Didn't you say you had more research to do?"

We'd talked about my dissertation earlier. Aunt Mae's reticence to revisit bygone days when Oak Ridge was a secret city had only reinforced my desire to dig into the issues people dealt with after the war ended. Things like guilt, shame, and the need to keep secrets, all centered around their very unique situation of working on the Manhattan Project. But while I would like to spend more time at the library, it didn't feel right, especially with Aunt Mae still recovering from her injuries. However, I was certain I could find chores back at the house to occupy my time and prepare for Aunt Mae's homecoming.

"I'll make some phone calls while I'm here," Dad said. "I need to find out what happened to Mae's car and look into any charges she could face as a result of the accident."

I made him promise to call if Aunt Mae took a turn for the worse, kissed him goodbye, and drove to the grocery store. Once I returned to the house, I made chicken and vegetable soup and left it on the stove to simmer. If all went as planned, Aunt Mae would come home tomorrow, and I wanted everything ready. With the windows open, letting in a warm summer breeze, and the radio in the kitchen tuned to music from the fifties, I had to admit the little house felt cozy. I could see why Aunt Mae wouldn't want to uproot her life.

I'd just finished cleaning the bathroom and had moved on to the living room when a knock sounded. Peggy ran to the front entry, barking and dancing a jig. Georgeanne stood on the porch when I opened the door. She held a bouquet of fresh-cut flowers from her yard.

"I saw your car in the driveway," she said. "How is Mae?"

I invited her inside. "She's better. Dad is at the hospital with her, so I came back to do some cleaning."

She handed the flowers to me. "I was going to take these to the hospital, but then that's one more thing you'd have to carry home. Figured I'd just bring them over now."

"They're lovely. Let me find a vase to put them in."

While I dug around in kitchen cabinets for something to put the flowers in, Georgeanne trailed me.

"I'm sure Harris is beside himself with worry over his sister." She settled in a chair at the table. "I fell last fall and bruised some ribs. You'd think the world had come to an end the way my kids acted. My daughter came and stayed with me and wouldn't let me do anything."

I found a Mason jar, filled it with water and the flowers, and set it on the table. "I'm sure Dad only wants what's best for Aunt

Mae. Unfortunately, her failing eyesight is a serious issue we can't ignore." I dropped into the other chair. "She's already had two car accidents. I know she doesn't want to leave Oak Ridge, but what will she do if she can't drive? Can't take care of things? There are a lot of unknowns right now."

Georgeanne patted my hand. "You and your family love Mae. I know you'll make the right decisions. You will all be in my prayers."

We chatted a little longer, then Georgeanne returned home. I finished straightening and dusting the living room, then poked my head into Aunt Mae's bedroom. Everything was neat and tidy. Clean sheets always felt good after an illness, so I set about stripping the bed. I opened her closet and was immediately met with the odor of mothballs. A set of sheets sat on a shelf above where clothes hung.

As I reached for them, I noticed the end of a metal box sticking out behind a folded blanket. It gave me pause, probably because everything about Aunt Mae's life was shrouded in mystery. Of course, there wasn't anything strange about a box in a closet. I had boxes in the closet of my apartment in Boston.

I moved the blanket to give a clear view of it. I was surprised to find the box had a padlock on it. What was so important that Aunt Mae kept it under lock and key?

I glanced at her bedside table. Could the key be in the drawer?

Guilt immediately washed over me.

Snooping wasn't cool. Even when I was a kid and my sisters begged me to help them find where Mom and Dad hid our Christmas presents, I refused.

I closed the closet door. I wouldn't want someone rummaging through my private things. Whatever Aunt Mae had in the box in her own closet wasn't any of my business.

It was late afternoon when more visitors arrived. I greeted

Velvet and Roonie and invited them in. They each had a dish in their hands.

"We brought Roonie's famous tuna casserole and a peach cobbler," Velvet said.

"Much better than hospital cafeteria food," Roonie added with a chuckle.

They deposited the items in the kitchen, then we settled in the living room.

"We stopped by to see Mae before we came here," Velvet explained. "She was sleeping, but Harris said she'd been awake earlier and ate some lunch."

"It sounds like she'll be able to come home tomorrow," Roonie added.

I nodded. "I've been trying to get things ready for her."

Velvet glanced at Roonie, an odd expression on her face, then back to me. "Laurel, we wanted to talk to you before Mae comes home. Roonie remembered something about our time in Oak Ridge during the war. Something involving Mae. He'd never shared it with me until yesterday. I must admit, I was surprised by it."

I met Roonie's serious gaze. "Roonie? What did you remember?"

He heaved a sigh. "I'm not one to spread gossip. Don't listen to it, either. That's why I never told Velvet about seein' Mae with a fella out near the S-50 plant site."

"S-50?"

"It was one of the plants where they enriched uranium. It sat next to the Clinch River. With S-50 being so far away from Townsite, only folks with business out that way were around. That's why I remember seein' Mae. I knew she wasn't s'posed to be there." He squinted, as though going back to the 1940s in his mind. "I worked on the railroad crew at S-50 for a time. One of my jobs was to help off-load building supplies and equipment from all those railroad cars they brought in. Tons of coal, too.

It was backbreaking work, I tell ya." He paused. "One day I saw this Army sedan go past. A fella was driving and had a girl with yellow hair with him. I started seein' them on a regular basis. They'd go on past the plant and disappear around the bend." He shrugged. "Figure they were goin' down to the river to do what young lovers do."

Could the woman have been Sissy, I wondered? "But you said you saw Aunt Mae too."

"I did. Same sedan, same fella, but this time the gal in the passenger seat was Mae. They passed right by me, and I could see her face plain as day in the window, lookin' way up to the smokestacks on one of the buildings. You see, I worked the railroad crew at K-25 too, and I'd seen Mae from time to time, going from one building to another. She was always on her bike. Then one day not long after I saw her with that fella, I found out she was a friend of Vel's."

"Roonie has a wonderful memory for faces and names," Velvet said. "Me, I can't remember someone's name two seconds after meeting them."

I tried to understand what Roonie was telling me, but I didn't see why this was troubling. "You said Aunt Mae wasn't supposed to be where you saw her. Was it against the rules?"

He gave a slow nod. "Sure was. If someone didn't have the right colors on their ID badge, they weren't permitted to be in certain areas. They'd find themselves in a heap o' trouble."

"Why do you think Aunt Mae was at S-50 with him if she wasn't allowed to be there?"

Roonie looked uncomfortable, almost embarrassed, before he answered. "They didn't stop at the plant. They kept on goin' around the bend, down to the river, same as he'd done with the gal with yellow hair."

His meaning widened my eyes. "Oh."

"Now, now," Velvet said, glancing between Roonie and myself.

"We don't know why Mae was with him or what they were doin'. I'd seen her with this same fella. He'd give her a ride in his car after work sometimes so she wouldn't have to take the bus. From what I observed, they didn't seem like a couple in love. In fact, I got the impression she didn't much care for him. She never smiled when she was with him."

"I wouldn't have brought it up at all," Roonie said, "but Velvet told me about Mae gettin' worked up at the hospital when the nurse came in and reminded me that Mae's roommate, Sissy, had been a yellow-haired gal that went missing." He gave a shrug. "I don't know if any of this has any meaning or significance, but we figured it best to tell you anyway. I know you want to help your aunt."

I sighed. "Thank you. I don't know what any of it means either."

The couple left a short time later. I put the casserole in the refrigerator, along with the soup I'd made. I wasn't sure if Dad would be home for dinner tonight, but we'd enjoy the yummy dishes the rest of the week. Once things were tidy, I let Peggy outside and sat on the porch steps while she wandered the yard.

Roonie's story about Aunt Mae stirred up more questions.

Was Sissy the yellow-haired gal that Roonie saw? If so, why was Aunt Mae with the same man? Who was he? Clive Morrison? It wouldn't make any sense for her to be with him, considering he'd filed an official complaint against her with the military police. Yet he'd also claimed they were romantically involved. The whole thing didn't make any sense.

The telephone jangled from inside the house. I hurried to catch it on the fourth ring.

"Hi, Laurel," Jonas said. "Is this a bad time?"

Just the sound of his deep voice brought a smile to my lips. "Not at all. I was outside with Peggy."

"How's your aunt? I haven't had a chance to go by the hospital today."

I filled him in on Dad's arrival and the hope that Aunt Mae would come home tomorrow.

"Velvet and Roonie stopped by." I paused. "Roonie remembered something about Aunt Mae from the days when they all worked in Oak Ridge during the war."

"From the sound in your voice, I gather it wasn't good."

I exhaled a long breath. "I don't know if it's good or bad, significant or unimportant. Honestly, I don't know if anything we've discovered even matters now. Like I keep saying, all of this happened thirty-something years ago."

He was quiet for a long moment. "I know you're frustrated. Would a burger and a milkshake at Hoskin's drugstore help?"

I heard the humor in his voice and grinned. "You read my mind."

"Great. My shift ends in an hour. How about I pick you up?"

"I'll see you then. Thank you, Jonas. I feel better already."

"That was the plan. See you soon."

I replaced the receiver, my mood lighter. Jonas was a great listener. He also had experience that came from being a cop. I'd tell him what Roonie and Velvet said and see what he thought.

"Peggy," I said to the little dog as we went inside. "I have a date tonight. If you're a good girl, I'll bring you some french fries."

She let out a yap of approval.

Dad was at Aunt Mae's house when Jonas and I returned from dinner. For some reason, I was nervous for the two of them to meet. I hadn't dated a lot since high school, so bringing men home was not something I did often. And although Jonas and I weren't officially dating, there was something about him and the way I felt when I was with him that told me he was special.

"Dad, this is Jonas Tyson. Jonas, this is my dad, Harris Willett. Jonas is the police detective I told you about who helped the day Aunt Mae had her accident."

The men shook hands.

"It's nice to meet you, sir," Jonas said. "I'm sorry about your sister. Mae is well loved in our community."

We settled in the living room, with Jonas and me on the sofa and Dad in Aunt Mae's favorite chair.

"I'm glad to know that," Dad said.

His gaze ping-ponged between Jonas and me. I could practically hear the wheels of his mind turning, wondering what was going on between his daughter and the cop. I'd phoned him at the hospital earlier to let him know I was going to dinner with a friend. I'd asked if I could bring him something, but he'd declined. What I hadn't said was that my friend was a man.

"How was Aunt Mae when you left her?" I asked. "Is she coming home tomorrow?"

Dad's expression grew serious. "She's been a bit confused this afternoon. The doctor isn't too worried, but they'll watch her overnight and decide in the morning if she should be released or not."

"I'm sorry to hear that. What do you mean when you say she's confused?"

His brow furrowed. "She didn't recognize me. Didn't know I was her brother. She kept asking who I was, and when I'd tell her I was Harris, she'd shake her head. 'Harry is only eleven years old,' she'd say. When an orderly came in with her dinner tray, she called him Garlyn. The young man looked at me for an explanation, but I've never heard the name before."

"I have," I said, surprising him. "Just the other day she mentioned a friend by that name. Someone she worked with at K-25. I got the impression she'd liked him, but they never officially dated. It's almost as if the concussion has made her mind travel back in time."

I glanced between the men. Jonas and I hadn't talked about Aunt Mae while we enjoyed our burgers, which helped get my mind off the mystery for a while. But now it felt right to share the latest information with both of them.

"Velvet and Roonie stopped by earlier. Roonie remembered something about Aunt Mae from the early years in Oak Ridge. I'm not sure what to make of it."

When I finished telling them the story Roonie had shared with me, Dad looked perplexed.

"I don't understand." He shook his head. "My sister has always been a woman of high morals. Our mama instilled biblical principles of honesty, integrity, and faithfulness in us from the time we were born. I'll admit I didn't always live up to them, but Mae did. She had a strong sense of what was right and what was wrong."

"Velvet didn't think Aunt Mae and the man she was with had a romantic relationship," I hurried to add. "They didn't seem like a couple in her opinion."

"But remember the complaint that Morrison fellow filed with the MPs," Dad said, concern in his voice. "He claimed he and my sister were lovers and Mae broke into his home in an act of revenge. I wonder if he was the driver of the car."

Dad had a point. "Then there's the other girl Roonie saw in the same car with the same man," I said. "She was blonde."

"Do you think it was Sissy?" Jonas asked.

I shrugged. "Maybe. The complaint Morrison filed said he believed Aunt Mae was jealous of his interest in Sissy. If the occupants of the car Roonie saw were Morrison and Sissy, and then Morrison and Aunt Mae, it would appear that Morrison did indeed have a relationship with both women. I wish we knew more about the timeline of when Roonie saw Aunt Mae with him. Was it before the break-in and the fire or after? Was it before Sissy went missing or sometime later?"

"Remind me what happened to Sissy," Dad said.

I told him everything we knew, which wasn't much. "When Aunt Mae saw the nurse with the same color of hair, her reaction was one of genuine fear for Sissy's well-being. It makes me wonder if something bad happened to Sissy. And if so, did Aunt Mae witness it? Does it have something to do with Clive Morrison? There are so many questions, but the only person with the answers isn't talking."

A troubled expression settled on his face. "I admit all of this has me concerned. I would have never thought my sister could have so many secrets in her past, but I guess everyone does." He paused. "Let's keep this to ourselves for now. We need to focus on getting Mae home and feeling better. I'm hoping I can convince her to move to Boston. With her eyesight failing, it doesn't seem wise for her to live alone anymore."

I reached for his hand across the small space between the sofa and chair. "I'm happy to stay with her until you and she decide what to do about the future. I don't need to be back in Boston until mid-August."

"Thank you, sweetheart. That'll help a lot." He heaved a sigh and stood. Peggy, who'd been curled at his feet, also stood and stretched. "I'm beat. I think I'll grab a glass of water and call it a night. It was good to meet you, Jonas. Thank you for all your help with my sister."

Jonas also stood and shook hands with Dad. "Glad to do it, sir. Let me know if there's anything else you, Mae, or Laurel need."

I gave Dad a hug, then he headed to the kitchen.

"He insists on sleeping on the pullout sofa," I whispered. "I'm sorry I can't invite you to stay for some lemonade."

"That's okay." We moved to the porch, listening as crickets

and tree frogs sang a peaceful melody. "I enjoyed hanging out with you tonight." His gaze held mine. "I know it's selfish, but I hope you stay in Oak Ridge a while longer. I like being with you, Laurel Willett."

My stomach did a little flip. I couldn't look away. "I like being with you too, Detective Tyson."

His lips lifted in a grin. "I'll see you tomorrow."

I watched him drive away, unable to stop smiling.

After Peggy went outside, I locked the door and made up the sofa bed for Dad. He came out of the bathroom while I was finishing up.

"Jonas seems like a nice young man," he said.

I nodded. "He is. He's been extremely helpful, both with my research and with Aunt Mae."

Dad chuckled. "I promise not to read too much into this, but you know your mother is going to have a thousand questions if I tell her about Jonas."

I groaned. "Then let's not. Jonas and I are just friends. Even if I stay in Oak Ridge a little longer, my life is in Boston. His life is here."

Dad studied me a lengthy moment. "All I'll say is, life is short, Laurel. You don't want to live with regrets. I'm starting to wonder if that's what my sister's life has been like all these years. Secrets and regrets."

His words followed me as I readied for bed. Peggy ditched me in favor of sleeping with Dad on the couch, so I stretched out in the dark and gazed out the window at the stars. I said a prayer for Aunt Mae, then whispered, "Lord, I don't know what's happening between Jonas and me, but I really like him. I know you have plans and purposes for each of our lives. Lead both of us as we spend time together."

Sweet dreams claimed me the moment "Amen" crossed my lips.

CHAPTER TWENTY-SEVEN
MAE

I'D NEVER HAD A HANGOVER, but the way I felt when I arrived for the morning shift at K-25 must surely be close. My head throbbed. My stomach rebelled at the thought of food. My eyes were bleary and bloodshot. But unlike the girls in the dorm who sometimes suffered the malady from too much strong drink, my condition was brought on by something far worse.

I'd awakened to a pitch-black room sometime after midnight. My body was stiff from lying on the hard wood, and I'd been confused as to why I was on the floor. The bulb on the lamp had burned out, but the moment I flicked the switch to the overhead light and saw Sissy's Christmas gifts from her family, fresh agony flooded my entire being.

Clive killed Sissy.

Those awful words rolled through my brain, over and over, like a record album with a deep scar. There was no other explanation for Sissy's sudden disappearance. While I had assumed she was home with her family, they thought she was safe in Oak Ridge.

Her mother's letter, however, revealed the truth. Clive had lied. About everything.

I'd stayed awake the rest of the night, vacillating between grief and despair, fear and revulsion. I'd cried until I had no more tears left. After that, I became angry. I railed at God for letting this happen, demanding answers. Sissy believed in him, so why didn't he protect her? Why allow Clive to get away with the evil things he'd done?

After I readied for work and caught a bus to K-25, different questions poured into my mind.

What should I do now? Who could I tell? Would anyone believe me?

The evidence pointed to Clive's guilt, but his position at Clinton Engineer Works afforded him a level of respect someone like me didn't possess. Although I could hand over the documents hidden behind the headboard to the authorities, they would only prove that he was a spy. It would be much more difficult to convince anyone he was involved in murder. Other than finding Sissy's badge in his trailer, I had no tangible proof of his guilt. No proof that Sissy was even dead.

A grisly thought nearly brought me to my knees as I clocked in for the day.

Only the discovery of Sissy's body would lead to Clive's arrest.

The very idea brought on nausea, making me grimace when I walked into the maintenance shop. Mr. Colby stood just inside the entry, talking to one of the workers, but when he glanced my way, his expression told me I must look a fright.

After he finished with the employee, he said, "Willett, my office. Now."

Once the door was closed and we'd each taken a seat, he asked, "What's going on, Mae? You look awful."

The fact that he'd used my first name caused tears to spring to my eyes. How I wished I could tell him the truth, but I'd sound like a raving lunatic. Until I had more evidence, I had to pretend everything was fine.

"I didn't sleep much last night. I don't feel well."

"You don't look well." He hesitated. "Is there something else you want to tell me?"

My head shot up. Had Clive gotten to my boss? Told him more lies? "About what, sir?"

His gaze narrowed on me. "Ever since that MP showed up, you've been different. I have a mind to call Morrison in here and get to the bottom of things."

My eyes widened. "Please don't do that, sir."

He studied me for a long moment before he leaned back in his chair. "Did you know I have a daughter?" At the shake of my head, he continued. "Belle is ten years old, and as precocious as they come. I'd do everything in my power to keep that girl safe. I'd do the same for you, too, Willett. So, if there is anything—*anything*—you want to tell me, now is your chance."

My heart hammered.

How I longed to blurt out the entire, horrific story, right here in the privacy of Mr. Colby's office. But the only thing I could prove with any certainty was Clive's traitorous behavior. If he was arrested for spying, would the military police look into Sissy's disappearance? Doubtful, since people left Oak Ridge every week with little to no notice. It wasn't unusual for someone to simply not show up for work or disappear from the dormitory. The authorities would be more concerned about Clive's espionage than a missing girl. As much as I loved my country and despised what Clive was doing, proving he was responsible for Sissy vanishing was far more important to me than the secret documents he snuck out of K-25 and gave to the Russians.

I shook my head. "There's nothing to tell, sir." *Not yet,* I added silently. But I would keep searching, keep watching Clive, until I knew what happened to Sissy. Then I would take Mr. Colby up on his offer and make sure Clive Morrison paid for what he'd done.

My boss didn't look happy with my answer but didn't press the subject. "Go home, Willett. You can't do your job if you're sick, and I don't want you spreading something around to the other employees. If you need tomorrow off too, take it."

I thanked him and left the office. I knew I wasn't contagious, but I welcomed the time off. To think. To process. To plan.

The same guard who'd checked my ID badge when I'd entered the plant a short time ago checked it again as I exited. I thought he might question me, but he simply returned the badge and moved on to the person behind me.

Because it wasn't time for a shift change, there were no lines when I arrived at the transportation terminal. I walked toward a bus going to town, but a glance to the west brought my feet to a halt. I stared at the tree line beyond K-25 to where a dirt path disappeared into dense foliage. It was the same road Clive had taken the evening he told me about Oak Ridge's secret. The same road he took when he and Sissy drove out to the river, including the day she vanished.

I shivered, but it had nothing to do with the crisp December air.

If Clive killed Sissy, as I was now convinced, he would've had to bury her body somewhere. By his own admission, they'd driven to their favorite spot just past S-50 to talk. While I couldn't bear to think about what happened to my friend that day, if a fresh grave existed, it would be easy to detect. Finding it was the only thing that would convince the authorities to arrest Clive for murder as well as espionage.

And I was the only one who knew where to look.

If I was going to do this, I had to get to S-50. It was only a couple miles, I guessed, but someone walking down the road would draw unnecessary attention. I didn't have clearance for S-50 and would be in trouble if I got caught. Even if I could get one of the bus drivers I was familiar with to ignore rules and transport me to the plant this one time, I didn't want anyone to know where I was going. The fact that I even knew about another uranium enrichment facility could cast a shadow of suspicion around me.

With my mind made up, I turned toward the west and started out on foot. I'd simply have to keep aware of oncoming traffic and dart into the woods before anyone saw me. Luckily it hadn't rained lately, so the road was dry. I'd traipsed around our mining community my whole life—up and down hills and hollers, and along animal paths in thick woods—so walking long distances wasn't difficult. Yet the terrible mission I was on made my steps heavy. I didn't know why the burden of proof fell to me, but Sissy had been my roommate and friend. She deserved to have the person responsible for harming her held accountable.

Every so often, I turned to look behind me. It felt as though the trees had eyes, watching my every step. Thankfully only one car passed by, but I'd ducked into the brush. I wasn't certain what I would say should someone stop and ask what I was doing way out there. Maybe I'd tell them Mr. Colby sent me on a confidential errand. With so many secrets in play in Oak Ridge, no one would know if I was telling the truth or not.

The sound of a train rumbling on the other side of the woods to my right brought me to a standstill. I couldn't remember if the tracks crossed the road or ran parallel, but I didn't want an engineer or railroad workers to spot me. I let the train pass before I resumed my journey.

After walking for nearly an hour, S-50 came into view. Once again, I found it shocking to see the plant. The train I'd heard pass was now stopped near a large structure with three tall smokestacks that belched some kind of smoke or vapor. Men worked to unload the string of railroad cars, although I couldn't see the cargo they toiled over.

With so many people nearby, I left the road and walked to the edge of the Clinch. Unlike most riverbanks, this one had been scraped clean of vegetation when S-50 was built, with no brush or trees to offer cover as I followed the water's edge past the plant. While I didn't run, I did pick up the pace and was soon around the bend, hopeful no one had noticed me.

When I reached the area where Clive had parked the car the day we'd come here, I stopped to catch my breath. Piles of unused building materials were scattered here and there. Thick forest grew untouched across the river, but the Clinch was wide. One would have to drive to the Gallaher Gate and cross over the bridge to get to the woods. To the north, behind S-50, were more woods.

My shoulders sagged. A grave could be anywhere.

Tears sprang to my eyes, but I wouldn't let myself give up. Sissy needed me to do this. I set about searching. The piles. The woods. Everything in between. I had just sat on a fallen tree to take a rest when I heard voices.

"Let's check over here," a man said. "She can't be far."

My heart nearly leaped out of my chest. I couldn't get caught. I'd lose my job. I might even be arrested. As quietly as possible, I scrambled to crawl behind the log and pressed my body up against it, trying to still my ragged breath.

Brush rustled loudly nearby. "I don't see anything," another man said.

A horse snorted, followed by someone saying, "Easy, girl."

I gulped.

The men must be mounted military officers. I'd seen them on their horses from time to time, patrolling the riverbanks near K-25. I'd always wondered why it was necessary to have such intense military presence and security measures throughout the Reservation. After Clive revealed the secret mission everyone in Oak Ridge was working on, whether they knew it or not, things made sense.

"Let's go. Whoever was out here is gone. It was probably just someone taking a walk on their lunch break."

I waited until everything was quiet again before I peeked over the log. The men and their horses were nowhere in sight. I retook my seat on the rough tree bark, frightened and discouraged. Tears rolled down my face unchecked.

I hadn't found any signs of freshly turned dirt or mounds of debris. No signs of a struggle or a terrible crime. Was I wrong? Had Clive been telling the truth when he said he drove Sissy back to the dorm?

"What should I do, Lord? You know where Sissy is," I whispered, the words choking me. "Help me find her."

In the stillness of the woods, I listened.

A Canadian goose honked. A chipmunk squeaked. A splash drew my eyes to the wide river. The Clinch snaked around a bend, making its way south.

My pulse began to race as I stared at the moving water. "No," I breathed.

But suddenly I knew.

Without care for the mounted patrol, I ran out of the woods and didn't stop until I stood at the river's edge. The water flowed at a lazy pace. Dark. Dangerous.

I dropped to the ground, my body shaking.

Almost like a scene from a horror movie, the image of Clive carrying Sissy to the river filled my mind's eye. I shook my head and covered my face, sobbing.

There was no grave, I realized. No freshly turned earth. No body for the authorities to discover.

Sissy was gone.

The river had carried her away.

It was nearly dark when I dragged myself up from the riverbank and started for home. I didn't care if the mounted men found me. I didn't care if I lost my job or even if they arrested me. Sissy was dead, and I was the only one who knew the truth.

As I'd lain on the hard ground, weeping, I came to a conclusion. I would tell Mr. Colby everything. Today. Now. He often worked late hours, and I hoped he would still be in his office when I returned to K-25. If he wasn't, I'd wait all night until he arrived in the morning. Clive needed to be arrested. To rot in prison for what he'd done. I would see this thing through for Sissy's sake.

Bundled in my coat against the chilly night air, I crept past S-50, thankful for the shadows. No one called out an alarm. I continued on until I reached the main road. Night sounds filled the woods on either side of me. When two cars approached, I hid in the brush. Neither stopped.

More than an hour later, I crested a rise and nearly wept. I'd never been so relieved to see the massive structure of K-25 rising up out of the Tennessee soil, illuminated by outdoor lights. I quickened my pace. The sooner I got to Mr. Colby's office, the sooner all of this would be over.

I'd almost reached the edge of the compound when headlights from an approaching car landed on me. There wasn't anywhere to hide this time, but it didn't matter. I had every right to be at K-25.

The car swerved into my path and stopped, forcing me to step off the road. With lights blinding me, the door opened, but I couldn't see the reckless driver.

"Hello, Mae."

Clive's voice sent a wave of terror crashing through me, and I stood, frozen to the ground. He walked to the front of the car and leaned his hip against the hood, blocking one of the headlamps. With a casualness that belied the situation, he took a cigarette from his pocket, lit it, and took a long drag. All I could do was stand there like a hunted animal, too afraid to move.

"I looked for you today. A girl in Mr. Colby's office said you were out sick, so I went to your dorm. Funny thing is, no one had seen you all day. Not even your housemother, who checked your room. When I got to the barracks a little while ago, I overheard some of the MPs talking about a woman down by the river. 'Surely it's not Mae,' I said to myself. 'Why would she be down there?' But two plus two always adds up, so I came to see for myself." He took another drag and blew out the smoke. "What were you doing, Mae?"

Anger and disgust replaced my fear. I was done letting this creep intimidate me.

"I was looking for Sissy's body."

I let the words hang in the cold air. If he tried to silence me, as he'd done to my roommate, I would fight with everything I had in me. I'd left my purse in the dorm that morning, the knife still inside, but it didn't matter. Justice and anger would be my weapons.

I couldn't see his face because of the bright light, but I could well imagine his surprised expression when he heard the truth come from my lips. Did panic roll through him at finding his crime had been exposed? That would be satisfying.

But he simply puffed on the cigarette one last time before tossing it to the ground. With methodical movements, he ground the butt into the dirt with his shoe. Then he took a step toward me.

My body tensed, prepared to run. "Stay away from me, Clive Morrison. You may think you've gotten away with your crimes, but I know what you've done. I won't rest until I see you behind bars."

We stood facing each other for long moments. A standoff of good and evil.

He leaned against the front of the car again and crossed his arms. "You think you're smart, don't you, Mae?" He laughed, although the sound was not pleasant. "Here's some advice. Don't ever play poker. You just gave away your hand."

I frowned. "What are you talking about?"

"You've got nothing left. No leverage. No ace up your sleeve. You just told me exactly what you plan to do."

My heart sank. He was right. I shouldn't have blurted everything out.

"I see I was right." He straightened. "Here's what's going to happen. You're going to get in this car, and I'm going to take you home. We're going to pretend this conversation never took place. The day after Christmas, you'll give me the documents, then I'll bid you farewell. We never have to speak to each other again."

I shook my head. "I don't give a rat's behind about the documents. Sissy is dead. I'm sure of it."

"There you go, letting your wild imagination rule out common sense. Sissy took off because she was embarrassed and hurt. She's home with her family in the backwoods of Georgia right this minute." He turned and walked to the driver's side of the vehicle. "It's getting cold. Get in the car and let me take you home."

I stared at him in disbelief. "You're a liar. Sissy's family hasn't seen her. Her mother sent—"

I clamped my mouth shut. I'd done it again. I'd given away too much information.

He stood perfectly still. "What did her mother send?" When I didn't answer, he took a menacing step forward. "You don't want to mess with me, Mae. There's too much at stake to let some simpleton ruin everything. First one from Georgia, and now one from Kentucky."

My blood surged. He'd all but confessed to killing Sissy.

"This simpleton from Kentucky has you figured out." I bent down to pick up a good-sized rock and drew my arm back as if to throw the stone at him. "Get in your car and leave. Don't ever bother me again or you'll be sorry."

Neither of us moved.

"You've made a huge mistake, Mae. A mistake that will cost you." His voice was calm. Too calm. "I've done some checking around, and I know all about your family. With my connections, it wasn't hard to find out where they live. I don't imagine it would take much for a coal mine shanty to go up in flames, do you? It would be particularly tragic if someone were trapped inside because the door was nailed shut. Tsk-tsk. What a terrible end that would be, especially for a boy who hasn't made it to adolescence yet."

I sucked in a breath. "No! You wouldn't." Yet my entire body shook with terror, because I knew he would.

Oh, what had my foolish bravado done?

He offered no response. He simply turned and opened the driver's door. "Get in the car, Mae. I won't tell you again." He didn't wait to see if I would comply. He got behind the steering wheel and closed the door.

Everything inside me told me to run. Run as fast as I could through the woods to K-25 and find Mr. Colby. He'd know what to do. I could send word to Mama and Pa and tell them to get someplace safe until Clive was captured. I'd quit my job, take the next bus home, and be done with burdensome secrets and Clive's terrible crimes.

But my feet didn't move.

Clive wouldn't leave me alone now that I knew the awful truth about Sissy. I'd been a fool to reveal she hadn't returned to Georgia, but it was too late to take it back. I'd put my family in danger with my own stupidity. Clive had set fire to his trailer to cover his tracks. He'd gotten rid of Sissy because she knew too much. My parents and little brother were next if I didn't cooperate. Not even Mr. Colby could protect them.

The stone fell from my hand.

Defeat poured through me like a raging river, swallowing up every good thing in my life. If I walked away from truth and justice and ignored all that had happened up to this moment, there would be no turning back. No peace. No freedom.

No forgiveness.

But I didn't have a choice.

I walked to the car, opened the door, and climbed inside.

CHAPTER TWENTY-EIGHT
LAUREL

DAD AND I WERE UP EARLY the next morning, hoping Aunt Mae would be released from the hospital. I hadn't been able to sleep last night and ended up going over notes from the interviews I'd conducted thus far, as well as things I'd jotted down at the library. While I greatly appreciated Georgeanne and the others sharing their personal stories with me, Aunt Mae's refusal to share hers made me more determined than ever to dig into the secrets and heavy emotions people who worked on the Manhattan Project experienced then and now.

When we arrived at the hospital, the doctor was with Aunt Mae. We greeted them both, then Dad moved to the opposite side of the bed and took her good hand. I noticed she was wearing her new glasses.

"How's my favorite sister doing today? I trust you're behaving yourself, Maebelle."

Aunt Mae didn't smile at his teasing. "I've been a model patient, Harry, but if they don't let me go home today, I may have to change tactics."

Dad looked relieved. I knew he'd been worried about Aunt Mae not recognizing him the previous day. Except for the yellowish bruises on her face and small cast on her wrist, it seemed she was back to her usual self.

We looked to the doctor for his response.

"I was just telling Ms. Willett that while she has improved, she is still experiencing symptoms from the concussion." He glanced down to Aunt Mae. "You had a very restless night and experienced confusion regarding the nurse's identity. But"—he included all of us in his gaze—"she's better this morning. We were discussing whether she should spend another night in our care."

"And I told him I would sleep better in my own bed." Aunt Mae's face bore a scowl. "I don't see what all the fuss is about. Just let me leave and get on with life."

The doctor didn't seem offended at her gruff words. "The fuss, Ms. Willett, is that brain injuries take time to heal. It could be up to a month before you feel normal again. Headaches, fatigue, mood swings, memory problems, and even seizures are all part of the healing process. These symptoms aren't to be taken lightly."

"She lives alone." Concern edged Dad's voice. "Do you recommend someone stay with her until she's recovered?"

"I don't need a babysitter, Harry," Aunt Mae said, clearly annoyed by the suggestion. "I can take care of myself."

"I disagree," the doctor said. "It would be best if you weren't alone for the first week or two, depending on the level of symptoms you experience. We don't want to see you in the emergency room again because you lost your balance and took a tumble." He turned to Dad. "I'm willing to release her into your care today, but I strongly caution against resuming her independent lifestyle right away."

"I understand." Dad glanced at me. "Laurel has volunteered to stay with Mae, through the summer, if necessary."

Aunt Mae's gaze shifted to me. After a long moment, her expression softened a bit. "That's very kind of you, Laurel. I'm sure it won't come to that, though."

"I'm glad to be of help, Aunt Mae." We exchanged smiles.

Dad and the doctor left the room to tend to paperwork. With a nurse's help, we got Aunt Mae dressed in the clean clothes I'd brought with us. By the time Dad returned to the room, Aunt Mae sat in a wheelchair, ready to escape the hospital.

"I hope we're doing the right thing," he said as the nurse pushed the chair toward the exit. "Another night in the hospital might not be a bad idea."

"It's a terrible idea." Aunt Mae kept her eyes fixed on the glass doors ahead. "I want to go home. Have you been taking good care of Peggy?"

I assured her the little dog was fine but missing her, which seemed to please her. The drive didn't take long. As Dad pulled his rental car into the driveway, Aunt Mae got emotional.

"It's good to see my little house again," she said, her voice wobbly.

She was weak, so Dad and I got on either side of her and slowly made our way to the house. Peggy danced and yapped, making us all laugh.

"At least *someone* is happy I'm home," Aunt Mae said once she was settled in her chair, with Peggy in her lap.

Dad's gaze met mine. He rolled his eyes, then took the small suitcase to Aunt Mae's bedroom.

"It's a bit early for lunch, but can I get you something to eat?" I knelt in front of her and petted Peggy's head. "Velvet and Roonie brought tuna casserole and peach cobbler."

"That was nice of them," she said. "I had a decent breakfast, although the bacon was soggy. We'll save the casserole for supper."

A knock sounded at the front door.

Aunt Mae huffed. "I'll bet a nickel it's Georgeanne. She's probably been glued to her front window, watching for us."

I hid a smile and opened the door. There stood Aunt Mae's neighbor, holding a covered dish.

"I saw y'all pull into the driveway." She pushed the container into my hands, stepped past me, and went directly to Aunt Mae. "You certainly gave us a scare, Mae. I'm glad you're home, safe and sound, but dear me, what an ordeal. I've never had a concussion, but my daughter's youngest boy had one last year. Fell off his bike. She had to sit with him all night to make sure he didn't slip into a coma."

Aunt Mae's mouth was a straight line. "I'm fine."

Georgeanne settled on the sofa, clearly prepared for a lengthy visit. "You can't be too careful though. I happened to drive past the police station yesterday and saw your poor car sitting in the lot. 'It's a wonder Mae and that other fella weren't hurt worse,' I said to myself. Guess you'll have to get a new car."

I watched Aunt Mae's expression harden. She opened her mouth to reply just as Dad entered the room.

"Hi there, Georgeanne," he said. "I thought I heard your voice. How's the family?"

Georgeanne greeted Dad and launched into one story after another about her kids and grands. After long minutes of bragging about her grandson's skills in Little League baseball and her granddaughter's ballet classes, Dad cleared his throat.

"It was kind of you to come check on Mae, but I think it's best if she rests now," he said. "The doctor encouraged her to take things nice and easy."

Georgeanne took the hint and rose. "Of course. I made a chicken and rice casserole for your supper, although I know Velvet brought over some things, too. Y'all let me know if there's anything I can do. Take care, Mae."

The woman chattered as Dad walked her outside. As soon as he returned and closed the door, Aunt Mae heaved a sigh.

"I know Georgeanne means well," she said, "but I've often wished I'd bought a house one block over so I wouldn't have to live next to her. That woman wears me out." She motioned me over. "Take Peggy outside, please. I think I'll lie down for a bit."

While I took the dog out, Dad helped his sister to her room. Her eyes were already drifting closed by the time I returned. Peggy put her front paws on the side of the mattress and whined.

"Come on, sweet girl," Aunt Mae murmured. "Let's take a nap."

I lifted the little dog onto the bed where she tucked herself up against Aunt Mae's hip, then I tiptoed from the room and closed the door. Dad waited for me in the living room.

"I think I'll go down to the police station and see Mae's car for myself. Then," he said, followed by a heavy sigh, "we need to figure out a plan of some sort. I'm grateful you're willing to stay with her for a while, but that's a temporary fix. The doctor believes her eyesight is only going to get worse. She's going blind, Laurel."

The news was devastating. "Oh, Dad. Poor Aunt Mae. I wish she would agree to come to Boston."

"So do I. I'm going to do everything I can to convince her. I may need your help."

"Of course."

He left a short time later. I put the clothes Aunt Mae had worn the day of the accident into the washer with some towels Dad and I had used, then set some of the soup I'd made on the stove to simmer. With the delicious aroma filling the house and birdsong coming through the open windows, everything felt peaceful and calm. It was good to have Aunt Mae home again.

She slept most of the afternoon. Dad and I ate lunch without her, discussing different options for the future. While he called

Mom to give her an update, I went out to sit on the front porch. I'd just settled there when a police cruiser turned into the driveway.

My stomach fluttered as Jonas exited the vehicle, looking handsome in his uniform.

"Hi, there," he said with a smile as he approached. "I thought I'd come by and see how the patient is doing."

"She's happy to be home, but the doctor doesn't think she should be alone. Now or in the future. She's going blind, Jonas."

His face filled with compassion. "I'm sorry. I know that's not what you and your family wanted to hear."

"No, it's not, especially with everything else that's going on." I heaved a sigh. "I can't help but feel the stress of keeping secrets about the past played a role in Aunt Mae's accident. Who knows. Maybe it has something to do with losing her eyesight too. Stress can wreak havoc on us, mentally *and* physically. I'm convinced that whatever happened to Sissy is at the center of Aunt Mae's emotional instability, but until she's willing to talk about it, all we can do is speculate."

Jonas nodded. "Unfortunately there aren't any records from the 1940s that mention Sissy."

"I wish we knew where she lived after the war. If we could locate her, she might be able to help us understand why Aunt Mae is so afraid. Doesn't the police department have a database with information on people?"

He nodded. "On criminals and suspects, but I've already checked it for a Sylvia Galloway. I also looked for Clive Morrison, but nothing came up on either of them."

"I haven't mentioned anything about Sissy to Georgeanne," I said, glancing at the small house next door, "but if we don't get answers soon, I may ask her. If there's anyone in Oak Ridge who might know something, it would be Georgeanne."

Jonas chuckled. "She's definitely a deep well of information."

Dad's voice drifted through the open door. It sounded as though he was talking to Peggy.

"Do you want to come inside?" I asked Jonas.

He shook his head and stood. "I'm on my way to work, but," he paused, a slight grin inching up his face, "if everything is okay here tomorrow, maybe we can have dinner."

I couldn't help but smile. "That sounds nice."

"Good. I'll call you later."

Dad arrived on the porch as Jonas was driving away. He gave me a knowing look as he took a seat.

"We're just friends, Dad," I said, returning to the chair I'd been sitting in when Jonas arrived.

He chuckled. "I may be old, Laurel Ann, but I remember how I felt when your mother and I met. Your eyes light up when you're with Jonas."

I'd never been able to hide things from Dad. "I admit I like him. A lot. But my job, my family, my life is in Boston. His life is here, in Oak Ridge. A relationship beyond friendship would be too complicated."

We sat in silence for a while, looking out toward the tree-covered hills in the distance.

"Oak Ridge is a special place," he said. "Not only because it was a secret city during the war and has a fascinating history connected to the Manhattan Project, but I became a man here. Mama was frail and worn out by the time Pa passed and we moved from Kentucky to live with Mae. I was only fifteen, but I got a job after school and had to grow up. When I graduated from high school, Mae was adamant that I leave Oak Ridge. I'd planned to attend the University of Tennessee in Knoxville so I could still take care of Mama and Mae. During the war, UT started the V-12 Navy College Training Program, which offered students a path to a Navy commission. That was my plan, but Mae put her foot down."

"Wow," I said. "You were going to join the Navy?"

He nodded. "It seemed like a good option, but Mae didn't want me in the military. The war was hard on her. On everyone. She convinced me to leave all that behind and go into business. My high school accounting teacher had graduated from Boston University and helped me apply to the school. He wrote a letter of recommendation and somehow I ended up with a partial scholarship." A gentle smile touched his lips. "Mama was so proud. She told me to spread my wings and fly, so I did."

"I wish I could have known Grandma."

"She would've loved you and your sisters." He took my hand. "If I hadn't listened to Mae and changed my plans, I would have never met your mother. Life is too short to be set on one certain idea and miss all the wonderful surprises that come along. Surprises that can alter what we thought was the right path for ourselves but actually ends up being the very thing we needed to make us happy."

His words stirred something deep inside me. A hope for the future that had nothing to do with degrees and jobs. "I hear what you're saying, Daddy."

He kissed my knuckles. "Now," he said, a teasing tone in his voice, "I'm not telling you to move away from us. There are plenty of jobs for cops in Boston."

I had to laugh at that.

It was after five o'clock when Aunt Mae roused. She was groggy and weak but wanted to sit in the living room and watch the evening news.

"Remember what the doctor said about overstimulation," Dad reminded her. "Television, radio, and reading are to be limited until your brain fully heals."

"I just want to hear what Walter Cronkite has to say, then we can shut it off." She rubbed her temple. "I do have a bit of a headache."

"Can I get you some aspirin, Aunt Mae?" I jumped up from my place on the sofa, ready to help.

"No, dear, but thank you. I took some a little while ago."

I watched her closely, concerned about the slight slurring of her words. When I glanced at Dad, he nodded, indicating he'd noticed it too. He clicked on the television set and turned the knob to switch channels. Walter Cronkite's familiar voice soon filled the room.

The Dow Jones was up, while treasury bill rates dropped. A leak caused the 800-mile Trans-Alaska pipeline to be shut down. Race car driver Bobby Unser broke a three-year victory drought.

Then Cronkite's voice turned serious.

"In news from Great Britain, the trial of Letty Gladding, the woman arrested for spying for Russia, is over."

Aunt Mae uttered a strange sound. When I looked her way, I found her wide eyes fixed on the television screen.

"Mrs. Gladding was found guilty of violating the Official Secrets Act, legislation that provides for the protection of state secrets and official information," Cronkite continued. A mugshot of Mrs. Gladding filled the screen behind him. "During World War II and in the years that followed, Mrs. Gladding worked in British government offices as a secretary. She has been found guilty of passing classified information to the Soviets, including materials regarding Tube Alloys, the British atomic weapons program during the 1940s. She is the latest of what are being called 'atomic spies' to be prosecuted. Here in the United States, it is believed many spies within the Manhattan Project have yet to be positively identified."

The jingle for a laundry detergent commercial replaced his solemn voice.

"It's crazy that they're still uncovering spies all these years later," Dad said.

"Mrs. Gladding was arrested the day I came to the house and

asked you all those questions about Oak Ridge," I said. "I wouldn't know about the Secret City if I hadn't walked into the faculty lounge while Dr. Baca was watching the news."

I turned to see what Aunt Mae thought about the fascinating story.

"Aunt Mae, have you ever . . . ?" My voice trailed. Something was wrong. Her face had gone pale, eyes glazed over. Her body shook. "Aunt Mae?"

Dad and I rose simultaneously.

"Mae?" Dad knelt in front of her. "Can you hear me, Mae?"

"I didn't want to do it," she whispered, panic in the words. "He made me. He was going to hurt Harry and Mama and Pa, just like he hurt Sissy. I couldn't let him do it. I couldn't let him." She began to sob uncontrollably.

Dad gathered her into his arms. She clung to him, desperation in her tight grip.

"I'll get some water." I ran to the kitchen and filled a glass. I also grabbed a dish towel, wet the edge, and hurried back to the living room.

Dad gently pulled out of Aunt Mae's frantic clutches. I handed him the glass.

"Have a sip of water, Mae," he said, his voice full of worry. "You need to calm down and tell me what's happening." He tipped the glass to her lips, but she pushed it away, sloshing it onto her lap.

"You don't understand." Fear flooded her eyes as her gaze darted around the room. "He knows. He knows where I live. Where Harry lives. The girls. He'll hurt them if I ever tell anyone. Oh, Sissy, Sissy. I don't know what to do." She covered her face with her hands and sobbed. "I don't know what to do."

Dad stood and motioned me into the hallway. "I think we should get her back to the hospital. It was a mistake to bring her home so soon."

"I'll call the emergency number," I said and hurried into the kitchen to use the telephone. When I returned to the living room, Dad was crouched beside Aunt Mae, holding her hand while she muttered unintelligibly.

The sound of a siren soon echoed in the warm evening air. I opened the door as it came closer. Not only did an ambulance arrive within the next minute, but a police cruiser too. Jonas climbed out and strode to where I stood on the porch.

"I was on patrol and heard the call," he said, concern in his eyes.

My voice trembled as I quickly told him what had happened. We followed the ambulance attendants into the house where they gathered around Aunt Mae, blocking our view of her.

"Ms. Willett, do you know where you are?" one of the men asked. Aunt Mae mumbled something that sounded like *home*. The attendant asked more questions, then turned to Dad to get the full story on the situation.

When one of the men stepped to the side, Aunt Mae's gaze landed on Jonas.

Her eyes grew wild, and she let out a piercing scream. "Don't arrest me. Don't arrest me. He made me do it. I didn't want to take the papers. I didn't want to, but I had to protect my family. I couldn't let him hurt them. I couldn't."

She grew more hysterical, fighting the ambulance attendants. Dad tried to calm her, but it was as though she didn't hear him. As though her mind had carried her away to another time and place. A place where she lived in fear.

It was excruciating to watch. Tears rolled down my face. Jonas put his arm around me and pulled me against his side.

With Dad's permission, the men sedated Aunt Mae. In a matter of seconds, she grew quiet. While one of the men took her pulse, the other motioned us outside to talk. When we gained the porch, I noticed Georgeanne stood beside her mailbox with several people. I'm sure Aunt Mae and the ambulance were the talk of the neighborhood.

"I believe your sister suffered a panic attack," the man said. "Her blood pressure is elevated, but it isn't alarming. I don't see signs of stroke or any other serious condition that would warrant hospitalization. However, we can transport her to the emergency room for observation, if that's your wish."

Dad's face bore his concern. "I don't really know what to do. She seemed fine this morning when the doctor released her."

"She may have more episodes of panic and confusion while her brain heals from the concussion," the attendant explained, "but unless she's in danger of hurting herself physically, I don't believe it's necessary to hospitalize her. Her doctor can prescribe a mild sedative you can administer at home, but it's your decision, sir."

Dad's worried gaze met mine. "What do you think, Laurel? Can we handle things here?"

I bit my lip. "I'd hate for her to have to go back to the hospital."

"I feel the same." He returned his attention to the ambulance attendant. "I guess we'll see how things go here. I'll contact the doctor and let him know what's happened. We appreciate you fellows coming out."

The men helped us get Aunt Mae into her bed, then packed up their equipment and left. Dad, Jonas, and I moved into the kitchen. I set about making a pot of coffee. We needed something stronger than lemonade.

"I wish I knew what upset her." Dad dropped onto a chair. "We were watching television one minute, then she was out of control."

"Laurel, didn't you say Walter Cronkite was talking about the woman who was a Russian spy when Mae became agitated?" Jonas asked.

I nodded. "It's the same story that led me to discover the secret about Oak Ridge." I repeated as many details about Letty Gladding's arrest and trial as I could remember. "That's when I noticed Aunt Mae acting strangely. She started talking about someone hurting Grandma, Grandpa, and Dad. She kept saying she didn't want to do it, but *he* made her."

Dad frowned. "I have no idea what any of it means."

Jonas's serious expression told me he was in detective mode. "When she saw me, she begged me not to arrest her and said she hadn't wanted to take the papers. That *he* made her take them."

The three of us looked at one another.

Dad's eyes grew wide. "You don't think she meant—"

He didn't finish the question, but I knew what he was going to say. "That she stole secret documents while she worked at K-25?"

The loaded question hung in the silence.

"That's impossible," Dad said, yet he didn't sound convinced.

"I can't imagine her doing anything like that either, but it would explain why Aunt Mae has been so secretive. Why she doesn't want to talk about things that happened during the war." I glanced at Jonas. "If someone forced her to commit a crime, that would explain why she's so frightened about revisiting the past. But," I paused, shaking my head, unable to believe what I was about to say, "could the kind and wonderful woman we all know and love be guilty of . . . *espionage*?"

"I'm afraid that would be my guess at this point," Jonas said, his voice and expression somber. "We won't know until she's lucid and able to tell us what's going on." He looked every bit a policeman in that moment.

Dad slowly rose, his gaze fixed on Jonas. "Are you going to take my sister in to be interrogated?"

Jonas shook his head. "No, sir, I'm not. That isn't what I meant.

But," he glanced between Dad and me, "if Mae is guilty of espionage, the authorities will need to be notified."

I gasped. "No," I said. Dad grasped my hand, and we clung to each other. "It happened a long time ago. Even if she did steal confidential documents, it doesn't matter now. Letty Gladding worked for the British government for years. She's been supplying them information throughout the Cold War. That's why they arrested her."

A look of compassion filled Jonas's face. "I understand that, Laurel. But a number of people have been prosecuted for spying during the Manhattan Project. If Mae passed confidential information to the enemy, she is guilty of espionage too."

My heart raced, and Dad's grip on my hand tightened.

"The only thing Mae is guilty of is having a wild hallucination, brought on by an injury to her brain," Dad said, his voice firm. "I appreciate your kindness to our family, Detective Tyson, but I think it's time for you to leave."

I shot a look at Dad. He was dead serious.

"I understand, sir." Jonas's gaze met mine. "Let me know if I can be of help."

I nodded and watched him leave, torn between wanting him to stay and wishing he'd never come in the first place. That a police officer had witnessed what might be Aunt Mae's confession to espionage was alarming.

Dad's shoulders slumped once the door closed behind Jonas. "What in the world has my sister gotten herself involved in?" He rubbed his face with both hands and sank down onto the sofa. "This could turn into a real mess. Especially now that your cop friend knows."

"Jonas is a good man, Dad. He wouldn't do anything to hurt Aunt Mae."

"You heard him, Laurel. If Mae is guilty of passing secret documents during the war, she could go to prison, just like Letty Gladding."

The sobering truth punched me in the gut. "What do we do now?"

His grim face said it all. "Wait for Mae to come to her senses and tell us what the devil is going on."

CHAPTER TWENTY-NINE
MAE

CHRISTMAS CAME AND WENT. The new year arrived. The war continued. People moved to Oak Ridge nearly every day to work on the secret project. I'd heard there were more than seventy thousand residents on the Reservation now. Everyone carried on as usual.

Everyone except me.

My life ended the day Clive Morrison threatened my family. I thought I'd be rid of him when I returned the stolen papers to him the day after Christmas . . . but I was wrong.

"I know Mr. Colby gives you certain documents to take to the incinerator," he'd said, a smug look on his face. We sat in Clive's car in the parking lot at Jackson Square. I hadn't wanted anyone to see me with him, so we'd agreed to meet away from the dorm.

My stomach had twisted with his words. I knew what was coming.

"I want those documents, Mae. Instead of taking them directly to the incinerator, you'll bring them to me. I'll keep the ones that interest me and give you replacements. No one will be the wiser."

"I'll be the wiser," I'd hissed, sickened by what I'd become involved in. "I'll know. Mr. Colby trusts me. I won't do it."

His eyes had narrowed on me. "Yes, Mae, you will. I'm sure I don't need to remind you of the consequences if you refuse."

Sissy's sweet face had filled my mind's eye. Mama's, Pa's, and Harris's too.

I'd climbed from the vehicle, unable to see through my tears.

That was the day I went from being an accomplice to Clive's crimes to committing full-fledged espionage. I'd aligned myself with a murderer and a spy. There was no going back. The authorities wouldn't care that I'd had no choice.

Everything was different after that. I didn't want to be around anyone for fear they'd suspect the truth. Guilt kept me from going to church, and I ate my meals by myself, refusing my friends' offers to sit at their table. Garlyn noticed. Each time he'd invite me out on a date, I'd make up an excuse of why I couldn't go. After weeks of this, he finally asked, "What's going on, Mae?"

I'd hated to do it, but I'd lied to him one last time. "I don't think we should see each other anymore. I'm sorry."

The hurt in his eyes pierced my heart, but I didn't take back the words. I saw him from time to time at K-25. He was always friendly and polite, but I knew I'd wounded him.

Mrs. Kepple assigned a new girl to my room, which thankfully prevented Clive from demanding I hide documents in the dorm again. Dorothy was a nice girl, but I wouldn't let myself get close to her. It was too dangerous. If I accidentally let something slip, we could both find ourselves at the bottom of the Clinch River.

Sissy's mama mailed more letters to her daughter after Christmas, but I sent them all back, unopened, with the words *Return to sender; not at this address* written across the front. The letters eventually stopped coming. I wouldn't let myself think about the woman's fears and heartbreak. No amount of tears or wishes could bring Sissy back. I consoled myself with the belief that she was in heaven, far away from the evils of the world.

Even Velvet felt my rebuff. If I noticed her waiting for the bus, I'd pretend I hadn't seen her friendly nod and walk the other way. On more than one occasion, Clive insisted on driving me home in order to exchange stolen documents if we hadn't had a chance to do so earlier. Garlyn happened to be at the bus terminal on one of those days, not long after I'd broken things off with him. He'd watched me climb into Clive's sedan, a question in his eyes when I'd glanced his way. I longed to run to him and tell him everything, but that would only put him in danger too. It was best to act as though my heart didn't break a little more every time I saw him.

By March, I'd passed dozens of confidential documents to Clive. I didn't know why they were important to the Russians, but Clive claimed they would help keep the world safe. I often found Mr. Colby's eyes on me, but he seemed more concerned than suspicious. I did my job and kept to myself. If anyone noticed a difference in me, no one questioned me about it.

The truth is, a lot of people were having difficulties dealing with news from the war, losing loved ones, and the constant stress to keep our lives in Oak Ridge secret from everyone. Dr. Clarke, the chief psychiatrist on the Reservation, brought in additional employees to help with the heavy load of patients seeking relief. I'd considered visiting him myself but ultimately decided it wasn't a good idea. The issues that kept me awake at night weren't something I could discuss with anyone.

By April, news from Germany gave us all hope the Allies were gaining ground in the war. Hitler was reportedly ill, holed up in a bunker in Berlin, watching his army fall apart. Everyone was shocked when we learned he'd committed suicide. Germany surrendered unconditionally a week later.

The war in Europe was over.

I sat in my dorm room that night, watching the celebration in the streets from my window. Crowds of Oak Ridgers sang and danced, shouted and cried for hours after the news reached us. Although I was as elated as everyone else, relieved that our boys would come home, the news meant only one thing to me.

I would be free from the strangling grip of fear Clive Morrison had on me.

He would no longer need me to steal documents. He wouldn't need me to hide his terrible secrets. K-25 and the other plants would close. I would go home, return to my life, and try to forget everything. With the threat from Germany and Hitler gone, there wasn't a need for the terrible weapon we were all working on. Clive had told me earlier that General Groves, the man in charge of the project, was worried Hitler would develop an atomic bomb first. The world, Clive had said, would never be the same if that happened. But now, that fear was gone.

The day after victory in Europe was announced, I went to work as usual. Even though I felt lighter than I had in months, I wasn't the same naive girl who'd left Kentucky a year ago. I now bore scars no one could see. Yet home beckoned. Somehow I would manage to carve out a life, despite the dark secrets I carried inside.

Mr. Colby called everyone together shortly after I arrived at K-25. I joined the other employees of the maintenance shop at what would hopefully be the last meeting we had before the plant closed.

"I know you've all heard the news about the war in Europe coming to an end," he said. People responded with a loud cheer. "You no doubt have questions about the future of K-25, your jobs, and Oak Ridge. I admit I don't have all the answers, but what I can tell you is that K-25 is still open for business and will be for the foreseeable future."

Another cheer went up.

I, however, stood still, staring at my boss.

What did he mean? Weren't we going home?

"The war in the Pacific is still raging," Mr. Colby continued, his voice somber. "Lots of our boys are dying over there. We here at home must stay on the job until all our soldiers are safe."

Murmurs and nods of agreement filled the small space.

My shoulders fell. Tears sprang to my eyes. I looked down at my feet so no one would see them. Of course I wanted all of our soldiers home safe, but with Hitler dead and the fear of him developing an atomic bomb no longer a threat, why was enriched uranium still necessary? Why couldn't we all go home?

The other employees dispersed and went back to work as usual. I walked to where I'd left my bicycle the day before. I needed to get away to a quiet place and think.

I'd just hopped onto the seat when Mr. Colby approached.

"Willett, please take these documents to the incinerator." He held out a manila packet. It didn't matter that it was stamped "Secret" in red ink or that it was sealed. I couldn't count the number of envelopes I'd opened over the past four months.

Nausea swept over me as I reached for the despised packet. The sweet freedom I'd almost been able to taste just moments ago had turned bitter in my gut.

"Mr. Colby, can I ask you a question?"

"What is it?"

"How long do you think the war in the Pacific will last?"

He gave a slight shrug. "There's no way to know. But," he paused, "our work here in Oak Ridge is important to the war effort. What we're doing could help speed things up."

I knew he meant the development of a new bomb. I still didn't understand how an atomic bomb was different from those that were being used already, but Clive seemed to believe it would be far more powerful. I wished I could ask Mr. Colby to explain it all, but that was impossible. I wasn't supposed to know what was happening here at K-25 and the other plants. I wasn't supposed to know that uranium that had been enriched in Oak Ridge had already made its way to another secret city in New Mexico. According to Clive, that location was where the bomb was being built.

"I hope so, sir," I finally said.

I pedaled away, the packet of documents in the wire basket. I was tempted to take it directly to the incinerator and bypass Clive altogether, but I'd tried that once. He'd found me later that day, livid.

"Don't ever do that again, Mae," he'd said, his teeth clenched. "I know when Colby is finished with certain documents. I know who comes and goes from the incinerator. You don't want to cross me. You don't want me to tell the people I'm working with that you aren't cooperating. It would be easy for them to go to backwoods Kentucky and deal with *things*."

The threat shook me to my core.

I left my bike on the cell floor and found Clive on the third level pipe gallery with two other men. When he glanced at me, I had the packet clutched to my chest. Without making it obvious, he looked up. That was the sign I should meet him upstairs on the operating floor. Although people moved about on that floor, large machines and dark corners offered privacy.

I made my way there and waited. It wasn't long before Clive arrived.

"Here." I shoved the packet at him. "Hurry up before Mr. Colby comes looking for me."

"Why, Mae, you don't look happy," he said, his usual smug grin creasing his face. He took the envelope and began to carefully open it. "You must be the only person on the Reservation who is glum today. The war in Europe is over. Hitler's dead. We just need to whip the Japs and everything will be back to normal."

I stared at him. "How can you say that? Hundreds of thousands of people have died." I wanted to add that Sissy was dead too, but I'd learned it wasn't wise to mention her to Clive. I still didn't have proof that he'd killed her, but I knew it was true. "Lives have been forever altered. Countries bombed and torn apart. Nothing will ever be normal again."

He wasn't listening. He removed the documents from the envelope, flipped through them, then stuffed them all back inside. "I don't need these. They're similar to some I've already passed."

While I was relieved he wasn't going to keep any of the papers today, it made me ill to think of how many top secret documents I'd helped him steal over the past months. It was a small comfort knowing they went to Russians rather than to Germans or Italians, but I hated what I'd become involved in. Hated that I'd betrayed my country and the brave men and women fighting overseas.

Hated that I was a coward.

Oh, that the war would finally come to an end and set me free.

By the time August arrived, sultry summer temperatures had everyone grouchy. The war with Japan dragged on. The secret was old and burdensome. Tempers flared on a dime. In order to stay cool, people flocked to the spring-fed swimming pool in town, and ice cream was in high demand.

With Mr. Colby's permission, I'd begun working seven days a week. I had no desire to have a day off, not even to take a dip in the chilly water. Too many hours with nothing to do allowed my mind to wander to places I'd rather not go. My roommate Dorothy thought it the strangest thing I'd done so far, according to Prudence Thorpe.

"I probably shouldn't tell you this," she'd said last night when

I returned to the dorm after a long Sunday shift, "but Dorothy thinks you're an odd bird."

I'd been too tired to take offense. "She may be right."

Prudence had given me a curious look. "You haven't been yourself since Sissy left. Any word from her?"

My back had stiffened. "No."

She'd pressed her lips together, a sure sign she was about to say something I wouldn't like. "I've noticed you've taken up with Clive Morrison. Seems a little strange, considerin' he was Sissy's fella and all."

I'd nearly choked. "I haven't taken up with him. I can't stand the man."

"But I've seen you with him on several occasions."

My heart had dropped to the floor. I'd thought no one had noticed my meetings with Clive, but I was obviously wrong.

"There are things about our jobs at K-25 that sometimes require—" I'd covered my mouth, feigning surprise. "Oops, I nearly said something I shouldn't. You know what they say about loose lips."

I'd turned and walked away without giving her a chance to respond.

Monday began as any other day. Mr. Colby had assignments for me, but thankfully none required transporting documents to the incinerator. Halfway through the morning, he called me into the main office. A crowd of other maintenance personnel were already there.

"I received word that something important is going to be announced over the radio," Mr. Colby said. I'd never seen him so anxious. He fiddled with the knob on the radio while others in the room speculated on what we were about to hear.

"Maybe the Japanese surrendered."

"Or the emperor is dead, just like Hitler."

"I bet the Russians invaded Japan."

I didn't glance at the man who'd spoken that last statement. Reports about Russia's Red Army made me nervous.

Mr. Colby called for silence. Static and a hum came from the radio.

Finally, we heard President Truman's voice.

"A short time ago, an American airplane dropped one bomb on Hiroshima, and destroyed its usefulness to the enemy. That bomb had more power than 20,000 tons of TNT."

As people in the room gasped, I stood frozen, unable to breathe.

Was President Truman about to unveil the secret?

"The Japanese began the war from the air at Pearl Harbor. They have been repaid manyfold. And the end is not yet. With this bomb we have now added a new and revolutionary increase in destruction to supplement the growing power of our armed forces. In their present form, these bombs are now in production and even more powerful forms are in development."

He paused. "It is an atomic bomb."

I grasped the bib of my overalls, unable to believe what I'd just heard. My heart hammered in my ears, to the point I couldn't hear what the president was saying. Something about harnessing the powers of the universe and the sun.

"We are now prepared to destroy more rapidly and completely every productive enterprise the Japanese have in any city. Let there be no mistake—we shall completely destroy Japan's power to make war."

The people gathered around the radio cheered.

The president continued his speech, but I couldn't get past the fact that the United States had used the secret weapon we'd all been working on. The weapon Clive had told me about. I don't think I'd ever truly believed him until this very moment.

I focused on the voice coming from the radio again. President

Truman spoke about a meeting that took place at Potsdam, a place I'd never heard of, where an ultimatum had been given to Japan's leaders to surrender.

"If they do not now accept our terms," Truman said, "they may expect a rain of ruin from the air, the likes of which has never been seen on this earth."

The threatening words filled me with a sense of dread, and I found myself praying the Japanese would give up their stubborn fight. No one else needed to die.

"We have spent more than two billion dollars on the greatest scientific gamble in history—and we have won."

Mr. Colby whistled. "Two billion dollars."

"Both science and industry worked together," the president continued, "under the direction of the United States Army, which achieved a unique success in an amazingly short time."

I thought back to the day I learned about S-50. Clive said the liquid thermal diffusion plant had been built in less than three months.

"The Secretary of War, who has kept in personal touch with all phases of the project, will immediately make public a statement giving further details. His statement will give facts concerning the sites at Oak Ridge near Knoxville, Tennessee," the president said, followed by whoops and hollers from my coworkers before Mr. Colby shushed everyone, "and at Richland near Pasco, Washington, and an installation near Santa Fe, New Mexico. Although the workers at the sites have been making materials to be used in producing the greatest destructive force in history, they have not themselves been in danger beyond that of many other occupations, for the utmost care has been taken of their safety."

The president's speech ended with his promise to recommend Congress set up a commission to monitor and control the uses of atomic power in the United States. I couldn't help but think of the classified documents Clive had delivered to the Russian government. What did they intend to do with the knowledge they'd stolen from our country? All I could do was pray that whatever secrets I'd passed to Clive would never be used to harm Americans.

After Mr. Colby clicked off the radio, he faced us. "I'm sure more information will come out in the coming weeks, but for now, just know that your hard work—everything we've all been doing the past two years—was for this day."

A triumphant cheer filled the room. Everyone spoke in excited voices at once. Some were astonished that Oak Ridge had played a role in making the powerful weapon, while others appeared relieved the secret was finally out.

I quietly slipped from the office. I wasn't sure why, but tears filled my eyes. I hurried to the restroom and locked the door. My knees gave way, and I sank to the tiled floor and wept. I cried for all the soldiers who'd died because of this terrible war. I cried for the innocent victims. For Sissy and her mama. For myself.

But it was finally over, or it would be soon. Surely the Japanese would surrender after having such a terrible weapon used on them. President Truman didn't say how many people were killed, but one would assume it was a great many, considering the power the bomb unleashed.

Three days later, a second atomic bomb was dropped on Japan, this time on a city called Nagasaki. I'd sat in Mr. Colby's office, stunned by the radio announcement. Why hadn't Japan's leaders surrendered after the first bomb? Why had they put their citizens at risk? When would all the death and destruction finally come to an end?

On Tuesday, I woke to the sound of happy voices and car horns out my window. Groggy from sleep, I glanced at my wristwatch. It was after noon. I'd worked the late shift last night and had fallen into bed in the wee hours of the morning.

A warm August breeze came through the partially open window. I pulled back the curtain and saw a repeat of what had taken place when Germany surrendered. Crowds of people and cars clogged the streets, celebrating.

I hurried into the hallway where a young woman ran past.

"What's happening?" I hollered after her.

She skidded to a stop and stared at me. "Haven't you heard? Japan surrendered. The war is over!" She didn't wait for more questions and disappeared down the stairs.

I stood there in my nightgown, stunned.

Could it truly be over? After all these years, had the war finally come to an end?

I covered my face with my hands and sobbed.

CHAPTER THIRTY
LAUREL

THREE DAYS PASSED before Aunt Mae felt well enough to leave her bed. Dad and I took turns tending to her, although neither of us broached the subject of what had caused her breakdown. We'd agreed to wait until she was stronger before tackling everything she'd been hiding for more than thirty years.

I heaved a sigh as I handwashed the breakfast dishes. I still found it strange that Aunt Mae didn't have an automatic dishwasher. We'd always had one in our Boston home. Mom even had them replaced when newer, better models came out.

But my mind wasn't on dishes or how best to clean them.

I hadn't heard from Jonas since he walked out the door the night of Aunt Mae's breakdown. I hadn't felt at liberty to reach out to him, considering the way Dad made it clear Jonas wasn't welcome. Until Aunt Mae told us what happened during the war, it wasn't a good idea to communicate with Jonas, no matter how much I wanted to discuss it with him. He was a cop, after all. A man sworn to uphold the law. While we weren't sure any laws had been broken, Aunt Mae was our first concern. Everything and everyone else came afterwards.

Dad joined me in the kitchen. "Mae would like to talk to us."

The gravity in his voice stilled my hands. "Did she say what this is about?"

He shook his head.

I dried my hands on a dish towel and followed him into the front room. Aunt Mae sat in her armchair, a crocheted afghan across her lap despite warm air coming through the open window. The sweet scent of lilacs wafted up from the purple bunch Georgeanne brought over the previous day, displayed in a Mason jar on the coffee table.

Dad and I sat on the sofa, shoulders tense, and waited.

Aunt Mae took a deep breath, exhaled, then met our gazes. "I know you have questions. I'll try to answer them in due time, but first . . ." Her voice quavered. "First I need to tell you something. I'm ashamed to reveal such things to you, my precious family, but it's time. I've kept this secret for far too long."

"Mae—," Dad started, only to be stopped by his sister.

"Let me do this my way, Harry. Please."

Dad nodded.

"When I came to Oak Ridge in 1944," Aunt Mae began, "I was sheltered and naive. I knew nothing of the world beyond our small Kentucky community, but I'd wanted to do my part to win the war and bring our boys home."

She told us about the day she arrived on the Reservation, being assigned to a dorm, and about her roommate Sissy Galloway.

"Sissy was pretty and sweet," she said, her face taking on a pained expression, "but she was just as naive as me. She met a fellow named Clive Morrison." Her voice turned hard when she spoke his name. I recognized it from the MP's report. "He was a spy, although Sissy didn't know it at the time."

Dad and I sat perfectly still as a mind-blowing story unfolded.

She told us about Sissy's diary, her disappearance, and Aunt Mae's certainty that Clive murdered her roommate. Then came the trailer fire, and a frantic search of the riverbank for a fresh grave. Finally, she divulged the threats that forced her to become involved in espionage.

"One of my responsibilities at K-25 was to take packets of confidential documents to the incinerator. Mr. Colby, my boss, trusted me to do this for him." Her chin trembled. "Clive insisted I bring the documents to him first. He'd take the ones that interested him, then I completed the job of destroying the ones that remained."

"Who was he spying for?" Dad asked.

"The Soviet Union."

Images of Letty Gladding's arrest raced through my mind. She wasn't much older than Aunt Mae.

"This is bad, Mae," Dad whispered, a tremor in his voice. "This is really, really bad."

She met his gaze, tears glistening in her eyes. "I'm sorry, Harry. I'm sorry you have to learn that your big sister is a traitor. I had hoped to take this terrible secret to my grave."

"You're not a traitor, Aunt Mae," I said. "You're a victim. You were forced to do it. Clive threatened you. You were just a young, frightened woman who found herself in a horrific situation."

She wiped tears from her cheeks. "That may be true, but in the eyes of the law, I betrayed my country. I betrayed my family and everyone who worked on the Manhattan Project. It's time now for me to be held accountable for what I've done."

"No!" Dad jumped to his feet. "No one needs to know about this. The only people who know the truth are in this room. Jonas might be suspicious," he said, glancing at me, "but he has no proof." He began to pace. "We need to get you away from here. Move you to Boston as soon as possible. I'll make some calls and—"

"Harry, sit down." Aunt Mae's voice brooked no arguments. Dad sat.

"I'm done with secrets and lies. They've been part of my life for far too long. I'm resigned to facing the consequences for my actions."

"You want to go to prison?" Dad asked, his voice raised.

"Of course I don't want to, Harry, but it's what I deserve."

Dad sank back against the couch cushion, arms crossed over his chest. "This is nuts."

I glanced between the siblings. I knew how Dad felt, yet I admired Aunt Mae for finally facing her giant.

"I have two requests," she said. "First, I need to speak to Velvet. I don't want her to hear this on the television news."

Dad groaned and closed his eyes. "The news." He shook his head, then looked at Aunt Mae. "What's the second request?"

Aunt Mae's gaze shifted to me. "I want to give my confession to Jonas. He'll know what to do."

A sob escaped my throat, but I nodded.

"My poor family." Her voice cracked. "I'm so very sorry to put you through this. I know you're ashamed of me. I won't blame you if you never want to see me again."

Dad and I went to Aunt Mae, where we wrapped our arms around one another.

"We'll always be here for you, Mae. We're a family," Dad said. He wiped his face. "We'll get through this somehow, together."

Aunt Mae asked me to call Velvet and invite her and Roonie to the house. Velvet must have heard something in my voice, because she said they'd be right over. When they arrived, Aunt Mae burst into tears. While Velvet sat and held her hand, she told her friend the shocking tale.

"Oh, my poor Mae." Tears slid down Velvet's cheeks. "How I wish you would have shared this with me all those years ago.

I knew somethin' was wrong, but I could have never imagined this."

"I didn't want you to hear about it from anyone else. I've treasured our friendship through the years, but I betrayed you. I'll never forgive myself for being a coward and a traitor. You deserved better. Everyone did."

Velvet knelt in front of Aunt Mae and grasped her by the shoulders. "You listen to me, Maebelle Willett. You are the dearest friend I could ever ask for. I would never hold this against you. You're a good person with a good heart."

Aunt Mae's face crumpled. "I'm not. I lied to everyone. I stole classified documents and gave them to the enemy. I let Clive get away with Sissy's murder," she sobbed. "It's too much. God can't forgive me. No one can."

Velvet gathered Aunt Mae into her arms and let her weep. When she quieted, Velvet met Aunt Mae's tormented gaze. "You were trying to protect the people you loved, Mae. You had to make choices you would never have made under normal circumstances. God knows your reasons for doing what you did, and he has already forgiven you. The day Jesus hung on the cross, he paid the debt for your sins. He looked into the future and knew all the wrong and sinful things you would do. That each of us would do, and he died for them."

Aunt Mae shook her head. "I wish I could believe that, but I can't. I did things that were illegal and immoral. I betrayed my country. I betrayed Sissy's family. They never knew what happened to her because I was a coward. No, those things aren't forgivable."

"Mae," Velvet said, her voice soft, "think about the man on the cross next to Jesus. He was a criminal. We don't know what he was guilty of, but it doesn't matter. The Bible says he even mocked Jesus as they hung there. But as the hours went by and death was near, that same man asked Jesus to remember him when

Jesus entered his Kingdom. Did the Lord deny him because of his wrongdoing? Because he'd done things that were illegal and immoral? No. Jesus looked into that man's heart and saw the things only God can see. Things that convinced Jesus the man was sorry for what he'd done. Then he told the dying criminal that he would soon be with Jesus in paradise."

Velvet grasped both of Aunt Mae's hands. "Mae, have you told Jesus you're sorry for what you did? Have you confessed your wrongdoing and asked for forgiveness?"

Aunt Mae nodded. "Over and over, but I don't feel forgiven. I've tried to do penance. I've given aid to the needy, money to the poor, volunteered at church, but nothing helps. Nothing takes away the guilt I feel, deep in my soul."

Velvet wiped Aunt Mae's tears with her own embroidered handkerchief. "Guilt has a way of making us think God is too angry to forgive our sins. That we're too far gone to be saved, but grace says otherwise. Grace says our sins are washed in the blood, bringing with it a time of refreshing and renewal. Jesus died so you can be free, Mae. Free from sin. Free from guilt. You just have to accept the amazin' gift of grace he offered to everyone from that terrible place on the cross."

Aunt Mae stared at her friend, longing in her eyes. "To be free is all I've ever wanted. Free from Clive. Free from the terrible memories. Free from the heaviness I've carried all these years. It can't be that easy."

A gentle smile came to Velvet's face. "'If the Son therefore shall make you free, ye shall be free indeed.' When we acknowledge our sins before God and repent—when we turn away from wrongdoing—we're no longer slaves to sin. It loses its grip on us, and we become the redeemed, beloved children of God."

Aunt Mae's breath came in hard gulps. "I'm forgiven?" she whispered.

Velvet nodded. "Yes, Mae. You are forgiven. You're free. Now it's time to live like it."

Aunt Mae's sobs shook her entire body as she fell into Velvet's arms.

The change in Aunt Mae was immediate. She still felt deep remorse over her long-ago actions, yet her face shone, almost radiant, with peacefulness as she spoke to us about what was next.

"Laurel, please call Jonas and tell him I'm ready to turn myself in," she said. While she'd been resigned earlier to confessing her guilt and paying the price, now she had a sense of serenity about her that was nearly tangible.

"Are you sure you want to do this?" Dad asked. He'd been quiet while Aunt Mae shared her story with Velvet, but I saw in his eyes he didn't agree with her plan. "What you did was wrong, yes, but it happened a long time ago. Whatever the Russians may have learned from the documents you passed to Morrison is obsolete by now. We don't even know if Morrison really was a spy or if he was just some lunatic."

"What do you suggest Mae should do?" Roonie asked, his voice gentle.

Dad glanced at each of us. "I don't see the need for her story to leave this room." When Aunt Mae began to protest, he held up his hand. "Hear me out, Mae. If you had actually been the one stealing the documents and passing them to the enemy, then I'd have no choice but to let you turn yourself in. But you weren't a spy. You were blackmailed and threatened by a murderer. You didn't commit a crime. You were a victim, like Laurel said."

"If that's true, then everything will work out." New confidence infused her words. She nodded at me, indicating the plan was still in play.

I left the room to make the call to Jonas. The woman who answered the telephone at the police station said Jonas was out of the office but she'd pass my message to him over the radio. I thanked her and returned to the living room. It wasn't long before I heard a car enter the driveway.

Dad looked out the window. His shoulders grew stiff. "Tyson is here."

Aunt Mae reached a hand to him. He grasped it like a lost little boy. "It's going to be all right, Harry."

I met Jonas at the door. Our eyes locked.

"Thank you for coming," I said as he entered.

He nodded to each of the room's occupants, then went to Aunt Mae. "I'm glad to see you're feeling better."

She offered a peaceful smile. "I am, Jonas. Much better than I've felt in years."

"I understand you wanted to speak to me." He glanced around the room. "I'm going to assume you're all aware of what this is about."

"I've told them everything," Aunt Mae said.

Velvet and Roonie volunteered to leave to give us privacy, but Jonas requested they stay. Dad brought in a chair from the kitchen for Jonas and set it facing Aunt Mae. As he and I sank down onto the sofa next to Velvet, with Roonie standing nearby, I bit my lip to keep it from trembling, unsure what was going to happen after Aunt Mae confessed her crimes.

"Whenever you're ready," Jonas said to Aunt Mae.

She took a deep breath and began her story. Jonas listened intently, never interrupting her with questions of his own. He didn't take notes or look troubled or shocked. He simply let her tell the tale that still seemed unreal to me.

When she came to the end, she wiped a tear that trailed down her cheek. "I'm very sorry for my actions. I wish I could go back and change everything. I've lived my whole life trying to keep this secret buried. Telling all of you about it today is like coming out of the darkness into the light. I'm ready to accept the punishment I deserve for betraying my country."

"You're a very brave woman, Mae," Jonas said.

"What happens now?" Dad asked. His tone told me he was still angry. "Will you take her into custody?"

"No, sir," Jonas said. "Espionage cases are handled by the FBI. There will be an investigation. Mae will have to tell them what she's told all of us." He faced Aunt Mae. "You said you still have Sissy's diary with the entries about Morrison?"

She nodded. "I also have documents I took from Clive's trailer, as well as handmade copies of some of those I gave to him. I drew them myself in case I ever needed evidence. Laurel," Aunt Mae said to me, "would you go to my closet? There's a metal box there, behind some things. Please bring it to me. The key is taped to the underside of my top bureau drawer."

I hurried to do her bidding. I knew exactly where to find the box.

When I returned to the living room, Aunt Mae unlocked it. A pained expression filled her face as she lifted out a small book.

"Sissy's mama gave this diary to her before she left for Oak Ridge." Tears filled her eyes. "That poor woman never knew what happened to her daughter."

"You believe Sissy drowned in the river?" Jonas asked.

Aunt Mae nodded, her grief obvious. "After the war ended, Clive was transferred out of Oak Ridge. On his last day at K-25, he warned me to keep silent or else my family would suffer. Thankfully I never heard from him again. I searched and searched for Sissy's grave but never found one. I'm convinced she's in the

Clinch River. I can't tell you how many times I started to write to her mama about what happened. About Clive and my suspicions. But every time I'd convince myself I could do it, I'd remember Clive's threats, and I'd let fear win."

My heart broke for Aunt Mae. She'd been a young, innocent woman when she arrived in Oak Ridge, ready to do her part to help with the war effort. What happened to her and Sissy was a travesty.

She put the diary back into the box and handed it to Jonas. "Tell the authorities I'm ready to cooperate with them."

Jonas stood and included all of us in his gaze. "Until the FBI finishes their investigation, it's important not to talk to anyone else about this. We don't want it to reach the news outlets until everything is settled." He looked back to Aunt Mae. "I appreciate your honesty today, Mae."

Velvet and Roonie left a few minutes later, promising to cover Aunt Mae in prayer. Jonas, too, made his way to the door, assuring us he would keep us informed of what happens next.

I walked him to his car. "Thank you, Jonas, for treating her so considerately."

He offered a sympathetic nod. "I meant what I said. Mae is a brave woman."

"How long do you think the investigation will take?"

"I don't really know, but with the Gladding case in the news, they may jump on this fairly quickly." Our gazes held. "What's your plan now? Will you head back to Boston?"

"I'm not really sure. With Aunt Mae's health situation, she shouldn't be alone. Dad and I discussed moving her to Boston, but now with all of this . . ." I shrugged. "I guess we'll have to see what happens, but I should be here for a while longer."

I thought that might please him, but he didn't smile. "While the investigation is underway, it wouldn't be appropriate for us to see each other socially."

Disappointment washed over me. "I understand."

He opened the car door and set the metal box inside. "With the FBI handling the case, I may not know a lot, but I'll pass along anything I hear."

"I appreciate everything you've done, Jonas." I took a step back. "Goodbye."

I watched him drive away, a heavy feeling of loss in my heart. If Aunt Mae was convicted of espionage, it wouldn't be wise for Jonas to be found dating the niece of a spy. His career could suffer. It seemed our relationship was coming to an end before it even had a chance to get started.

Back inside, Aunt Mae apologized again for everything she'd done and how it would affect us. "I love you all very much. I hate that my family will suffer because of what I've done."

"We'll be all right," I said. "Remember the verse Velvet quoted?"

A look of peace settled on her face. "'If the Son therefore shall make you free, ye shall be free indeed.' It's from the book of John. I've read those words many times through the years, but I never believed I could be free of the guilt and shame. I didn't believe I deserved it after what I'd done. I may go to prison, which frightens me, but I'll walk through those doors without the heavy burden of guilt that has weighed me down for far too long."

I went to her and grasped her good hand. "I'm so proud of you, Aunt Mae."

"I'm proud of you too, Sis." Dad rose and put his hand on top of mine. "Mama and Pa would be as well."

Her eyes filled with tears. "That's more than I deserve, but it's everything I've ever wanted."

CHAPTER THIRTY-ONE

LAUREL

THE FOLLOWING WEEK, two FBI agents from Washington, DC arrived. Dad and I remained outside while Aunt Mae told the men her story. When they left several hours later without taking her into custody, we hurried into the house, anxious for details.

She sat in her chair, seemingly astonished. "You aren't going to believe this, but they knew all about Clive Morrison. How he'd stolen documents and passed them to the Russians. He'd been involved in the Communist Party here in the United States, but because he wasn't an official member, he was allowed to join the military. After he left Oak Ridge, he worked on other government projects and did the same thing there that he'd done here."

"Was he caught?" Dad asked.

She shook her head. "He died in a car accident in the 1950s, shortly after the Rosenbergs' trials. The FBI was on the verge of arresting him, but they think word leaked out and reached the people he was working with."

I gasped. "The car accident wasn't an accident?"

"There's no way to know for certain, but it's a possibility."

"What about you?" Dad said. "What happens next?"

A bewildered expression came over her. "They said I won't be prosecuted. They took my statement and kept Sissy's diary. Because I haven't worked for the government in some time, they aren't worried about me giving away secrets. In fact, they said that although the information Clive passed to the Russians was confidential, it was actually a spy in Los Alamos who provided vital information to the Soviet Union that helped them create their first atomic bomb."

We sat stunned by the news.

"All these years, I feared what would happen when anyone found out what I'd done." Aunt Mae grew somber. "I should have told the truth from the very beginning, but I was terrified. For myself. For Mama, Pa, and you, Harris. I gave up everything because of fear."

She told us about her friend Garlyn, wondering if anything would have come of their relationship had she been honest with him. The life she'd led in Oak Ridge had been solitary and full of lonely, guilt-ridden years. We were still talking when Jonas's Bronco pulled into the driveway.

"I heard the good news," he said after greeting each of us. "I'm glad things worked out, Mae. I came by to tell you about a discovery I've made."

Aunt Mae frowned. "A discovery? About what? There aren't any more secrets to uncover."

With a gentle voice, Jonas said, "It's about Sissy."

Aunt Mae clutched at her heart. "Sissy?"

"Yes, ma'am. After you said you thought she drowned in the river, I did some investigating. If you feel up to it, I'd like to tell you what we believe happened."

Dad put his hand on Aunt Mae's shoulder. "Maybe now isn't a good time for this."

She disagreed. "I want to know. I need to know what became of her."

Jonas nodded. "The time of year, water levels, and Sissy's weight all factor in to when and where she would surface if she had indeed gone into the river. We believe it would have taken approximately two weeks. The area where S-50 was located is about ten miles upriver from Kingston. I drove over there and spoke to the police chief. I told him I was looking into a thirty-five-year-old murder case and asked if there were any old reports of an unidentified woman being found in the river." He paused. "He called me this morning with his findings."

I knelt beside Aunt Mae and grasped her hand.

"Tell me what happened to my friend," Aunt Mae whispered.

"On December 12, 1944, the body of a young woman was pulled from the river just south of Kingston. She was blonde, had blue eyes, and was somewhere between the ages of 17 and 25. The only identifying article found on her was a gold necklace with a locket, but the photograph inside was ruined. No one had filed a missing person's report and no one came to claim the body after a notice was posted in the newspaper. She was buried in an unmarked grave in the pauper's cemetery in Kingston." Jonas looked at Aunt Mae with compassion. "I'm very sorry."

Aunt Mae wept for her friend. "I knew in my heart she was gone," she said. "I wish I'd told the authorities what I suspected happened to her. Even if they'd arrested me for spying, it might have helped identify Sissy and given her family some closure."

"I'm not sure it would have made a difference," Jonas said. "According to Dad, a missing person wasn't unusual back then. Lots of people were fired or quit their jobs and simply left town. But even if you'd been able to prove Clive's involvement in Sissy's disappearance, Oak Ridge was a government-run secret city. News of a murder and a body in the river would have brought too much attention. I doubt Sissy's family would have been notified."

"You're probably right," Aunt Mae said. After a long moment, she sat up straight. "I want to go to the cemetery, now, and pay my respects to Sissy. It's the least I can do."

Jonas volunteered to drive. As Dad helped Aunt Mae into the back seat of the vehicle, I met Jonas's gaze. "Thank you." He nodded.

We drove west on the turnpike, past K-25. When we arrived at the small cemetery on the outskirts of Kingston, we found the fence in need of repair and the plots overgrown with weeds. Small, square granite markers with numbers carved on top indicated gravesites. Only a few had headstones with names and dates. Dad and I stood on either side of Aunt Mae as she surveyed the neglected graveyard, distress on her face.

"Poor Sissy," she said, wiping her nose with a tissue. "To end up here, unknown, uncared for, when she had a loving family in Georgia waiting for her. I hope her brother Joe made it home from the war and brought comfort to her parents in their old age."

Jonas led our solemn group to a grave at the end of the row. "According to cemetery records, this is where they buried the young woman."

We stood in silence while Aunt Mae's heartbroken sobs rose in the summer sky. She asked Dad to pray, and he offered a beautiful blessing on Sissy's family. With emotion in his voice, he also thanked God for sparing Aunt Mae from going to prison.

When Aunt Mae was ready, we loaded into the Bronco.

"I don't need to come here again," she said as we drove away. When I turned to glance at her, I found a peaceful expression on her face while she gazed out the window. "In fact," she faced Dad where he sat next to her, "I don't need to stay in Oak Ridge any longer."

Dad's eyes widened. "What?"

She heaved a sigh. "All these years, I've felt stuck. Stuck in the past. Stuck in my shame. I couldn't move forward to something new, and I couldn't go back to change the things I'd done. But now," she said with a soft smile, "now I feel free. Freer than I've ever felt before. I'd like to take you up on your offer, Harry, and move to Boston. I want to be near my family."

The happy surprise on Dad's face mirrored my own, but in the best way possible.

Back at the house, Dad walked Aunt Mae inside while I remained in the driveway with Jonas.

"That was unexpected," he said once we were alone. "It's like she's a different person."

I repeated Velvet's words about freedom in Christ and how the guilt Aunt Mae had carried all these years seemed to melt away when she accepted them as truth. "That's what we all need, isn't it? To know God's grace and plans are perfect, no matter how it seems."

"Speaking of plans," he said, his eyes locked on to mine. "If Mae moves to Boston, I guess you won't have any reason to come back to Oak Ridge."

I couldn't look away. I knew what he was asking. I just didn't know how to respond.

"I suppose I might return. I still have research to do."

He cupped my face with his hands, his gaze intense. "Laurel, I don't want you to come back for research." He grimaced. "That didn't come out right. What I mean is, I *want* you to come back. I want to continue getting to know you. I want to continue . . . *this*."

My heart pounded. After hearing Aunt Mae's story—a story about a lifetime of dashed hopes and unfulfilled dreams—I didn't want to look back on this day with regret. My reply to Jonas's heartfelt declaration could ultimately change the well-laid path my life was currently on. Was I willing to take a risk and possibly alter everything?

My galloping pulse slowed. I knew the answer. "I want this too."

We closed the gap between us. His lips met mine, sweet and full of passion. I felt his arms go around me, and I clung to him as we kissed. Nothing around us mattered. When it came to an end, we were both breathless.

"That went better than I thought it would," he said, followed by a mischievous grin.

I remained in his embrace, my hands on his muscled chest. "When I came to Oak Ridge, I didn't expect to find you, Detective Tyson."

He pulled me closer. "I'm sure Dad will take all the credit, since you were interviewing him when we met."

"As I recall, you weren't exactly Prince Charming that day," I teased.

He laughed. "Guilty as charged." He caressed my cheek with his thumb. "You'll find I can be pretty protective of the people I love."

The ardent look in his eyes sent a delicious sensation racing through me.

"I can live with that."

EPILOGUE
LAUREL

OAK RIDGE, TENNESSEE

DECEMBER 27, 1979

A fresh layer of snow blanketed the yard when I awoke and looked out the window. The wintry weather had turned Oak Ridge into a picture-perfect Christmas scene. I was grateful the storm had held off until my plane landed in Knoxville late last night. I was also grateful it was toasty and warm inside. Jonas and his dad had volunteered to keep an eye on Aunt Mae's house after she moved to Boston at the end of the summer, and they'd repaired the ancient heater last week after it conked out.

I glanced at the clock on the bedside table. I still had thirty minutes before Jonas was due to arrive. As I padded across the hall to the bathroom, I thought back to his trip to Boston last month for Thanksgiving.

Aunt Mae had proudly given him a tour of her new apartment in the basement of Dad and Mom's house. After sleeping in my old bedroom while the renovation took place, she'd happily moved into her own space the previous week. She and Mom spent hours decorating, enjoying each other's company. A new watercolor of the Tennessee mountains Mom painted for Aunt Mae hung prominently over the sofa, a reminder of her former home. Even my sisters spent time with our aunt these days, learning how to make clothes on the old sewing machine and bake cookies. The best news was Aunt Mae's eyesight had greatly improved, stumping her ophthalmologist. Aunt Mae simply stated that God had healed her of many things when he set her free, including her failing eyesight.

I'd just finished applying a little makeup when Jonas knocked on the front door. I missed having Peggy bark her greeting when someone arrived, but she was queen of the Willett's Boston house now. Mom and my sisters adored the little dog, and I'd even caught Dad sneaking treats to her from time to time.

"Good morning," I said when I opened the door. Jonas looked like a ruggedly handsome lumberjack in his plaid flannel shirt, jeans, and boots. We'd planned to go hiking in the Great Smoky Mountains National Park this morning and attend an Oak Ridge Boys concert in Knoxville tonight. I hoped the snow wouldn't put a kibosh on our plans.

"Good morning, beautiful."

I was in his arms a moment later, his warm lips on mine.

When we parted, he held up a brown paper bag. "Fresh donuts for breakfast."

"You read my mind." I led the way to the kitchen and started a pot of coffee. "It seems so strange that Aunt Mae lives in Boston now instead of here in her house."

Jonas sat at the table, opened the bag, and peered inside. "Correction. Your house."

I joined him while we waited for the coffee to brew. "I still can't believe she gave me the deed to her house for Christmas. I'm sure my jaw dropped to the floor when I opened the envelope."

He smiled. "It was definitely a very generous gift."

"Later, when I was alone with Dad, I asked him what he thought about it. I mean, he's her brother. If anyone should have inherited the house, it's Dad."

"What did he say?"

"He's happy for me to have it." Bashfulness came over me as I looked at Jonas, but I didn't turn away. "Especially now. Secrets brought me to Oak Ridge six months ago, but you're the reason I want to come back."

He reached for my hands. "I know we have a lot of things to work out, logistics being one of them, but there isn't anything we can't overcome together."

We kissed again.

"I have something cool to tell you," I said, grinning, "but I didn't want to share it over the phone. It's too juicy and wonderful."

He laughed. "That sounds interesting."

"Do you remember Aunt Mae telling us about the young man she dated during the war?"

Jonas nodded. "She broke things off with him because she felt guilty for what she was doing."

"Well, he lives just outside of Washington, DC."

His brow rose. "How do you know that?"

"It's the craziest thing. Dr. Baca has a friend who teaches history at Georgetown. Last semester he invited guest speakers to talk to the students about the Manhattan Project. Dr. Baca suggested I contact his friend and get the names of the guest speakers, with the hope of interviewing them."

Jonas squinted. "You're not going to tell me—"

"Retired Lieutenant Colonel Garlyn Young was among them. Of course, I had no idea who he was. I contacted him, told him about my research, and asked if he'd be willing to talk to me. He said he was going to be in Boston during the holidays, so I invited him to the house." I grinned. "He and Aunt Mae saw each other again for the first time in thirty-something years."

Jonas's mouth gaped. "What was Mae's reaction?"

"She was shocked and very shy at first, but they were soon chatting like old friends. He's a widower and has a son who's in the Army. He confessed that when he first heard my last name, he hoped there was a family connection to the young woman he'd known in Oak Ridge."

"Did she tell him about her secret past?"

"She did. I was so proud of her. Garlyn got very emotional. He said he wished she had told him what was going on back then, because he'd always suspected Clive Morrison was up to no good. Even Mr. Colby, Aunt Mae's boss, had hinted that he didn't fully trust Clive and told Garlyn to keep an eye on him."

"That's wild. Are they going to see each other again?"

"I hope so. Garlyn got Aunt Mae's telephone number and promised to call."

"What a great ending—or beginning—to their story."

While I rose to pour us each a cup of coffee, Jonas took two chocolate frosted donuts out of the bag. "The Kingston police chief called yesterday. He said the memorial stone Mae ordered was installed at the pauper's cemetery last weekend. Sissy's brother Joe and his family came to the public ceremony."

I returned to the table with the coffee. "Aunt Mae will be so pleased. She said writing to Sissy's family to tell them everything that happened was one of the hardest things she's ever done. But in the letter Joe sent in return, he expressed his gratitude for her friendship with his sister and for giving them closure. His parents never gave up hope that their daughter would come home someday. They've both passed away, but Joe still lives on the family farm and has a daughter named Sissy."

"It must've been hard for her parents not to know what happened," Jonas said. "According to the chief, when the mayor read the inscription on the memorial about Sissy and the other people buried there being known and loved by God, it brought some of the attendees to tears. A group of people stayed after the ceremony to clean up the cemetery and place flowers on all the graves."

"Would you mind if we drove out there today?" I asked. "I'd like to take a picture of it for Aunt Mae."

"Your wish is my command, Miss Willett," he said before he stuffed his mouth with a big bite of donut.

"Good," I grinned, "because I have a whole list of things I need to do and places I want to see while I'm here. Dr. Baca thinks my dissertation will be good enough to publish once I finish it. I'm thinking about titling it *Secrets from the Secret City.* Thanks to Georgeanne, I have several interviews lined up with some of the women she worked with at Y-12, as well as one with your mom. I also want to go back to K-25 and take a closer look. When we were there before, I didn't appreciate everything Aunt Mae experienced. Then there's the area that used to be Happy Valley where Velvet lived, and—"

"Whoa, now." Jonas chuckled. "You're only here for a week before school starts up again. I kind of hoped to have your undivided attention."

I heard the teasing in his voice. I slowly put down my coffee cup, stood, and plunked down in his lap, with my arms around his neck. Delighted surprise registered in his eyes as I gazed at him.

"Is this undivided enough for you, Detective Tyson?"

He laughed and pulled me into his embrace. "As long as I get to hold you like this every day you're here, then yes, this is enough. For now."

"For now," I whispered before our lips met in sweet passion. Promise, hopes, and a multitude of happy dreams overflowed from those two simple words.

I'd come to Oak Ridge with the sole intent to uncover secrets about the Manhattan Project and the people involved in it.

What God had planned was so much better.

Keep an eye out for the next historical from Michelle Shocklee

COMING IN STORES AND ONLINE IN 2027

JOIN THE CONVERSATION AT

A NOTE FROM THE AUTHOR

I GREW UP in Santa Fe, New Mexico, thirty miles south of Los Alamos. When the first atomic bomb was detonated in the desert of New Mexico at 5:29 a.m. on July 16, 1945, my grandmother witnessed the intense, white flash. The test, code-named Trinity, took place approximately fifty miles from where my grandparents and my mother, a teenager at the time, lived in Truth or Consequences. Grandma said the flash through the kitchen window was brighter and whiter than daylight. A false government-issued statement for newspaper and radio said ammunitions at a nearby military base had exploded.

Beginning in 1943, thousands of young women were recruited to work on a secret project at an undisclosed location in the hills of Tennessee. Nearly 10,000 of them worked at the Y-12 electromagnetic separation plant where they unknowingly helped to enrich uranium. These women were called "cubicle operators," but in the early 2000s, the term "calutron girls" emerged. I had Mae work at the enormous K-25 gaseous diffusion plant where employees really did ride bicycles due to the sheer size of the building. All that remains of K-25 is the "footprint" of where the building once stood, but the nearby K-25 History Center is informative and was a highlight of my trip to the area. Recorded interviews with former Oak

Ridge employees reveal most had mixed feelings about their role in the creation of an atomic weapon. While the Manhattan Project and use of the atomic bomb continues to be debated today, my goal in writing *The Women of Oak Ridge* was to honor the women and men who simply wanted to help bring the war to an end.

A real spy worked at Oak Ridge. George Koval, an American engineer, spied for the Soviet Union throughout the war. He believed in communism and had family ties to Russia. After the war, he fled to Europe, never to return to the United States. The truth about his espionage came to light in 2007, when Russian Prime Minister Vladimir Putin posthumously awarded Koval the Hero of the Russian Federation medal. While I took bits and pieces of information from Koval's story, the character of Clive Morrison and everything he's involved in is fictional.

Another World War II spy that inspired parts of the novel is Melita Norwood. Mrs. Norwood was a British citizen who worked in various government offices throughout her long career. She joined the Communist Party of Great Britain and eventually became a spy for the Soviet Union. Her family and neighbors were astonished when she was unmasked in a 1999 book written by a former KGB archivist. Mrs. Norwood was never arrested.

While researching life in wartime Oak Ridge, I discovered that a young woman did indeed go missing from the dormitory and was rumored to have died from drinking tainted moonshine. Years later, several former employees said people often disappeared from the Reservation. Not due to criminal activity, but because people were fired or quit on a regular basis. A drowning did occur during the Manhattan Project, but it was in Los Alamos. The story of John Hendrix predicting the existence of Oak Ridge many years before it was built is true.

I hope you enjoyed learning about the women and the secrets of Oak Ridge as much as I did!

ACKNOWLEDGMENTS

IT'S NO SECRET that my husband, Brian, has been my best friend and favorite person on the planet since I was a twenty-year-old college student. He's my research buddy, chauffeur extraordinaire (even if I do offer "suggestions" from the passenger seat), first reader of all my books, and the best coworker I've ever had. I love our life, Mr. Shocklee.

Taylor & Erica, and Austin & Kaley—my children—I'm proud to be your mom, momma, and mother-in-law. I have great expectations for all that God is going to do in your lives, your marriages, and your families. Each one of you is an answer to my prayers.

Dear friends and beloved family, you are rare, beautiful, and priceless jewels. Your lives have touched mine in ways you will never know, and I'm grateful for every single one of you.

Being part of the Tyndale House Publishers family fills my heart with profound joy. Karen Watson, Elizabeth Jackson, Kathy Olson, and the entire team: thank you! I am incredibly honored to partner with so many talented, creative, faith-filled people. Thank you, too, to my agent, Bob Hostetler. I sincerely appreciate all you do on my behalf.

I could not have written a novel about Oak Ridge if not for

the meticulous work of author Denise Kiernan. Her book *The Girls of Atomic City: The Untold Story of the Women Who Helped Win World War II* was invaluable as I immersed myself in the history of the Secret City. *City Behind a Fence* by Charles W. Johnson and Charles O. Jackson, as well as *Sleeper Agent: The Atomic Spy in America Who Got Away* by Ann Hagedorn, were both incredibly helpful resources throughout the writing process. Photographs taken by Ed Westcott, the only person allowed to take photos of Oak Ridge during the war, brought the Secret City in the 1940s to life for me. Thank you to Ray Smith, official historian for the city of Oak Ridge and the Y-12 National Security Complex, for answering my questions. If there are any historical discrepancies within *The Women of Oak Ridge*, they're mine.

To each and every person who has read and enjoyed my books, thank you! Your wonderful reviews, social media posts, and encouraging personal notes truly warm my heart and make the long hours of research and writing worth it.

Guilt is a heavy thing to carry, yet so many of us do. Like Mae, we'd rather take that guilt to our grave than allow it to come out of the darkness and into the light. We're certain that not even God can forgive us. But his Word says otherwise. His grace is sufficient—for everyone and everything. John 8:36 says, "If the Son therefore shall make you free, ye shall be free indeed." Those are "red-letter" words, spoken by Jesus himself on a long-ago day, yet they are as relevant to you and me as they were to the people who heard them. I am eternally grateful for the freedom I've found in Jesus Christ.

Soli Deo gloria.

DISCUSSION QUESTIONS

1. Mae says, "Not every secret needs to be told. Some just need to be forgotten." Do you agree? How have secrets and regrets affected Mae's life? Are there secrets or regrets that have had a lasting impact on your family?

2. Jonas points out that the government couldn't hide something on the level of Oak Ridge in the 1970s, and that's even more true today. When it comes to government secrets and strategic planning, what are some of the pros and cons of today's technological advancement, with its twenty-four-hour news cycle and ever-present cell phones?

3. Mae tells Sissy she's learned we need to trust God with everything, including the people we love—but admits it's hard to let go of that control. Why do we feel like we can (or should at least try!) to control outcomes for our loved ones?

4. When Mae is feeling threatened and vulnerable in light of Clive's threats, her supervisor at work shows kindness and compassion and asks her what's wrong. Should she have confided in him? How might things have turned out differently if she had?

5. Roonie tells Laurel that we can ask God's forgiveness for "things known and unknown" and that he believes God in his mercy doesn't hold people accountable for what they don't know. Do you agree? How do you see this playing out both for the characters in the book and in your own life?

6. Mae feels that what she's done is beyond God's forgiveness, but her friend Velvet tells her that isn't true. Have you or someone you care about ever felt beyond God's forgiveness? What are some truths we need to remind ourselves (or others) of in times like that?

7. Velvet says, "Guilt has a way of making us think God is too angry to forgive our sins." Why is it that our feelings so easily block out things we know, intellectually, to be true? How can we overcome that?

8. Laurel and Jonas talk about dealing with the past as a key to letting go of fear and unforgiveness. How do we see this play out in the novel? Do you know of a real-life example you can share?

9. Laurel's father tells her, "Life is too short to be set on one certain idea and miss all the wonderful surprises that come along." What does this mean for Laurel? What might it mean for you?

ABOUT THE AUTHOR

MICHELLE SHOCKLEE is the author of several historical novels, including *All We Thought We Knew*; *Count the Nights by Stars*, a *Christianity Today* fiction book award winner; and *Under the Tulip Tree*, a Christy and Selah Awards finalist. Her work has been featured in numerous Chicken Soup for the Soul books, magazines, and blogs. Married to her college sweetheart and the mother of two grown sons, she makes her home in Tennessee, not far from the historical sites she writes about.

Step back in time with more great historical fiction from Michelle Shocklee

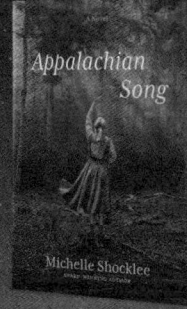

"Though set years ago, this title resonates today. . . . With its haunting message of forgiveness, this is a must-buy for any Christian or historical fiction collection."

Library Journal on *Under the Tulip Tree*

AVAILABLE NOW IN STORES AND ONLINE

JOIN THE CONVERSATION AT

CONNECT WITH AWARD-WINNING AUTHOR MICHELLE ONLINE AT

michelleshocklee.com

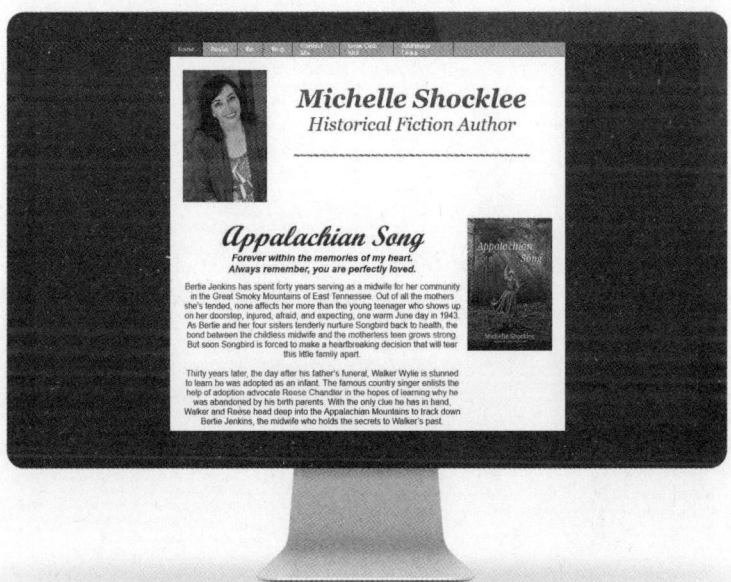

OR FOLLOW HER ON

f AuthorMichelleShocklee1

◉ michelleshocklee

g Michelle_Shocklee

𝕏 shellshocklee

TYNDALE HOUSE PUBLISHERS IS CRAZY4FICTION!

Become part of the Crazy4Fiction community and find fiction that entertains and inspires. Get exclusive content, free resources, and more!

JOIN IN ON THE FUN!

- crazy4fiction.com
- Crazy4Fiction
- crazy4fiction
- tyndale_crazy4fiction
- Sign up for our newsletter

FOR GREAT DEALS ON TYNDALE PRODUCTS, GO TO TYNDALE.COM/FICTION